Dead
in
Time

ANNA REITH

"Rock 'n' roll is dream soup; what's your brand?"
~ Patti Smith

Prologue

August 28th 1976

It started as a long, hot summer. Only now it wasn't just heat but a dry, sucking, breathless thing. Still, stagnant air that choked all it touched, malicious and unrelenting... and it scared him. He stared at the polystyrene tiles on his bathroom ceiling. Longest summer of his life, and now he wouldn't see the end of it.

Shit, man.

His lips, parched and sticking, pulled back into a grimace. This wasn't funny anymore. He flexed against the vinyl, not quite feeling his hands or feet and not quite managing to move his head.

Nope. Definitely not good.

How long had he been lying here? Hard to be sure. He remembered... not much from the last twelve hours, he decided, but then it *had* been turning into a hell of a party. Yeah, and that was a thought, wasn't it? There had to be plenty of people still in the house. Someone would be bound to find him. Bound to come blundering up the wrong stairs, back into these private rooms, this small sanctuary—because they always did, and that's one of the things Inez got pissed off about, right? —and they'd find him.

Inez.

Consciousness started to slip away from him again. He tried once more to turn his head and groaned when the pain hit, searing and crushing, his whole skull gripped by some huge claw. His neck was on fire, but his feet felt cold. Trippy. Weird, but not as weird as seeing part of his own temple smeared across the side of the maple sink cabinet. A few strands of hair waved in the convection of the shower heat, and there was blood... a lot of blood, painted stark against the white basin.

Oh.

Funny, he didn't remember doing that.

His body spasmed in an attempt at a retch. Coughing, he barely felt the bloody ooze and the phlegm slide down his face. His vision blurred again, the bathroom walls misting in a jumble of melting shapes. Steam coiled across the room in a liquid prism of unimaginable colours.

"Whoa, man," he murmured, because... because, like, this could really be it.

The end.

This time, maybe. And it was so quiet. He hadn't expected that. The house lay far enough from the road for him not to hear the cars. Secluded—the reason he'd bought it. You weren't s'posed to hear cars in the country. He realised that no birds were singing in the trees outside, either. He noticed that now, now that he'd got used to it. The birds almost replaced the dim thrum of the traffic he'd grown up with... rarer, sweeter, but still the same; still the sounds of life, the sounds of living. All swallowed up in silence now.

It made sense, then. Maybe things went that way when you... y'know.

Everything, just a final hush.

He hadn't thought much about death before. Not actual death, as in the ending of his own life. Oh, there'd been times he'd ducked fists, knives, or screaming girls—scarier, in a way —and times he'd been really hammered, or done bad shit and thought he'd die because nobody could be that utterly, completely fucked up and live... but he hadn't really *thought* about it. He wasn't sure he wanted to start now, but the pain kept getting worse.

He should have told Inez he hadn't meant it.

No. Fuck it, he *would* tell her. 'Cos... 'cos she'd come back, wouldn't she? Yeah. She would, and she wouldn't be happy about this. She'd just sigh, like he'd proved her right about something she hadn't even bothered to accuse him of... sigh, and roll her eyes. And she had a point, he knew. This *was* really stupid.

Someone would have to call an abulamance, he realised.

An... amblibance.

Blue light. Noise. One of them things.

What the fuck's happening to my head?

Insistent bony fingers of panic prodded at his brain.

No one's coming. No one's there.

You are entirely, completely alone.

3

No more chances.

"Nnn...." He tried to speak, but his tongue seemed dry and too big for his mouth.

On the plus side, after what he'd gone through when he woke up, there couldn't possibly be anything left in his stomach, so if he *was* going, it wouldn't be like Jimi. 'Cos he'd never wanted that. Not that and not, like, flat on his back with a needle in his arm, nor slipping away on some slick, rainy, midnight road. None of those clichéd rock star jags, man. That... that just proved people right, y'know?

But at least something like that could be quick and full of impact.

Not like this.

Not this way.

He thought he heard a door close, somewhere out on the landing. *There.* Someone would walk in, any minute now. Someone would save him.

Shit, why am I so tired?

Blood still seeped from the broad, ugly wound on his brow. It stung his eyes. In his mouth, the sweat-salt of blood and... tears? Christ, he was an idiot. He wheezed sharply, surprised to find his chest tight and cold. The numbness kept spreading. Fear snaked through him as he fought for breath with rhythmic, bloody gulps of panic. It *was* it.

Please, no. Not like this. Not alone.

Wait.

No, *not* alone. Somewhere... in the bedroom? No. Across the hall. In his studio, in his sanctified, private, special place with crooked wall and exposed beam and view of river. *No!* Someone... messing with his tape deck. Inez? He moved his lips, his mouth slack and cold now, trying to say her name.

Music. He heard the sound of his own voice, sketchy and thin as he worked his way around the embryonic ideas that got him out of bed at three in the morning. She shouldn't be in there. That was his shit, man... Inez knew better than that. Better, unless she was really pissed off. Like when she ransacked his wardrobe in a temper, with pinking shears and paint. Or broke the windscreen on the Jeep.

Couldn't she forgive? Just one time?

He could.

Footsteps, on the landing. He flexed his fingers, trying to brace himself against the slick floor, to sit up, but his body wasn't listening. The door creaked, and he scrabbled with faint feet and fingers at the lavatory, the sink, the tiles, trying to haul himself up and only dimly aware of losing control of his bladder.

A soaring guitar line, sharp and raw, curled around him, knitting like a solid thing into the steam as he stared for the last time at the ceiling, strangely aware of how cold the floor felt beneath him.

I ain't never gonna get that lick right now.

S'a real bust, man....

He thought he felt a warm hand on his shoulder—for a moment, almost companionable—and then he was moving so fast, up and up, and he wanted to scream because he knew nothing but the pain.

That it ended soon wasn't much of a consolation.

He dropped back to the tiles and, naked except for the plastic shower curtain that fluttered down to half-cover his body, Damon Brent died.

Chapter One

Brighton is nice in the spring. It has its charms all year round, but is, I think, at its best when the weather is pleasantly warm, but not yet hot enough to melt the tarmac or encourage otherwise sane men to go out in public in nothing but shorts, sandals, and a sheen of sweat. I lived in a flat on the edge of Kemp Town village—ten minutes to the city centre and only five minutes' walk to the seafront—and, while I might not have exactly been happy, I'd started getting my life back on track.

I even had a sea view, just. You had to sit on the window seat and press your nose to the glass, or get someone to hold your legs while you hung out of the tiny bathroom window, but you *could* see it. Nothing but a murky grey band on the horizon, of course; the suggestion of white caps to swelling waves rather than the panoramic views you got with the expensive apartments further along the seafront. My building—a Victorian townhouse, carved unceremoniously into flats by developers sometime in the Seventies—hardly matched up to those high-class Regency extravaganzas, built like limestone and stucco wedding cakes, but it was comfortable and fairly convenient for the university.

I'd begun the second year of my social history PhD—*Ad nauseam: images of women in advertising 1900-1970*—hoping less for the thrill of becoming *Doctor* Ellis Ross than the security of landing myself a junior lectureship. I'd have taken a museum post, too, or even archive work. Anything that interested me, paid a regular salary and wasn't one of the 'women's jobs' that, aside from marriage, had been the only route out of the home for generations of girls in my family. Old-fashioned, I know, and probably a stereotype I could have fought against more violently if I'd wanted, but however stuck in the mid-twentieth century I thought my family were, I still owed them a lot.

No. Nursing, teaching, and secretarial work; not bad choices, but not *my* choices. And that mattered.

It also explained why I came to be working so late on Thursday night. And it *was* late… more specifically, about half a bottle of Rioja and four cups of black coffee away from Friday morning. Perhaps I'd been overdoing it a little bit. Friends had gently reminded me that student all-nighters usually stopped after undergraduate finals, but there I sat all the same, sifting through a pile of facsimile adverts from 1932 for automated floor cleaners.

The top page featured society brides of the preceding year and told the thoroughly modern, independent new women of the sophisticated Thirties that they, too, could be liberated from the shackles of housework in order to look nice for their prospective husbands.

'Will any of these modern girls be scrubwomen at forty?' it asked in bold, loud print.

Hmmm. Almost as good as the 1968 slogan for grape-flavoured Tipalets: *Blow in her face and she'll follow you anywhere.*

The lies human beings are capable of telling each other—and themselves—had never failed to amaze me. How we worked our way through life as a species like that, founding our worlds on tissues of fibs and porkies, was the central point behind my thesis.

I poured myself another glass of wine. Behind me, Mr. Tibbs dozed peacefully on the sofa. A large, black tomcat of indeterminate age, he'd turned up three days after I moved in and had never left. Beneath his gentle feline snoring and the occasional soft yowl as he disembowelled some many-legged dream critter, the stereo played softly, blocking out the general static of the night.

Stretching, I yawned and wondered if it would be worth going to bed. The stereo whirred faintly, slipping another CD into place. I blinked, briefly confused, because I hadn't expected anything else in the playlist. The confusion turned to surprise as a heavy four-four drum intro echoed out of the speakers, split by a tight, wailing guitar in the third beat. When the hell had I put *that* in there?

I recognised it, even before a voice—a light, agile tenor, dripping with the imperious sex appeal of black leather trousers —curled into the room, working over a hard, fat blues in E.

Got me gunnin' for ya baby,

Got you in my eyes tonight
Down at heel, on my wheel,
Girl we gonna make it right

I smiled to myself. The title track from Brother Rush's *Rush On Love* album of 1975. The disc was an expanded edition, part of a boxed set that I'd bought for Mum, a gesture of reconciliation after years of mocking her taste in music.

A true child of the revolution, she'd been a glam kid all the way, littering my own childhood memories with twangy glitter guitars, primal four-four rhythms, and kitschy vocals that didn't need to make sense. Good honest rock 'n' roll, she'd called it, and she had danced around the house, dusting, vacuuming, cooking, all to the strains of T. Rex, Suzi Quatro, Slade, and Alice Cooper. While other kids' mums doted on inoffensive, cardigan-wearing crooners as an early sign of menopausal mayhem, my sister Becky and I had a parent who still treasured mementos from the Marquee Club and laughed at all the in-jokes in films like *Velvet Goldmine*.

But Brother Rush... oh, how she'd adored those four shaggy-haired boys from Bermondsey! When I was small and my sister had gone out to school or Guides or some such thing from which age or chronic shyness precluded me, Mum and I had danced our way together through such classics as *Saturday Loving, Darby & Joan,* and *Sit Tight, Baby.* As I grew, I found it embarrassing, then cringe-worthy—but funny in an ironic and post-modern kind of way—and, eventually, I grew old enough to enjoy being a child.

Mum didn't dance anymore by then. But, when the boxed set came out, I'd bought it for her, even though she still owned all her vinyl. She unwrapped the package during a sit-down birthday meal in the Cricketer's Rest near Thorley and touched the cover art like the cheek of an old friend. She drank two gin and tonics with her steak and ale pie and told my sister and me about the day Damon Brent died. Even then it made her cry... although that could have been the gin mixing with her pills.

The day it happened, she said, she'd met up early with our Auntie Jan and Auntie Gail (whose kinship was purely honorific, but who'd been in our lives since we were in knitted booties just the same). It was that long, hot, anarchic summer of '76, when everything smacked just a little of sex and violence, though the majority of it seemed to bypass East Hertfordshire's pretty villages and quaint market towns. Mum, Jan, and Gail had been planning on a swim at the new Grange Paddocks pool, then maybe some shopping before drifting off to their various part-time jobs in the local boutiques and, in Gail's case, the Cecil Rhodes museum.

They caught the announcement on the news, Mum said, on a twenty-two inch screen in the window of Jerry Dickson's TV & Radio Hire (in Medlar Lane, just off the High Street, as was), as they crossed the road on their way up to the sports centre.

She said it took less than twenty minutes to get home at a run and, though Granddad never approved of modern music in general, and men with hair below their ears in particular, parental arguments and work commitments alike got swept aside with the full force of inconsolable, desperate teenage tears. The three of them leapt aboard the train from Bishop's Stortford within the hour, more or less, and by half past four that afternoon, they'd become part of the throng that was flowing into Gloucester station. People, mostly girls, pooled for taxis, buses or sympathetic local drivers to take them to the hamlet of Rodley and the renovated sloop captain's house with electric gates that lay between it and a muddy, shallow strip of the Severn.

The TV reports soon showed drifts of limp flowers and pale faces, clustered in silent despair at the end of the driveway. Mum said the most striking thing was the quiet. Even when the rain came, a real downpour, the first breakthrough rainfall of that drought year, they never really noticed it, just standing, watching the cars come and go, uniformed officers redundant in the damp stillness and the blue lights of panda cars reflecting in puddles.

At least, that's how she told it.

Brent had been idolised enough—and the transport, in those years of three-day weeks and power cuts, was bad enough —for the vigil to last days, with more people arriving well into the night. By dusk, Mum said the rock star death reportage, moving from full flow to torrent, was suggesting Brent had died in his bathroom, encouraging the assumption that a drug binge had ended finally and messily on the tiles.

CROAKED BY COKE?
DAMON BRENT DRUG DEATH HORROR!

The Sun had proclaimed by the evening edition, although they later apologised and retracted the allegation. *The Times* carried a discreet four-line obituary on page five, and even *The Express* took a day off from their anti-immigration bashing of the '4-star Malawi Asians' to run a condescending opinion piece or two. Mum and Auntie Jan had all the cuttings, carefully pasted into the sad final pages of their Damon Brent scrapbook.

The initial shock of it soon got subsumed by the scandal of drug investigations and the clamour of the tabloids preaching, while simultaneously dishing out their column inches to 'insider' exposés from guests and former friends of the deceased. Worse—or luckily, depending I suppose on what kind of PR team you had—there had been a party at the house the night before and, even as the police carted Brent out in a body bag, nearly two dozen rock and pop luminaries of the day were being expected to give urine samples and full witness statements.

Of course, the inquest quashed much of this ghoulish fun by establishing that Brent, although well under the influence of both drink and drugs, had merely slipped, fallen, and hit his head. The whole thing was chalked up as a stupid accident, the misplacement of foot on soap and an advertisement to the young to stay clean. It crashed his image somehow, wrecking any chance of rock martyrdom. Shunned and embarrassed, Brother Rush split before Christmas, their music fell from fashion, and Damon Brent's death, if at all remembered, simply became an unfortunate and foolish codicil to a life and a career cut short.

The CD had played on while I was thinking and now a live cut of that classic standard *Sit Tight, Baby* twisted out of the speakers, the sound of the band broader and harder over the top of a screaming audience. Mum had always said how incredible Brother Rush were live. Brent's voice vibrated in the air, shining as the chords tumbled around him like sweaty roses.

She got a face like the Mona Lisa

(Sit tight, baby)
But she ain't smilin'
And I can't see her....

A strident guitar lick topped the four-four bass in a drawn-out crescendo, pierced by the characteristic Damon Brent battle cry: the sound of a vibrato bar pushed to the limits and a jubilant, orgiastic '*Yeeeeeeaaaaahhhh*' closing in a breathy leer right up against the microphone. You heard it on nearly all the live sets, but it vanished in studio recordings, somewhere in amongst the mumbling and the synthesisers.

"Not bad for a man with a dodgy perm and lurex trousers," I murmured, taking off my glasses to rub eyes bees-winged enough to be buzzing.

"Well, that's charming," he said. "Thank you *very* much."

Huh.

I blinked, and replayed the moment over in my head.

No… I definitely had heard it.

I wished, in a way, that I'd been having weird experiences for months before. It might have proved me crazy, but— knocking pipes, catching strange reflections in the mirror, hearing things on the wind—I hadn't had any of that. That's what made it so odd. So believable.

So clear.

I stared at the papers in front of me. They still lay there innocently, black-and-white photo repros and colour plates, page after page of my chicken scratch notes. My wineglass and my coffee cup to the side. The computer screen flipped to its screensaver. Very retro toasters flapped through endless space.

I'd have to turn around eventually. I tried to picture the

worst possible thing I could see and, considering that, what I saw wasn't half as bad as it could have been.

He sat... no, that wasn't the right word. Nobody could just *sit* like that. He sprawled, but in an extremely stylish way, on the window seat, one knee drawn up with his right arm propped carelessly across it, his foot tracing circles on the sheepskin rug and a cigarette smouldering in his left hand, threatening to deposit a pillar of ash on his bright purple loon pants.

It was pitch dark outside. I hadn't bothered to draw the curtains; the window wasn't really overlooked, so I rarely did and, in any case, I liked the moonlight. The dim tanné glow of streetlamps further down the road gave the blackness a warm edge, backlit him with an odd, pale aura against the dark glass... in which he had no reflection, I couldn't help but notice.

He wriggled a bit on the window seat, turning his head as if looking out into the night, trying to see the sea. You couldn't, not at that angle and not at this time of night. Nothing but the smudges of pavements seeming wet under the lamplight and, in very late or very quiet moments, the distant sound of the waves, somewhere in the blackness beyond. I swallowed heavily.

I'd seen Mum's famous scrapbook more than once. Oh, the blond perm seemed a little more natural-looking and—apart from a lot of heavy, Theda Bara-style kohl—he had none of the stagy make-up he'd worn on half a dozen different album covers.

Definitely Damon Brent, though.

I reasoned, in what I gathered to be my madness, that it must be him. Quite clearly. If a flesh-and-blood look-alike had broken into the flat, I would have heard him, after all. I licked my lips and turned my chair around. In addition to the purple crushed velvet loon pants, white patent boots with spangly silver stars and a two-inch stack heel encased his feet. A tight green babycord jacket buttoned over something gold and shiny and a very long, very stripy scarf completed the picture. On one lapel of the jacket, a gold starburst brooch set with red stones— either truly tacky costume jewellery, or something genuine, Victorian, and very expensive—glittered, catching the light.

He looked at me, all poise and self-assurance and smiled, with perfunctory dimples. I looked at his cigarette, wondering how long he'd been sitting there for it to burn down like that, and it occurred to me that I couldn't smell the smoke. I opened my suddenly very dry mouth.

"Um...."

"Mm?"

"Sorry. Do you need an ashtray for that?"

I *could* have been surprised at myself. But, equally, I could just have hyperventilated. Damon Brent looked at the cigarette, as if seeing it for the first time. He smiled at me again, and it seemed more genuine.

"Yeah, thanks."

I handed him my mainly empty coffee cup, waiting to see if it smashed to the floor.

"There you go. Er," I said, as a pale but very solid hand grasped the handle, "I'm afraid that's the best I can do. I don't smoke and I wasn't expecting visitors."

"Oh, there's only one of me, baby." An amused sarcasm touched his eyes as he knocked the ash off his ciggie into the cup. "Did I give you the horrors?"

The clipped consonants were pure theatre, just like the way the window framed him, but a hard, flat South London accent prowled behind the thickets of crisply trimmed vowels. I flapped my mouth for a bit, the small lucid part of me wondering what the etiquette might be here. 'Yes, you did. You're dead,' seemed a bit brusque.

"Sort of," I said eventually. "Um…?"

Mr. Tibbs still lay fast asleep on the back of the sofa. So much for feline psychism. Or maybe this delusion would stay totally self-contained.

"Sorry," said the—what?—apparition, dropping the butt of his cigarette into the cup and setting it down on the narrow band of painted windowsill. "It's difficult to know how to make an entrance. Didn't think *I'd* ever say that, but it is." He raised an eyebrow. "You did solid though, baby. No screaming or anything. Very calm. Nice."

"That's only because I'm clearly either mad or dreaming."

The shade, or spectre, or fevered imagining, or whatever he was, of Damon Brent looked at me and smiled kindly.

"You can see me," he said. "Hear me. Right?"

I nodded. "Er. Yes. But—"

"Then you're only slightly more sane than everybody else, love. I wouldn't worry about it."

As I wondered just what he meant, his smile spread into a grin, and he wriggled forward on the window seat, pulling a pack of Camels and a silver lighter from the pocket of his jacket.

"You'll be all right. Ah, can't tell you, though, babe…. This is so cool! I knew you'd come through. Hey, mind if I smoke?"

I blinked. He rattled the packet at me.

"Oh. Er… sure," I said, partially out of curiosity.

Mystic ghost ciggies? I wondered. He put the slim white tube between his lips. It didn't look at all unusual and neither did the pack, not... really. It had no glaring black health warnings printed on it, and the artwork seemed dated, though the carton was clearly new.

"Thanks." He looked up at me over the lighter's flame and flashed another dimpled grin. "Helps me when I'm nervous."

I said nothing. *Him*? Nervous? The cigarette's tip flared red, and he took a long drag. I expected the bitter, acrid smell of tobacco, and the lack of it disorientated me.

"You do know me, though?" he asked suddenly, earnestly, taking the ciggie out of his mouth. "You know who I am?"

"Damon Brent," I said, before I really meant to.

For all I knew, there could have been some sort of Rumpelstiltskin thing to the passing of the words. Naming him might have made him invincible, or real, or consigned me to the underworld for six months of the year or something. You never can tell, after all.

But there was no puff of pantomime smoke. He just nodded, looking relieved, his expression that of a man whose ego had been well-stroked.

"Good. Okay. That's a good start."

"Start? Start to what? How can...? Why are you—no, wait. *How* are you here?" A note of panic rose in my voice, and I tried to quash it. "I mean, you're.... It's been more than thirty years. You're—*what* are you?"

"Oh, baby... that hurts." He pouted, mischief in his eyes, and then a half-formed smoke ring slipped from his mouth like a laugh. "Nah. I'm all I ever was, Ellis. Well, near enough."

"How—? No." I pinched the bridge of my nose. "I'm not even surprised you know my name. But why... why are you—?"

He turned to knock cigarette ash into the coffee cup on the

sill. Then, unfolding his legs, he stretched away from the window seat like a languid and very trashily dressed cat. He seemed taller than I'd thought.

"This doesn't make any sense." My fingers dug ineffectually at the collar of my baggy overshirt, pulling it tighter around me. Had the room grown colder? "Out of all the people I've known who've died, nobody's ever popped back to say—"

"None of them were murdered," said Damon Brent softly.

He moved to the fireplace, ostensibly looking at the row of framed photos I kept on the mantel. *Murdered?* I couldn't tear my gaze away from his boots. They sank slightly into the pile of the carpet when he walked, and there wasn't a thing that looked odd about it; so he must have mass, I reasoned, physical existence of a sort. Yet he left no footprints, no traces of himself. I heard no rustle of velvet, nothing that signified his presence. As if wherever he stood, just for that moment, he could be as solid and real as anyone... but for that moment only. Like trying to catch a shadow seen from the corner of the eye.

"Murdered? No," I said, running off at the mouth, unthinking. "There was an inquest. It was an accident. My mum said—"

"I was there, sweetheart," Brent said dryly, turning to glance at me over his babycorded shoulder. I had never before seen such old eyes. "She wasn't. So take it from me, yeah?"

I blinked, my mind racing to catch up.

"But.... How? I mean, you...."

He took another pull on the cigarette. The fingertips of his free hand brushed along the white gloss paint of the mantel, his head tilting a little to the side. He seemed lost in thought. He exhaled and turned back to me, the cigarette smoke wreathing fantastical arabesques around him.

"Someone smashed my brains in for me, baby. I think that's pretty conclusive, don't you?" Brent lifted one pale, nicotine-stained hand and waved the smoke away. "Look. This is a bit of a head trip, I know…. Have you got any scotch?"

"No, but there's, um, there's gin, I think."

He nodded and looked hopefully at me.

"Oh," I said belatedly. "Right, yes. I'll, er…. Do you—I mean, *can* you…?"

Something in his face made it seem like a silly question. I got to my feet—pleasantly surprised to find that my legs still worked—and edged out to the kitchen, never quite turning my back on him.

I wasn't entirely sure what would happen if I did.

In the kitchen, I stared for a while at the white melamine cupboards, because there are few things in life more statically, irrefutably normal than melamine. Everything out here was just as I'd left it on my last coffee break, right down to the teaspoon I hadn't bothered to wash up and the unwiped worksurfaces. I opened the cupboard, pulled out the bottle of gin I'd bought last Christmas, and fetched two cut-glass tumblers. A quick fumble through the fridge-freezer yielded ice cubes and some slightly flat tonic… and the fact that I still wasn't panicking surprised me. The simple, deliberate actions of ice, glasses, and tonic, the metallic spin of the lid on the gin bottle, occupied my mind and hands entirely, and I found I'd started worrying about not having any lemon or lime slices.

Murdered.

Well, that made both more and less sense, but… why now? Why, above everything, *me*? I turned around with a glass in each hand and nearly dropped the lot as I found Damon Brent far closer to me than I could ever have reasonably expected. Like standing in front of an open freezer, a bone-gnawing chill seemed to pull me in. I gasped with the sudden shiver and promptly felt like I'd been really rude, even as I stepped backwards.

"Sorry, baby," he said, looking crestfallen.

I could see the beginnings of lines around his eyes, the places the kohl had started to settle. Embryonic lines around his mouth, too, and tiny filaments of golden beard growth; the frizzy, untamed bits of hair, the thick dark blond sideburns, and each one of the bridge of freckles dusted across his nose and cheekbones. The mole on his neck and the pulse beating there... both so wrong and so strange, but not as strange as not being able to smell him. He should have absolutely reeked of cigarette smoke, and there should have been the scent of aftershave—lots of aftershave, if I was any judge—but I couldn't pick up a thing.

I hurriedly cleared my throat, realising I'd been staring.

"Is that why... why you've.... Is it why?" I managed, keeping my voice even. "To avenge your own murder?"

I held out one of the G&Ts. He grasped the tumbler with long, callused fingers; the glass seemed to crawl against my skin for a brief, horrible moment, cold and slippery. I did my best not to shudder.

"Nah." Brent wrinkled his nose, and the intensity of things lessened slightly. "Not exactly. No avenging, anyway. That's very frowned upon."

He smiled and, despite myself, I let out a short laugh.

"Drink up," he prompted, raising his glass.

He waited, watching me drink before taking his first sip.

The gin barely touched the sides, but it didn't much help. I could still see him, for a start. I cradled the tumbler in front of my chest.

"I don't understand," I said, in a masterpiece of understatement. "Why me? What—"

"Shh. Come sit down, yeah? That's a girl. You're all right."

He reached out as if to usher me back into the other room, but his hand stopped, half-curled, halfway to my arm. He flashed that perfunctory, dimpled smile again and, taking a big slug of his G&T, stepped back to allow me past. I—unusually for me—obeyed and went through, looking carefully at the carpets, curtains and ceiling, as if my flat had somehow conspired to betray my sanity. Nothing had changed. No melting walls, no wonkier than usual floors…. I toed off my brogues and curled into my armchair, watching Damon Brent prowl across the floor.

"You—you said somebody…." I trailed off, not quite willing, or not quite able to voice it. "How? I mean, who—"

"If I knew that, would I fuckin' be here?"

The venom in his voice took me by surprise, and almost instantly I saw the apology on his face. Abruptly, Brent paced to the window, nervy and jangling, like a stop-motion film. Something of that lingered in his movement, and it hurt my eyes trying to follow it, though I couldn't look away.

"Look," he said. "It's not…. It's complicated, all right?"

I wanted to suggest that this drifted close to further epic understatement, but he looked at me with such seriousness that the words stuck to my tongue. He took up his place on my window seat again, one foot slung over his knee, drink cupped elegantly in his hand with his cigarette smouldering in two extended fingers. Like he owned the room, like nothing could shake him. He turned his head and looked out again towards the general direction of the sea, apparently watching the line of silver-grey light starting to rise along the road. Was he waiting for the dawn? *Rush On Love* played on in the background. His left hand, resting on his knee, tapped absently to the rhythm of a phasey middle eight.

"It ain't," he said carefully, "like if some bastard shivs you inna ribs and you get a good look at him on your way down, right? I mean, I was rat-arsed... but I didn't do all that to myself, Ellis. You gotta believe that."

Brent took a short, urgent pull on his cigarette, still watching me as he exhaled. I swallowed, my interest caught by his words as well as the lunacy of his presence. Murdered...? Oh, if Mum had only known...! He'd missed his perfect avenger.

"So, what?" I groped for a little clarity. "Somebody struck you?"

"Yeah." He nodded, gaze flicking down to his drink. "I remember—I mean, I think I did take a purler—I was laying there on the floor... waitin' for help. Dunno how long. Could've been minutes, hours.... No way of telling, 'cept it bloody hurt."

I wanted to look away. When he spoke again, it came almost as a whisper.

"There is.... I mean, I didn't even know that it was really real, y'know? But it's the last thing. I didn't wanna be on my own. I tried to get up, an' I couldn't. And there was music. My tapes. Then the door opened and... and I thought I was gonna get help, yeah?"

My heart leapt in my throat. He must have seen, then. Something, at least. Some suggestion, some clue. Perhaps he read my mind, because he shook his head.

"I didn't see who it was. I just…."

"What?"

He glanced up at me, pausing to take a swallow of his drink.

"Like I meant nothin', y'know? Just picked me up and—" He grabbed a handful of hair at the back of his head, jerking it roughly upwards. "—*blam*. That's it. Finished the job, right?"

He lifted the cigarette to his mouth, hair dropping back around his face. His jaw moved tightly, as if he was chewing the smoke. I frowned.

"But, if that's true… how did the autopsy not pick that up?"

Brent snorted.

"I had enough in my bloodstream to put half the runners in the National under, baby. S'what the pathologist said. And the old Bill were so busy bustin' everyone there with so much as half an ounce of grass that no one thought…. Nah. Time they put me in the ground, I was just a clumsy drunk, wasn't I? Good funeral, though. All those people. I'd never've thought…."

He rubbed his palm over the knuckles of his left hand, making the ice cubes in his drink bob. It didn't seem like a good moment to ask who he thought might have wanted him dead. I watched the cigarette smoulder in his outstretched fingers as the vampy riffs and twangy guitar breaks of *Cheeky Half* echoed from the CD player, Brent's voice cresting them both in taut, aching style:

> *Baby let me be your one and only*
> *'Cos only tonight'll do*
> *Baby if you make me lonely*

I won't share half with you

I remembered Mum circling a roundabout four times on our way to tea with my gran while that played on the car radio and she tried to find a way to answer my simple child's question —'What's it about?'—without using the word Mandrax. I shook my head.

"This is mental. I'm talking to a… what?" I faltered. "What am I talking to? I mean, I don't understand how you…."

Those Theda Bara eyes flicked briefly over me. Damon Brent pulled himself out of whatever memory he'd been idling in and took another drag on his cigarette.

"It's what I was tryin' to tell you, baby," he said. "I'm still me. When you—*y'know*—all that stops is what the world makes you be. What you're left with is the part of you that says 'I am', yeah? The little voice behind your eyes. Your centre, right?" Brent touched splayed fingers to his peacock chest. "This is everything I am, everything I've ever been. And it stays the same. Ten years, thirty years… means nothin', baby. Time and space are just ways of slicing it all up."

I frowned at him over the rim of my glass. Hate though I did to admit it, I understood his point. All human measurements—cubits, turves, feet, acres—started off as relative to the body itself, all derived from how much a man might lift, plough, carve or carry. As what we call our civilisation got more complex, our systems for counting did too, our ways of quantifying—all right, slicing up—the world. Trying to understand it. And still, so much remained unknown. And yet… I had questions. So many questions they filled my mouth like cotton wool.

"But… *death*? Death isn't important?"

He opened his mouth, like he planned to make some flippant remark, but perhaps something in my face stopped him. He swigged his G&T, and I watched that so carefully, trying to understand how it worked. Brent shook his head.

"Nah, it is. It-it's the biggest thing, baby. But it's not… it ain't what you think. No more up, down, left, right, no more worryin' about the bills and the politics and remembering to keep your heart pumping and your pancreas… pancreating," he said vaguely, and I realised that Damon Brent, glam rock god, might not be all that bright.

"Look," he went on. "What stays, yeah? What stays is everything else. The you that made every memory you've got, had every thought, wrote every line…. You believe what you like, Ellis, but believe every little thing you do's important, baby. 'Cos it's all you're left with, in the end. And eternity's a bloody long time to spend being totally aware of every last little piece of yourself. Y'see what I'm saying?"

I stared. *That's it, I've lost it.* Clearly, totally, and completely.

He took a long drag on his cigarette and then held it out, thumb tapping on the butt, its smouldering tip pointing straight up at the ceiling. A thin column of smoke coiled from it, dissipating in a halo around his head. I bit my lip. Though my upbringing hadn't exactly been religious to start with, having all my preconceptions rearranged by a man wearing more eyeliner than me felt unsettling, to say the least.

"Heaven or Hell, maybe," he said, the corner of his mouth twitching in a mirthless little smile. "Depending on how much you like yourself."

"*Kata ton daimona eaytoy,*" I said, not thinking.

It's the inscription on Jim Morrison's grave, in that cramped, shabby corner of Pére-Lachaise. It means 'according to his own demon', though for the Ancient Greeks, the word daemon had more to do with demi-gods and fallen heroes, guardian spirits and genius locii than pitchforks and leathery wings.

"Do what?"

I blinked, aware that I'd lost him.

"It's Greek," I said and I would have explained, but Brent grinned broadly at me.

"See?" he crowed, pointing with the hand that now held both cigarette and drink. "*See?* That's what I'm talkin' about. Fuckin' Greek… that's brains right there, girl. I knew you'd be the one."

"Huh?" I looked up sharply. "What does that mean?"

"Mm." He waved dismissively at me as he reached around to get his coffee cup ashtray from the sill. "Hang on, honey."

He unfolded himself and crossed to the sofa, pulling the coffee table a few inches closer to it so he could have both ashtray and drink in easy reach, and pushing aside with apparent disregard the stack of conference flyers and paperwork I'd left on its surface. He sat down among the patchwork throws and inexpertly embroidered needlepoint cushions—not what I'd chosen for myself, but had inherited from Gran just before she died—and grinned sybaritically.

Mr. Tibbs chose that moment to wake up. He stretched, jumped gracelessly off the back of the sofa, and regarded Damon Brent with the malicious yellow-eyed disdain he reserved for all visitors. An amazing sense of relief washed through me. Finally, definitely, *it wasn't just me.* Then the cat, the great hairy black tom that had been known to duff up badgers, rolled onto his back, four chunky legs in the air. Brent's hand descended and, absently, he began scratching the furry black belly.

"Now, thing is…. I'll do my best to keep this cool for you, baby," he said, shooting a puff of smoke from the corner of his mouth. "But it's easy to blow it, and I've been waiting a long time for another chance at this. I don't wanna screw up." He tilted his head, another photoshoot pose. "'Cos there's Rules. Y'know?"

Mr. Tibbs began a wheezy, rusty purr. I frowned, distracted.

"Sorry. Rules?"

Brent made a gesture of hopeless laissez-faire with his cigarette hand.

"Yeah, y'know… like, bureaucracy, baby. I've wanted this sorted out for years, but it's not easy. You still, like, got to bow to the Man, y'know?"

"What?"

He opened his mouth, tip of his tongue up against his teeth, then winced.

"I can't…. Look, I told you there'd be things you'd ask that I couldn't—"

"Oh, come on!" I swigged the last of my gin and tonic, finally finding a voice for all the disbelief. "If—*if*, okay?—this is really happening, you can't just expect me to swallow it all without having questions. I mean, the planet's crawling with people who say they know all the answers, whether they read it in a holy book or the Archangel Gabriel came down and dictated it all to them on golden notepaper with exclusive rights to the merchandising...what difference would it make to tell me?"

Outside, a car passed; the unmistakeable bass thump of a customised gas-guzzler tearing up Marine Parade. Somewhere, spotty teenagers had spent the night comparing spoilers on the prom and pissing off the local residents' association. Life went on, I supposed.

Brent stared at me, and I couldn't decide if it was with amusement or respect. Slowly, he took another long, considering drag on his cigarette. He held it, but I didn't want to wait.

"Just give me something. Come on...the worst I can do is sound off like any other bloody kook. I mean, I only even know your name because of Mum," I snapped, feeling that familiar, metallic anger scraping inside me.

Damon Brent flinched. I saw it. Oh, it was over fast, but I saw it.

He narrowed those kohl-rimmed eyes, exhaled a thin wisp of smoke and, when he spoke, his tone was low but the words were like snake strikes. He leaned forward, knocking ash into the much-abused coffee cup on the table.

"Look, what d'you wanna hear, mama? Heaven's a gas; all the angels wear mohair suits, and God's a great guy, even if sometimes He thinks He's Marc Bolan?"

For some reason, in that whirl of frustration, it pleased me to see that I'd goaded him.

"I just want answers."

"Answers ain't gonna help you, Ellis. You need to keep your head straight. You know what I'm sayin'? Reality...

reality's a bitch, right?" He took another pull on the ciggie, taking it down to a miserable stub of a dogend. "So many different maybes, all pressed in together. Until you see the bigger picture, you can't even begin to.... Look. Nothin' is simple, yeah? Nothing's ever just one thing."

He crushed the cigarette out on the side of the cup, letting the butt fall into the gritty dregs.

"That's why I can't tell you, Ellis. I can't let you blow your mind on this, not when I need you solid, baby. I need you to be straight on this. Okay?"

"Wait...." I leaned forward in my chair, realisation slowly dawning on me. "Hold on. Y-You're saying, what? You're here because you believe you are, or because I do?"

Brent pulled another Camel from his pack. He laughed softly.

"See? Said you'd got brains," he said. The unlit cigarette wagged as he spoke. "Told you. Nah, it's... it's both. Y'see what I'm saying? But it's hard, really hard, to find somebody that can, right? Anyone who can really see.... I mean, I tried, baby. I really did. For the longest time."

He struck the lighter and stared gloomily at the flame.

"Inez just threw a plate at me. My own old lady and she just freaks out... then swears blind she never saw anything. Couldn't, you know? Or wouldn't. I dunno. But, huh, if you knew half the hoops I had to go through to get here tonight...."

He trailed off, playing idly with the lighter. An inscription caught the light on its polished surface, but I couldn't read what it said. I rubbed a hand over my face. This was crazy. *I* was crazy... but he had my interest. And the bastard knew it. The sky paled, the inevitable morning making the cosy warmth of electric light seem dull and deceitful.

"I want answers too, baby," he said, still looking down at the lighter. "And I want... I *need* help. Will you help me, Ellis?"

The dawn had come. Weak gold sunlight started to filter across the rooftops. Traces of a sea mist would be clinging to the road outside. From the floor below us came the muffled sounds of my neighbour, whose name I'd never known, crashing into his furniture. He did that some mornings, and most evenings he descended gently into oblivion by way of the bong but, all in all, he kept pretty much to himself and only made intermittent noise, except for that time he'd woken the whole building up at four a.m., screaming about invisible pink spiders.

I sighed. "I don't see what good you think I can do, or why.... I mean, wouldn't you have been better off going to someone in the police? Or a criminal historian... a lawyer, even? Why me?" I asked, aware of that slightly hysterical whine creeping back into my voice and hating it.

"It's... connection, baby," he said wearily, with a look that suggested I wouldn't understand even if he tried to explain. "You'll see."

"Wh—"

"Shh, look... I know you can do it, right, girl? It ain't about why, it's about *can*, Ellis. And you're talking to me. Believe me, baby, that is a serious step up. Anyway," Brent tipped his head to the side, giving me a thoughtful stare as he lit his cigarette, "how many chances like this do you get in a lifetime?"

I glared at him, because I disliked being manipulated. Though he had a point. His proposition intrigued me, certainly in terms of evidence... or, rather, the lack of it. I could picture it now: *'The prosecution calls the deceased to the stand. Total silence in court, please, and would the jurors all join hands around the table?'*

But I had commitments. This stuff belonged to speculative journalists, cranks and, yes, crackpots, not…. My train of thought foundered, and I realised, for probably the first time in my life, I *was* the crackpot.

And what the hell did he mean by that 'connection' crap?

Brent exhaled a lazy pool of cigarette smoke, still staring steadily at me through narrowed eyes. I shifted uncomfortably in my chair.

"Point taken." I frowned. "But I don't understand why…? What am I supposed to do? How? And I still say there are hundreds of people better than me for…. I mean, there'd be real fans out there. Anoraks. People who'd jump at the chance to—"

He snorted, leaning forward to knock more ash into the coffee cup. I decided I'd have to see if I couldn't find that atrocious volcanic ashtray Auntie Jan had brought me back as a present from Pompeii, several years ago. I'd put it in the back of the kitchen cupboard, hadn't I? With the good wineglasses I normally only used at Christmas. Brent regarded me with a hooded gaze familiar from numerous publicity stills.

"Yeah… right. People who'd take it as calm as you, baby? People with brains, who'd listen? People smart enough, believable enough to go where I can't, ask the questions that need asking… see things and make them seen? No. You're sensible, Ellis. Christ, girl… you wear *brogues*."

I looked down reflexively at the shoes I'd left by my chair, feeling suddenly sensitive about my choice of footwear.

"Which is fine, of course," Brent added quickly, having the grace to look slightly embarrassed.

I stood up, pacing across the room, hands shoved deep in the pockets of my overshirt. I needed answers. Perhaps not as badly as he wanted them, but it occurred to me that, just maybe, I could be the one in control here.

"One question," I said, facing the door. "Before I say I'll do it."

Idiot! screamed a tiny part of my brain. But, I reasoned, why not agree? Either I had a chance at something I could never have imagined, something no one could possibly pass up because this—this tasted of truth, a real opportunity to walk the void—or, and the possibility did remain, I'd gone bonkers in the night and none of it would matter anyway.

I turned and found him within inches of my nose.

"Argh! Don't *do* that… that's one thing. You don't get to do that," I snapped, lurching backwards.

"Sorry, baby."

He stepped away, and that strange coldness that had struck the pit of my stomach lessened just a little. I felt dizzy and steadied myself with a hand on the back of the sofa.

"What's the question?" he asked.

From below, I heard Mr. Downstairs' flat door slam, followed by the front door and running footsteps receding down the path, then the pavement, thinning into the distance. A car passed and, somewhere, a dog barked.

The sunlight glinted off Damon Brent's hair and off his horrendous brooch. Gold and red. His cigarette smouldered and deposited a few flakes of ash on my carpet.

"Exactly how long have you been here? Watching, waiting…?"

"Ah." That sarcastic little turn to his mouth, back again.

"Long enough. Long enough to make you listen."

"Oh, G—" I began, beginning to feel queasy.

"Hey! Scout's honour." He held up three fingers. "No bathrooms, no bedrooms, and definitely no knicker drawers."

"Hah!" I narrowed my eyes. "Were you actually ever a Scout?"

He shrugged. "Went to Cubs every Wednesday down Thorburn Square. Well, for a couple of months... would have been about '57, I s'pose. Gave it up after my dad bought me my first guitar."

I watched him contemplate that memory for a moment and tried hard not to think about roomfuls of small boys in shorts singing *Ging Gang Goolie*. If, I thought, this was a phantasm—some figment of my fevered imagination—it had just hit a whole new level of weird. Plus, I wasn't sure I trusted him about the knicker drawer bit. Or the bathroom, come to that.

"All right," I said, part defeat, part admission, part acceptance... part everything, I supposed. After all, who could ever expect something like this? "I'll do it."

Brent grinned hugely at me.

"Cosmic!" He flicked his half-spent ciggie into the coffee cup and clapped his hands together. "So, where d'you wanna start, baby?"

I groaned. Sleep would have been a preferable place.

Chapter Two

August 28ᵗʰ 1976

"*How* much? You're joking! She is... it's a bloody laugh. Jan... Jan, she wants three pounds for the wreath," Caro complained, nodding at the woman behind the counter who stood, implacable, her arms folded.

Jan rolled her eyes. She had been peering through the florist's grubby window, trying to catch sight of Gail. Her view was cramped, restricted by the peeling white lettering that, from outside, read WEDDING FLOWERS BY IRENE and the cork noticeboard with assorted small ads and leaflets pinned to it that sat on the sill, leaning against the glass. With relief she finally made out the figure of her friend, asking directions from someone outside the grocer's.

"Caro, no." Jan turned to her sister, shaking her head. "We

can't spend that. We'll need money to get home, then there's food, drink… we're going to need to think about somewhere to stay, as well." She turned to the woman, presumably the Irene of the wedding flowers, though she seemed to lack the *joie de vivre* for the job. "What else have you got, please?"

The florist nodded to a display stand of plastic buckets, bottle green and filled with tired gerberas, hanging their orange heads between slightly off-white sprigs of gypsophila. A few spiky dahlias, their petals drying up at the ends, sat in the end bucket, together with a ragged bunch of pom-pom-headed chrysanthemums, already starting to shade from white to brown and giving off a distinctly sour smell.

"No." Caro shook her head. "Jan…!"

Jan sighed.

"Nothing else?"

Presumably-Irene sniffed and folded her arms.

"Well, it's on account of the increased costs, isn't it? You've no idea, my girl, what it's like keeping this lot fresh. We've had standpipes, you know, water rationing. The lot. Have you *seen* the trees round by the hospital? Worse for the flowers. I've lost whole loads of stock, thanks to this bloody weather… not to mention growers' crops failing. Entire market's facing ruin, you mark my words. Now, do you want them or not?"

Caro gave an exasperated growl, and it looked to Jan like she might cry again, so she pulled her purse from her pocket.

"At least the chrysanths are white. How much?"

"Sixty pence a bunch. I'll do you a nice big one, with some gyp."

Jan took her sister's arm as Caro mumbled something about gyp being bloody well right and nodded.

"Fifty a bunch, and we'll take three."

Presumably-Irene pressed her narrow lips together.

"Fifty-five."

"Fine." Jan ignored Caro's squeak of protest and handed over the money. "Thank you," she said as Presumably-Irene came out from behind the barricade of her counter to haul the flowers from their stagnant bucket.

The girls watched her make up three generous bunches, wrapped tight in waxed blue paper and held with red elastic bands. Jan gave the flowers to Caro and hustled her back outside before she could cause an incident. Gail met them by the door, sweltering in a long seersucker skirt and short-sleeved blouse, freckles standing out like beacons from her forehead to her fingertips. She stared at the flowers.

"Oh, no... was that it?"

"I know." Caro glanced over her shoulder. "Bloody bitch in the florist wanted three pound—"

"Look," Jan cut in, "we've got the flowers. That's the important thing."

"Yeah, but," Caro began, the threat of tears clouding her eyes again.

Jan glared at her. "Gail, did you get directions?"

"Yes. A man in the grocer's knew where it was. Well, sort of. He said we want the A48 and we have to go to Minsterworth, then turn right at the Severn Bore pub, go up the hill, and he thought it was around there somewhere. He said he didn't 'rightly know exactly'."

"Which way's the A48?" Caro squinted along the road, back towards the station, the light thick and hazy.

Jan wiped the back of her hand across her forehead. The

sun beat back at them from the pavement, and the gold crucifix she wore at her neck was uncomfortably hot against her skin.

"We have to go that way to pick it up." Gail pointed, still unsure. "Past the cathedral. Look, it's more than eight miles, Caro, and we don't even know where the house *is*.... I asked how we could get there, and he said best try for a bus. They go from the bus station out that way, but he didn't know how often... there's not so many in school holidays. But it might be cooler to wait down there, mightn't it?"

"We'll be stuck there for hours." Caro was already stepping down from the kerb. "We're better off hitching."

"Caroline! You know what Dad said...!"

"Grow up, Jan. Anyway, there's three of us," she added, darting out into the road to wave down a passing car.

Jan and Gail watched her make attempt after attempt at attracting the attention of the vehicles going by and exchanged weary looks. Finally, a grey Morris Minor coasted to a halt. They broke into a run and caught up with Caro, explaining their predicament to its cheerfully perplexed middle-aged owners.

The car was hot and cramped. They shared the back seat with the couple's shopping and an elderly, smelly Yorkshire terrier, sitting on a folded tartan blanket among the bags of fruit and veg. It wagged its tail as they got in, widdled on Gail's skirt as she slid across the seat, and then went to sleep, the pervading odour of doggy ammonia mixing with the steadily wilting (and increasingly reeking) chrysanthemums. The Fullers, as the couple introduced themselves, appeared not to notice, and Gail, not liking to say anything, sat quietly and tried to spread her wet skirt out as best she could on the upholstery. The couple were politely sympathetic to their young lady passengers, yet seemed not to have heard of the tragedy at Westleve House, or even of Damon Brent, although Mr. Fuller did remark that "th'are a lot of cars about, yun't there?"

The Fullers took them to Minsterworth, stopping the car outside the village's pretty redbrick school. They waved, set off towards the bridge that would take them on to Elmore Beck, and wished the girls luck in finding a lift to Rodley. The Morris puttered away into the heat haze. A warm, gentle wind bowled along the road in its wake, rippling through the pollen-heavy verges and trees. Gail scowled.

"It peed on me! The bloody thing *peed* all over my leg!"

"It doesn't show. Honestly." Jan took a tissue from the pocket of her frayed denim shorts and dabbed ineffectually at the damp patch. "See?"

"That's not the point. I smell like dog wee."

"You don't. Not really. Honest."

The sound of ducks and miscellaneous waterfowl drifted up from the river, echoing among the trees that framed the school's sharply-pointed roof, light glinting along the line of tiles that cut into the sky. Caro strode out towards the village church, looking for a car to flag down, cream sundress billowing in the dusty breeze.

"What time is it?"

Jan crumpled the tissue back into her pocket and looked at her watch. "Nearly quarter to two."

She peeled off the checked shirt she'd layered over her t-shirt and tied it around her waist, fanning the still, thick air uselessly with her hand. Gail sighed, letting the flowers droop in her grasp.

"We're going to be stuck out here forever."

Jan peered over at her sister, arm extended as a dark blue Volvo turned past the end of the road. Caro kicked her sandal against the tarmac and, Jan thought, probably swore. Just like at New Year, when Dad had let them go to that party at Naomi's house, up in Cambridge (he hadn't known that her parents would be away for that weekend—*quelle surprise!*) and it had seemed like such a great idea to all walk down to the river and try to look cool in front of the partying students, which had worked amazingly well and they'd had a wild time... until they realised that Naomi and the other girls had gone home without them, and they didn't know how to get back to her house. Jan wondered what Dad would have done if he ever found out about that night. It had been sheer dumb luck that they'd got back to Naomi's place in one piece, but of course Caro had that in her veins, didn't she? Luck, charm, bloody-minded determination... and the looks to go with it.

Jan felt the sister's prerogative of bitter criticism stir at the back of her mind and pushed it firmly away. Not today. A patriotically grubby red Ford Consul pulled up at the side of the road, the first success of Caro's efforts, and they ran to join her.

"You're for Westleve House are you, girls? Jump in."

The voice sounded cheerful and rounded. It belonged to a dark-haired woman of much the same appearance, red-cheeked and smiling compassionately.

"How did you know?" Caro asked without a trace of irony, taking the passenger's seat. Jan and Gail slid into the back, fighting the odiferous chrysanthemums for space.

"Just a hunch. Heard all about what happened on the radio this morning... everyone's been talking about it. Terrible business. Such a shock. Awful. Now—are we all in?—I'm on my way home, but I'm sure I can drop you down at least as far as Rodley." She tapped the fuel gauge. "D'you know where you're going from the Methodist Chapel?"

"Er, not really. Well, not exactly," Gail volunteered. Jan nudged her in the ribs. "Is it near the Severn Bore pub?"

The dark-haired woman crunched the gearbox and swung the Ford around the corner with jolly abandon, not back onto the main road, but out into the network of impossibly narrow, leafy country lanes riven with jack-in-the-hedge and rabbits. Popularly known as 'local roads', for few tourists knew about them and fewer still had the nerve to tackle them.

"Close," she said. "The pub's about a mile or so that way, back on the main road. Really, if you want to avoid the traffic, you need to get up to Goose Hill, then on for another couple of miles 'til you come to the Chapel, then you go right and follow the lane up to Westleve, though I understand it's quite a walk."

Caro gaped, blue eyes wide in the rearview mirror.

"Do you, like, *know*...? I mean, have you—"

"Oh, good grief, no. Never been up there myself, though Westleve House is quite the local landmark. One of our historic buildings... I say 'our', I'm from Salisbury, actually. Still, surprising it's not a listed building. The local history society was absolutely up in arms about it when Mr. Brent bought the place, but I'm told he's done a lovely conservation job. Did, I mean. Gosh, it's dreadful, isn't it?" She tutted and pushed the Ford through another agonising gear change. "Of course, he was very well-known, locally. When he was 'at home', as they say. Used to come into the butcher's in Westbury—it is very good, does lovely game and everything—and he always came in himself, you know.... Very pleasant chap. Of course, all the girls in my

6B class are absolutely struck on him... they'll be devastate—
um."

She glanced in the rearview mirror, took in the three pairs
of wide eyes, the three mouths rounded into 'o's of amazement,
and cleared her throat.

"I teach at the school in Minsterworth, just where I picked
you up, you see," she said cheerfully.

"You *met*...?" Caro melted a little against the seat. "Ohh...
you actually *met* Damon Brent? Cor!"

"Miss Lenham, incidentally. Dora Lenham. Nice to meet
you."

"Oh. Um, Caroline Ross," Caro said absently. "That's my
sister Janet, and our friend, Gail Masklin."

There was an associated shuffling and muttering of
greetings from the back seat.

"What was he like? What'd he say? What was he wearing?
Did he—"

"Caro...." Jan warned.

Dora Lenham smiled. She threw the Ford around another
bend, flinging the brakes on to allow safe passage for an
oncoming tractor.

"Like I say," she said diplomatically, "he was a lovely man.
Very polite. So, have you three come far?"

"Hertfordshire," Caro replied, surreptitiously gripping the
edge of her seat.

Miss Lenham sucked her teeth and waved at the tractor
driver as his vehicle inched past, pushing against the hedgerow
with a graunching series of splintering, woody twangs.

"Quite a way."

"We had to, Miss," said Caro, her voice starting to crack,

"soon as we heard."

"I see." Miss Lenham waited for the tractor to chunter further down the lane and the young girl beside her to stop quietly weeping. "Um. Very... very laudable. Yes. There do seem to be quite a lot of people coming, don't there? Popping up all over the place. Er. Lucky the Bore's not rising this weekend, I have to say... especially with the bank holiday. You can't move for tourists when the tide's up and the river's putting on a big show! The Severn's a tidal river, you see," she added, lapsing into the broad, comforting tone of her profession as she propelled the Ford back out of the hedge. "The Bore rises up and pushes all the way in from the sea. Very powerful. Most impressive to watch when there's a big surge. Naturally, we do get a lot of silly so-and-sos coming to surf it. There was one lad taken to hospital back in March, but I suppose they won't be told.... Years ago, centuries, there used to be a harbour down Rodley way, you see. Matter of fact, Westleve was originally a captain's house. Dates from somewhere in the sixteenth century, I think... at least, originally. Good grief, will you look at all these people!"

Miss Lenham rounded the turn into Goose Hill and drew the Ford to a rather abrupt halt. Here, gaggles of teenagers, white-faced and waiflike even in the heat, clutched flowers. Cars crawled like sun-baked beetles, people weaving in and out of their paths with the same dull stride. The silence seemed nearly as hard, as oppressive as the heat.

"Like pilgrims," Caro whispered.

The Ford edged into the formation, and they crept along the length of the hill, up towards the Chapel, where a hastily painted sign had been erected offering tea, use of a telephone, and parking facilities. A uniformed police constable directed cars to the gravelled forecourt beside the grey stone building, and the minister stood in the doorway, proffering a handkerchief to a red-faced, near-hysterical girl in a yellow dress.

"Right. Best let you out here, I think," Miss Lenham said, drawing the Ford to a standstill on the narrow verge. She rummaged in the glove compartment for a few moments, came out with a paper napkin and a biro and wrote down her telephone number, which she pressed into Caro's hand. "Now, listen. You take this, all right? That's my telephone number. You promise you'll call me if you get stuck."

"Thank you, Miss."

"It's no trouble. I would have said the pub'll be doing cheap rooms, but looking at the number of people here…. Are you three all right for money?"

"Yes. Thank you," Jan cut in, because she believed there should be limits to the kindnesses of strangers. "We really are. Thank you ever so much."

"All right, then. Take care."

"We will," Caro promised, and the three of them left the car, Jan and Gail still struggling with the flowers.

Dora Lenham inched the Ford back down the lane, and the girls walked on towards Westleve, just glimpsing the house's roof, black against the darkening sky, its bulk obscured by the thick hedges that lined the lane.

"I can't believe it," Caro murmured as they came into the heart of what was, to all intents and purposes, an impromptu camp. "Can't believe it."

They noticed the flowers first, pooled around the gates,

forming great drifts either side of the dirt-and-grit turning circle. The fragrance of lilies, marguerites, and a dozen other summer blooms mixed in the air, leaving it heavy with pollen and heat, tinged with the dust and hot metal of the cars. A couple of police vehicles, accompanying the uniformed officers that stood by the gates, enforced a nominal cordon of yellow tape. A St. John's Ambulance crew waited in attendance, and journalists, sated on the morning's diet of famous faces and scandal, loitered in the shade of the beech trees, smoking and talking amongst themselves, the occasional burst of laughter breaking the quiet. And it was quiet... unbelievably so. Mourners lined the grass verges and hedgerows. Sitting, standing, huddled, but all recognisable by shocked, pallid faces and hollow eyes, most united by long hair and flashes of old denim and bright colours. Beside a battered camper van, parked at the far end of the lane, a young man in a pair of cut-off jeans patched with jewel-like glimpses of different coloured fabric sat, cross-legged, playing an acoustic guitar in a manner not really very much like Bob Dylan. His hair hung down his bare, brown back as the strains of *Shelter From the Storm* filtered over the gathering, the sound of muffled crying mixing with his tearful rendition of the song.

Caro, Jan, and Gail found themselves pushed through the ragged crowd, propelled in part by jostling elbows and in part by the strange wave of emotion that pulsed through the assemblage; half grief and half awe, almost made tangible, it drew them like iron filings across paper, without thought or control, just response. Within minutes, they stood before the gates themselves, the pathetic bunches of dry, wilted chrysanthemums in their hands.

The tributes had been piled high, some bound to the gates, some propped beside them, the scents of summer in waxed paper wraps and crinkled cellophane, peppered with the pastel *In Loving Memory* cards of a dozen florists. The messages on them, in so many different hands, were a tumult of silent voices driven by a sense of outraged justice, of sorrow and desperation, clamouring to know why, struggling to understand.

Tears ran hotly down Jan's cheeks as she laid her flowers down, and one of the WPCs on gate duty—with a kind smile and nearly as many freckles as Gail—guided them along the lee of the gate, helping them add their tributes to the swell and helping them support Caro when, with a wail, she collapsed into floods of desolate, jaw-cracking tears.

The WPC took the time to settle the three of them back behind the cordon—on a grassy patch of verge beneath the hedge, close enough to the gates that the scent of the flowers still enveloped them—and made sure that Caro remembered to breathe. Jan untied the shirt from her waist and spread it out on the ground. She sat beneath the oaks and ashes and held her sister as she cried, her own tears making Caro's hair damp. Gail went with the WPC to fetch some water from the St John's crew, returning with a paper cup and a wad of napkins

"Here you are." She sat beside them on the grass, dabbing at her own wet cheeks and streaming nose. "God, I didn't think it would be so…."

She sniffed noisily and blew.

"You should have been here this morning, poppet," the WPC volunteered, pulling a soft bar of chocolate from her pocket and breaking off a few rapidly melting squares for Caro. "There you go, eat that. There… better? Blimey, I don't know!

Six fainters, four hurlers, and one who needed oxygen. Mind you, she *was* asthmatic…." She glanced up at the sky. "Is it me, or is it clouding over a bit? That'd be nice. Could do with it cooling off… last thing you need with this lot is heatstroke." A whistle pierced the air behind her, and she turned. "What?"

"Oi, Vonny. Incoming."

Jan stared. Behind the gates—*the* gates, the actual gates—a man with a walkie-talkie, long hair, and a large moustache was calling to the WPC.

"She's coming," he said. "Frank reckons about five minutes."

The WPC's face fell. "Oh, God… *why*? The Super's going to go ape. He wanted her kept out of the way, 'specially with this lot hanging around…!"

She glanced over her shoulder at the assembled journalists. The long-haired man shrugged.

"Ain't much I can do, love, 'cept let you know."

The walkie-talkie crackled, and he exchanged a few words with the voice on the other end, though Jan, listening from behind her hanky, could barely make out anything beyond his curt reply.

"Roger that." He turned to the WPC. "Hey, if I was one of your lot, Vonny, I'd be saying you ought to get yourselves on standby."

"Great. And you said there's no back way in? Oh, bugger… all right. Thanks, Tim."

"Pleasure."

The long-haired man winked and moved off. Jan watched the WPC, with the studied nonchalance of one caught in the middle of something very urgent indeed, talking to her colleague at the other end of the gate. The policeman nodded, and the two constables went to confer with their compatriots, leaning quietly against the panda car and sharing a smoke.

"Psst." Jan elbowed Gail in the ribs. "Something's going on."

"What?"

"Look."

She pointed. The police had started to tighten up the cordon, edging people back along the lane.

"What are they doing?" Gail asked, sliding Caro's head from her shoulder, pushing forward to get a better view. "What's happening?"

They heard the commotion from beyond the dog leg in the lane, the hollering and thud of running feet, together with the short, sharp pulses of a car horn and the stern calls of policemen trying to assert authority without causing a riot. Simultaneously, from behind the gates, there came the sounds of crackling radios and slamming doors. They heard shouting, saw the gaggles of people part, and the journalists spring into action with well-oiled pack co-ordination, even as the car turned into the lane.

It was a saloon, the colour of pallid, dusty oatmeal rather than the black that might have been expected. The windows weren't even tinted. The rear door opened before the car had fully halted, and with the crunch of heels on grit, Inez half-stepped, half-fell from the vehicle. Apparently oblivious to the barrage of camera flashes and shouted questions, she lurched towards the gates, a pair of huge, tortoiseshell sunglasses shielding her eyes, a high-collared dress in a psychedelic print of cerise and purple showing off her tanned limbs and shoulders.

"Let me in," she said over and over as the young policewoman with the freckles tried to take her by the elbow. "Let me in! I need to get in... I need to see— Will you just let me through?"

The young WPC plugged courageously on with the speech about coming down to the station probably being best and how they were terribly sorry, but madam really couldn't do anything here, the area still officially being a closed scene and.... It did little good.

The crush of people behind pressed Caro, Gail, and Jan closer to the cordon, jostling them in the excitement. Almost on a level with the gates, they heard the raised voices within, the sounds of running feet, scuffling bodies, and the rough whirr of the gates themselves starting to open. Staff—in the informal uniform of black tees and worn jeans—and police darted to and fro, trying to instigate damage limitation before the grieving widow did something everyone would regret. Nearly close enough to reach out and touch, close enough to smell her French perfume and see the thickness of her make-up, the girls watched Inez Blackman—tennis star and celebrity wife—bob helplessly in the whirl of movement. The journalists hit with the ferocity of water on a break wall, questions flying up like foam and cameras clicking wildly.

"Inez! Inez, this way, sweetheart—you weren't at the house when it happened, were you? Where were you, darlin'?"

"How did it feel when you found out, Inez? Can you tell us who told you? Was it the police?"

"Have they given you details? Is it true it's an overdose?"

"Did Damon often throw parties when you were away,

love? Were you having problems? Inez?"

"Would you say your husband had a drug habit, Inez?"

"Come on, sweetheart, one little comment!"

"Inez!"

The last shout came from the crush at the gates. A tall figure in worn blue jeans and an overtight t-shirt barrelled through. Inez looked up, and her mouth twisted, caramel lips framing a terrible, choking cry. Her hands reached out, dark red nail varnish livid against the pale fabric of his shirt.

"Charlie...! Oh, God... oh, God," she repeated, a stifled mantra as she sagged against his chest. "Oh, God, Charlie... what happened?"

Beside Jan, Gail squeaked. Jan glanced at her friend: wide blue eyes, hands clasped over her mouth, and a deep blush fading up to her cheekbones. Not three feet from them stood Charlie Davies... and it looked like Gail might wet herself.

Brother Rush's bassist was a tall, broad man, built like a rugby player but with a great shock of tightly permed mouse-brown hair, thick sideburns, and heavy, straight brows framing his face. His tight t-shirt highlighted the firm planes of muscle beneath it and demanded FREEDOM FOR TOOTING in a sparse, black font. He frowned and put a protective arm around Inez, pushing back the more overeager hacks.

"You wanna jump back, man? Give her some bleedin' air! C'mon... can we get the lady inside? It's all right... come on, girl. I know," he soothed. "I know. It was a stupid accident. It just— Look, man, you wanna get out of my face?"

It seemed for a moment that punches might be thrown. The offending photographer backed off and held up his hands, his voice wheedling.

"Hey, chill, Charlie... just want to show the real story, right, friend?"

The bassist's eyes narrowed. "I'm not your friend, you evil little sod. Now fuck off."

Amid the jumble of sight, sound and tension, Inez's voice carried on a high, ethereal chant.

"Oh, God," she moaned again, sinking to the ground, hanging between Charlie and a uniformed police constable for a moment, the tears coming fast now.

The pushy photographer made another sortie at Inez. Charlie shoved him hard enough to send the man spinning and, in the ensuing fracas, the two stars were bundled through the gates, the pale car following at a crawl. The sound of Inez's weeping faded along the driveway, with the crunch of feet and wheels on gravel and the crackle of radios. The journalists dissipated, some departing to take another circuit of the perimeter in the hopes of finding low-boughed trees or ill-watched side exits and some sloping back to their cars. The WPC on the gate gently dissuaded a few of the more enthusiastic fans from trying to sneak in, and the photographer with whom Charlie had got physical stood, brushed himself off, and made a few choice utterances, met with jeers and heckles from the assembled fans.

"Frigging vulture!"

Jan glanced at her sister in surprise. Caro, hands still cupped around her mouth, looked embarrassed.

"Well?" She lowered her hands and made a pretence of smoothing out her dress. "It's no way to behave when the poor cow's just lost her husband."

"Wasn't he manful, though?" Gail crowed, still pink and

glowing. "*Him*. Couldn't believe it. Right there! Charlie Davies... right there! Actually, really... oh, *wow*...!"

The whispers passed through the lane like waves, those mourners that still lingered growing restless with the heat and the activity. Slowly, the sense of silent expectation settled back over the crowd. At the end of the lane, a young man with an old-fashioned ice cream cart mounted on a barrow had rolled up and started crying his wares.

"Got ice creams! Ice cream, Coca-Cola, sausage rolls...!"

Jan's stomach growled for the first time since breakfast. She'd been about to ask the girls whether they wanted something to eat when something patted against her bare shoulder. She looked up. Ragged grey clouds drifted across the sky. Another drop fell, then another, thudding into the grit, the first rain in months.

Gradually, like a curtain falling across a lit window, the rain pattered the length of the lane and beyond. The assembled crowd stood in silence, just watching. Then, as if a bung had been removed, a key turned somewhere, distant thunder began to grumble and the rain fell harder, thrashing against the ground, thrumming against the cellophane and the flowers. Some of the crowd whooped, some squealed, others wept, and others just stood and stared at the sky, squinting into the fall.

Jan held her shirt over her head, looking around to see where Caro had darted off to. The echoes of lightning paled against the clouds and, as the rain continued to steam down, the crowd began to break apart, and the young man with the camper van suddenly found himself becoming extremely popular.

Chapter Three

It rained on Friday. I woke to find a fine spray of droplets blowing in through my bedroom window—habitually left open for Mr. Tibbs—cursed, sat up, and groped for my dressing gown. The night could, in the face of all the grim and grey mundanity outside, have seemed like a dream, but it didn't. I didn't for a moment consider the possibility that it hadn't been... well, real. I had to admit, however, that it'd been the first time a rock star had kept me up all night. I suspected that I'd been a disappointment; Damon Brent, chain smoking and pouring out floods of names and half-connected stories, caught up in the excitement of having someone listen to him, had slowly realised that I'd never heard of most of the people he was talking about.

Around four a.m., he'd looked apologetic, and said I should go to bed, grab some sleep. There'd be, he said, plenty of time.

He smiled when he said it. Some kind of private joke, maybe.

I stumbled into the kitchen. Something familiar glinted on the worktop, next to the kettle. His brooch. Still sleep-mired and claggy, I stared at it for a long while before picking it up. It looked like something that might have lain hidden in an elderly aunt's jewellery box, only to catch the light like a prism when, some empty afternoon, it got taken out and examined for the first time in years. I shook myself. The thing felt heavy in my hand, cold, but it soon warmed against my skin. A folded piece of paper lay under the brooch, the writing on it large and rounded. Just one word.

Boo !

At least he had a sense of humour. He had a plan too: he wanted me to pose as a biographer, gaining access to interview his former bandmates, friends, associates, and... other suspects, I supposed. He thought I'd be professional, believable. I hadn't the heart to tell him I had no idea where to begin, how one went about finding people who, as far as I knew, hadn't been heard from in almost three decades.

The best place I could think of to start was Mum's scrapbook. It had been one of the few things of hers I couldn't bear to keep in the flat after she died, perhaps because it had been so important to her, so intimate. I'd kidded myself that I'd given it back to Auntie Jan because she wanted it. It had been half hers, too, I'd said. But now I wanted to look at the cuttings, the adoration... the tiny sealed moment of history when it had all happened and she—*they*—had seen it.

I showered, dressed, and caught the bus out to Broadwater, spending the whole ride thinking about how I would frame my questions. I could hardly tell her the real reason I wanted to know, but 'so, apropos of nothing, how about the Seventies?' didn't really seem the right way to kick things off. Still, I reflected, as I got off the bus and walked up from Sompting Road, thankful for the time to clear my head and prepare myself, I didn't know anyone more entirely sane than my Auntie Jan. I wanted to see her and to believe that somehow that would make it all fine again.

I got to the corner shop before I realised I'd be visiting empty-handed, so I stopped in and bought a packet of treacle tarts. They looked pathetic, even to me, and I felt like a heel.

Auntie Jan's place stood among the neat, pleasant, three bedroom post-war semis on the way to the golf course. All uniform, all... nice. She and Uncle Duncan had bought it when they married and never felt the desire to move. Not even now.

She was the first of the family to leave Hertfordshire, at least for a generation or so, and she'd been so pleased when I came down to the university for my postgrad study... I'd barely been able to convince her not to move me into the spare bedroom. I couldn't have faced that. Oh, I would have visited anyway, yes, but....

The door opened, and Auntie Jan beamed at me, her heavily powdered face lighting up like a sunrise.

"Hello, darling! Come in, it's so nice to see you."

She ushered me into the little porch with all the pomp of the Queen of Sheba and insisted on taking my coat, thanking me for the paltry treacle tarts.

"I was surprised when you rang," she said, leading me through to the kitchen. The immaculate state of that house never ceased to amaze me. "I wasn't expecting to see you this week, knowing how busy you are with all your studying."

"Oh, it's not so bad," I lied, trying to peer into the living room, the curtains pulled tight and the door only slightly ajar. "But are you sure I'm not disturbing you?"

"No, don't be silly. Sylvia came this morning. He's had his bath, he's all spruced up... knackered, of course, now. He's asleep, love. Be awake and with it again in a minute, I shouldn't wonder." She put the kettle on, rattling in the dark pine-look cupboards for plates. "Gives us five minutes off, though, doesn't it? Here you are, open up those tarts."

I plated up the treacle tarts, watching Jan make tea with a kind of automatic efficiency she had probably acquired as a nurse. It seemed easy to picture her applying first aid, taking pulses, and changing dressings with those strong, brown fingers, stripped of pearly nail polish and gold rings, her slim figure clad in a more conventional uniform than the baggy pink sweater and black leggings she always seemed to wear nowadays. Her lips, painted coral pink, pressed together in a line of pure concentration, and her big, round glasses lent an owlish air to her face, softened by her short, blonde-streaked haircut. She treated herself to a morning off once a week—when Sylvia, the physiotherapist, came in—and divided that precious free time on a strict rota. She would go to the hairdresser's for a touch-up to the roots and a cup of coffee she hadn't made herself, or to the chiropodist for a pedicure with added tea and scandal. Sometimes she went shopping, or met up with a friend for an early lunch and a whole hour or so of normality.

"How are things?" I asked. We sat at the kitchen table, addressing the treacle tarts. "Really?"

She shrugged. "All right. Nothing new. He's got his ups and

downs, same as ever. Some days, he's almost himself again, but others.... No. No, we're fine, love. Honestly."

She smiled, and I had sense enough to let her steer the conversation past the jagged rocks and into the shallows. She poured the tea, stirring two sugars into her cup with methodical rhythm, and I put my hand on her arm.

"Thanks, love," she said, because she would never have cried.

Not, at least, with me there. I gave her wrist a gentle squeeze and withdrew my hand.

"By the way," I said after a moment, lifting my cup. "I need to pick your brains."

"Ooh." She chuckled. "You can try, darling... but I don't know what good they'll be."

"I'll try and get some use out of them," I promised with a grin. "Listen, do you remember, it would have been about the mid-Seventies, when you and Mum and Gail went up to Gloucester?"

She frowned. "Gloucester?"

"You'd have been about fifteen, sixteen, I suppose.... It was when—"

A drawn-out moan came from the sitting room. Auntie Jan, with that cool efficiency, placed her cup back in its saucer, stood, and carried on talking in the same bright, even tone while she moved through the clean magnolia hallway.

"Oh, hang on... I know! You mean when Damon Brent died, love?" Her voice rose a little as she entered the sitting room. "Yes, we were there.... Of course I remember *that*. You come through, Ellis. He's decent, you're all right. It's Ellis, Duncan. Ellis. That's right, darling, your favourite niece."

I stood, licked the crumbs of treacle tart off my thumb, and followed her. Uncle Duncan, as usual, had been positioned to face the bay window. He liked, in his waking hours, to look out at the other houses, the cars and people passing by... particularly, as Auntie Jan observed, if they happened to be young women. It seemed an unnecessary trial to get him into his specially equipped bed for simple daytime naps, so—for his little rests, as she said—Jan would draw the heavy curtains and leave him in his chair with a pillow and a blanket. "He always lets me know when he's ready to get going again," she would say. He did so now, moaning and flicking his head to the side to articulate what he wanted, his fingers curling on the arms of the chair with the frustration of his flesh-prison.

His mouth contorted, small flecks of drool piling at the corner, as he shaped the word 'window' with an unwilling tongue. Pale blue eyes wheeled in my direction, and Auntie Jan pulled the curtains open, filling the room with thin, drizzly sunlight. Photographs lined the walls, covering those surfaces not taken up by the paraphernalia of caring and coping. Many of them depicted family occasions—birthdays, wedding receptions, anniversaries—and holidays, frame after frame of Auntie Jan and Uncle Duncan standing in front of famous landmarks, monuments, or moments of local colour. In one of them, Uncle Duncan sat on a camel, beaming with the same wide, toothy smile that opened up his face when he recognised me. That could take a few minutes now, on his worse days.

"Hello, Uncle Dunc," I said, pulling out one of the dining chairs that lived against the wall, overcrowding the room, and settling myself on the hard, Regency striped upholstery.

The dining room had been converted to house his sit-in

bath and adapted bed with the help of a disability grant but, despite everything she did for her husband, Auntie Jan refused to get rid of her reproduction faux mahogany dining set.

I held out my hand for Uncle Duncan to grasp with three hard fingers that shook with the effort. He gave me a smile, and his tongue flexed against the roof of his mouth in approximation of my name. I kissed his cheek, and he laughed.

The doctors, during the months of hospitalisation that followed the crash, said he might never relearn the brain functions that most of us take for granted—memory, speech, those little luxuries—but, slowly, he'd started to prove them wrong. The taut, waxy indentations at the side of his forehead, where a metal rod had pierced his brain as he lay, crushed beneath the train carriage, still showed the marks of the operations. "We're thankful," Auntie Jan would say, in what I thought at first must be some perverse Pollyannaism borne of desperation. "Because he wasn't burned. At least he wasn't burned."

True enough, though I wondered if the fire wouldn't have proved a more merciful disaster. The settlements had started, with all the investigations and inquiries finally completed, and it seemed that every few days the papers covered another victim awarded compensation. I asked Auntie Jan how the solicitor felt about their progress.

"It's going very well, apparently," she said, fastening the curtain tie-backs. "She's a lovely woman. Reckons it'll be over and done with by Christmas, which'll be helpful... 'cos he's not cheap, are you?"

She prodded his outstretched arm as she passed, sorting through the plastic cups, bags, and beakers that lined the sideboard. Uncle Duncan smiled. She returned with a moist tissue and wiped his face, carefully cleaning away the tracks and traces of his sleep.

"Mind you, you've never been cheap… I'll give you that. Have to, don't I? Always some new gadget or something, spending I don't know what on your fishing gear…."

He frowned and gave her a reply that I couldn't make out.

"Well, yes. Holidays, that's fine. Bit different, though, isn't it? That was something for both of us. Still," she continued, screwing up the tissue and dropping it into the rubbish bag that hung by the chair, "maybe, once all this is settled, we can afford a little break. A few nights in the Cotswolds or something. What do you think? It's not the Nile delta, I know, but it'd be nice, wouldn't it? What's that, love? Drink?"

Auntie Jan poured a cup of water, helped him drink it, never once breaking pace in her even, jovial speech, though now she directed that sunny, competent rhythm at me.

"It's all very well, this compensation lark, but you don't like to push yourself forward for it. Did you read about this bloke in the paper? 'Travel anxiety'. Enough to pay off his mortgage, just 'cos he didn't like the idea of getting on a train again… and when you look at some of 'em…! I don't know. Mind you, it's not the point, is it?"

She moved back to the sideboard, stacking the plastic cup with its companions for washing and tidying the rows of items with busy, efficient hands.

"It's not about paying for what you've lost," she said quietly, "it's about helping you build a life around what's left."

I opened my mouth, trying to think of something to say but not sure what. What response could there be? I looked at Uncle

Duncan, watching the woman from Number 23 walking back from the local school with her two small children and a little white dog. The youngest child, in an oversized blue jacket, skipped ahead on the pavement, oblivious to its mother's calls.

"Now," Auntie Jan wiped her hands on another tissue, buoyant and bright once more, "what was it you were asking about, darling? Ellis was asking about when Caro and I were teenagers, love," she added, for Duncan's benefit. "In the Seventies."

I nodded. "Seventy-six."

"Yes… you'd have been in the Army still, then, wouldn't you? That's right." She paused behind him, stroking the wisps of his sandy hair. "God, it's thirty-odd years, isn't it? 'Course, I shouldn't think anyone remembers Damon Brent these days."

If only she knew. I said nothing.

"What did you want to know about it for?"

Ah, the merits of preparation. I cleared my throat.

"Well, there's this guy in the Media Studies department at the—"

"Ooh, a young man?"

"Um, yes. Anyway," I hurried on, because there would be absolutely no stopping her if she headed down *that* road, "anyway, he's researching views of celebrity. You know, cults of fame, from Alexander the Great to Princess Diana… how the ways we think about people in the public eye have changed and how the public reacts to… well, to death."

I could hear myself sounding more and more uncomfortable. Auntie Jan pursed her lips and nodded.

"You mean, like the flowers and that? There's more flowers now, aren't there? Shrines. At accidents and things… you never used to see that as much. Not there on the roadside. Yeah, of course, darling... amazing what you can study at university, isn't it?"

Relief began to seep through me.

"All jobs for the boys," I said with a shrug, relying with sly cowardice on the respect I knew she had for my study, for my breaking out. "But I remembered Mum telling us about how you and Auntie Gail went up there and there was the vigil and... I was wondering if I could see the scrapbook?"

Auntie Jan folded her arms across her chest and sighed, gazing out at the grey sky. I hoped I hadn't hurt her. After everything, keeping the CDs I'd bought Mum was one thing, but I couldn't stand to keep the book. Not in my flat. Not where, every time I thought of it, sitting in a cupboard somewhere, I thought of her.

"I dare say it'll be in the back bedroom," Jan said after a moment. "Yes. I shouldn't wonder.... Oh, it was all the rage, then. All those pictures. Coming back, though, isn't it? Getting quite popular again, scrapbooking. Mm. Come on, we'll go and have a look. You're all right here for a few minutes, aren't you, Duncan?"

She patted Uncle Duncan's head, but he didn't seem to notice. Auntie Jan bent down to the level of his chair and squinted.

"Oh, I see. Number 26 is washing her windows. Dirty old bugger."

He grinned a little wider.

"Come on, love," she said, leading me back out into the immaculate hallway, up the stairs, and towards the box room at the back of the house.

More photographs up here: Duncan and Jan on their tenth wedding anniversary, pictures of Duncan in his Army uniform, with his unit and without, and of Jan, posing for a professional portrait she'd won in a magazine, too heavily made up against a cloudy blue background and smiling. There were pictures of their only child, my older cousin Marcus (in Canada now, working for a shipping company), in various stages of growth and high-flying success, and pictures of Mum, too, which still knocked me for six every time I saw them. Stupid, really.

The box room held several large, dark wood wardrobes, part of the old suite that had been in the master bedroom. I recalled, while Uncle Duncan was still in hospital, coming down from my university digs to help Auntie Jan move them out. It was an act of superstition, I think, but she couldn't bear to have his clothes, his shoes, his general mess and stuff, stay in the room. When he finally came home, she left the wardrobes in here, donated the rest of the set to the local hospice shop, and went out to buy herself a brand new bedroom suite. Faux Rococo. Snippets of its white paintwork and curlicues were visible through the partially open bedroom door.

"In here, I think," she said, kneeling to open the base drawers.

The little pendant handles clanked and rattled as she fought with the sticky runners and the piles of old curtains and table linen that now filled them. The smell of musty cloth wafted out into the room, tinged with cedarwood and lavender.

I hesitated in the doorway, the framed photograph of Mum on the opposite wall somehow putting me off the idea of entering the room. It felt… strange, seeing her young, pretty and bikini-clad—posing arm-in-arm with her sister—caught forever on some sun-drenched holiday.

"Here we go," said Auntie Jan, pulling a dog-eared scrapbook out from among the piles of old fabric. She followed my gaze and grinned. "Majorca, 1978. She looked lovely, didn't she?"

"Yes," I said softly. "So did you. Was it a good holiday?"

She looked thoughtful for a moment, then nodded. "Yes. Yes, it was. Very."

I smiled, but there was nothing I could trust myself to say. We both stayed silent for a moment; perhaps in tribute.

"Well, it's all in here. I'm sure there'll be something you can use, darling."

Jan brought the book out onto the landing, and we leant it against the banister between us. Blue card covers, A3 sized, held together thick leaves of grey sugar paper. The pages, brittle with age and glue, had been embellished with swatches of fabric, sequins, and biro tattoos, proclaiming the irrepressible optimism and energy of youth. Damon Brent's eyes stared out at me from the first page, and the whole thing reminded me of some kind of offering, desiccated but unburned.

My heart sank as I looked at that defiant pout, the smoky kohl, and the scary perm. Definitely a teen scream photograph; the stark black and white of the image highlighted every millimetre of cheekbone, created planes and angles, lifting Brent from simply handsome to ethereal. Hyper-real. Auntie Jan giggled. I blinked, not used to hearing that sound from her.

"There you are," she said. "Damon Brent."

She flipped through the next few pages. Brent again, again, and again. Generally, they were publicity shots. In most, the band flanked him, all four of them primped and posing for the camera. In some, his image had been carefully cut out from a wider shot. A few newspaper articles slipped in here and there, clipped mainly from tabloids and music inkies. It seemed Mum's fascination had started early in Brent's career and taken very serious root.

"Ooh, he was lovely, though, wasn't he?"

Jan grinned conspiratorially at me and turned another page. I smiled, beginning to feel ever so slightly dizzy. Brent, again. Stills from a live performance. Hip cocked, he was hammering hell out of a Telecaster, shoulder to lurex-lapelled shoulder with another guitarist whose dark poodle perm fought his own for the limelight. Both faces were contorted, streaked with sweat and sliding make-up. Behind them a taller, heavier guy on bass shared the by-now obligatory frizzy 'do in a mousey brown shade with big sideburns, pepped up with spray-on glitter. The accompanying live review, carefully clipped from the *NME*, saw one reviewer compare Damon Brent somewhat unfavourably to both Bolan and Bowie (I wondered briefly whether I should ask the accused what he thought of the phrase 'pin-up pimpette'), but granted an imperial thumbs-up to the band's 'sweaty, filthy, and at times transcendent rock grooves'. I rubbed my blackened fingertips together and felt a little more like an outsider.

"'Course," Auntie Jan said, gazing wistfully at the page, "your gran hated us going to concerts like that…. Dad too. Oh, you should have seen him when your mum and me were getting ready to go out! He was such an old git about it! Of course, y'know, you know *now* that it's all because they worried, isn't it? But, when you're young, you think you're immortal." She chuckled. "We used to leave our clothes at Gail's and change before we got on the train... mini skirts up to our armpits, you name it. I can't *think* now, what we looked like, but that's how it was. 'Nother cup of tea, love?"

I nodded weakly. We took the scrapbook downstairs, spread it out on the kitchen table. She poured tea and fixed faces to names. The pages smelled of patchouli and white musk.

"They were a four-piece outfit, you see. Damon, obviously, then you had Leon Fielding—he was a Yank, you know— Charlie Davies on bass. Your Auntie Gail thought he was the bee's whatnots, but me and your mum were always Damon's girls."

She giggled again, standing by my chair, looking over my shoulder at a full page close shot of Brother Rush searing the stage. I followed where she pointed; Fielding, the dark-haired poodle perm, clutching a sunburst Les Paul, lip curled like Elvis and knee bent like Berry. His long, oval face was capped by thick, dark brows and deep-set dark eyes, one framed by either a scar or a smudge of eyeliner... I wasn't sure.

Suddenly, something clicked in my brain.

"Fielding... didn't he do a comeback album a few years ago?"

Jan nodded. "That's right, love. It was— Hang on."

She disappeared into the other room for a few minutes, and I heard the sound of a cabinet being opened. I wondered how I could have been so dense, how I could have forgotten. Some bloody detective I'd be! It had been three or four years ago, a chance sighting of a TV ad, but... yes. Leon Fielding was still working. Being a thoroughly Anglicised American during George W. Bush's tenure in the White House gave him almost automatic left-wing credentials, and he'd slipped out of the woodwork with a new UK tour and an album of acoustic ballads. I remembered having mentally pegged him as a slightly edgier Tony Christie and mentioned it in passing to Mum... though it hadn't been one of her good days.

Jan came bustling back in, a stack of three CDs in her hands. She put them on the table in front of me and smiled shyly. I blinked. *No way.* Still, once a fan....

I looked at the cover art on the first disc: just a simple, moody headshot. Fielding had aged a little like Bob Dylan, losing the smoothness of youth for a slight hint of well-worn loucheness in middle age. The song titles had a distinctly anti-war, eco-rock sound to them—*Only the Rain*; *Love, Justice & Dust*; *Take Me Home Tomorrow*—I couldn't help but think what a long way it seemed from twelve bar electric boogies and three minute sweaty-palm pop songs.

"You take those if you like, love," Auntie Jan said. "Have a listen. It's really quite good."

"Um. Thanks," I said, still slightly stunned. I slid the discs into my bag. "I didn't know—"

"'Course," she muttered, and I realised that she hadn't been listening to me, that her attention had already turned back to the scrapbook. "You can see what Gail was on about, now. Look at him, strapping great big bloke like that...."

I followed her pink-tipped finger, tapping the picture. Charlie Davies, clad in bright yellow flares and a frilly orange shirt, stared intently at his fingering and appeared to be trying to ignore the audience.

Jan had a point.

But then there was Damon Brent, right up there in the centre of the thing, with his Telecaster yanked so high he could almost have taken his eye out with it. Spotlights striped the stage red, yellow, and blue, throwing patterns across his face; eyes tight shut, mouth wide open in what I guessed must be that battle cry I knew from the recordings.

"Who," I licked my lips, pausing to take a sip of my tea, "who was the fourth?"

I wondered if Jan heard me at first; her face had softened so as she stared at the picture. But her hand descended, patting me on the shoulder before she reached out to turn the page.

"Joss Napier, on drums. You can't see him in that one... here we go. He wasn't so much of a looker, but you wouldn't really kick any of them out of bed, would you?" She grinned and nudged me in the ribs. "Hm? God, it's such a time ago! All seems so silly now... it was wild, though, at the time. At the time."

She'd turned to another picture, clearly a centrefold from something, the staple marks still visible down the middle of what had once been a two-page spread, carefully torn out and reassembled.

I could identify Leon Fielding, a tumble of dark eyes and darker curls, sporting a silver lurex jacket with impossibly sparkly lapels; Charlie Davies, piercing green gaze and very macho expression both incongruous with the purple feather boa, and of course Damon, pouting for the camera, the old, fragile, and slightly pocked mark of the magazine's staple just above his right eyebrow. Behind him stood the band's last unfamiliar face: Joss Napier.

A tallish, gaunt figure—all sharp, pale blue eyes and long, rounded nose—he looked less bored and contemptuous than Davies, but nowhere near as at ease as the other two. His long dark hair hung below his shoulders in what looked like a naturally wavy style, feathered slightly in deference to fashion, his arms—crossed defensively across his chest—encased in the fluted sleeves of an unflatteringly tight red polysatin tunic.

"Like I say," Jan said softly, "it's stupid, really. Don't know why I kept the thing. Daft, getting like that about... well, we were kids, weren't we? Loving some silly song so much it hurts. Just hormones, isn't it?"

Her hand rested on the page, pearlescent pink-tipped fingers almost caressing the fragile paper. She gazed into the mid-distance for a moment, tutted, then flicked through another few pages.

"Oh.... Yes, this is it," she said, the smile leaving her eyes. "This is what your young man's after, isn't it, love?"

At this point, the offering became a shrine. Page after page after page of cuttings broke the news of Brent's death, over and over again, as if Mum and Jan had not believed the reports. Picture after picture, carefully pasted into the book, showed the house, the drift of tributes at the gates, and the grainy, pale faces of fans clustered outside. There were several similar pieces, with shots of a whole parade of famous faces being led out, white-faced and with blankets around their shoulders. Numerous column inches had been devoted to different versions of MY NIGHT AT DAMON DEATH HOUSE and HOUSE PARTY TRAGEDY: WHAT WENT WRONG?, featuring a lot of artists who should have known better.

A pressed daisy, yellowed and papery, slid from the crackling pages, and Auntie Jan sniffed.

"God, listen to me! I thought it was heartbreaking then. Well, it *was*, it *was* heartbreaking, really. Sounds stupid, doesn't it? For someone you didn't even know, but.... We had all the records, your mum and me, and we'd've gone to a hell of a lot more concerts, 'cept for your granddad. Mind you, he did give us the money to go up to Gloucester. Well, we went straight home when we heard what had happened—it was awful! I never thought he'd give us the cash... he was all set to round on us for making a fuss, but your gran said to him, 'Harold, you was young once,' and gave him a bit of a Look. You remember her Looks, I expect?"

I nodded. They normally preceded a very sore behind.

"Yes. Anyway, he gave us thirty pound! Can you imagine? Of course, we were just glad of it, at the time, but I always wondered about that. Still, we were down that train station like ferrets up a pipe, I can tell you... your Auntie Gail as well."

She traced a finger down a full-page photo of the iron gates, damp flowers bound to the bars, and sighed.

"Such an outpouring, you know. I 'spect it was 'cos he was so young. Only, what, twenty something? And the way it happened... everyone thought it was a drugs overdose, 'cos of course everybody did it then. Rock stars and that," she added quickly.

I nodded, privately intrigued.

"It took hours to get there. We camped in a tent, would you believe? Of course, the house was right out in the middle of nowhere. So many people, 'cos of the party, you know... quite famous, some of 'em... and it was *crawling* with journalists. Oh! I'd almost forgotten this. Look."

Jan flipped over the last leaf before the dismal expanse of blank pages that spoke more than all the column inches put together.

"Yes, this is it. God, your granddad didn't half go spare!"

The headline read: MY AGONY: INEZ SPEAKS OUT, and the full-page photo showed the gates of Westleve House. A woman in dark glasses and a printed dress was being supported by Charlie Davies, his arm outstretched as he pushed away a snap-happy hack.

"Here." Jan's tapping finger picked out three familiar faces in the crowd behind the police cordon. "In *The Mail*, no less." She smiled. "Could have wished it was different circumstances... people were talking to Mum and Dad about that for months after! Your gran said she couldn't set foot in the post office without old Mrs. Hinckley buttonholing her. Wouldn't give her the time of day before, but give the old cow a whiff of a scandal.... God, we all look so young, don't we? 'Course, here, look." She pointed to the woman in the psychedelic frock. "That's Damon's missus. Inez Blackman. Kept her maiden name, she did. Tennis player... don't know if she was a good one or not, but *I'd* never heard of her 'til she married him. Anyway, there we were, and she shows up, goes into histrionics, and out *he* comes... oh! Charlie Davies, almost as close as you are to me now. I tell you, your Auntie Gail damn near wet herself, she was that—"

From the other room, Uncle Duncan called out. Jan blinked and cursed.

"Oh, bugger.... I should have been thinking!" She pushed the scrapbook into my hands and dashed to the door. "Coming, sweetheart—just a minute! You take that, Ellis, love. I hope it helps your young man with his course."

"Thanks," I said feebly, following her back into the immaculate hall, just in time to catch the smell.

"Sod it." Auntie Jan pushed her fingers through her hair. Uncle Duncan began to holler. "I should have been paying attention! He'll only get upset, love," she added, patting my arm. "Go on, you run off now."

I hesitated. "Are you sure? I could—"

"No. Best not, darling. Go on."

She leaned in to kiss my cheek. In the sitting room, Duncan screamed in frustration. It sounded as though he was crying. Jan smiled at me from behind her owlish glasses and wrinkled her nose.

"Go on."

"I'll ring you over the weekend, okay?"

"All right, love," she said, handing me my handbag.

I hugged her, instructed her to give Uncle Duncan my love, when he felt... better... and let myself out while she went to fetch the marigolds and the antibacterial soap. I walked back down to the bus stop with the scrapbook clasped across my chest, feeling utterly and completely rotten.

Chapter Four

I got back from Auntie Jan's at about one, the scrapbook tucked inside my coat to keep it from the rain as I stepped off the bus, though I didn't want to go straight home. Not yet. What if I found *him* there?

Worse, what if I didn't?

I took the picturesque route, past my shabby fringe of Kemp Town and down to the Enclosures. These gardens, laid down in the early nineteenth century, formed the jewel of the Kemp Town Estate proper, jealously guarded by the residents of the ownership co-op. Years ago, there even used to be a constable, provided with his own cottage from which he could judge whether non-residents had dressed respectably enough to be allowed entrance. These days, things weren't quite as formal, though I'd heard there'd been whisperings among the committee to find bylaw loopholes proscribing the exposure of pallid beer bellies. They'd already managed to ban Estate houses having for sale boards outside them on 'aesthetic grounds'... I wasn't sure, but I suspected prospective buyers also had to know a funny handshake or two.

The gardens were still lovely, though, even in today's apathetic, muggy drizzle. There's a cut, a tunnel that runs down from the rose garden to the shore, under Marina Parade. The trees curve over it, they cosset the path and—in the spring—wreath it in mottled green and the heady scent of the flowers. I took that way, shadows dappling my steps. Lewis Carroll, in his mundane incarnation as the Reverend Charles Lutwidge Dodgson, had often visited friends at one of the houses in Lewes Crescent, and allegedly this path had inspired the rabbit hole down which Alice descended to Wonderland. For a moment, Grace Slick's voice ran through my head.

Hurriedly I walked on, down out of the patchy shade and onto the seafront. Watching the grey tide calmed me down, made me think that, despite everything, it might somehow be all right. A foolish notion, maybe, but there's something about the sea that makes you feel so small you know nothing's really important; it only seems that way.

I leaned on the railing, its wooden poles salt-bleached and its cheerful, turquoise-painted metal uprights rust-stained. I stared at the sea, breathing its sharp, sandy air. Mum's scrapbook crackled against my chest and, carefully, I slipped it from the confines of my jacket. This was insane. The metaphysics of last night aside, where was I even supposed to start? If the killer had gone undetected then and no questions had been asked since, how the hell could I find a scrap of evidence? And, even if I did, what would I do about it?

My fingers brushed the dry page edges. Out below the

clouds, a gull screeched, wheeling down on the wind.

"Nice here, innit?"

I stifled the incipient squeak of surprise, then closed my eyes with a sort of sinking dread. "How long have you been there?"

I thought, for a moment, I smelled a waft of cigarette smoke. As my eyes flew open, it dissipated and I looked to my right. Damon Brent leaned nonchalantly on the rail beside me. His bottle green velvet jacket appeared to move gently in the breeze, open over a blue crewneck with a silver foil print on it that looked suspiciously like agapanthus leaves. I found myself glancing at his feet—cherry red Cuban heels—and a pair of distressed (and distressingly) dark gold velvet flares. A cigarette burned in his fingers, pale flakes of ash carried away on the breeze. He turned and smiled at me.

"Not long. Thought I'd come out for a walk, y'know? See what the twenty-first century's like first-hand." He took a drag on the cigarette. "I love the seaside. Never had much chance to go when I was a kid... but I like the sound it makes."

"Uh-huh," I said, still watching the ash flutter.

Could it land, transmuted somehow into something cold, gritty and real? I had, that morning, almost been annoyed to find he'd rinsed up the coffee cup he'd used for an ashtray last night. I'd wanted to know what happened to the fag ends.

"And, um, people can see you?" I asked innocently. "Only, you said how you hadn't found anyone who—"

"People only see what they want to, baby," he assured me. "You're right, that's the trouble... but it's a blessing too. Y'know?"

He winked at me and, just for a split-second, I could have

sworn he wore nothing more glam than a pale blue shirt and washed-out jeans, with a pair of designer sunglasses and a stubby ponytail. I blinked, hoping that the sudden pain in my sinuses would go away soon, and turned my face back to the greasy swell of the waves.

"So," I said, because it was easier to talk than to be left with nothing to drown out my thoughts. "What d'you think of Brighton?"

"Yeah." Damon chuckled. "It's... different, now."

"You were here before?"

I glanced over at him. The rain—a mild and intermittent drizzle before—had begun to patter harder against the water. Drops spotted the railing between us, patted against my shoulders. He wasn't wet at all.

"Mm. Once or twice. London to Brighton and back in a day. Cheap place to come when I was a kid. All old geezers on deckchairs, or greasers havin' it out with a coupla wannabe faces on the beach. Not so much after everything that went down in '64, but you know.... There was a scene. Cheap boarding houses, with curtains that smelled like musty seaweed and frogs."

"Yeah," I said after a moment, wanting to break the trance, but still sort of wondering about the frogs.

It seemed strange to hear him mention the 1964 Riots, and I found myself wondering, from the way he talked, if he'd been a Mod. He'd have been, what? No more than a young teenager then, surely. How old had he been, exactly, when he...?

"D'you fancy going for a drink?" I heard myself say. "I mean, if people can... and, well, I know you *can* drink. I, um, I picked up this scrapbook from my Aunti—Aunt Jan. It's got

photos, cuttings and things that I could do with some help
with... and, well, I s'pose we need to talk about how we're going
to, sort of, do this. Really."

He took a pull on his ciggie and grinned at me. Overhead,
the gulls called hoarsely on the air.

"Yeah. That'd be nice," he said, crushing the cigarette out
on the railing and flicking it into the wind. "I haven't been—
Well, I mean, *obviously* I ain't been down the pub in years,
but... not just for a quiet drink, like. Y'know. After we hit the
big time, we were always rushing somewhere in the back of
some car, dodgin' some scene or other. I used to miss bein' able
to go out on the town, just me and a couple of mates."

A sadness tinged his voice on those last words that seemed
almost.... I nearly thought the word 'haunting', but stopped
myself just before I got there.

"Well, they say if you're not having a good time in Brighton
you're probably d— damn well in need of a good excuse for why
not," I corrected hurriedly.

I really had to concentrate more.

The rain still couldn't make up its mind, vacillating
between spitting showers and damp mistiness, though it seemed
to be clearing as we walked the few blocks to The Crown and it
had left the stonework of Kemp Town's elegant terraces damply
mellow, the pavements patterned with puddles. Damon
whistled, hands buried deep in his pockets.

I wouldn't have minded it, but I kept recognising the tunes.

* * *

The Crown had long been a welcome bolthole for me. Set

off one of the village's bystreets, between a wholefood shop and an independent clothing store, the old building still retained some of its dark wood beams. Fake extra beams had been added to the ceiling at some point, possibly in an attempt to capitalise on someone's idea of Olde-Worlde Charme. Eric, the current landlord, hadn't bothered to take them down, though he had bowed to the conventions of modern health and safety by pinning a notice to one that read 'Minde Yore Hedde'.

Lunchtimes were normally fairly quiet, and this one seemed to be no exception, so I went straight up to the bar and smiled at the goateed student polishing wineglasses behind it.

"Vodka tonic, please," I said, noting the look of unfocused confusion that passed, very briefly, over the barman's face when he looked at Damon, busy peering at the stock of real ales.

"And… what are you drinking?"

As I turned, he'd just moved from the ales to looking at a laminated list of cocktails and shooters. I prayed silently that he wouldn't order any kind of orgasm.

"Pint of bitter, mate. Thanks. Well," he added, smiling at me, "it's been years since I had a good pint. Guess you could say, recently, I've been more of a spirit dr— No? Okay. All right…."

I rolled my eyes.

"Don't," I muttered, ordering us two Plantagenet Potato Bakes (the Traditional Fayre Lunche Speciale) as well and paying for the lot. "Just don't."

He grinned. We found a table by the window, and I slid gratefully into the wine-red leather banquette. My sanctuary.

Damon frowned.

"What?"

"They usually play Led Zep in here?" he asked.

The tail end of *Black Dog* echoed faintly from the speakers behind the bar.

I shrugged. "Well, they did reform. At Christmas."

He stared at me for a moment, then narrowed those Theda Bara eyes.

"Get out of town! *Nobody's* still playin' together after," he paused for a second, counting quickly under his breath, "nearly forty bloody years. If you'd said, like, Son of Zeppelin or somethin', I might—"

"No, really." I sipped my vodka. "Honest."

"Hm." Damon looked incredulously at me as he lifted his pint. "Robert Plant's balls drop yet, then?"

I snorted, and the corner of his mouth twitched into a little smile. I supposed it must be strange for him. In what I hated to think of as his day, rock 'n' roll had already become bloated on its own success, sure... but there must still have been a freshness to it, a sense that its history was still being, *could* still be, written. Early twenty-first century heritage rock must come as something of a shock.

"Rolling Stones too," I said. "They've never really stopped."

I thought of Leon Fielding's CDs, still in my bag, and wondered if I should say anything. Damon shook his head, fiddling with the wooden spoon that had our table number written on it; another of Eric's rustic affectations.

"Shit, man," he murmured, reaching for his cigarettes.

"Uh-uh. No smoking. Smoking ban, affects all public places."

He groaned very theatrically. "Awww... c'mon. Seriously? But—"

"Yep, honest. After all," I added, unable to resist, "those things could kill you."

He narrowed his eyes again, but I slapped the scrapbook down on the table between us, derailing whatever he'd been about to say.

"Come on. Focus."

"Hah.... This is the book?"

To tell the truth, I felt a little bit worried about showing it to him. I'd told him that Mum, Gail, and Jan had been fans and I had mentioned the scrapbook, but actually *showing* him... that seemed rather like reading out extracts of someone's schoolgirl diary in the toilets at break. Damon looked at the cover and raised an eyebrow.

"Um," I said. "Sorry if it's a bit, er...."

"Oh, don't sweat it," he said, lifting his pint, carefully opening the book with his free hand. "Baby, you get used to it. So long as the pages aren't sticky."

"Er...."

He slipped me a big, sly grin. "Yeah, if you knew what we used to get... huh. Mainly after *Saturday Loving* charted in June of '72. Yeah. One minute, gigging over a pub in Clapham, next we're doing the fucking Roundhouse! Chicks going crazy all over the place. I'm telling you, baby," the grin slid even wider, "if I was, like, a smaller guy... I'd never have had to buy any underwear again, y'know? 'Course," he added, after a moment's lecherous consideration, "you'd want to wash 'em first."

I tried not to think about it, but it was already too late.

"Eewww!"

Damon laughed, a low, throaty sound. It stopped when he

hit the first live still. Him, with the Telecaster, almost on top of the mic, shoulder to shoulder with Leon Fielding, the latter's eyes on him, mouth half-open, fingers high on the neck of that sunburst Les Paul, forever caught in the beginning of motion.

"Christ." He frowned, fingers tracing the edge of the picture. "Leon…. That's been a long time."

I caught the bar-student's attention as he hove into view with our lunches. He brought the plates over and looked, again, momentarily confused. Damon still stared morosely at the scrapbook.

"Ooh. Chillier than it was this morning, innit?" said the bar-student.

"Um. Yes." I smiled and thanked him.

He toddled off, his expression slightly glazed.

"It was just us, starting out," Damon said to the world in general.

With a lingering sympathy for the goateed student, I speared a piece of lettuce from my side salad. "You and Leon?"

"Yeah. We were just kids. Never thought we'd… I mean, Leon thought he'd spend his whole life working in the bloody GPO. I wasn't much better… I had a job at Burton's. Tailor's assistant," he added caustically. "But it didn't matter, y'know? 'Cos we didn't care if we were broke. It's, like, every kid has those funky rock 'n' roll dreams, y'know? But you don't actually *expect*…. We didn't believe it when this A&R guy from Garten Records starts coming on all sweet. We did this gig up Chalk Farm way, see, Christmas 1970. This bloke—Dexler, his name was, Vince Dexler—says he wants us to come in for an audition. We're tryin' to be all cool, y'know, and Leon puts on this big front… 'Oh, well, we'll see what we can do.' Hah… bloke's out the door five minutes, we're swingin' off the freaking ceiling."

He chuckled.

"Well, we were seriously stoked, right? Biggest Christmas present ever. We thought there was going to be a big contract, record deal... all that shit. 'Course, it don't work like that."

"No?" I asked, dandling my fork in my potato bake.

Damon shook his head vigorously, curls bouncing.

"Mm-nn. Like I say, we were kids, we didn't know what we were doing. Dexler says we should sign this deal memo, yeah? 'Show a commitment to the project' and all that crap. So we do.... 'Course, we end up locked in on the label. Can't take any other auditions, can't hardly play a gig without getting our knuckles rapped. We just had to hang around, waiting for Garten to offer us something—anything, y'know?—or blow the whole lot." He sipped his pint, frowning slightly. "It could have all crumbled away then, y'know? Never got any further'n that. But we were lucky. Vince introduced us to Cris McIlroy, beginning of '71. Said he'd be the perfect manager for us. S'pose he was, really. It was Cris that brought Charlie and Joss on board. Not that me and Leon didn't get a say. I mean, we did, but...."

He flicked through the crackling pages, and I realised what he didn't want to voice: that 'choice' could be a flexible term, especially if you hoped to get paid. I thought again of the CDs in my bag and wondered if I should tell him that Leon still had a career. Maybe he already knew.

Would he know that, I wondered? And why did it worry me?

Damon cleared his throat, flipping past a collage of ticket stubs.

"I knew Charlie, vaguely. Seen him at the Crawdaddy Club... and Joss was a pretty well-known session drummer. Cris got us all together, and it gelled well, y'know? Worked great. Contract started moving. Cris even got us Maxwell Vost to produce the album for only four points—we thought he was a bloody magician!"

He glanced up, saw my incomprehension, and looked a little crestfallen.

"Vost was a big name in the Sixties. Real shaker, y'know? And he was responsible for a lot of our sound. We were lucky to get him. Produced everything up to *Rush On Love*... though he didn't stick on four points for long. Percent," he added kindly, making me feel like a complete idiot.

I watched as, for the first time, Damon picked at his plate. Lettuce only. I'd ordered for him without thinking but, I realised, I hadn't seen him eat before. I had to try hard not to wonder about where it went... how it all worked. Sunlight filtered through The Crown's thick bottle-glass windows, tracing the dust in the air.

"Vost made a lot of money out of us, by the end of it. Cris too." He stopped at a glossy black-and-white magazine photo. "But everybody takes their dues, y'know? Can't do nothin' about it. That's Cris McIlroy."

Damon tipped the book towards me. The picture had been clipped from an interview given to some nameless rag. Just a studio shot, showing a seated Damon Brent with a big acoustic dreadnought on his knee and a blank look on his face. Behind him, a balding man in his mid- or late-thirties, with tinted aviator glasses high on the bridge of his thin nose, held a cigarette in one skinny hand. He seemed to be gesticulating towards something in Damon's line of vision. I wanted to ask if he remembered the photograph, but he'd already moved on.

"Kinda weird guy, Cris. He was okay, but a little bit high-strung sometimes. Used to play with some freakout psychedelic outfit in the States, apparently, always said he was at Woodstock. I never saw him pick up an axe. But the cat could spot a trend coming, y'know? He was good for us. Though, after *Rush On Love*, we wanted to start branching out, y'know? Caused a bit of tension."

I pricked up my ears. "Tension?"

He curled his lip, lifting one shoulder in a kind of mini-shrug.

"No... well, yeah. Maybe. But not—I mean, neither him or Vost would have had anything to do with.... What?"

I stabbed my fork into my potato bake. "You haven't actually.... I mean, d'you have any idea who would have wanted to—you know?"

Damon shook his head—far too quick to deny it, I thought. I chewed pensively for a moment, wondering how to broach this. No one's squeaky clean, after all. Not entirely.

"So," I said, swallowing and reaching for my vodka, "no, um... I don't know... enemies? Nobody with a grudge? No spurned groupies, no—what d'you call it—creative differences within the band?"

He glanced up at me, a curious look on his face.

"Because," I ducked under the table for a minute, pulling notepad and pen from my bag, "it must have been somebody at that party, mustn't it? I mean, you said last night that you went upstairs about three... that's right, isn't it?"

"Yeah," he said. "'Bout three. Dunno how long I was out

for, but it all started catching up. I got myself to the bathroom… *really* needed that shower by the time I was finished."

"Nice."

"Yeah." He smiled sheepishly. "Well, that's rock 'n' roll, baby. I'd been, uh, I'd been drinking fairly heavily. I was… well, I was angry."

Now we were getting somewhere.

"How come?" I asked, keen to prod but careful not to push him.

He gave another of those dismissive mini-shrugs and rocked back in his chair. His hand wandered to the pocket that held cigarettes and lighter, the gesture turned into a brushing away of invisible lint as he obviously remembered he couldn't smoke in here. I wondered whether—if people only saw what they believed they saw—he could get away with it if he tried. After all, no one would smell the smoke… would they?

"Me 'n' Inez had this bust-up," he said insouciantly.

"Your wife?"

"Yeah. She never liked bashes at the house, y'know? She was…."

He trailed off, and I wondered what he'd been about to say.

She was… funny like that? Meticulous about not finding unconscious people on the floor in the mornings? Fond of her privacy?

I propped my chin on my hand.

"Tell me about her," I suggested. "She was a tennis player, wasn't she?"

"Mm." A strange sadness touched those Theda Bara eyes as he smiled. "Top ten seeded for British chicks in '73 when we met. She was… well, yeah, she was a fox, but she was a smart chick too, y'know? Ambitious, determined… she'd go all out for what she wanted, Inez would."

He pulled the cigarette packet from his pocket and tossed it down beside his plate as if it had burned his hand. I watched him trying to affect complete nonchalance while picking compulsively at the corner of the carton with one thumbnail.

"We had a—well, I s'pose it was a bit of an on-off thing at first—but we got spliced in '74. I asked her on New Year's Eve. She said yes, we tied the knot in June. Honeymooned in Portugal. It was nice," he added wistfully. "'Course, I'd bought the house, down by Westbury. S'pose I thought… dunno."

He prodded at a piece of potato with his fork and frowned. I watched him take an experimental, cautious bite. He chewed thoughtfully, like someone actually unused to eating. It made me wonder all sorts of uncomfortable things about physiology.

"I mean," he said, after a moment, "I always thought there'd be… y'know, I thought if she had a kid…. But she told me she saw this quack in Harley Street, and he said it was a no go, yeah? The rabbit just wasn't gonna die. I thought it was that, y'know, what kinda messed things up. That maybe…. But she didn't like talking about it. S'pose I was wrong to try and make her."

A fall of curls obscured his eyes as he bent his head. I drew a fresh column on my notepad. So, things had been… rocky?

"Was that what you argued about, before the party?"

He shook his head, still staring at his plate.

"Nah. She, um…. See, Inez hurt her leg. Bad injury, y'know? May of '76. Screwed up this tendon or something. She had an operation, had a cast on for, like, six weeks. She got pretty down about it and… well, I s'pose I didn't help, bein' away and everything, yeah? Long time. Then with the tour we done that year...."

Damon cleared his throat, looking up at me expectantly. I was supposed to save him from having to say it, I realised.

"You were, er, away a bit too much?"

His fingers drummed crisply against the fag packet.

"You could say that. Well, we was always touring, or there'd be studio work, gigs. I dunno, maybe if we hadn't moved out of London...." His chin dimpled as he chewed his lower lip. "She got down after the leg injury. Real down. June to July, we had a tour. West Germany, Holland, France... y'know. Our second wedding anniversary, I was playin' in Rotterdam, she was at home with a cast on her leg. I thought she understood how it had to be, y'know? How—well, p'rhaps she didn't. Anyway, day of the party, I... sort of found out what she thought of me. That she had this other bloke on the side."

He cleared his throat, grabbed the cigarette carton, and jammed it abruptly back into his pocket. I wasn't sure what he wanted me to say—at least this gave us a motive to work with— so I said nothing. Damon took a long swallow of his pint and stared into the middle distance.

"I dunno who," he said. "Thought prob'ly her coach, Graham Cooper. Smug little bastard, never liked him. But I don't know. S'pose I didn't wanna know, not really. But we started on at each other and, like, y'know.... Things were said." He cleared his throat. "Stuff was thrown."

"How did you leave it? You said you were drinking... angry."

"She left," he said shortly. "I told her she didn't need to bother comin' back. She said she wouldn't. Packed a bleedin' case right in front of me."

I nodded slowly.

"I'm sorry," I said, and I meant it. "But, um…. So, would you have, I don't know, divorced?"

Damon shot me a guarded look from behind his kohl.

"I…. No. Yeah. Look, I might've said it. I dunno. Like I said, y'know, girl? It was a tough year. We were touring, doing a lot of studio work… then, y'know, what happened… happened. What cuts, yeah, is that I never got to, like, to fix things up."

He looked away, digging back into the potato bake and flicking through the pages of the scrapbook, as if the subject was closed. I sighed inwardly. Despite all his talk about wanting answers, needing to know what had happened, he wasn't going to make this easy for me. I'd opened my mouth to ask, carefully, about the creative tensions he'd mentioned following the *Rush On Love* LP, when he lit with a soft crow of delight on a blurry, grainy black-and-white shot in the scrapbook.

"Oh!" Damon swung the book round towards me. "Oh, you gotta see this one, baby. This is… oh, you'll like this!"

I'd barely noticed the picture before. I'd thought—if I'd thought of it at all—that it was just a fan's shot of a live show. Of course, it was.

"Bowie's Nineteen Eighty Floor Show," he said proudly. "At the Marquee, October 1973. They filmed it for TV, closed the whole place down for three days. The very last time he did Ziggy…. It was incredible, man! Not a journo in the place that didn't keep forgetting to breathe."

I craned my neck and looked at the photo, but I couldn't see the glamour that he seemed to. I could see why it had found its way into Mum's book; there was Damon, cigarette and drink in hand, looking very young and—to be honest—completely pissed, amid a knot of other people. I spotted the rest of the band, weaving amongst the crowd. He still kept reeling off roll calls and anecdotes of rock celebrity, and I failed miserably in not being able to recognise anyone.

"And *that* is John Baldry…. Joss was like a schoolkid, yeah, that excited to meet him. Leon was just all over the man himself, y'know. *Big* Bowie fan. We were so lucky to get in there…. Great night. Really great."

As I looked, I realised that the shot had come from an inkie and that—whatever Mum's feeling about it had been—Damon and his boys were totally incidental to it. Strange that, even so, he'd managed to get himself caught, staring straight at the camera, right in the middle of the frame.

I shook my head. He really wasn't making this easy.

"It must," I said, trying to drag us back to the heart of the matter, however strange and distasteful it seemed against the pub's flock wallpaper and the fake beams, "have been just an opportunistic thing, though. Mustn't it?"

Damon was still wallowing in the footlights of memory, looking at shots of a live show, the band shining like so many sparkly satellites from a dark, thinly spotlit stage. He frowned.

"Hm?"

"The way you were… you know. It was pure opportunity. It had to be. No one could have planned that, could they? I mean, it was risky… the house full of people like that. It must have been someone who was there that night, someone who had a reason to be angry with you, someone who had a reason to want you, er… thingy," I finished, feeling hopelessly twee.

It just didn't seem right to say 'dead' with him sat right

there, looking dismally at me over half a potato bake and a pint. Damon curled his lip.

"Well, someone must have done," I snapped. "Unless it really *was* an accident."

He let the open page of the scrapbook drop from his fingers.

"No. I told you, I never done all that to myself, Ellis. Whatever they said. The... the pathologist said," Damon screwed up his kohl-rimmed eyes, brow furrowing in thought, "there was an... epidural haematoma. I didn't know what it meant. I always thought a haematoma was, like, a bruise, y'know?"

"Path—" I began, wishing I hadn't. He'd mentioned this in passing once before, but I'd been in no condition to think about it. Unfortunately, now I'd started to... quite unintentionally. "Oh, no. Oh, y— You were *at* your own autopsy?"

"Mm-hm." He nodded, picking at the remains of his lunch. "Well, everybody is, really, ain't they? But, I mean, y'know... bruise be buggered, right? Half my bloody head was smashed over the sink."

"Yuck," I said, without meaning to. "But you.... At the autopsy, you actually watched them cutti—"

"Oh, it's not that bad. Not really. Kinda gave me the heebies to start with, but once you stop thinking of it as yourself... well, it makes it easier. The first wound was here." He tapped a finger against his head, just above his right eyebrow. "The haematoma. Would've put me down... killed me eventually. That can happen, y'know? You, like, you can bleed in your brain for hours... have a headache an' that, but not know how bad you're hurt."

He paused to drain the rest of his pint. I said nothing. That first hit, though… well, that could have been accidental, couldn't it? He'd said how out of it he was. I sipped my vodka, looking guardedly at my own personal apparition. He hunched over the table, mouth pinched tight.

"There was another one," Damon said, putting two nicotine-smudged fingers to his left temple, "here. Couple of other bumps and scrapes. One on the back of my head. They, uh, reckoned I'd fallen out of the shower, hit myself on the sink… tried to get up, fallen again and, well, y'know. Not got up. Clumsy drunk, right? Only I could always hold my booze." He paused, gazing speculatively at the bottom of his glass. "Shouldn't have had those bloody pills off Leon, though. 'Ludes," he added, putting the glass down reluctantly and flicking me a quick smile.

"Dodgy gear?"

"Nah, not as such…. He always brought party favours, y'know? And he loved to, er, experiment. I mean, I never had a problem with that, yeah, but bloody quaaludes put me to sleep quicker than a mug of Ovaltine and a foot rub. Always did."

"Uh-huh?" My vodka and tonic paused en route to my lips as I contemplated that image.

"Yeah, y'know? You down, like, eight cups of tea just tryin' to stay awake then, if you can fight the first half hour, you get a nice buzz… makes the world all fuzzy. Takes the edge off things. That's why he gave 'em to me. Leon came down on the Friday afternoon, see? Me and Inez were still yellin' at each other when he turned up. Then she split and he, well, he wanted to help." Damon laughed softly. "Some bleedin' help… I ended up necking a fistful of reds just trying to stay awake. Did a couple of lines early on, prob'ly about nine... more after midnight. Kept drinking. I was... huh, I was gone, baby. But that's just the way it was, y'know? I wasn't a— It wasn't like they made out in here."

He stabbed a finger at Mum's scrapbook, and I saw he'd been flicking through the 'Death House Horror' reportage. He rubbed a hand over his mouth, and I wondered if he thought he had to justify himself to me.

"I wasn't a bleedin' junkie. It's not.... Look, 'cos when you're trying to make it, yeah? You know you got no chance unless you can make your face fit right, and to do that... well, there was always something going on, y'know? You had to keep up, be amped, all the time, so you pop a couple of hearts here, a bomber there. It only got more intense after we started getting some success. Tours, gigs, press, all that shit.... You go from a couple of pills to keep you pumped to a few lines of coke, y'know? Then, when it all stopped and you got a break, you needed something to bring you back down, and it'd go on like that. Y'see? 'Course, the booze was just there to keep everybody sociable." He gave a sour chuckle. "We all picked up bad habits. I wasn't half as bad as Charlie. I never was."

He'd flipped abruptly away from the pictures of police cordons and flowers, back to the feather boas and sparkly lapels. I caught sight of Charlie Davies' surly face, glaring at me upside down.

"So, Charlie had a problem?"

Damon chuckled mirthlessly from the depths of his pint.

"Long-running love affair with the white lady, baby. I mean, it's like I said, pretty much everybody'd do a line here and there, but with Charlie.... Well, it was a runnin' joke, wasn't it? Charlie and his... *Charlie*. It got so a couple of lines wasn't enough. And when you get that way with somethin' like coke, y'know, it—no matter how much—it's never gonna be enough. Eats you up. He was strung out most of the time by the spring of '74. When we were in the studio for the *Working Man* LP, he used to piss off for hours at a time. S'either Leon or Joss playin' bass on most of that, y'know. Came to a head when I went round to his place in Notting Hill one weekend. Found him passed out with a needle in his soddin' arm... I called Cris, and he got Charlie bundled into a clinic. He was in for a good coupla months, doin' all that twelve-step crap, y'know? Blamed me."

I frowned. "But—"

"That's the way you think when you're fucked up like that," Damon said gently. "I s'pose... yeah, he probl'y hated me for a while. 'Cos addiction takes away your choices, your control. Y'know? Makes you resent people interfering even more... and Charlie was an argumentative sod to start with." He smiled. "Doing all the N.A. stuff, though... it's a lot of rules, baby. And when you give people rules, some of them are gonna follow 'em, right? But some are just gonna learn how not to get caught next time."

The goateed bar-student wandered past again abstractedly, pausing to relieve us of our plates. He seemed less confused, looked directly at Damon for the first time. The walls didn't melt, and the bar-student didn't scream or faint, so I supposed things must be all right.

"Everything okay, sir?"

"Yeah." Damon turned the pearly grin on him. "Nice. Can we get another round?"

"I'll bring 'em over," the bar-student said, pottering off

again.

I meant to point out that it was barely two o'clock—and he was spending *my* money, thank you very much—but instead I bit my lip, and my frown deepened.

"You're saying Charlie didn't stay clean?"

"Nah. Not really." Damon flicked back to the later pages of the scrapbook, his expression hardening as he hit that shot of Inez collapsing outside the gates. "He handled it better, but he was still using. He'd still get wasted, still get a little crazy, y'know? Though it was coke more than junk... at least when he was working."

I nodded slowly, filing that away for future reference.

"So, he was high that night? At the party? Higher than most people were," I added, seeing Damon's raised eyebrow.

He smiled. "Prob'ly. I, um, I don't really remember that much."

I bit back a small laugh, any amusement at how much, for a moment, he looked like a sheepish teenager, quelled by the question of just how high you'd have to be before you lost your censor control as well as your inhibitions. *He hated me for a while.* Could Charlie really have hated him that much? Was that what it had been? Some immature, momentary snap of anger? I thought about pushing, about asking if he could have had some deeper motive, but Damon seemed preoccupied. He was frowning at the photo of his wife, at the gory headlines and the post-mortem dissection of her personal pain.

"It, er... it must be difficult," I said, because I had to say something. I couldn't sit there and watch the black waters close over him, cutting off any opportunity I had to prod a bit more, go over what he knew. "Seeing that. Um. Sorry."

Damon glanced up at me and, fleetingly, I thought he'd say something, but the bar-student came back with our drinks and, in an instant, the darkness left his expression. The fluid, graceful transition and the charming smile impressed me, but I wasn't fooled. They disappeared right along with the bar-student, and Damon shook his head, hands coming to cradle his second pint. His hair brushed the shoulders of his green velvet jacket, golden tendrils dragging a little against the nap of the fabric.

"It's cool, baby. Really." The edge of his mouth twisted into a cynical sneer.

"So… she stood to inherit the lot?"

Damon looked warily at me over his beer. I thought perhaps I'd hit a nerve, but he licked his lips and shrugged.

"Yeah. My royalty share too… I'd just negotiated a better split on points, that spring. Bleedin' typical, really…. But she wasn't there, babe. I don't know what you're thinking," he looked levelly at me, "but I told you: Inez left on the Friday. Stormed off in a whirl, said she was going to, like, stay at the flat. We had a place up Chelsea way. She used to stay there when she went for… well, shopping trips, she said."

"Mm," I said soothingly, though he'd stopped paying any attention to me.

"She *knew* that night was important to me." Damon rubbed a thumb through the condensation on the side of his glass. "There were people there, y'know, industry— I was talkin' to people at Decca, Universal… you don't understand, baby. They were gonna offer me blind terms, more cash. Vince had it all lined up! I *needed* her there. I needed— Well, it wasn't fucking fair," he concluded, taking a long swallow of the beer.

I blinked. What?

"Hang on," I said, glancing at my notepad. "Vince? D'you mean Vince... Dexler? The A&R bloke from Garten Records?"

"Well, he wasn't with Garten anymore by then. And he wasn't really still strictly Artist and Repertoire... got himself a gig with one of the big companies, y'know?"

I frowned. "And, what? You mean it was going to be a better deal for the band? A new contract?"

Damon gave me another one of those looks that seemed to suggest there should be a special institution for people like me, with soft, cushiony walls and large, stocky nurses strong of hand but kind of heart.

"No, love," he said carefully. "For *me*."

It took a moment to sink in but, when it did, I couldn't help but stare.

"Huh?"

He shifted uneasily, lifted one velvet-clad shoulder in a mini-shrug, and cleared his throat. "It's... well, it's, like... I mean, we'd all been wanting to get more wossname, y'know, artistic control for a while, baby. Y'know what I mean? It's, like, we had this fantastic live vibe—we always did, yeah?—and after *Rush On Love* came out, we did a lot of touring. And that sort of makes you think, y'know? Brings everything into focus."

"But you were going to quit? You were going to—"

"It's like I said, babe...."

"Oh, for goodness' sake!" I snapped, unable to believe that anybody could possibly be so obtuse. And he'd said he had no idea who wanted him dead? "You mean you were planning to lea—"

Across the pub, a familiar voice rang out, cutting through

my indignation. Damon looked incredulously at me and I wished I knew what would happen if I slapped him. It had never seemed so tempting.

"Ellis! Hello!"

A cuss softly passed my lips, and I closed my eyes. *Not now. Please.* I turned in my seat.

"Ron!" I pinched my cheeks into an unwilling smile. "How are you? Jerry with you?"

"Getting in the drinks in, love. You all right?"

My friend Ron was what is generally termed a pillock of the community. He got involved in pretty much all the local committees, both the Kemp Town residents' association and the historical society, the Neighbourhood Watch and, every year, regular as clockwork, he took some kind of voluntary officiate role at Pride, bustling among the crowds like a bantam. His partner, Jeremy, could usually be seen skulking somewhere in the background, looking faintly embarrassed.

They were, however, both lovely blokes, and I could forgive Ron his tendencies towards pomposity ever since the day I moved in, when they'd found me abandoned on the pavement by my cheapskate removal firm with all my furniture and boxes of books and clutter to hike up four flights of stairs. Ron had organised friends, neighbours, and those too weak to resist his bullying into an impromptu workforce, and Jeremy had lent tea, sympathy, and a strong arm on the dog legs.

"Can't complain," I said as Ron drifted over to the table, tall, skinny, and bespectacled, in a baggy t-shirt and washed-out jeans.

I supposed I couldn't. Not unless I wanted to get myself sectioned.

"You'll work yourself into the ground, you will," he chided, smiling broadly at Damon. "No telling these women, is there?"

Just for the briefest of moments, his words seemed to echo into a deepness that I knew wasn't there. This was The Crown. There were sepia photos of old Kemp Town and its elegant Georgian walkways on the walls, interspersed with more recent portraits of Brighton. Dust spun in the shafts of spring sunlight, and a faint hint of beeswax furniture polish lingered beneath the beer and the... cigarette smoke?

No. As soon as I noticed it, the smell dissipated.

"You said it... you can talk, but they don't listen, right?"

I looked between them; Damon—to my eyes, still a kohl-rimmed vision in King's Road and Camden chic—and Ron, the slight look of confusion passing over his face only briefly, replaced with his usual determinedly affable expression.

"You're telling me," he said, still beaming, then, as Jeremy hove into view behind him, holding two lagers and a packet of peanuts clenched in his teeth, he glanced over his shoulder. "Oh. Um, this is Jeremy. The ball and chain."

Jeremy waggled his eyebrows over the peanuts.

"'E-oo."

My mouth had gone dry. How the hell was I going to—

"Hi. Jack. Jack Yorke," Damon said, turning up the charm, and I had no idea where he'd pulled that name from.

We seemed to be getting away with it, however. I surreptitiously tucked away the paperwork, trying not to look amazed when he told them he was attached to the University of Sussex's Centre for Life History and Life Writing Research and we were writing a conference paper together on the social history of image branding. Had he been going through my bookshelves when I wasn't looking? Would I even have been able to tell if he had?

We exchanged a few more pleasantries, but both Ron and Jeremy had started to get that glazed look that my particular branch of academia tends to induce in people and said they should leave us to it. Jeremy winked at me as they headed off to the beer garden, and I groaned inwardly, knowing it wouldn't be long before I got the dreaded 'and who was *that*?' phone call.

The rictus of a smile didn't leave my face until they disappeared.

"Who the bloody hell's Jack Yorke?" I demanded.

Damon avoided my gaze. "Jack o'Lantern. In the *Eagle*," he mumbled. "He used to, um, like, catch French spies in the Napoleonic war and... stuff. Hey, I didn't hear you sayin' anything, baby."

He had a point, but I wasn't about to admit it. "You used to read the *Eagle*?"

He shrugged sheepishly. "Maybe a couple of times, when I was a kid. Look, I'm gonna nip out for a cough and drag. You want another drink?"

"No, I'm all right. It's my money you're spending, anyway," I added pointedly, glancing at my watch. "Might as well get home, I suppose.... Bugger. Of course!"

"What?"

Damon looked quizzically at me as I stood up. I shook my head.

"Nothing. Well, no, not.... I'll see you outside, okay? Just had a thought."

Had my mind not been racing with sudden possibilities and the contemplation of fate, it would have given me an ignoble but gleeful little twinge to leave him sitting there—looking thoroughly nonplussed—while I nipped out into the beer garden.

Ron sat out by the trellis and the ill-tempered and untrammelled clematis that rambled along it. Jeremy was just rounding the glass-paned door between the bar and the terrace, back from a trip to the gents', and I collared him before he could go any further.

"Just a minute… Jerry?"

He turned, raising an eyebrow. "Yeah? What can I do for you, Ell?"

"Um. Do you still write for that agency?"

A pained look crossed Jeremy's face, and I almost felt sorry for bringing it up, but providence had dealt me one of those slaps upside the head that can't be ignored. Jeremy had told me once before that, when the market for freelance features journalism got a little slow, he hooked up with an agency specialising in red-top rag human interest and 'real life' stories. Not so much writing, he said, as re-sequencing the phrases 'love rat', 'hardening nipples', and 'totally gobsmacked' into the correct house style and judiciously applying a bad pun for a strapline, but it paid the bills.

"Not… regularly," Jerry said cautiously. "But I am in touch. Why?"

I cleared my throat. "If—just supposing—I wanted to find somebody, for an interview, say, how would I go about it?"

"Interview?" he echoed, looking confused.

I sidled closer, slipping a nervous glance out to the beer garden. I really hadn't wanted to bring Ron into this—or Damon, come to that.

"Just say, for the sake of argument, if I did, it could be done, right? I mean, I remember you saying there were, er... facilities, for finding people. The office that you worked w—"

"Well, it doesn't guarantee they'll talk to you," Jeremy said cagily. "But, yes... electoral roll searches, databases, direct mail companies. You can find virtually anybody if you know where to look. It costs, but if.... Why'd you say you wanted to know?"

I ad libbed generously. "Um, Jack has a, er, book proposal that we're, uh, going to be working on. So, I just wondered...."

Jeremy grinned. "Oh, yeah?"

"Yes. No, it's not— Jerry! Stop it."

He sniggered, failing to look remotely chastened.

"Oh, come on, Ellis... he's *lush*! Where'd you dig him up?"

I winced. Bad word choice. "Sod off... no, I mean it. Seriously, Jerry. Could you find someone, if I asked you?"

"All right." He relented, but not without another chuckle. "Yeah. Yeah, it shouldn't be too much of a problem. You need as much information as you can get upfront... name, age, date of birth, the general area to look. But if you can give me that, I'll see what I can do. What's the book about?"

My tongue almost caught at the back of my throat. Shit. A more than reasonable question, but I hadn't been prepared for it.

"D... um, Damon Brent," I said, relieved to see the total and utter lack of recognition on Jeremy's face. "Old, er, Seventies pop star. He died in '76 and it's, um, well it's sort of a biography.... Cults of fame," I added, grabbing desperately at the lies I'd told Auntie Jan and tying them up with the plan Damon already had for me... the plan I hadn't, until now, tried to voice. "You know. How people react to, well, celebrity death.

Um."

That, I thought, could have sounded better.

"Gruesome." Jeremy wrinkled his nose. "Hang on, did you say Brent? He wasn't out of that band... oh, *you* know.... They had that song. It was on that advert last year, for that car. Oh, what was it called?"

"*Hope Diamond*," I supplemented, not thinking and immediately cursing myself for it.

"Yeah, that's the one... God, Ron remembers them. Bloody hell. All right, I'll see what I can do."

"Thanks, Jerry. You're a life saver. I'll, um, I'll email you the names and stuff, all right?"

"Sure. Take care, Ell."

"Will do," I said, smiling as I turned to leave and rather glad that I'd sent Damon on ahead.

When I got there, he was leaning against the wall outside the pub, just to the side of the weedy and slightly shabby hanging baskets, cigarette smouldering in two elegantly extended fingers, his face tipped back to catch the sun, eyes closed.

"All right, baby?" he said, not bothering to open them.

It took me aback, but only for a moment.

"Yeah. Let's go."

Damon cracked open one eye and peered at me. The light flamed off his hair and the foil print on his shirt. Even his bloody flares seemed to sparkle.

He smoked while we walked, talking more about how we planned to start things off. I explained about Jeremy and how he might be able to help us track down anyone not immediately accessible through a quick trawl of Google and a couple of social networking sites. That led on to explaining about the internet in general, which fascinated him, and me saying that Leon Fielding—given that he still seemed to be working—should be relatively easy to approach. The spring sunshine warmed the pavement, and Damon laughed so hard I thought he'd swallow his cigarette.

"He is? For real? Ah, babe.... That's brilliant. I mean it. What's he doin'?"

I dug the CDs out of my bag and showed them to him. Hooting with glee, he read all the titles and liner notes carefully before making me promise to play them in full when we got home.

Chapter Five
July 16ᵗʰ 1976

The raw heat tapered off as day passed into late afternoon. A clear, blue sky grew hazy where it met the acid yellows and greens of the trees; birds called in the beeches. Inez ran slowly along in the lee of the grassy slope that circled the south-eastern side of the garden, and her feet crunched on the parched lawn. She approached the stone and weatherboard bulk of Westleve House, rising dark against the bright sky, and her pace grew uneven. The smaller, older west wing cast a welcome shade over the crescent of stone steps that led up to the terrace; pots of garish pink dahlias and fragrant thyme scented the air.

Panting, her white shorts and t-shirt sticky with sweat, Inez headed up the steps and into the cool shade of what had once been the old scullery, now fitted out as a small country kitchen. She lurched to the Deal table, catching its solid edge with the heels of her palms, clumsy enough—her vision still streaked blue from the bright sunlight—to stumble against the wood and stub her toe. She cursed, hanging on to the table part in support and part for resistance as she bent her knees to a series of lunges. Inez gritted her teeth at the pain, letting out a grunt of frustration at her own weakness. This being the quietest part of the house, her anger echoed back at her, a blunt reinforcement of her failure. She began a set of stretches, her eyes at last adjusting to the dimness. She didn't like the poky rooms back here. Stuff the elm beams and the Georgian cupboards; if she'd had her way, they could have knocked it all through when the east wing had been extended and made room for a south-facing sun lounge. But Damon had his fantasies, didn't he? And it was his house, his money… he'd left the whole of this wing virtually untouched in the two years since he'd bought the place, apart from the odd lick of paint or fitted carpet, chosen with the kind of care he normally reserved for a new guitar. Inez groaned and bent towards the cool slate floor, her muscles protesting.

Like watching a bloody bird nest.

And he'd talked about babies.

It drove her crazy. How could he even…? As if she would be happy to let this injury be the end of her career! At least she'd heard the last of that one. For now, anyway. But, that he could think she'd be happy to sit back and breed, when she needed to hear that she could still get back to her peak, she could get back on top….

On the third repeat, she touched her palms to the smooth stone and, with a gasp, allowed herself to stand. Graham understood that. Who knew what she'd do without Graham, although he wasn't going to be pleased with her. Not after this. She swore, limping across to the refrigerator that sat incongruously beside the mellowed yellow pine of the cupboards, their iron hinges wrought like lacework. Still panting too... fucking ridiculous. That circuit, four months ago, would have been a mere warm-up, the sort of thing she'd do before going onto the hard court that Damon had had built for her, and getting in a few hours' practice. She wouldn't have broken a sweat over it, but now... no. Clammy with perspiration and as out of condition as she was breath.

If only it wasn't so fucking hot!

Inez grabbed a glucose drink from the fridge and leaned against the table while she drank, wiping the cool bottle across her brow, eyes closed against the pain, the frustration, and the things that kept her awake at night. Having to watch the Open on the bloody television had been bad enough, then that Czech bitch, Hovorka, had actually had the nerve to send her two tickets to the Wimbledon women's final, along with a cutesy little note that made her want to spit blood.

Better Luck Next Year.

She'd show the cow. Inez glanced at her watch (solid gold, first anniversary present, virtually unreadable dial) and then at the clock on the wall. It had put her in a filthy mood, and now it felt like her whole day had been wasted.

Graham would be by later. Oh, of course *he* would lecture her about trying to build up her stamina too fast, running on the leg too soon, expecting too much. But she could talk to him. She would tell him about the Czech bitch, about the pain... and about how important it was that he stayed with her. She could make match fit for Melbourne in January, she knew it. What else was she supposed to do? Don a pinny and stay in this fucking kitchen, making pastry and kneading bread?

Kick back, kick off her shoes, and get pregnant?

Not bloody likely.

Inez drained the bottle and threw it at the bin, scoring a perfect shot. At least something still worked. She wiped the back of her hand across her brow and left the kitchen for the passageway that lay beyond. Once, it would have connected the service rooms, the business end of the house, with the parts set aside for show, for aspidistras and William Morris upholstery. Inez supposed it did the same job now. The thought made her chuckle, but the smile turned to a grimace as the tendon, that insidious cord of nerves and cells that twanged and strained under her skin, burned in protest at the exercise. She gasped, stretching out one hand to push against the dark burgundy wall of the corridor, bowing as if she'd just received a punch to the gut. She tried to save herself from the fall, and her hand brushed against the framed photographs that lined the walls, knocking one to the ground.

Inez watched it tumble, crash to the slate tiles. Glass cascaded around the toes of her tennis shoes. The shot from their engagement party, the one that had launched a dozen magazine covers. She looked wonderful: bronzed, fit, and fully made-up. Beside her—upstaging her—Damon smouldered disreputably in something white by Yves Saint Laurent.

She gazed at the mess for a moment. Then she collected herself and walked tightly past the doors that led to the other private rooms, to the end of the passage, where the hallway spilled out into the partitioned lobby that connected east with west, front with rear, real with fake. She kicked off her shoes, dangling the scuffed white pumps in one hand as she buried her sore, tired feet in the thick cream shag pile, and looked with trepidation at the pine staircase that separated her from the long, hot bath she now desperately wanted to have. She heard the movement from the other side of the glazed partition, but didn't look round. Oh, good. The boys were back. Well. Just perfect.

The door opened, and Damon emerged, unshaven, cheesecloth shirt open at the neck, sleeves pushed up to the elbows, a huge hurricane glass full of melding layers of brightly coloured alcohol in his hand. His leather trousers were slightly too tight, and he was beaming with a goofy serenity explained by his pinprick pupils.

"Hey, baby! I tried to call, but you weren't home, then things got all crazy on the motorway, and there was this truck, and... aw, check it out, you're running! How's your achillea? You all right?"

Inez turned, smile already fastened in place. That she felt, looking at him, neither pleased nor annoyed surprised her. It was just a cool, dispassionate act of observation, and nothing more.

Was that wrong?

"It's Achilles," she said simply. "An Achill-*es* tendon. And it's just as bad as when you left. I've barely managed three quarters of a mile. Did you just get in? I thought you were staying in town 'til after the weekend."

"Mm-hm," he said, leaning against the wall. "Was going to. But I'm sick of hotel rooms... all the buses and shit, y'know? An' I didn't wanna stay at the flat, I wanted to come home, even if it's only for a few days. I wanted to see you." He took a thoughtful sip of his cocktail. "Hey... three quarters of a mile? That's a bummer, baby. Look, Leon and Charlie came back with me. We're gonna go over those tapes. You wanna come chill out by the pool? Cheer you up."

"Not really." Inez ignored the pout he struck. "Graham's coming up to talk about the physio. I want to have a bath first."

"Aw, c'mon, baby...." He sidled closer, the scents of rum, French aftershave, and the heavy little dogends he said didn't affect him at all mixing in an uninviting miasma. "One little drink?"

Inez leaned back as he stroked his fingertips down her arm.

"'Cos I missed you, mama. And you and me, we need to, like, talk, y'know?"

"No." She batted his hand firmly away. "For starters, that's not a little drink, it's about six of them in the same glass. And not now. Not with them here. I'm going for a bath; I don't want to sit around listening to you three shit each other. I just... look, jump back, will you?"

"All right!" Damon held up his hands, cocktail and all, and stepped away, swaying very, very gently. "Jeez, baby...."

Inez snorted and shook her head.

"Look at you. I cannot *believe* this! W-will you just tell me you didn't drive like that?"

"What? Nah... we had the driver, baby. Y'know I hate those freakin' speed limits. Anyway, I'm solid. We're all stoked; it's gonna be great. Charlie's got this crazy idea for—"

"Not... now." She exhaled through gritted teeth. "I'm going for that bath."

"All right, baby. If you don't wanna. I'll tell the lads. They wanted to see how you were, but...."

He fastened his lips around the straw in his drink and gave her a look that might have belonged to the last puppy in the shop, once it had struggled out of the weighted sack, swum to the river bank, and been kicked by a passing child wearing leather football boots. Inez sighed.

"Oh, all *right*. I'll be down in a little bit. I'll come say hi."

Damon beamed happily. "'K. Love ya, baby."

"Sure."

"Inez?"

She turned, her hand on the newel post, its acorn carving worn smooth with time. Damon squinted at her.

"It's gonna get better, yeah? I.... I know you can do it, baby."

She looked at him for a moment, contemplating a time when she would have leant over the banister and ruffled his curls, or when—just for a moment—she might have believed him. She smiled sadly.

"Yeah."

"Okay."

He waited, seeming uncertain, as she made her painful way up the stairs. Inez reached the landing and heard the glazed door close again. She sighed. Three doors led off from here: one, to the glossy white and maple bathroom, two, to their bedroom, with its king-size bed and mirrored wardrobes and, three, to the euphemistically titled 'spare' bedroom. Spare, because guests always stayed in the east wing. Euphemistic, because it had no bed, just an old leather sofa and a wall of shelving. Damon kept his records, his tape deck, and his moods in there. His studio, he said, despite the fact that he'd paid to have one of the old outbuildings fitted with all that expensive equipment.

Like a bird. With all the attention span.

Inez went into the bathroom and dropped the plug into the

tub. She spun the hot water tap on and dandled her fingers in the stream. Wiping her hand on her shorts, she began to root through the cabinets for her bath oil, pausing only to push the door closed with a soft *click*.

* * *

Water lapped against the concrete edging of the pool. Sunlight dappled the terrace through the sharply green leaves of lime and beech trees, and Damon Brent leaned back, sinking that little bit further into the bean bag as he stared up through the glass panes of the conservatory roof at the beautiful blue and white jumble of the sky. He brought the roll-up to his lips and took a pull, inhaling before blowing a thin plume of smoke up towards the pattern of glass and steel, watching it curl in dissipating ribbons. He was chilled. No pressures, nobody wanting a piece out of him, no politicians blowing bad news on the airwaves, just... cool.

He felt a sharp prod in his knee and raised his head just enough to squint down at the sun-warmed floor. A light breeze blew through the open french doors, and Hendrix was *All Along the Watchtower* on the record player.

"You're bogarting the doobie, man."

Leon Fielding raised a decorous hand from the floor and snapped his fingers. Damon passed the joint down to him wordlessly and, linking his own hands behind his head, listened to his friend take a deep drag.

"Oh," Leon murmured. "*Yeah....*"

They had known each other since the age of fifteen, when the Feldmans, as they'd been then, left the pre-Gateway blight and concrete expansion of Newark, New Jersey, for a return to Mrs. F.'s native London.

The Elephant and Castle did not, for the Feldmans, swing as much or in quite the way as had been expected, but the young Leon—notwithstanding certain insecurities about his nose, his hair, and his accent—found an instant love for the city's grimly hip, denim-clad bustle. For Damon Brent, still struggling to make the hire-purchase payments on a Lambretta and skipping two meals a day in the hopes of shedding enough puppy fat to squeeze into a pair of drainpipe Levis, the friendship represented something both genuine and transfiguring. They smoked cheroots outside Habitat together, posing in high hopes and tight jeans, saw Dylan at the Albert Hall, and endured each other's epiphanies, struggles, and heartbreaks over women, money, and barre chords. By the dawn of the new decade, the Brent/Fielding partnership was itching to bust out of the button-down scene of work-a-day jobs and weekend parties. They'd never realised what hung around the corner, or just how stupidly lucky they were gonna get.

Damon watched Leon smoke and stare at the glass ceiling through half-closed eyes, thinking vaguely about old times and new faces; how things might have been different in another place, another time. He looked up, hearing the glazed door from the sitting room open, and a lazy smile spread over his face as Inez, freshly bathed and wearing something short, chiffony, and very sweet indeed, breezed into view. She looked past them, out to the pool where the sound of splashing water had ceased, replaced with the wet slap of footsteps on paving.

"Hey, foxy lady! You got the time to take a dip with me?"

Damon tilted his head back, about to admonish Charlie for

hitting on his lady, although neither the flirting nor the reprimands normally had any effect. The words died in his throat as he gazed at the bassist's dripping, naked figure, hands on his hips, member at half salute, and a broad smile on his face.

Beside him, Leon started to giggle.

* * *

Inez nodded coolly. "Hello, Charlie."

Damon failed to restrain his laughter, sliding from the bean bag to the floor and snorting loudly. Inez glared at him until he rose unsteadily, still convulsed with laughter, to take a towel from one of the rattan chairs. He threw it at Charlie, who retreated, grinning, back to the terrace.

"Sorry, baby." Damon paused to kiss her cheek on the way to the drinks cabinet. "You have a nice bath?"

"Mm."

She glanced at Leon as he sat up, still chuckling. The joint dangled from the corner of his mouth.

"Hey, Inez. How's the leg?"

"Same old."

She sat down in the chair that Damon positioned for her between the french doors and the enormous cheese plant that took up one corner of the conservatory. His hand lingered on her shoulder, and she reached up to touch his knuckles from habit, turning out her heel to show Leon the scar from the operation.

"I just had the cast taken off, like, this week. Hoping to be back on the court in a couple of months, then it's just a matter of building up again, for January. That's what I'm aiming for, anyway."

"Good luck, baby." Leon wrinkled his nose, pushing back his dark, curly mop with the hand that now held the roll-up, and coming dangerously close to setting himself on fire. "It was a fuckin' tough break, I know. Real down for you."

He held out the joint. Inez shot a sideways glance at Damon, mixing another round of Zombies and talking in quiet earnest to Charlie, who had reappeared, red towel knotted around his waist. She took the little white cylinder between her thumb and forefinger. Well, it would hardly matter now.

"And, uh, the... y'know." Leon shifted uncomfortably, hooking his arms around his knees. "The other thing too. Are you okay?"

Inez paused, staring at him for a moment. *Thing.* Yes, that's all it had been, hadn't it? A thing, a minor episode. Mid-May, just after that stupid party at Charlie's, when she'd let herself get wasted because she was angry, jealous... she'd known she'd have a morning after, though she hadn't expected the bleeding. The sharp pain, then the awful realisation of what was happening.

Too early to call it a child, it had been a mess, a blotch of cells... a thing. Nothing more, so the hormonal reaction had surprised her, even though she supposed it was normal. The doctor had said so, hadn't he? Maybe it had been that which had made her push herself on court, made her try to forget that bodies had limits. Maybe she'd deserved the ruptured tendon. Inez hated the thought, but there it coiled, sneaking and insidious, all the same.

She wished she'd never told Leon, that she'd never needed

his comfort or his pity. At least he'd kept if from Day, or if he hadn't, they'd had the sense to pretend otherwise. If there was one thing Inez couldn't have stood, it would have been hearing from Damon that the... thing... didn't matter. He'd have said that, she knew, though it would have changed everything for him. She waited for the hot burn of the hit, the smoke filling her throat. Damn Leon. She'd never wanted him to help. She wished she'd been able to keep it to herself, like she would have done if... well, if she'd seen to it on her own.

Inez exhaled through her nostrils and smiled. "Yeah. Well. Perhaps for the best, y'know? Maybe it wasn't the right time. S'like Day always says. We've got plenty of time." She blinked. It had hurt more than she could ever have known it would. Almost as much as the injury to her leg. "So," she said, quick to change the subject, desperate to evade his terrible sympathy, "should I ask how Holland went?"

"Aw, fuckin' A, y'know? They loved it!" Leon grinned. "Loved *us*. It was a blast... real easy, too. Just keep throwing out all that old material, you still got chicks creaming three rows back. Right, man?"

Inez's gaze flicked to her approaching husband. She took a final drag and handed Leon the joint back as Damon passed her a drink and perched on the arm of her chair.

"New stuff went down well too," he murmured, sweeping her damp hair to the side and planting a kiss on her neck. "It's worth building up. Eindhoven, Rotterdam.... 'S gonna be worth keeping it sweet, y'know."

Charlie threw himself into the remaining chair with his usual abandon and snorted.

"Oh, yeah. Fuckin' centre of world affairs. Let's all get

matching velvet monkey suits and try for a residency at one of them nice Continental hotels, just by the airport. Fuckin' brilliant."

Leon frowned.

"Hey... didn't hear you complaining, man. Certainly not in Nie... Nidge...."

"Nijmegen. I was just doing my duty for international relations."

"Hah! Yeah, man. That's right. What was her name? The chick with the...." Leon gestured vaguely in the direction of his chest, which probably lay somewhere beneath a purple tunic embroidered with gold peacocks. "And she was all... Dutch. And stacked. And the girl with the green eyes. They were green, weren't they?"

"How the fuck should I know?" Charlie shrugged. "I wasn't lookin' in her fucking *eyes*, man...."

Inez switched off as the banter descended into crudity. You expected it, but you didn't need details. Just another thing that happened. The tours, gigs, promos, and parties; none of it really needed to be real.

She'd watched Damon for the first year of their life together, how he'd take his persona out of the wardrobe, dust off the lapels, and slide it on just like a suit. Oh, it was all about playing to the crowd, stroking the ego that lived under the surface, maybe even feeding that desire—no, the *compulsion*—to play, to create... and a well-loved suit does become a part of the person that wears it.

Inez had, she admitted even to herself, only seen the pretty, glittering reflection at first. When she met him, she'd been seeing a racing driver, himself a part of that premeditated collusion of sport and glamour designed to get the big bucks flowing. It was the only reason they were at the party, and then she'd seen Day, zapped on uppers, dancing like crazy and talking unbelievable jive with a glossy, glitzy set of fashion people, music people, who knew what.... She'd made her decision. She knew that. Even so, she felt she hadn't been entirely prepared for the reality. Not the coldness, not the business of it, but how unremitting it was, how relentless.

The first time she'd sat in on a studio session (oh, how he'd preened then! And how she had sat, beautiful and dutiful, behind the glass with the engineers, watching them tweak consoles and levels, and trying to find useless things to say to her), she realised just how calculated it could be. Cris McIlroy, the manager, had been there, in some god-awful lounge suit, smoking some foul-smelling cigarillo and droning on and on about hooks. It had to be a hooky album, the public loved hooks, The Stones were very hooky, it was so big.... Not long after that, she'd first witnessed—what was it?—creative differences at work.

These days, Inez found herself wondering how anyone could bear to listen to music.

Charlie was still going. Some disjointed ramble about America now, delivered at double speed and half coherence. She watched the sweat trickle down his temple. Well, how could he have passed through Amsterdam again and stayed clear of the junk?

Inez looked at the cocktail in her hand. Zombies were one of Damon's specialities; invented in the Thirties by Donn Beach, the tiki king. Smooth, fruity, expensive to create and pretty to look at, vaguely redolent of B-movie Hollywood, and reputed to pack more brain-rotting power per quarter gill than three Manhattans. *What a good idea.* She took the straw between her lips and gazed dreamily out at the pool, allowing the conversation to ripple around her as Damon's fingers crept insistently beneath the shoulder strap of her dress and towards her right breast. It was her prerogative not to listen. Her right. Anyway, there was no need. Here, her only functions were decorative, aesthetic and sexual, and that was where her power lay. Easy once you looked at it that way.

Inez sipped her cocktail and crossed her legs, right over left, one elbow resting upon the arm of the chair, supporting the enormous glass, the other arm lying across her husband's knee. She flexed her freshly polished fingertips and began to trace small, idle circles on the supple leather covering Damon's thigh. Outside, a gentle breeze rippled the surface of the pool, and swallows dipped over the water in a complex pattern of dares and challenges.

"Are you even listening, man?"

Charlie sounded annoyed, his voice rising in pitch before he even got to the end of the sentence.

"Hm?" Damon disengaged himself from Inez's earlobe. "Yeah. Yeah, sure, baby. Uh... New York, right?"

Inez tensed, sensing the prelude to another fight. Charlie opened his mouth, loosely trying to round up the words and spit them out in the right order, but he was mercifully interrupted. A soft knock sounded at the conservatory door, followed immediately by the implacably substantial presence of the housekeeper, Mrs. Staplow, who saw no need to wait for permission to enter. Inez couldn't understand how a woman like that could ever work in service; she didn't seem capable of recognising that anyone else could possibly be above her. She wore, damn it, she wore that damn floral housecoat like a bloody silver mink.

"'Scuse me," the housekeeper said, blunt as ever, apparently oblivious to the heavy smoke and the profanities hanging in the air.

Inez rolled her eyes. Mrs. S. was a stout, square woman of the type apparently bred to Government order during the interwar years, a little like the National Loaf. She looked at the world with her head held back and her eyes half-closed, as if always assessing everything and finding it dismally lacking. Now, she cast her gaze around the room until it fell, with rigid indifference, on Inez.

"Mr. Cooper's here for you. Ma'am," she added, purely—Inez suspected—to annoy.

Inez thrust the remnants of her drink into her husband's free hand and extricated the other one from her bosom.

"Thank you, Mrs. Staplow," she said, struggling for a sense of superiority when she discovered her balance was a little off. "Boys," she acknowledged.

Damon touched her back, a question seeming to pass across his eyes for a moment, until she shook her head. Leon ripped off a GI-style salute, and Charlie wriggled his fingers, watching their motion through the air with wonderment. Then he blew a kiss at the retreating Mrs. Staplow and flashed his towel open. Damon threw a cushion at him, and Leon laughed until rum almost came out of his nose.

The door shut after Inez, the mellow gold of late sunshine and useless conversation closing around her departure like syrup.

Chapter Six

Finding people turned out to be easier than I'd pictured, which seemed strange. Surely, I thought, anyone with something to hide would have covered their tracks and—from what Damon said—everybody must have had at least one skeleton tucked away under the bed. Figuratively speaking, obviously....

I made contact with one Elena Schimmel, former president of the Brother Rush fan club (West German contingent), who now ran a website dedicated to preserving their, and Damon's, memory. She proved very helpful, emailing me stacks of scanned newspaper articles, further links and information. If I'd been surprised at Leon Fielding's transformation, I shouldn't have been; his seemed to be the least dramatic. Joss Napier, after a stint in a none-too-successful prog rock outfit, had retired from the music business in the early Eighties and now seemed mostly noted for the string of hits he'd penned for an early boy band and the organic farm he ran near Bristol. Damon laughed until his eyeliner ran when I told him. However, he found Charlie's early Nineties splash all over the tabloids less impressive.

Charlie Davies had apparently struggled in the long term with his addiction issues, batting in and out of rehab long before it became fashionable. Eventually, it seemed he'd made a last ditch effort, marked by an outpouring of soul-baring, saccharine interviews to the red-tops that had dogged his steps. We had copies of them all, complete with scans of grainy photographs. From a Sunday tabloid dated in early 1993:

"I'M SO SORRY, MUM"

– EX-ADDICT STAR BEGS FORGIVENESS

The picture showed Charlie, a little older and a lot less glam, outside a drug outreach centre in Tottenham. He'd grown a moustache. The body of the article concerned his alleged personal torment and tortuous reformation.

"'Damon's death was the turning point for me,'" he claimed, "'I knew then I had to kick my habit. I couldn't end up like he had.'"

A little over eighteen months later, he'd given another interview, marking his new qualification as a substance abuse counsellor.

"'Knowing what I know and having gone through what I have, I hope I can help other people to stand up to their demons and come through the other side. I will always remember the terrible sense of loss when Damon died and the senselessness of the way it happened. He continues to be my inspiration.'"

I read the segments aloud over cheap red wine and takeaway pizza, one evening of many we holed up in the flat, paper universes splayed out on the floor around us. Damon stuck a finger in his mouth and made gagging noises.

"See?" he said bitterly. "Still bloody blaming me."

Elena Schimmel, despite her enormous collection of cuttings and seemingly bottomless dedication to the cause, couldn't tell us where Charlie had ended up but, after much searching, we found his name listed among the staff of a private clinic in Northwick Park. I sent an enquiry email—the falsehoods coming more easily to me now—and felt slightly secret-agent-ish about the whole thing. There was a sense of triumph even to laying out leads we couldn't follow; Maxwell Vost had died in a car accident eight years ago, and Vince Dexler, the A&R man, fell victim to an overdose in '78. We found no sign of Cris McIlroy, the old manager, nor of Inez, though I hoped Jerry would come up trumps there. It would just be a question of waiting, as I tried to explain to Damon, in all his eager impatience.

I didn't expect to hear back so soon from anybody, least of all to receive a call from Gavin Malpas—Leon Fielding's personal assistant—on one otherwise unremarkable Thursday afternoon.

"Erk?" I said, clutching the phone to my ear, jerked unceremoniously from the notes for a seminar I was supposed to be giving the following week.

"I have got the right number, haven't I?"

Fielding certainly had a smooth team. I had to admit that. Malpas' vowels sounded like the confident, rounded plumminess of an old Harrovian, though I doubted he'd really been a public schoolboy. More probably a fresh-faced media studies grad from some London college, judging by his unquenchable enthusiasm and self-conscious chirpiness: Mr. Fielding was so terribly excited about the project, Mr. Fielding had said what an awfully interesting proposal it was, everybody definitely agreed he certainly should contribute and, of course, he'd said he was really looking forward—ever so terribly much —to meeting me.

I sincerely doubted *that*.

All the same, we fixed up an appointment a few days hence at—Malpas' suggestion—an über-trendy Dulwich restaurant which should fit in with Mr. Fielding's schedule. I could do nothing but grit my teeth and accede, wishing I really did have the advance paid on the book I wasn't really writing. Malpas rang off, leaving me with the unspoken suggestion that—given Mr. Fielding's much-vaunted schedule—I should consider myself lucky to have this opportunity.

I didn't feel lucky. Standing in front of my wardrobe that Sunday afternoon, balancing a clothes hanger in each hand, and with two days until the interview, I felt pretty feeble.

"If I *really* had to choose, I'd say go with the green blouse."

For just a second, I caught my breath, as if I could have imagined it. When I turned, Damon was leaning against the jamb of my bedroom door, clad in a white smocked cheesecloth shirt with red embroidery, a pair of very, very vintage drainpipe jeans, and scuffed brown moccasins. He wasn't wearing any eyeliner. He gave one of those elegant, eloquent uni-shrugs.

"Blondes can do green. It'll bring out your eyes... professional, but human. Compassionate, like, yeah? 'Course, it could do with being a different cut."

He brought the obligatory cigarette smouldering in his fingers up for a quick drag, watching me.

"I thought you said you stayed out of bedrooms, bathrooms, and knicker drawers," I snapped.

Another semi-shrug, though a smile hid at the corner of his mouth.

"Yeah. Did, didn't I? I dunno... you could at least have gone out and bought some Janet Reger undies, tried to tempt me or somethin'."

My mouth was empty. I'd expected to have some smart comeback, some sharp response, but found nothing there. I chuckled softly.

"Now," he said, rubbing his hands together. "Have you got a decent skirt to wear? You can't spend your whole life in jeans."

He brushed past me like the cold draught under a door and, after a moment, a black skirt flew past my head and landed on the quilt.

"Er.... I think I'm quite capable of—"

"'Course you are, baby," Damon said, and I knew it was only a different set of word-shapes hung on the sentence *You dress like a colour-blind nursery teacher on a cold, wet Friday afternoon.*

He emerged from the wardrobe, holding up a cotton sweater in a greyish heather colour, just as I was framing something rude about taking fashion advice from a man with a perm and the dress sense of a camp magpie.

"Be nice," he reprimanded, quirking an eyebrow at me. "And stand up straight. Does this fit?"

"Of course." I took the sweater and held it up against me.

"I've been a student for the past four years. It's hard to put on weight with beans on toast and cornflakes."

Damon didn't look convinced. I sucked my abs in a bit and pulled the material tight.

"See?"

"And you haven't got anything... like...." He gesticulated loosely in the general area of bosoms. "Lower?"

I blushed and then felt ridiculous about it. No, I hadn't, because I didn't have much to show off... that didn't mean it felt good to have what I *had* got under critical scrutiny. Even if he was dead.

Actually, *especially* as he was dead.

"No," I said. "Not really. But then I'm trying to present a professional image, not a glamour portfolio."

"All right, baby." He held up his hands, conciliatory and almost apologetic. "I'm just sayin'... it wouldn't hurt to, y'know, maybe hip it up some, yeah? Maybe... flirt a little bit."

I stared incredulously at him, which wasn't easy to do when I was still using my chin to pin the sweater to my chest. I lifted my head and let the garment fall into my hands.

"Excuse me?"

"Oh, c'mon baby...." Damon winked at me. "I *know* Leon. He always had an eye for the canaries, yeah? Anyway, after thirty years, a little female flattery and some focus on the fact he used to be a sex symbol's gonna appeal to any man. I ain't sayin' you've gotta do anything awful. Just... y'know. Put a little somethin' on show. Break the ice."

I continued to stare. He'd gone back to rifling through my clothes.

"So, tell me," I said. "Did feminism just pass you by, or did you stick your head under a blanket and wait for it to go away?"

Damon laughed. Properly. I wasn't used to hearing that, but it sounded nice. Unaffected and unselfconscious. The only unstaged bit of him, I thought, and instantly regretted it.

"Nah," he said, camping up the Bermondsey vowels. "Where I come from, babe, the women round there would of ate Germaine Greer for breakfast."

I wanted to ask him to elucidate—my so-called biography was decidedly light on his earlier life anyway—but he seized a pair of brown tweed trousers from the wardrobe and held them against the sweater in my hands with a look of abject horror on his face.

"Oh, come on," I said. "It can't be that bad."

"No?" He looked at me and raised an eyebrow. "Don't you *have* any skirts, babe?"

"Only the one you threw over there. And the long one that I wear with my boots. I prefer trousers, really, and—"

Damon grimaced. Then, in one of those horrible moments of blurred movement that made my sinuses hurt, he was holding the black skirt and looking at it critically.

"It's the wrong length for you," he announced. "What are the boots like?"

I sighed. It wasn't like Fielding and I would be doing cocktails at the Ritz. I tossed the sweater on the bed and rooted out my knee high black boots. Damon actually whimpered.

"What?" I snapped, beginning to get exasperated.

"Well... no, nothing, baby. Really. It's just... they're... sort of...."

"Yes? What?"

"Chunky," he said quietly.

I sighed.

"But they'll probably be fine," Damon said, wisely in view of the look that must have crept into my face. "Yeah. Solid, right?"

"Solid," I said.

A worried look flitted over his eyes. "What about jewellery?"

I picked a pillow off the bed and threw it at him. It hit with an extremely satisfying *thunk*.

* * *

The following Tuesday, I arrived at West Dulwich station at about midday. I hauled into the lee of the Victorian brickwork and reached up to twiddle the sapphire stud in my ear: the only 'real' jewellery Mum had ever owned. She'd gone in for costume and paste, of course, but these had been a gift for her twenty-first birthday, from Gran and Granddad. It had seemed only right that, today, something of hers came with me. I pulled the map from my pocket and squinted at it. Then, hoping that Leon Fielding was a born-again macro vegan who only ate small portions of lettuce and drank tap water, I set off to find a cab and get myself to the restaurant.

The place looked far more traditional than the media hype suggested; a building of mellow golden stone, set in a small but beautiful garden, flanked by charming terraces and touched by warm, sandy light that filtered through the trees. Carefully trimmed wisteria and honeysuckle cloaked the mansion house itself while a reclaimed steel sculpture in the front courtyard— possibly of some sort of Japanese crane, or possibly a deformed heron—added to the general suggestion that this, though still the heart of London, had achieved a state of existence far more laidback, and therefore far trendier, than mere mortals could ever hope to approach.

I found my suspicion that I wasn't the place's usual kind of clientele quickly confirmed. The maitre d' peered at me with his nostrils right up until the point I said:

"I'm meeting Mr. Leon Fielding."

A quick check of the list and an unctuous smile. Within moments, I had been ushered to my table. Obviously, despite its painfully trendy décor, the restaurant couldn't lay claim to that many celebrity diners.

"We put you over here by the window, Miss Ross. Nice and quiet."

"Thank you."

The table had been laid in crisply minimalist style and set back in an alcove beside a huge sash window. I settled myself and ordered a bottle of fizzy water to occupy me while I waited. The chairs had been designed for impact over comfort, moulded from some hard plastic that made it difficult to move without sounding like you'd farted. Some bright spark had also decided they should be coloured to match the starkly funky—and starkly orange—concrete floor.

Cool modern jazz played quietly in the background, and the sunken spotlighting glinted off the chunky cutlery. I tried not to fidget as I wondered how late Fielding would be. Fashionably, or superstar? Of course, he wasn't that anymore. Not that he—*they*—ever had been, whatever Damon liked to pretend. Brother Rush might have had their share of screaming teenybopper fans, they'd played the right venues, had great sales and chart successes, but they'd never broken the top crust of the big time... or America.

I'd just started to wonder whether they'd been big in Japan when, across the sea of funky orange concrete, I saw the dark wood double doors open, and Leon Fielding breezed in with the maitre d' at his heels.

I would have recognised him even if I hadn't seen his most recent press shots. The perm was gone—his dark hair peppered now with grey, shortish and slightly wavy—and he'd thickened rather in the waist and jowls since his centrefold days, but the face had stayed very nearly the same. And then he had all that presence. Strange, really. Only medium height, medium build, but he knew how to draw the eye. Certainly, more than the occasional head turned as he walked past. He flashed me a broad, extremely white smile, bearing down on me in a plain, dark suit (casual, almost certainly Italian. Silk blend. Wow.) and exceptionally nice shoes. Very *distingué*, with just a hint of the rake. I wondered if he had a stylist, or if it was all down to him.

"Hi. You're Ellis Ross, right? No, don't get up, please.... Leon Fielding. Hello. So sorry I'm late."

He shook my hand. Broad voice, broad accent—part Stateside, part London—broad palm. His strong, warm grasp, solid and reassuring, spoke of years of schmoozing and a well-practiced, easy charm.

"Totally unforgivable, I know, but I'm afraid I was in a meeting with my publicist. She's really very interested in your project," he added, signalling a waiter.

In what seemed like nano-seconds, we had menus in our hands and the sommelier dancing attendance. I decided I could get used to this. I started to say something along the lines of how pleased I'd been when he'd agreed to take part, but he cut across me.

"They do the most incredible black cod here," said Fielding, examining the menu. "Really. It's great."

"Um," I said. "I'm sure."

We both ordered it—I'd never had French-Japanese fusion cuisine before, so it seemed safest to stick with something which someone else had survived—and allowed the sommelier to persuade us towards a pricey Sauvignon Blanc.

Well, pricey for me.

"So." Fielding smiled at me, lifting his glass.

Something, I realised, lingered behind that genial expression of his. Something else in his eyes, in his voice.... He didn't want to be here.

He *really* didn't want to be here.

"So, Ellis...," he said sweetly. "You don't mind my calling you Ellis? Great. Gavin told me all about the book."

"Did he?"

I suddenly felt painfully aware of my own banality.

"Mm... I'll be honest with you. At first, I said I wouldn't do it. But," he said, his pause just long enough for effect, but not long enough for me to speak, "everyone seems to think it's a good idea. It's... good publicity," he added with a faint expression of disgust.

I understood his pain, or at least an echo of it. Now that it had become more or less acceptable to make a comeback after fifty, hauling himself out of the great PR graveyard that rockers went to when they hung up their Marshalls wasn't enough. I'd done my homework, and Damon and I had listened to the albums Auntie Jan had so loyally bought... and they were good.

Genuinely good. Fielding had a gorgeous voice, all smoky timbre and warmth; he played subtly, and his writing walked a delicate line between poignancy and wit. Yet, of all the notices he'd had in the press, each one had prefixed his name with the phrase 'former Seventies pop star'.

And now here was I. That had to hurt.

"Well," I said, "I'm very glad you decided to—"

"So where d'you wanna start? This book."

I noticed, for the first time, the scar beneath his right eye. I'd thought it was a wrinkle, but then I remembered it from his picture. When I looked closer, the skin seemed slightly tighter there, almost puckered. I blinked. This wasn't going at all the way it should.

"Um, well, I, uh—" I began, mentally kicking myself. Hard, and repeatedly.

"Why are you writing it?"

He was direct, at least. I waited a beat before I answered, making the most of the sip I took from my glass. Really exceptionally good wine. And he really did have that intense thing down well. I marshalled the cover story Damon and I had concocted for just this kind of answer.

"I've always," I said, praying I'd gauged it right, "been very interested in contemporary and visual culture... and how music relates to that. It's a big research area of mine and, well, my mum was a Brother Rush fan in her youth. That's how I discovered the music."

The right mix of truth and illusion, Damon had said. I watched the cringe in Fielding's face... in my mother's youth.... That's right. Makes you feel old, huh? Not too flattered, because I'm young enough to be gauche. That's what worked, he'd said.

"So," I continued, "when I found there hadn't been anything written... I just thought it would be great to do something. I'm," I added, with a small smile that, yes, I had practised, "currently doing my doctorate, you see, and I needed to find a subject. Life writing and biography, so it seemed... right. Besides—"

I took a breath. Damon's instructions on what to say and how to say it had been strict, and I was about to ad lib. If I blew it, I knew he wouldn't forgive me. He'd probably haunt me for the rest of eternity and be in a really filthy mood while he did it. Not a pleasant prospect. Across the table, Fielding arched one thick, penstroke eyebrow.

"He didn't deserve to be forgotten," I said. "Or remembered just for how he died. It isn't fair."

A small silence settled, cool and thoughtful. Around us, the jazz continued to ooze, and cutlery clinked in the lapping of quiet conversation. Fielding studied me from beneath those heavy brows, drawn in apparently serious contemplation and, for a moment, I thought I really had blown it and I'd never be able to go home again.

Then he grinned and let out a relieved sigh which I very nearly echoed.

"Thank God for that!" He leaned back a little. "You're based in Brighton, right? Yeah.... Gavin said you were something to do with the University. I had this awful fear you were gonna be some kind of incredibly serious student, all hung up on how he was an icon for youth revolution, or something stupid. Day would have hated that. But I don't think that's your angle, is it?"

"No," I agreed. "I'm not out for angles. Except possibly

getting my PhD. If that's an angle, I mean...."

Fielding smiled. Not the big, white beam, but a real smile. For just a moment, he reminded me so much of Damon it was disturbing.

A neatly coiffed waiter appeared, dressed in a rather Orwellian soft grey ensemble with comfortable, square-toed black shoes (low heel, lots of arch support. I recognised this well; my entire undergrad career had been augmented with shifts at Pedro's Mexican Bar & Grill—a fiesta for the whole family—and I suppressed a shudder at the memory). When we had been supplied with bread and salad, Fielding seemed to loosen up a little.

"So," I said, not wanting to give him another chance to take charge of the conversation. "I understand that Damon and you went back a long way."

"Sure." He nodded, still guarded. "My parents and I came over in '64, from New Jersey. I was young, insecure... all I wanted to do was be part of something." He laughed softly, picking at his bread roll. "There was a hell of a lot to *be* part of.... You know. Swinging London? It was a copywriter's wet dream but, I was so green right then, to me it all still really did feel like the start of somethin' new."

The Orwellian waiter reappeared with our black cod. It had been artfully arranged in several tiers, carefully balanced on square white plates. I wasn't sure whether to photograph it or eat it. We thanked the waiter, and he melted back into the ether, leaving me to ponder the best way to deconstruct my dinner without dropping it down my cleavage.

Fielding continued to talk. His words didn't come in great rushes, but neither did he seem at all slow or indecisive. I had the feeling that each sentence was being taken down from a shelf and dusted off after a time left unused. A time spent packed away, but not forgotten. He leaned forward in his chair, arms on the table and fork in his right hand as—a picture of artless elegance, if not one of classic table manners—he addressed his fish.

"The first time I met Damon was at a party, y'know, some artist's show, down in Holborn. I don't remember who the artist was... some proto-psychedelic freak, as I recall, only not very good. I think he went on to do some stuff with the *International Times*. I don't remember the paintings, but I remember a lot of people sitting on the floor smoking pot and talking about politics. Like I said, I was a kid. I'd only found out about the thing by chance. Tagged along and blagged my way in." He smiled. "Damon saw right through me first off."

"How do you mean?"

The black cod actually wasn't at all bad, and I could identify some of the things in the salad, which was encouraging. Fielding shook his head.

"This place... the guy's flat, it was kinda dark. Very moody. This girl in a miniskirt with a Mary Quant haircut gave me a joint. First time I ever smoked weed. Barely knew which end to stick in my mouth, you know, how hard to draw. So, I'm standing there, pretending not to cough, trying to work out what the hell is going on and how not to look like a complete idiot, and this voice behind me says—"

He struck a pose—chin down and fork held out like a cigarette—and the impression was nearly note-perfect. I had to stifle a yelp of laughter.

"'You and I are the only two sober people in this room,

man. We either need to split this scene, or start pissin' on the houseplants.'" Fielding chuckled, spinning the fork round again in his fingers. "He was... aw, he was funny. And he could see a scene for what it was, y'know? So, we got to talking... both hated the pictures, both thought the Marxists were pompous asses, so we ditched. Ended up getting really stoned, standing on Southwark Bridge at two in the morning, just... talking about life."

Fielding shook his head again; not disbelief, not regret or awe at his younger self, I realised. Just an acknowledgement of days long gone.

"Damon had all these big plans, all the things he was gonna do. Move up north, get digs somewhere it was all happening. King's Cross, or Ladbroke Grove... he never took it all as seriously as some of the guys up there, of course. Not, like, real Underground stuff. Y'know? But he wanted to be part of it, whatever *it* was, because it had to be better than missing out. Better than *not* doing something. 'Course it never came off. That was the year his dad died."

I realised that my fork, laden with cod and mizuna, had stopped half-way to my mouth. Fielding took a sip of his wine.

"It was... I don't know. The beginning of things, I suppose." He speared another bite of fish philosophically.

I swallowed my mouthful and reached for my pen. "You... uh, would it be all right to talk about that?"

My study of online and library-loaned journalism primers had not been in vain. Lead your subject gently with your questions, but don't forget to show compassion. It makes them open up. Watch for emotional responses and get ready to play them. I'd studied hard. Trouble was, it didn't seem to impress

Fielding. And, if he had an emotional response to that, he didn't show it. His eyes darkened slightly, nothing else.

"Day never really spoke about it. He didn't talk about his family, his home life, to the press."

He put the same twist on the word 'press' that you might find in the phrases 'cat turd in the herbaceous border' and 'weeding without gloves', when they occurred in the same sentence. He'd thrown me a little off-balance too; I'd not been expecting such a flat refusal. Though, I had to admit, Damon hadn't talked to me about his early life, either. Or about his parents. I cleared my throat, affecting nonchalance and ad libbing generously.

"It was difficult, then? I mean, I realise that—"

"Look," Fielding said shortly, "Day grew up in a shithole of a place off of the Old Kent Road…. I mean, those houses went electric barely two years before Bob Dylan did. But Damon, he never made a thing about it, y'know? That's two things he never did. Kiss and tell, and pretend to be a martyr. He did everything else… but not that. That wasn't his style. So, if you'll forgive me, Miss Ross, I'd much rather leave you to do your own research."

Uh-oh, back to surnames. I licked my lips, trying to work out how to turn this one around, but Fielding wasn't even looking at me. A small part of my brain had been busy with mental arithmetic. Nineteen… sixty three? My personal apparition had never mentioned a childhood in the last of London's tenement slums.

"I'm sorry," I said. "I suppose I was just looking for some background. A fuller picture, maybe."

"Yeah," Fielding said, not unkindly. "Well, working class poverty didn't usually make the interview spread in *Jackie*."

He took a mouthful of wine, raising his eyebrows with the weary air of a man who has been asked his favourite colour more times than anybody can answer and still remain responsible for his actions. I smiled and decided we'd better give this angle a break.

"Okay…. So, I understand you two worked closely together, right from the start?"

"Oh, yeah." He nodded earnestly. "Yeah. We always bounced ideas around. When we first started playing together, it was all about sounding like The Yardbirds, but that passed… a bit."

He seemed to respond to me asking about the music. His eyes sparkled as he talked about the time he and Damon had spent in squalid Kentish Town digs, just on the border of the burgeoning Camden scene.

"Before it was really fully regenerated," he explained. "It was only a coupla years after the *International Times* launch party… y'know, the legendary one where Paul McCartney dressed up as a sheikh, Marianne Faithfull came as a dirty nun, and there was the six foot high giant jelly? It's, like, canonical now, or something."

I started to get wide-eyed, despite my best efforts, and he laughed.

"I know… I wish we could've gone to that. But that was what we wanted *in* to, y'know? That place where things were happening, things were *new*…. The Roundhouse didn't see that many more parties like that one, but there were some fantastic gigs. We went to everything we could… and Day always seemed to know someone in the right place, y'know? I don't know how he did it, but it was incredible."

He asked me questions back, asked what I knew about this band, this artist, this venue… it kept me on my toes. Although I found myself pushed for a few answers, I offered up silent thanks to Mum, wherever she was. I'd never realised I'd learned so much at her knee, or how unsuitable for a small child most of it had been.

We talked about the antics and anecdotes of the time, about Damon, and how—in the December of 1970—they'd played a gig in a room above a pub not far from Chalk Farm tube station and had, by chance, caught the attention of an A&R man called Vince Dexler.

"He'd been over at the Roundhouse, happened to drop into The Anchor for a pint after the gig and liked what he heard… or so he said." Fielding grinned. "Not high tact, of course. Asked if the drummer was with us, Damon said we'd only just met him that week. Dexler says, 'Best not let him have your phone number, baby'. Nice, right? So, by the end of the night, he has us thinking we've practically got a deal. Of course, what he *said* was that, if a band could be put together, we *might* get something. Subtle difference."

"But crucial," I said. "So that's how you were put in touch with Cris McIlroy and then Maxwell Vost?"

"Yep." Fielding nodded. "Took the best part of a year, with us hanging around like spare parts, just waiting. But when it started to come together, it moved fast. Before we knew it, Charlie was on board, then Joss, and the whole thing just blew up."

We ordered up dessert (French apple tart with a wineberry and vodka coulis), and he talked about the years with the band. He talked about the explosion of their careers in '72, and the pressure and the unbelievable highs, of which he admitted, with tongue in cheek candour, he'd had more than his fair share. After that came '73, the year Brother Rush had been in their prime, riding in the tail of the comet. They'd been up against the mania of T. Rextasy, kept busy aping the ChinniChap hits machine that had produced such quantum success for Suzi Quatro, The Sweet, and others. Although falling short of the expansiveness of the Electric Light Orchestra and the mixolydian gravitas of Led Zeppelin, somewhere—in the middle of the glitter and the cash-ins—they'd found success, and respect, of a kind.

"So, '73.... That was the year he met Inez, wasn't it?" I asked, looking up from my notes.

Fielding nodded. "Yeah, that's right. They got together sometime... uh, yeah, sometime in the summer, I think. Met at some bash. She, oh, she was a real knockout, y'know?"

"She was a tennis player?"

"Mm-hm. Talented. Top flight, Inez... that was their only problem."

"Sorry?"

"Yeah." He smiled sadly. "So was I. Y'see... Damon wanted something steady. He needed that. *She* was very career-driven —rightly so, y'know? 'Cos she was good. And, Inez... she had that, uh, star quality, you'd say, I guess. They were perfect. Just... just so much glam in one room." Fielding shook his head. "But he couldn't see that she was never gonna settle for a house in the country and a baby or three. And Day still had stuff to get out of his system."

I was going to ask what stuff when Fielding sighed and frowned deeply. He rubbed his fingers over the rim of his wineglass, tapping a broad, thickened thumbnail against it.

"He treated her very badly. Bought that pile down near Westbury, just before the wedding. He was all hyped up about it. He says to me, 'I'm leaving London. We're just gonna go, man, start clean over. Gonna be,'" Fielding pulled a face, "'Garden of Eden'. That's what he said. He was pretty wasted at the time, but... I told him to watch out for snakes."

"Snakes?"

"He just set her up in that house—oh, he built her a tennis court, a pool.... But you can't play dolly house with people. You can't expect them to fit the roles you put them in. And he didn't always behave himself, either."

It didn't remotely surprise me. I raised an eyebrow in gentle enquiry.

"D'you mean—"

Fielding fidgeted, backtracking before I had a chance to pin him down.

Damn.

"I'm not saying anything specific," he said, loyal even beyond the end. "Just, they could both have been different people, y'know? And, if they had, perhaps things would've been quieter, but.... I dunno. Perhaps if they'd had a kid. I don't think they could—she couldn't, I mean. And that was what Day wanted, more than anything."

"Family?"

"Stability," Fielding corrected. "That's how it worked, in his mind. I don't know, I shouldn't really.... We didn't often talk about his marriage, him and me. See, I didn't much like the way he treated her. This one time, I told him I thought she deserved better, and Day just blew up in my face, y'know? So I tried to leave well alone. Be the best friend I could to both of 'em... and I felt for Inez. I really did."

He fiddled with his spoon, made a pretence of being interested in his apple tart and, for a minute, I thought I wouldn't get anything else out of him... but there seemed to be something else he wanted to say. Dark eyes flashed up to catch mine, keen and incisive.

"Have you spoken to Inez yet?"

"Um... I've enquired," I said, technically truthful. "She's not exactly been easy to track down."

"No." Fielding smiled ruefully. "Last I heard, she sold Westleve, moved back to London for a while. Couldn't bear to stay there, after.... Thing is, I'm not going to give you the dirt out from under people's feet, okay? You'd need to talk to her, if she'll.... I mean, you'll know she ruptured her Achilles tendon that spring. It was in all the papers. Bad injury... she made match fit again, but barely. It was never the same, and she never got it back, y'know? She lost everything that year. Her career, the baby, Damon. She was left with nothing." He raised his glass to his lips, pausing as his eyes darkened. "Well, except the money. And the house."

My pen scratched to a standstill on the paper. Baby? What baby? He spoke with such graceful composure and easy self-confidence that little phrases like the double whammy he'd just dropped on me were very nearly missed. *Nothing except the house and the money, huh?* I wondered if he'd really meant to imply what he had.

Leon frowned into the depths of his glass. "Poor girl, though. Y'know? She never wanted Day to know about the miscarriage," he explained, in response to my confused look.

"Just a few weeks before she hurt her leg. Really sad, looking back. Y'know, he was so hung up on what he thought he wanted. The house, kids... whole package. And she tried. She really did."

The rabbit just wasn't gonna die, right? That had been how Damon said it, and I'd seen how it hurt him. But if Inez had kept the loss of the baby from him... how had Fielding known? The look on his face suggested he regretted having said anything, so I thought maybe I should strike while the wound was fresh, see if a little guilt couldn't squeeze him.

"You said she tried to keep it from him. So, um, how did you—"

The Orwellian waiter reappeared to remove our dessert plates. I silently cursed him. Places that overcharged this much should have staff who knew when not to intrude.

"Like I said, I really shouldn't.... I mean, it was hard on everybody to lose him like that. It was a shitty year, y'know?"

The waiter receded, and I inclined forward a little over the table.

"She told *you* about it, though."

Fielding exhaled, long and low, looking decidedly uncomfortable. I expected him to tell me to take a hike.

"I guess I was just in the right place at the right time. When she needed a shoulder to... y'know. She, uh, she made me swear not to tell," he added, doubt painted on his face.

I gave him my best semblance of a confidential smile, sombre and respectful. *So why are you telling me now?*

"It's not something I'd think about including without speaking to her."

Fielding looked relieved, but it seemed to me I'd passed

some kind of complex, clandestine test. I shifted slightly on my hard, uncomfortable chair, trying in vain to avoid the fart-squeak from the plastic. If he heard it, he didn't acknowledge it. I prayed I wouldn't blush, while inwardly cringing.

"She was a strong lady, Inez," he said. "She.... Well, you gotta remember, y'know, that at his best Damon Brent was a sexy bastard. At his worst... well, Inez was more than his match." Leon toyed with the stem of his wineglass and smiled at some distant memory. "I mean, this one time? She found out about some groupies we had hanging around at a gig—not that we ever had that *many* groupies, unfortunately." He grinned at me. "And not that I'm sayin' Day did anything wrong. But Inez could get.... Well, like I said. She was more than his match, y'know? She took the windscreen right out of the Jeep. With a brick. And his clothes... my God. Y'know, most of those threads were irreplaceable. Day used to shop like," another, wider grin, "well, like my mother. He was terrible, but he had a hell of an eye. Y'know. Everything was Alkasura, Let It Rock, Mr. Freedom, Granny Takes a Trip... I mean, there was even some Ossie freakin' Clark in there. And she trashed the lot. Pair of pinking shears and a can of green paint. He was inconsolable for days."

I could picture it all too well... and I couldn't help but wonder about the clothes I'd seen Damon in. Mystic ghost raiments? I pushed the thought away, postponing it until—if I had to have it at all—another time. Another time, a long time away, preferably.

"Wow," I said instead. "So... things were volatile?"

Leon stiffened, vacillated, and treated me to another pained wince.

"I'm not saying *that*... y'know, all told, they loved each other. And he'd have done anything for her. I know that."

And that was that. Subject closed. I could see it in his face. More than that too... I could see echoes of Damon there. It was —there was no other word for it—spooky. That same moody, challenging look. I girded myself.

"Would, um, would you mind perhaps talking about the night he died?"

"Sure."

The word came out too fast, too insincere, and Fielding winced when he said it. I actually felt guilty. That amazed me, though it shouldn't have done. If one thing had come across clearly this evening, it was the affection that he'd had for Damon. I'd known they went way back, but.... It still unsettled me. The man made me feel like a fraud and a cheat, and that pissed me off. Plus, something seemed wrong, but I couldn't put my finger on what. I wished I had more experience at this.

As he spoke of the death, Fielding's demeanour changed again. He grew eerily tranquil. All the fidgeting, the gestures and the expressiveness of his movement seemed to stop, replaced with a strange, stiff composure.

"Mm," he said softly. "I remember the party. In bits, anyway.... Day was excited, 'cos there were gonna be all these big names there. Reckoned after that he was going to be in with the players, y'know? Then he had this fight with Inez... I don't know what it was about," he added, meeting my eye steadily.

I knew he was lying. He'd been there, offered pills and sympathy, but I couldn't call him out on it. *Damn.* I cleared my throat.

"You don't have any idea, though? I mean, money, or...

something else? It must have been fairly major for her to leave before the party like that."

"Oh?"

Whoops. Hadn't meant to overstep myself.

"Well," I said, "just the newspaper reports and so forth. But it does seem a little odd. That she wasn't there, and then sh—"

"Like I said," he countered, "we didn't really talk much about Inez."

I wouldn't get anything else—he even clammed up the same way Damon did, damn it.

"So, um…. You found the b-body?"

Fielding drained the rest of his wine in one smooth motion but didn't put the glass down, his fingers working on the base and stem as he turned it in his hands. I wondered how many times he'd told this story before. How much it hurt each time. He scowled morosely at the wineglass, and I knew he wasn't there anymore, but rather going back through every footfall, every step on the way to that room.

"Yeah," he said, after a while. "So it was fairly early, on the Saturday morning. Place was still swinging. I notice he's not there, think, y'know, I've not seen him for a while, I'll go check he's okay. 'Cos it was weird not to see Day bein' the centre of *somebody's* attention. I remember feeling really generous, thinking I'd share some uppers with him." Fielding laughed dryly. "So I went up into the west wing… he 'n' Inez had private rooms up in there, y'know. The house wasn't actually that huge, but I guess Day liked it better that way. I… I could hear the shower. Then I saw the door was open, and—I guess he didn't lock it—I thought that was weird. So I go across the landing and… and that much blood." He stopped, staring at the wineglass. "I don't care what people say. You can *smell* it."

Abruptly, he stood the glass down. I stared at it, watching the light glance over its bowl. I blinked.

"He was still warm," Fielding said, clearing his throat. "I thought... I thought there'd be a pulse. Shouldn't have touched him, I guess, but I thought.... He was laying on his back, on the floor. The shower curtain was down, like he'd... I don't know. There was blood on the sink, on the john... like he'd been trying to get up and couldn't. Struggling like some kinda trapped animal, y'know? It was awful. And his head... there was skin missing. He musta hit that damn sink so hard. Musta hurt. So much."

He fell silent, and the sudden absence of his voice dropped the bottom right out of everything. I realised I'd been holding my breath. Fielding topped up our wineglasses. I wasn't sure I was going to be able to stand up after all this, much less get home without a wheelbarrow, but I didn't dare stop him in case he started to think.

"I-I remember," he began again, slowly, "knowing I needed to get help. I think I realised he was dead, but I didn't—I couldn't understand it." He emptied the last of the Sauvignon into his glass, watching the last drips cleave to the lip of the bottle before giving it a final shake. "He wasn't there anymore. You know what I mean? I think it was then I freaked out. I mean, I was messed up to start with. I don't remember much at all after that... I know I gave a statement. We all did. And I remember the press arriving and, later, Inez showing up. I... may have said things I later regretted."

My pen paused on the paper. "May I ask what you mean?"

Fielding blinked and glanced up at me. He shrugged

dismissively.

"Just stupid shit. Somehow, I thought… if she'd been there. Y'know. It was all just what ifs. I know he fought with Charlie about her that night. Charlie used to flirt with Inez somethin' awful, and… well, it never mattered, y'know. Only, that night, Charlie said something—I don't know what—and Day took it all wrong. Threw a couple punches. I don't really know," he said quickly. "I wasn't in the room."

Fielding's frown deepened, and he swallowed. I could see him thinking about what he'd said, thinking about backtracking again. Worse than that, I couldn't think of a single thing to prompt him with, anything to say that wouldn't sound plastic.

"It would never have happened like it did," he said, his words carefully clipped, "if he hadn't been so fucked up. And he was fucked up because he was cut over her. Over whatever…. And it was so… *stupid*. A stupid, stupid accident. It wasn't right. Never was."

I took a gamble, hoping to play myself onto his side. "The press coverage was certainly unkind."

Fielding looked at me with something like derision in his eyes, and I realised I'd screwed up. Shit.

"Not really. It *was* stupid. And it all fell apart after that. Y'know, no one cared anymore. I suppose it's because of when it happened, as much as how. I mean, it was all heartbreak and tragedy at the time, but the press was just so keen to muck-rake. I guess everyone closed ranks. After that, the interest kinda petered out… 'cos then there was '77, you know? And that was one hell of a year. Whole new set of currents, whole new set of splashes." Fielding shook his head. "Whole lot of waste too. Seemed like a lot of people were gone that year. Steve Biko,

Peter Finch—I mean, *Peter Finch*—Elvis. We're never allowed to forget about that, are we? And poor Marc…. That was really awful. And Forrest Bess: I have one of his pictures. God… all right, I've depressed myself now."

He said it with an ironic little smile and a sip of the Sauvignon, but it became clear he'd reached his limit. There would be no more about Damon Brent. Not tonight. I tried to push a little bit, go over some of what we'd talked about and press for details. Fielding continued to be charming and graceful, but I couldn't move him. Eventually, I had to admit I'd been beaten and pay the bill.

We parted on good terms, or near enough. He said it had been a pleasure to talk to me, though I wasn't sure I believed him. He made me promise to call Gavin Malpas if I needed anything else, and I gave him one of the partially fake business cards I'd printed on my PC. We shook hands, he kissed my cheek, and I was appalled at myself because I blushed. He had a subtle scent of oranges and vetivert about him—some kind of designer cologne I almost recognised—and more than a touch of the satyr in those dark eyes. I wasn't sure which was more unsettling; finding a man more than twice my age attractive, or reminding myself that he could potentially be a murderer.

Still, it had grown late when we weren't looking. Leon insisted on making sure I got a cab to the station, and he insisted on seeing me into it.

He played the consummate gentleman, and it was just enough to scare me.

Chapter Seven
June 3rd 1976

Rotterdam: the last stop on the map. This time tomorrow, they'd be back on English soil and, for Cris McIlroy, it couldn't come quickly enough.

Front of house, eight thousand fans were on the rail. The Dutch roadies had dropped at least one amp, which the sound engineer had patched up with duct tape, chewing gum, and prayer. The lighting guy kept complaining about the depth of the grid, and the band's rider had no M&Ms. Worse, Cris had left his spare pack of cigarettes back at the hotel, and someone had just told him how much of the band's money the promoters had spent on inflatable armchairs.

They had, for some reason, decided to make it the theme of the night.

Every gig had a theme, as every promo moron tried to outdo the others along the tour route. In Eindhoven, it had been 'precious jewels', after *Hope Diamond*, that crappy B-side they'd released that had been so popular out here last month. You couldn't move for chunks of coloured glass hanging off everything. It had been like being stuck inside a Lalique lamp, and Cris hated the damn song anyway.

> *You shine like a star*
> *You're burnin' me too steep*
> *But you're cursed, you are*
> *I know, 'cos I can't sleep*

What the hell was that all about anyway? Damon could do better. And in Nijmegen... well, Cris didn't understand the logic behind it, but there had been tiki lights and a topless bartender. She'd been jiggly enough, sure, but unfortunately she couldn't make a Cosmopolitan to save her life.

Tonight, the whole backstage area had been kitted out with shiny, round plastic furniture in candy colours. Inflatable bubbles, kinda like transparent beach balls, hung from the ceiling. The general buzz of pre-show activity was disrupted by the occasional bang and sorrowful, drawn-out squeak of somebody accidentally—or otherwise—puncturing something.

A group of roadies huddled in a corner, smoking dogends and chattering in Dutch. Cris waved his arms at them and swore in a vague, half-hearted kind of way, like a man trying ineffectually to frighten geese. One of them muttered something as he passed by, and the other three laughed. People milled aimlessly about up here... had there been so many people in Eindhoven? It seemed like the number of hangers-on increased with every town. Who knew where they came from, or what they were for. He almost collided with a girl in a silver dress and red lipstick, her eyes wide in her skull.

"Who the hell are you?"

She said something in English so heavily accented he couldn't understand it, and darted off. Cris cracked on his gum and exhaled tightly. It would be so much easier if they brought their own crew. Just one set of bozos for the entire tour, instead of this ramshackle fragmentation. This time tomorrow, he promised himself, and pushed open the dressing room door.

"Boys? Five minutes, all right? I don't want to hear— Hey. Is it me, or are we two short? Where are they?"

The facilities weren't bad, considering they were basically playing a university campus. Sure, so the Erasmus Universiteit was shiny and new, all white concrete and practical spaces, but it still felt bare and flat. Back here, pale fluorescent light washed the low, square room. The assorted chairs and a couple of overstuffed couches had been pushed up to the walls. Tables, floor, and shelves were littered with things that crackled and clinked, a general detritus of wrappers, bottles and—Cris cracked on his gum again—yes, more transparent beach balls.

Charlie was sitting at one of the tables, pawing at his nose like a dog with toothache. A very empty space had been cleared in front of him, and Cris chose not to look too closely at it.

"Bad ice cube," Charlie said, like it was the funniest thing he'd heard all evening.

From one of the couches, Joss, wrapped around a bottle of Remy Martin and some chick with red-gold hair down to her backside, pointed vaguely behind him. Cris grunted, popped his gum again, and picked his way across the floor. He missed his Tipalets. He could hear Leon throwing up even before he got into the bathroom. As he opened the door, he noticed that the telephone cord was tracking underneath it.

"Ohhh… oh, Jesus. Oh. Oh, Christ! Sweet Jesus God, I'm—oh, Christ—I'm gonna fuckin' die," Leon moaned between retches, plaintive voice echoing from one of the stalls.

Damon, phone receiver clamped to his ear and its cream plastic cradle dangling from his fingers, was pacing the tiles. Every time he got to a wall he stopped, twitching lightly and shifting from foot to foot.

"But, sweetheart…. No, I didn't say that. I—"

"Oh, God, no…! Oh, Jesus… Jesus *Christ!*"

Damon sighed dramatically and glanced over his shoulder. "Look, I dunno what you think Jesus is gonna do, man. You're Jewish. No, Inez, not…. Nah, babe, I was talking to—"

"Fuck off! Oh, *God*, no…!"

There was another explosive and vile noise. Cris closed his eyes. Just twenty-four little hours. All he had to get through. He took a deep breath and pinched the bridge of his nose. From the stall, Leon whimpered.

"Day? Day, are you there?"

Damon pressed the phone into the shoulder of his maroon velvet jacket. Silver dragons coiled the length of his sleeves.

"Yeah. What?"

"I think I just lost another filling…."

Damon glanced up at Cris, as if seeing him for the first time. Cris cracked on his gum and decided that it had most definitely lost its flavour.

"What the hell?" he asked needlessly.

"Don't sweat it, man. He'll be fine." Putting the phone back to his ear, Damon crossed to the row of sinks and filled one with cold water, listening to the voice on the line. "Yeah, I know, baby... but you got the flowers, right?"

"You know you've got, like, five minutes?" Cris prompted, hanging back in the doorway. It smelled worse than a nightclub bathroom in here.

Damon shot him an exasperated, if unfocused, glare.

"You mind, man? It's my fuckin' anniversary!" He frowned, bringing the phone back up to his mouth. "What? Well, yeah, I know. No, I *know*, honey.... I— Look, I'll make it up, all right?"

"Day?" Leon whined from the cubicle. "Day? Where'd you go?"

"And it's not like it's forever. I promised, didn't I? Well, there you are, then, girl. I'm here," he added, muting the phone on his shoulder again. "Christ, it's like having a little sister. Are you finished?"

"I...." There was an uncertain pause and some spitting. "Yeah. I think so."

"All right. C'mon, man, we gotta get you cleaned up. Cris, you wanna get us some clean towels in here or something?"

Still holding up the doorjamb, Cris realised he'd been watching the whole scene with a kind of horrified fascination. And now he was being told what to do, like any other fucking lackey. The cubicle door opened, and Leon tottered out, deathly pale except for red-rimmed eyes and running nose.

"I told you to leave that shit alone," Damon chided, holding out a wad of toilet paper. "Here."

"Fuck you," Leon muttered, snatching the tissue and going to the sink to sponge himself down.

Damon sniggered.

"It's not fucking funny, man! Christ... state of me," Leon

moaned, holding on to the sink to stop himself from swaying as he peered into the blotchy mirror.

Cris looked critically at Leon and his chalky, sweaty throw-up face.

"Is he really okay?"

"Yeah, sure... it's, y'know, it's fine. Five minutes. What? No," said Damon, returning what remained of his attention to the phone. "I'll be home for that. It's gonna be sweet. I promise."

"Well," Cris began doubtfully, aware that Damon was actually having the nerve to usher him out. "Five minutes. Okay, baby? 'Cos, y'know, we need to get this thing moving."

He watched the door close in his face and spat his gum on the floor before going to see about those towels. This had to be the last time.

Whatever it took, man, this *was* the last freaking time.

* * *

Damon shut the door firmly. Everything echoed in here... just like the voice in his ear. Inez, waiting for a response. He never knew what to say to a crying woman.

"Then I'll see you when I get home, baby. Yeah. I gotta go. Love you."

He hung up, sighed, and shook his head. After a moment of consideration, he threw the phone against the wall. The plastic splintered and it made a big crackling, impressive sort of noise, tinged with the ping of metal, but it didn't make him feel very much better.

He looked over Leon's shoulder at the white, wan face in

the mirror.

"You sure you're up to this?"

Leon nodded with the kind of care that suggested he thought his head might fall off. "Mm. Kinda tired, though. You got any of those r—"

"No! Come here."

He turned Leon, floppy like a rag doll, around and propped him against the sink as he rinsed out the wad of tissue. Eyes fluttering closed, Leon smiled at the feel of cold water on his brow.

"S'nice."

"Yeah, well, chuck on me and die, right? You dig that?"

"Mm. I'm all right."

"Bollocks are you."

Leon cracked open one eye and watched Damon sponge down the front of his blue satin tulip jacket. It wouldn't survive any longer than tonight, that was for sure. But at least it wouldn't show under the lights.

"You're good to me," he mumbled. "Y-You always been good to me."

Damon dipped the tissues back in the sink.

"Yeah. Well, you make me look better, don't you? Idiot."

* * *

There had been two fainters in the front row by the time the band got out there. Cris, having sent a runner to scour the place unsuccessfully for Tipalets, settled reluctantly for a pack of Djarum kreteks the promoter had tucked into his hand with a knowing smile. Yeah, so they were expensive... but the clove flavour made his tongue itch.

Now, he hunched up in the wings, smoking too much and watching the boys get ready to go. The lights came up, washing over the polished stage in flares of green, blue… pink? Jeez. At least it made Leon look like he had a little colour.

Cris moved aside as one of the roadies finished fixing up the cables and shambled offstage, slowly, apparently totally oblivious to the ranks of massed, yelling fans. The guy brushed past, on his way to do whatever it was roadies did when they stopped doing anything else, and Cris realised that he'd bitten down on the end of his cigarette. It tasted foul. He saw Damon, centre right like always, glance off to the side, getting his last levels check, and then—chin tipped, sliding up to the mic—he hit the first two E7#9 chords of *Love You (Like a Brother)*, letting the notes ring out until they were almost swallowed in the screams.

"You all right?!"

The crowd roared. Cris prayed he wouldn't keep it up too long. It got wearing very quickly. He sucked on his kretek and counted to five. The third chord sounded, the drums crashed in, and Charlie was late on the bass line. Still, at least Leon hadn't passed out. He was even facing the right way, looking determinedly tight-lipped and picking up a fat, heavy riff on his wine red Les Paul Deluxe. Head bent, hair falling over his eyes, he'd started to get into it by the time Damon stopped vamping it up and slipped in a tight, intricate little lick that Cris hadn't heard before.

"*Yeeeeeeaaaaahhhh!*"

And then there was Damon's tic… that whole fake climax thing, leering up against the mic. Cris took a long drag on the kretek, wincing slightly and, gradually, becoming aware of the girl standing beside him. Charlie brought up the bass line, coming forward in the spotlight, doing some long runs up and down the neck that—almost—disguised the fact Leon had screwed up.

Cris glanced at the chick, surreptitiously at first. Onstage, Damon broke into the verse:

> *Well life is like a mother baby*
> *Ain't nothing like it wants to be*
> *Only thing I know is how to show*
> *How to do what you do to me...*

She looked pretty enough, though her mouth and her eyes seemed kind of big, like she'd never really grown into them. He thought at first she must be a fan who'd got past security, but she was acting way too calm. Cris took the kretek from his mouth as Joss pounded seven kinds of hell out of the bridge. He looked over the freckles, the ridiculously long sweep of red-gold hair... the dimpled chin. Leon had picked up like he'd never made a mistake, coming forward on his mark. Sure, he sounded a little shaky on the first bar of the chorus, but it resolved itself.

> *Well I love you (Yeah I do)*
> *That much I know is true*
> *Love you like a brother baby*
> *And brother ain't I good to you!*

The Les Paul's thick, dirty sustain drew out, the chord shift strident under Damon's ad lib lick. If Charlie tried for a bass run any funkier, it would sound like God moving furniture. The kretek drooped between Cris' lips, and he turned to the redhead, sudden realisation slipping coldly between his shoulder blades.

"Jessica?"

She glanced at him, but only briefly, her attention consumed by the show.

What the hell was she doing here? Now? Christ, he'd be in so much trouble if anyone found out. Ghosts from the past were one thing, but when they interfered with the future…. He made to grab her by the arm, pull her away, but she swayed out of his grasp. All the grace of a dancer.

Her toe tapped, and her whole body shivered lightly against the rhythm, just the ripe side of skinny in a short, figure-hugging dress patterned with rusty gold daisies. A silky, crocheted white shawl whispered against her shoulders.

"I'm not doing anything wrong, Cris. Am I?"

He snatched the cigarette out of his mouth, spitting the smoke.

"What did… when did you get here?"

As the second verse gave way to a blues-rock stomp, she just looked at him and shrugged.

Chapter Eight

I got in late and had to wade through the heavy blue smoke that wreathed the stairwell courtesy of Mr. Downstairs. Nobody really knew what he did all day, but he kept very strange hours, and his manner just didn't tempt anyone to ask in more detail. Pink spiders and four a.m. panic attacks aside, he gave off the impression of being a little... special, to put it charitably. Although, with recent events being what they had been, I had to admit I wasn't in the best position to call anyone else crazy. I unlocked my front door, glad to be back, even though the flat smelled of sandalwood and... curry? I edged in cautiously. Damon stood by the fireplace, ostensibly studying the photos on the mantelpiece, though he glanced up as I came into the room. He was barefoot, a pair of black leather trousers hugging his hips. A v-neck tunic with fluted sleeves in a slinky, silky sea-green fabric looked as if it ought to rustle when he moved, though I knew I wouldn't hear it. Smoky kohl and a cropped red waistcoat with black and gold edging completed the picture.

"All right, babe?"

He held a very short gin and tonic in one hand, with a half-smoked cigarette in two extended fingers and, in his free hand, the empty jewel case of Fielding's latest CD. The darkly sweet acoustic guitar of *Only the Rain* filtered from the stereo, along with Leon Fielding's voice, soft but insidious. I wondered how long Damon had been here, drinking and listening to the songs.

"Hey." I dumped my bag and kicked the door shut behind me. "All right?"

He took a mouthful of his gin, not really the kind of dimension that could ever be called a sip, and swallowed.

"Mm. You wanna drink, baby?"

"I'll make some tea."

He appeared to stifle a belch; I wondered if he could get drunk. It stood to reason, after everything I'd seen him put away, though it brought me back to all those questions about his physicality... about mine, too, really. Actually, about everything. Reality seemed a lot less static these days, and I was getting sick of questions that flapped loose without answers, like unbuckled shoes.

I went through to the kitchen. Fielding's voice curled from the stereo, burred with a slow melancholy:

> *Don't know why it seems like*
> *Every drop's the same*
> *Whiskey or water I know it's*
> *Only the rain.*

I put the kettle on, going through the comforting ritual of

rinsing pot and mugs, finding spoon and leaves, organising the kitchen worktop the way one might calm and order a fractured mind. I shivered lightly and turned, that cold ache on my bones again. Damon trailed after me, a little too close for comfort. The cigarette dangled from his lips, his eyes heavy with more than the kohl.

"So, what'd he tell you?"

I leaned back against the cooker, fighting the urge to wave away smoke I couldn't smell.

"Well, we talked about how it started. Your first contract and... the years up to—" I stopped short of phrasing it. "Y'know. All the biography stuff. He told me how you met, at some psychedelic art show."

His face softened a little at that, and he took the cigarette from his mouth long enough to exhale in a sort of half-laugh. I wondered what had upset him—the thought of Leon being a suspect, or the fear that he'd revealed something Damon wanted kept hidden. I decided to probe a little bit, with all the grisly experimentalism of butting one's tongue against a sore tooth.

"The year your dad died," I said.

He blinked, and I saw how rubbish he'd be at poker. The kettle boiled, and I turned away, grateful for the opportunity to deal with the tea instead of him.

"He tell you about that? Leon?"

"No," I said, a trifle testily, perhaps still wanting to push him, perhaps cross with myself for having the impulse in the first place. "You don't have to worry. He was very loyal. About as forthcoming as a shed door when it got to relevant details. You know what? If you don't *want* me to dig, I don't know why you—"

Damon slumped against the worktop, ankles crossed in his best attitude of elegance *dishabille*.

"Not this again," he grumbled, shaking the half-melted ice in his glass.

"Well, there was no bloody point picking me in the first place," I snapped, tired of these circuitous games, "if I never get told anything. I don't know why you bothered."

"Connection," he muttered from the depths of his glass. "I *tole* you, baby. I tried so many times... came up short. You gotta find a connection, a way to—"

"Oh, *connection*. What does that even mean?"

I shot a look at him over the teapot. Head thrown back, his hair spilled behind him, the white angles of his neck cast in sharp relief. He leant back on his elbows as he stared at the kitchen ceiling, drink and ciggie both dangling artlessly from one hand. Thick, honey-gold sideburns ended at perfect parallels to the points of his jaw. I realised I was staring when he raised his head and looked at me, like he'd reached some kind of decision.

Damon took a last drag on his cigarette and dumped it in the glass. He put it down on the worktop and left it there, looking faintly like modern art.

"S'about a lot of shit, babe. You know that, and you know I can't... I can't let you blow your mind on this, Ellis."

I snorted derisively.

"But," he said, and the word cut through me, "I'll tell you one thing."

I said nothing, sitting myself down at the kitchen table. Green-painted gate-leg thing, secondhand; if I'd wanted, I could have tried to call it shabby chic. I arched my eyebrow at him, trying to look insouciant. "You understand," Day said simply, and slid into the chair opposite me.

It was one of those red-rag-to-a-bull statements.

"*What*?"

He shrugged wordlessly, pulling the lighter and the pack of Camels from his pocket. From my chair, I reached a chipped saucer from the worktop and plunked it down in front of him. I really never thought I'd need to own ashtrays, and I still couldn't find the one Auntie Jan had bought me.

"No," I said sharply. "Come on. What the fuck am I supposed to understand? Hm?"

Damon drew a cigarette from the pack, suddenly and evasively interested in lighting it, but I wasn't about to let this one go.

"Seriously," I snapped, "exactly what is it that you mean by that? I mean, this has got to be good... what do I *understand*?"

Dark eyes flicked to me over the intricate cupping of hands around cigarette and lighter. He stopped and slowly took the unlit cylinder from his lips, dropping the lighter to the table. For the first time, I saw the inscription; just a row of letters and numbers in a calligraphic font.

$$D \sim 3.6.74 \sim I$$

I wondered if *she'd* bought it for him. And I wondered if she'd ever told him about the baby.

Damon cleared his throat, tapping the cigarette against the carton. He opened his mouth, fumbling around the words—the first time I'd seen him really struggle—the tip of his tongue pressed against his teeth.

"This... this stuff," he said eventually. "You're... you can see, y'know what I'm sayin', babe? You're open. All your books, your college jive an' that, yeah? All that changes how you think, the way you... the way you see things."

I poured tea into the two mugs, dumped in short rations of milk and his customary two sugars, adding one for me as an afterthought I probably needed, and put the cosy on the pot.

"Oh?" I said curtly, pushing the mug across the pitted surface of my cheap table and watching him grasp the handle.

Damon lifted the mug halfway to his mouth before stopping to add another thought, snatched from the air before he lost it.

"Like your... wossname. Thesis," he said, and looked faintly proud of using the word. "S'all about how people see things, isn't it?"

"Wait... you've been reading my work?"

He gave me one of those eloquent little mini-shrugs, from which I supposed he must be perking up.

"I might've had a look. It's very... well, it's good, innit? I didn't understand most of it, but you can tell it's... y'know. I said, didn't I? You got brains. I can see why they're all proud of you. I mean, they might not get it, but they're proud."

"Wh—" I began, before I realised. He'd been poking through my work and he'd been looking at the photos I kept on the mantel. Pictures of Becky, my sister, with her husband, Mark, and the two kids... pictures that sort of made up for the fact we didn't have anything in common and didn't really get on, except for the forced civility of Christmas and the occasional visit during the summer holidays. Pictures of Jan and Duncan, of my grandparents, of friends from uni. Even a couple of pictures of Mum that I'd been nearly ready to look at again.

It had been me, not Becky, who had taken her effects out of her flat.

I shook my head. "You don't know what you're talking about."

"I do." Damon put the unlit cigarette back between his lips and rubbed his thumb across the polished surface of his lighter. "I know what it's like to have to get out. To know you gotta do anything 'cept what they did. Knowin', no matter how much you love 'em, you can't be like that."

I looked up sharply but found no trace of condescension, no hint of anything in his face but a strange sadness, blurry and a little ethereal. It passed as he struck a flame from the lighter. His cheeks hollowed, and he dragged those deep Theda Bara eyes up to mine again.

"D'you know Bermondsey at all?"

I shook my head.

"We lived just off the Old Kent Road. You know where that is... little cheap brown one on the Monopoly board, yeah? Y'know... you buy that, an' Whitechapel, and you stick hotels on 'em, and it still don't make you rich. Pages Walk," he added, by way of explanation, just as I'd started contemplating the Damon Brent Monopoly Board Theory of Social Inequality. "Guinness Buildings. They were housing for the London poor... like the Peabody Trust, yeah? These big, like, Victorian.... You had four flats to a floor, right? Baths and that in a block outside, shared lavvy and sinks on each landing. Just one bedroom, one main room, and a cooker. We got electric in '63." He exhaled a coil of fag smoke, waved it away from his face. "My dad was a roadworker for Southwark Council. Mum used to do cleanin' jobs, here and there. They were both young... y'know. She was eighteen when she had me. Prob'ly never expected anythin' different out of life. Lot of people didn't, y'know what I mean?"

I nodded slowly, taking a mouthful of my tea. The same cultural syndrome my own mother had been victim to, though it had been old-fashioned by then. She'd got so sick of being told she could—and *should*—have it all that she'd ended up rejecting the whole bundle. No husband, no career… no pigeon holing. She'd had a sort of thing about that.

Neither Becky nor I had really known our fathers, and Mum had always been adamant that whatever we wanted to do, we should do because *we* chose it, not because we'd been told it was a good choice to make. Secretly I'd always suspected that we had both disappointed her; Becky, by 'settling', as Mum saw it, for an early marriage and a home life punctuated only by occasional part-time clerical work. Me, by… well, by any number of things. Choosing academia, being too nice to my grandmother, never making the family choke on their tongues like Mum had. She'd always loved rebellion.

Outside, the customised gas-guzzlers tore up the prom again. Rain hit against the glass, falling like a curtain of echoes through the night. I glanced up at the black window, picking out the washes of streetlights beyond.

"M'Dad used to drink at a pub up the Road," Damon said, exhaling a thin, tight line of smoke. "He wasn't…. I mean, he didn't *drink* drink, y'know? An' he wasn't a mean drunk. He was a good bloke. Peacemaker. S'what he was doin', night he…. There was, like, this fight, yeah? Y'know, it weren't uncommon. He gets involved, tryin' to break it up, takes a knock on the head, comes staggerin' home. Mum blows her lid 'cos she thinks he's pissed. I slipped out for a bit, let 'em get it all over with."

He flicked ash into the chipped saucer and made a little shrug of guilty self-justification.

"I was sixteen. I'd left school, got that bleedin' job at Burton's. I didn't want their hassle, y'know? All I wanted was to leave home, move up north, somewhere it was all happening. Me 'n' Leon were gonna get a place together. Change the world."

He ran his thumb along the rim of his mug as he took a long drag on the cigarette. When he spoke again, the merest wisp of smoke trailed from his lips.

"It was all quiet when I come back. Went to bed, next thing I know, Mum's screamin' blue murder. He was dead. See, we didn't know," he said, pausing to take another pull, "we didn't know you could die slow like that, if you got hit… thought it was quick. Same as with me. That first blow woulda put me down in the end, regardless. S'easy to do. And you might not even know, yeah? Ironic, really," he added, glancing up at me. "Y'know. Fatal head injuries runnin' in the family like that."

A desperate attempt at flippancy, it made my chest hurt. He looked at me like he expected—needed—something, and I wasn't sure I could give it.

"Bit more extreme than male pattern baldness," I ventured.

Damon smiled. "Yeah," he said, sniffing as he knocked the ash off his cigarette. "You kinda wonder though, y'know? I mean, it's fuzzy, but when *I*… well, I remember lyin' there. I remember it bloody well hurt, y'know? I dunno if he felt it, or if he was sleepin'. Just slipping away, all quiet. He was cold, though. Mum'd been in bed with a corpse half the night. S'what did for her, y'know. I mean, you can imagine…."

I tried not to. In the other room, Fielding's album was still playing. The rain thudded ever more heavily against the window.

"She went a bit... sensitive, after that. Y'know?"

Day drained the rest of his tea and waved the mug at me. I refilled us both and got up to get the milk. I'd had no idea. As I looked at the contents of my fridge, another, sneaking thought struck me. No. Surely not.

I went back to my seat, putting the milk down between us. From the other room, a light thump sounded. My heart leapt in my throat for a second, and then I saw Mr. Tibbs—wet, bedraggled and apparently in a truly filthy mood—pad, stiff-legged, into the kitchen. He peered at us with yellow-eyed malevolence and stalked over to his bowl—a brown china affair that had the word DOG printed on the side of it, with a picture of a Jack Russell Terrier. Mr. Tibbs began to crunch his evening fish-biscuits, and Damon took another drag on his cigarette.

"She never got over it, see?" he said. "I couldn't leave her. Not then. Um. Leon... did he...?"

I shook my head. "Not a word. He mentioned that your dad died, but nothing else. No details."

A faint look, something like pride, crossed his face. "Right. Well, he said I should get her help, make her see a doctor, y'know? Took a year, but I got her to go... bastard didn't do nothin' but put her on Luminal, and that did fuck all. Barbiturates," he explained, crushing the cigarette out on the saucer as if it suddenly disgusted him. "I complained. Squeaky wheel, y'know... so he switched her to Valium. Huh. Mother's Little Helper. That was a bust an' all. She was still—"

He took a gulp of tea and pulled another cigarette from his pack. Unlit, it wagged between his lips as he spoke, and I heard the bitterness, the long-buried anger in his voice. My heart sank with the realisation that he'd been right: I did understand. To need the medical profession is one thing; to have to stand by and watch them, as far as you're concerned, fuck up, is quite another.

Oh, I understood that.

"It got bad, y'know." Damon picked at the surface of the table with one thumbnail. "I'd say goodbye to her in the morning and, by lunchtime, she'd be out in the street, pitchin' hysterics 'cos she couldn't find me. Mr. Wood, the porter, he was very kind. Him and his missus kept an eye on her. Doctor said the only thing left to do was, hah, consider a residential alternative. But I wasn't puttin' her in the bleedin' nuthouse." He struck a flame from his lighter and drew savagely on the cigarette to light it. "I prob'ly should of done."

I looked at him over the rim of my mug, recognising that dark note of remorse. I knew it well, because it was so easy to have, with hindsight. But you never consider those things, not at the time, because that's like admitting the change is permanent. That she's not coming back.

Mum had changed fast, to start with. The depression, the occasional moments of confusion that, once, she would have laughed off but that, for some reason we couldn't see, made her so angry. She had a prang in the car... when she'd complained of pain in her neck, I'd told her it was probably down to that. Whiplash, or something. Not long after, the first tremors had started.

"Leon was up Kentish Town way by then." Damon exhaled slowly. "I used to go up there when we were playing, crash out at his, come back an' find her climbing the bleedin' walls. He said to me, 'It can't go on, man. You gotta do something. You gotta get out.'"

I watched him knock ash off his cigarette, then take another deep, shaky drag on it, and my throat got heavy.

"Y'know, I thought it'd get better," he said, not looking at me. "They were gonna pull Pages Walk down. Y'know, to remodel? It needed it... but she didn't wanna go. I said we didn't have to go far if she didn't want. There were Guinness buildings in Snowsfields, and Kennington Park Road... we coulda put ourselves down on the lists, gone there, had our own bath an' everything. But she flipped. Like she thought she was leaving Dad or somethin'. We argued about it. I got pretty steamed up, I know. It was 1969, yeah? They'd put a bleedin' man on the moon, and I couldn't even get off the Old Kent Road. Last thing I said to her, that was. Before...."

Oh, no. I knew what he was going to say. Please no. My eyes started to fill, and I felt so stupid, because they weren't tears of sympathy, or even anything to do with his pain. I knew exactly what he would say, but I looked at the world through a tunnel, like everything was linear, inescapable.

Somewhere, out over the sea, thunder rolled. The rain lashed against my kitchen window, and lightning painted the underside of the sky metallic yellow. If my mind had been anywhere but Mum's bathroom in that moment, I would have laughed at the melodrama of it.

"It wasn't even like takin' a sodding bath was that easy," Damon said softly. "Mr. Wood only opened the block two days a week. You waited 'til the boiler'd been stoked, and you'd give him tuppence, and he'd put this little brass, like, tap, on the spindle, so you got just your ration of hot water—no more— and he'd run your bath. And you'd go in the cubicle, and he'd leave you to it. And she'd've stood there while she waited, talking to him, holding her towel and her lily of the valley soap —y'know, 'cos her name was Lily—and she'd've *known* she was gonna—"

He stopped abruptly and took a hard pull on the cigarette. His jaw moved as if he was chewing the smoke. Eventually, a thin plume of it slipped from his lips.

"She'd've thought it'd be Mr. Wood, y'see. Not me. 'Cos... 'cos she always used to try and be last in, so she could be quiet. Linger a bit. And, usually, he'd still be there, keeping an eye. Y'know. Only, Mrs. Wood—she used to get these chest infections, right? Real bad ones, and she was took poorly that week, so he slips off to go and check on her. No worries about Lily. Lily's fine... she'll clean up." Damon gave a low, bitter laugh. "Good old Lily. Even if she lives on her nerves a bit since her old man died, Lily's all right. Yeah...." His mouth twisted, and he took another pull on the cigarette. "I-I'd been up London Bridge after work, talking to a bloke about a gig. We... me an' Leon, we were actually startin' to make a little bit of cash. And I'd got a booking. I thought she'd be pleased. Come back, but she weren't in the flat. She... she didn't go out much, by then. Not on her own. So I knew something was wrong. Went down to Mr. Wood's flat, asked if he'd seen her, and he said the last time was at the baths. I-I think I knew what she'd done, then. Somewhere, inside... I knew."

I drained the remnants of my tea, fighting down the nausea. Oh, you knew. I'd known what Mum had done. I'd suspected when she didn't answer her phone that day. Convinced, by the time I let myself into her flat, that I knew.

Yet finding her like that, in the bath, had still been a

surprise. A shock... and it never should have been. Maybe there's only so much preparation you can do.

"So we went down to the bath block. Mr. Wood's getting all breathless and worried... I couldn't get the door open. Took a jemmy to it in the end, knocked the hinges through." Damon sucked the air over his teeth, pulling another cigarette from his pack with frantic fingers. He'd barely finished crushing the previous one out, the end still dying red on the chipped saucer, the dirty, bent tube like some half-squashed grub. "Water was cold. But she looked... peaceful. Like that painting, y'know? Only... chick in that never had th-these great big things on her wrists. Horrible, all.... She done it with nail scissors. I-I never knew it'd bruise. But they were. Bruised, yeah? They were all...."

He gestured vaguely in the air, fingers flexing before dropping to fumble for his lighter. He took a deep breath as the tip of the ciggie flared red. And it was a very bright red, all that blood. Warm water, I supposed, kept everything fresh.

She'd cleaned up so well beforehand, that was what got me. Mum had been so untidy in everything, so messy in her disorganised passion for life, that it had surprised me. The empty pill bottle, on the side of the sink (freshly cleaned; I remembered the smell of lemon), the folded towels she'd known she wouldn't use. The only thing that looked careless was the packet of blades, dropped on the bathmat. Even the cuts were neat. Comparatively. Clean. Washed that way in the water, I supposed. A red tide mark on the tub. I'd scrubbed and scrubbed and it just never seemed to come off. We'd ended up having the whole suite replaced before we sold the flat, Becky and I.

But… she'd looked so small. I remembered that. Thin. Shrunken and deflated. Everything that was her, gone. Just what she'd been afraid of the illness doing to her. I had found it—still found it—so hard to see at what point her fear had become her solution.

I looked across at Damon, pale and kohl-smudged, smoking like a satanic mill, staring back over the years.

"Were they deep cuts?" I asked, finding my voice at last.

It was the best thing I could do, to not insult him with useless platitudes and empty words. He looked up, and I knew he was seeing me for the first time in the past few minutes. He seemed to look so much younger than he had before.

"Not really," he said.

"Then it's possible for bruising to start to form. I read that somewhere."

"Oh." He nodded slowly. "She was bleeding for a long time, wasn't she?"

"Probably," I said.

Damon exhaled a long curl of smoke and stared at his cigarette for a while, his fingertips tapping lightly on the table. I cleared my throat.

"D'you, um, want me to make some more tea?"

"Mm."

I stood, making my way to the comfortable security of kettle, sink, and such. Mr. Tibbs had long since finished his dinner and sat on the worktop next to the microwave, washing the rainwater from his fur with an expression of intense disgust.

So. There it all was.

And, yes, I understood. I supposed it was what he'd been trying to tell me… connection. Shared experiences, shared—

what?—guilt, maybe. It's our experiences, after all, that shape the way we see the world. And, as he'd grown so fond of telling me, in that infuriatingly vague way of his, I could *see*. What had he said to me, that first night?

You believe what you like, Ellis, but believe every little thing you do's important, baby. 'Cos it's all you're left with, in the end.

God, that suddenly seemed so much less heartening.

Outside, the thunder rolled again. Mr. Tibbs gave an affronted yowl and leapt down from the worktop, sending a flurry of clutter flying.

I swore, turning around to pick up whatever I'd been fool enough to leave lying around in here—probably that paperwork I needed for my meeting with my supervisor the day after tomorrow—and saw Mum's scrapbook lying in the middle of the kitchen floor. I didn't remember leaving it out here.

I couldn't help but think of her showing it to me that last time, after I bought her that boxed set of CDs, and the whole story had come pouring out over lunch in the Cricketer's Rest.

She'd always laughed so much, so often smiled or had one of a thousand expressions, that seeing those drift away into the tautened, waxy masks that Parkinson's forced onto her had been like watching her die in slow motion. I remembered thinking that, a sudden cold shiver of fear that she'd end, shrunken and decrepit, in some bland institution that smelled of piss and disinfectant. I should have known, should have guessed, what she planned, should—

"'Cos there's nothing you can do," Damon said, apropos of little. "Is there?"

I looked over at him, wondering if he'd read my mind.

"No."

"Thing is," he said slowly, "you always think you should of done somethin', yeah? And... an' you go over and over it, and you end up realising—"

"That you wouldn't have stopped her, even if you could have," I said, finishing both his sentence and mine.

We looked at each other in silence for a moment. Eventually, he nodded.

"Yeah. S'it. Is that... is that really bad?"

I took a deep breath. I wasn't qualified to answer that. I remembered wishing I could be stronger, that I could have helped... somehow. Not pushed the pills down her throat, but—

"No," I said. "No, it's not."

This was both our failing and our redemption, I supposed. Either connection or penance. But he understood it, and so did I. I bent down to pick up the scrapbook. The one thing of hers I hadn't managed to keep in the flat.

Just too much of her in it.

"I, um.... Look," Damon said. His voice had started to get husky with the cigarettes. He cleared his throat. "Ellis, if I could've said—if I *could* say—baby, you know I'd...."

He trailed off, looking wretched. I shook my head, the scrapbook cradled to my chest. The faintest hint of white musk emanated from its dry pages.

Offering, shrine... paper cathedral.

"It kills that I can't, babe. It does."

White musk, and something else. Something heavy, sweet and woody. I frowned. Damon crushed out the sad remnant of his cigarette and cleared his throat again, looking up at me like he'd made a choice. I shook my head. I'd never wanted any of this… I didn't even feel like I wanted answers anymore.

"'Miss you, Tiger Cub.'"

Damon looked embarrassed. My breath caught in my throat and, without wanting to—wanting to do anything rather than cry—I felt my cheeks getting wet. After everything, and he gave me that?

It had just been something she'd said. Just once. Her idea of being cute. I blamed Mud, and that stupid song of theirs. *Tiger Feet*. Of course, it had stuck, but I hadn't heard it for years. And it was no kind of answer at all. I closed my eyes in the face of sobs that I couldn't stop.

In less than a minute I heard his chair move, and a chill passed around my shoulders, like the cold breeze on a lake. I realised he was rubbing my back. I cracked open one eye and saw a clean, white, linen rectangle being dangled in front of me.

"Hanky," he said, his voice just by my ear, the texture of it running across my skin like iced water.

I looked at the hanky and sniffed.

"Thank you."

I took it, and it felt real. Warm. I wished he did. I pondered this as I blew my nose, mopped my eyes, and with the pang of chagrin that inevitably follows the use of linen hankies, stuffed the thing in my pocket and promised to wash it.

Chapter Nine

Jeremy called round the next morning. I opened the door, red of eye, sallow of skin, and claggy of hair, and he looked at me as if he couldn't decide whether I was coming down with flu or had just had the night of my life.

"Your friend Jack about, then, Ell?"

"Sod off," I muttered, clutching my ratty terry-towelling dressing gown around me. I'd had to prise it out from under Mr. Tibbs while I buzzed my unexpected visitor in, and I really wasn't in the mood. "C'min. Ignore mess."

Jerry chuckled and edged around the pile of books by the door. I scanned the room for signs of abnormal habitation, offering up silent thanks that Day's fag ash had been confined to the kitchen last night. A light breeze fluttered the curtains at the open bay window, and Mr. Tibbs leapt up onto the window seat, yowling softly. A chill touched the room, and I narrowed my eyes.

Don't bugger about.

"Well, I've got to make it quick." Jerry pulled a wad of papers folded into quarters from his pocket and smoothed out the creases. "But here you are. I did what I could with what you gave me. She was a bitch to find… but then I suppose anyone would be, in her situation. Did you know people used to go to the house, try and nick souvenirs? Tile from the bathroom her husband died in turned up on eBay last year, apparently."

It took me a minute to catch up with him but, when I did, I thought too hard about it.

"Yuck."

"Yeah…. Anyway, there it is. Um."

He loitered, shifted his weight on the balls of his feet, obviously desperate to pump me for information but not quite sure how to start. Just a few weeks ago, I realised, I would have taken pity on poor Jerry and spilled the whole story… or at least some form of it that I could have shared without him thinking me completely insane. Now all I wanted to do was get him out of the door.

I peered at the papers he'd handed me, sucked my apparently furry teeth, and nodded. "Oh. She stayed in Gloucestershire… we thought she— Uh. Yeah. Thanks a lot, Jerry. I owe you on this one."

He made no move to go.

"Are you…. I mean, you're okay, are you?"

"Yes. Yes, I'm fine. Very fine. Thanks. Hunky dory, all that. Yeah."

I virtually pushed him out into the hall. His mouth set into a hard line, biting back whatever reprimand he wanted to give me.

"I'll leave you to it, then," he said icily. "Got to go and talk to God on the big white telephone, have you?"

I managed a sick sort of smile, appropriate under what Jeremy assumed the circumstances to be, and closed the door. I heard him huff his way down the corridor, fading out to the sound of hurried, grumpy footsteps on the stairs. I'd hear all about this later, I just knew it, though it somehow failed to worry me. I looked down at the papers in my hand. Eileen Shawcross, she went by now. Middle name, apparently. I wondered if there had ever been a Mr. Shawcross. I assumed so; for all I knew, maybe more than one ex-husband stood between Inez and her past.

I called her that morning. Somehow, it seemed right to take a shower, put on some clothes, and fix my hair and make-up before I did… not that it was video-phone or anything. I'd seen neither hide nor hair of Day. To be perfectly honest, I preferred it that way; I had no desire to try wheedling an interview out of Inez with him standing over my shoulder gesticulating. Anyway, I wasn't sure what I'd say to him, after last night.

I sat with the phone cradled to my ear, my knees drawn up against my chest, and the leather of the window seat pleasantly warm beneath me. The sun sparkled on the glass; a bright, seaside summer to come, maybe.

"Hello?"

I almost bit my tongue. "Oh… hello. Is that, uh, Mrs. Shawcross?"

"*Mizz.*"

"Ms. Shawcross… I'm sorry. I—"

"Who is this?"

"M-my name's Ellis Ross. I was won—"

"I'm not interested in sales calls."

The harshness of her voice made her sound older than I'd pictured her somehow. Silly, really, because she'd be at least fifty by now, surely. I didn't know what I'd been expecting—the glamour puss from the photos, the tempestuous siren Leon Fielding had described.... What sort of woman ended up being Mrs. Damon Brent, anyway?

"I'm not selling anything. I wanted to ask you for an interview," I blurted.

"What?"

That curt tone reminded me of my grandmother. Just as with her, I started to speak far too quickly, rushed to get the words out before her inevitable and irreversible judgement landed on me with a solid thump.

"Please. I'm writing a— I wanted to talk to you about your tennis career." Who knew? Maybe the lie would work. "Just a few words; maybe I could make an appointment?"

The briefest of silences—*Please don't hang up. Please.*—and I thought perhaps I'd appealed to her vanity. I was wrong.

"Oh, God... you're one of *them*, aren't you?"

She rang off and left me clutching nothing but a dial tone and a half-formed cuss.

"Bugger," I said to the world at large.

"I coulda told you she'd be like that."

I closed my eyes. I'd much rather not have had Damon witnessing my failures. He'd already seen into my darkest moments, watched my defences and my breakwaters crumble away. *Connection.*

Oh, I'd give him bloody *connection*....

A chill draught whispered to my right. I sniffed, opened my

eyes, replaced the phone in its cradle, and turned, bright and cheery and unflappable. Damon stood with Mr. Tibbs in his arms, tickling the cat under the chin. I stared. Damn animal barely ever let me pick him up—every trip to the vet for boosters ended up in a military campaign and a battle of wills—but he seemed to nestle quite comfortable against Day's shirt. Today's comparatively conservative ensemble comprised just a moss green cotton v-neck, frayed at the cuffs and hem, untucked over a pair of pale blue velvet flares; it surprised me.

"She never liked press. Not after we got spliced. 'Cos it wasn't about the tennis anymore. Nah, it wasn't," he added, making a kissy face at Mr. Tibbs and scritching him under one shaggy black cheek.

The sodding cat had started to purr.

Oh, you're gloves. You are gloves.

"I think she got jealous, y'know? I mean, it's one thing to buy into it all... but 'til you see it from the inside out, have to put up with all the shit that goes with it.... She hated that people weren't interested in her game, just her outfit. Y'know?"

I nodded and recalled what Jeremy had said about bathroom tiles cropping up on the internet. Given the note of melancholy that crept into Day's voice when he talked about Inez, it didn't seem wise to mention it.

"Mm." I gave a non-committal grunt and went to make some more coffee.

Anything but look him in the eye and say I'd screwed up. Truth be told, I hadn't even expected to see him again so soon after what I supposed I should think of as our little heart-to-heart. I would have expected him to slope off somewhere, for there to be some dark, lingering mood over the place. It would have given me a chance to get back, however briefly, to my research and my thesis, dealing for the first time in a week with the latest batch of concerned emails from my supervisors—worried by the way I'd rushed through seminars and missed audit lectures—and perhaps even writing a little bit more.

Not that I would have been able to really engage with it, my mind caught in the brambles of what I now thought of as my 'other book'. Oh, I'd write his biography. I knew that... although I hadn't told Damon yet. It wasn't as if I needed his approval, of course. It had been his idea in the first place.

I just felt that I owed him the courtesy of asking. Nothing more.

He'd followed me into the kitchen. I could tell without looking now, without needing to notice the chill or the change of the texture in the air.

"You don't need to worry, babe. She'll come around. Inez was always like that. Ask once, she says no. Ask twice, you get a maybe... third time's a charm. You just, like, keep on, yeah? She'll do it."

I retrieved the sugar from the cupboard and slammed the door, but a not-quite-grumpy smirk tugged at my upper lip.

"That's a patented seduction technique, is it?"

Day snorted. "Nah, I.... Well, maybe. Persistence is good, y'know? Big white limousine works too."

Reaching for the milk, I noticed something stuck to the fridge door. A small blue leaflet, badly photocopied and with a scratchy block font, advertised the monthly Open Mic Night at The Crown. I frowned, because I didn't remember picking it up, but there it was, tucked neatly under the magnet that reminded me *No Coffee, No Workee*.

I decided not to mention it. For now.

Instead, I sloshed milk into two mugs of tea and tried not to think about the nature of reality. It had been getting easier to do, which probably wasn't good. It no longer seemed strange—*he* no longer seemed strange—and, I had to admit, I was glad he'd come back. He sat down at my kitchen table and addressed the easy crossword on the back of the morning paper. I stood for a moment, holding the tea, and watched Damon Brent frown, chewing thoughtfully at the end of a biro.

"Tea," I said and set the mug down in front of him.

"Thanks, love."

I took my drink into the other room, slouched back in front of my computer, and wondered where we were supposed to go from here. If Inez didn't want to talk.... Well, the only thing I could do was to keep trying. Persistence, like Day said. Maybe try another angle. Write to her, call back on a different tack. Try not to get myself arrested for harassment.

I sipped the tea. Our list of suspects—though both of us seemed a little squeamish about that word—hadn't really changed. Sure, a lot of people had been ruled out by reason of being dead or overseas. The list Damon had drawn up of everyone who'd had a finger in the pie of his daily life seemed virtually incomprehensible to me: roadies and small-time dealers known only by their nicknames, a number of lawyers and label people who'd dealt with the finances, plus the ephemera of hangers-on, facilitators, and disposable faces who flitted in and out of the band's ken. 'Not mainly people you'd call friends,' he'd said dismissively. 'Not for long. Y'know?'

I didn't, not really, but I'd nodded and agreed. A lot of them had been at the party that night, and some of them might even have had motive. I privately suspected that sheer irritation value could have played a part in Day's death, from the way he spoke about people—if it wasn't 'that chick who looked after the fan club stuff. Y'know. Brunette. Kinda stacked. Dunno her name...', then it was 'that weedy little twerp we had in for A&R after Vince left the label'.

Still, it kept coming back to the same faces, that same inner circle. The wife, and the band. Leon, I had my doubts about. Damon wouldn't hear a thing against him. I knew that, so I held my concerns close to my chest, but I hadn't quite found it in myself to trust him at Dulwich.

I was wondering just why that had been when the phone rang. It jerked me out of my reverie, and I snatched up the receiver, brain not quite switched on.

"Hello?"

"Miss Ross?"

The voice sounded young, female, well spoken. Totally unfamiliar. I reasoned it must be a sales call, except that she waited for me to respond rather than pitching straight into the manifold wonders of double glazing. I did a quick mental check of any bills that I might have forgotten to pay.

"Yes," I said cautiously. "Who's this?"

"Christy Brooks. I'm Mr. Napier's assistant. Lovely to speak to you at last. Now, Mr. Napier sends his apologies; he said he would have been delighted to call himself, but we have a British White in breech with twins, so he's waiting for the vet."

I took a moment to process this, but it failed to hit any buttons.

"Ah-hah? Oh dear."

"Anyway, he wanted me to make an appointment with you

for the interview. He's been very enthusiastic about it. Would you be able to make, say, Friday? I realise that's rather short notice, but Mr. Napier will be off to Stockholm for a fortnight at the weekend, and he's very keen to talk to you before he goes, if possible."

I ruffled frantically through the paperwork on the desk in search of pen and notepad. Things cascaded to the floor. I bit back on a curse, aware of Damon's appearance in the room. He mugged at me, looked confused when I pointed at the chaos and flapped my hand urgently, while smiling into the phone and saying:

"Oh, absolutely... I'd be delighted. I must say, I wasn't expecting to hear back so soon."

Ms. Brooks chuckled and remained irritatingly sunny as she fixed up my appointment and give me directions to Old Wallow Farm. I scribbled down things of import, like the nearest train station and the time I needed to be there, on the back of an overdue gas bill.

"Good, er, good luck with the twins," I said vaguely, before hanging up.

The receiver clunked back into its cradle. I heaved a sigh and shook my head.

"Weird."

"What?"

Damon wafted behind my chair; in a moment of strange, unconnected flickers of light, the papers I'd knocked to the floor reappeared beside my keyboard.

"He seems... keen. Joss Napier. I don't know. Maybe it's me."

Day lolled against the edge of the desk and regarded me

with his head to one side. He curled his lip dismissively. "Yeah? Well, he always thought he was Mr. Articulate... prob'ly got some project he wants you to write in."

Catty. I raised an eyebrow. "You two didn't get on, then?"

"Nah, I'm not sayin' that." Damon fidgeted, hand straying to the pocket that held lighter and fags. "He's all right. It just, like, it wouldn't surprise me. Y'know? If there was one person who knew his way around the media, it was Joss."

I pursed my lips and said nothing. Just what I needed. A media-savvy former drummer with one arm up a cow.

* * *

May 24th 1976

Joss really wasn't keen on TV appearances. Everyone always told him they got easier with time, but they didn't. He hated the whole experience, from the way just having the cameras there screwed with the flow of the gig to the horrible invasion of having one stuck right in your face. He never knew what to do and ended up grimacing at the unseen viewers like an awkward cousin at a wedding. He brought his cigarette to his lips, took a pull, and leaned back against the dressing room door, watching the endless flow of people nipping to and from the studio.

He'd been in, taken a look at the set-up, seen Cris shading his eyes under one of the big, face-meltingly-hot spots and having some kind of argument with a skinny kid clutching a clipboard. He'd seen the host knocking around somewhere too. Short German bloke with a terrible hairpiece that looked like something he'd scraped off the autobahn and slapped on his head.

They'd be shooting partially in the round, down on floor level. Joss' drum kit had been wedged in between the amp stack and two blocks of scenery, just plain white cubes, redolent of the clean, bright concrete that most of West Germany appeared to be built from. Leon had been whinging about it all the way from the airport. Why this, why that, how come it all looked the same? Joss had tried to explain about how they'd rebuilt after the war, how concrete was cheap and quick and gave off this air of optimistic modernism. However false, however shallow it was, it made people believe there could be something better. Something brighter. Just like the music did.

Bullshit, of course. He knew that.

Camera people, lighting people, sound people. They were the same in any language. So were the roadies. Joss noticed one guy he knew only as Rusty Jimmy—Damon's main man for the few days they were over here—wander up from the corridor, twirling a spare cable in his hand.

They'd have to be out there before long. Joss took another drag on his cigarette. He wanted a drink. He—no, he *needed* a drink. If he'd be expected to do this thing, to keep smiling and looking like he enjoyed it when they stuck a lens right in his face... he needed a drink. It would have been better if there could have been some kind of respite. Some buffer between the studio work and all its grinding, incessantly depressing baggage —that whole oppressive *thing* Charlie and Day had going—and the nadir of all things horrible that loomed before them on the horizon. Another European tour. That's what this stupid TV appearance was supposed to promo. Joss winced.

Not that he hated touring, not per se. Sure, he hated the buses with the windows that wouldn't open and the heaters that wouldn't work, and the inevitable arguments, and the ancient, endless hours of boredom. And he was sick and tired of pale, anonymous towns he couldn't remember from the last time he'd visited and always believed he would never see again, full of pale, anonymous teenagers clinging to the ragged coattails of fashion. Sick and tired of being *obligated*. Sick and tired of being nice and being enthusiastic and, most of all, putting up with all of the shit and—right now—really, truly, sick of West Germany and all its forced, brittle, claustrophobic, clean-scrubbed false optimism.

Joss stubbed the cigarette out on the rim of the litterbin beside him and dropped it in. He flicked his hair off his shoulder and turned to push through the door, damn near colliding with Charlie, midway into a good long cuss.

"...completely and fucking utterly, man! What'd you do? Huh? I'm not doing— I mean, I've had a sodding *basin* of it so far this year, y'know? Bloody state of—"

"He can't help it, all right? It's just—"

Damon looked uncertain, which Joss wasn't used to seeing. He raised an eyebrow.

"What's going on? Did somebody find my traps case?"

Charlie waved dismissively at the door. "Roadie got it. Whatshisname. Jimmy. Left it on the bus. S'all right. Point is, man, he can't go on like that," he said and nodded to the beige vinyl couch at the other end of the room. "You can't cover for him in front of the camera, y'know?"

Joss turned to the couch. Leon was sitting on it, knees pressed tightly together and his upper body hunched. He held his left hand curled up by his mouth, gnawing at the edge of one nail, while the fingers of his right hand worried at the cuff of his embroidered purple tunic, twisting the cotton into a thick coil. He was sweating heavily, and his hair stuck out at even wilder angles than usual. He glanced up at Charlie, eyes wide and slightly unfocused.

"I'm not going on! I can't.... Like, nobody should, y'know man? It's not... no. No."

He shook his head, stuck the finger back in his mouth, and chewed with renewed vigour. Charlie swore under his breath. Damon sighed and looked to Joss for assistance. Joss fumbled for something to say, some excuse to get himself out of it, and failed. A smear of blood marked the bed of Leon's nail. Damon noticed and batted the hand away.

"Hey. Don't. Hands are worth money, man."

Leon blinked owlishly. "I can't," he murmured, shaking his head from side to side in a kind of rhythmic judder. "I can't go out there. I-if I go up there, man, it's all gonna.... Nah, 'cos you don't understand, right? S'all gonna blow up. *Kcccchbbbbbooooom!*"

Leon's hands clenched around an imaginary mushroom cloud somewhere in front of his pallid face. He stared at his curled fingers and began, very slowly, to rock back and forth.

"Can't," he said. "Boom."

A studious silence fell. Joss reached out a hand, going to touch Leon companionably on the shoulder. Damon stopped him.

"I... I think this is, er, one of those things, man. Y'know?"

"He's lost it." Charlie crossed his arms. "I *said*. Didn't I say? Fuckin' acid casualty, that's what *he* is. See?"

"He is not," Damon retorted. He glanced at Leon, then at the door, and frowned. "Anyone else seen this?"

Joss shook his head. "I was standing out in the hall; I'd have seen if anyone else had come in."

"Right." Damon shot him a determined look. "Then he's fine. Joss? Pass us that bottle of vodka. I think I've got…. Yeah, here we go."

He fished in the pocket of his flares and pulled out a small square of foil, folded into four.

"Oh, you're *kidding!*" Joss said, watching Day tip three small red pills into his palm. "You can't give him anything else. Who even knows what he—"

"Just shut up, all right? Gimme the booze."

Damon snatched the vodka bottle and hunkered down in front of Leon, who was still staring off into some hidden universe, quiet apart from the occasional whimper.

"Leon? Red time, baby. Come on."

"Charlie, aren't you gonna…? Isn't anyone going to say anything?" Joss rocked back on one foot, hands on his hips. "I mean, I'm not just gonna stand here while you kill him."

Charlie muttered something under his breath, scowled, and paced over to the door. Leon opened his mouth, and Damon slipped the pills in, one by one.

"You'll feel better in no time. There. See? Who's good to you, eh?"

"Mm-nn."

Leon turned a little green around the gills as Day tipped the bottle up and helped him wash down the reds. Joss stepped back, just in case.

"Can't trust the useless little berk to do anything right,"

Charlie complained. "We're all gonna look like complete nonces."

"Yeah, like you need help making yourself look stupid," Damon muttered.

Charlie angled for a reply, but was interrupted by the door opening. Cris poked his head into the room in a cloud of grape-flavoured smoke and worried anticipation.

"All right, boys? Two minute call, and we're ready for checks. Okay?"

Joss glanced at Charlie, who seemed about to say something, but instead just shrugged and turned away. Joss could, he supposed, have spoken up, but what would have been the point? Why bother now, at the last minute? And it had felt like the last minute for a long while now; lots of last minutes, stretched out and piled on top of each other, until every breaking point just got crested like another dip in the road. Damon and Charlie kept bitching and scrapping in some kind of pretence at machismo, while Leon disintegrated slowly on the sidelines.

They hadn't been in West Germany for eighteen months, but Joss remembered sharing a hotel room with Leon on the last tour. He'd listened to his stupid midnight roach-musings, his lame jokes... he'd never been this bad then. They'd snuck out of the hotel, gone to a Bier-Keller of Doom where all the red-cheeked, moustachioed locals stopped in their steins at the sight of two long-haired, denim-washed hippies entering the dim bar. It had been fun; he'd felt like a kid bunking off school, and he'd seen Leon in a new light. His *own* light, not Damon's reflected glory.

Joss slapped a hand on his back, hating it when Leon

flinched beneath his touch.

"You all right, man?"

Leon stared up at him with wide, hollow eyes. "Yeah," he said, and his voice sounded breathy, like an echo. "I'm being daft, that's all. It's fine."

He blinked a few times and flicked on a nervous grin.

Joss frowned.

"Well," he said doubtfully, "if you're sure."

"Aw... yeah. Yeah."

"Oi!" Damon stuck his head back through the door, impatient and tight-lipped, and whistled between his teeth. "You girls comin' or not?"

Leon wobbled to his feet.

"I'm there, man. I'm... yeah."

Joss rolled his eyes and followed on behind.

It wasn't their first TV gig. Whispering Bob Harris, *The Old Grey Whistle Test* and of course *Top of the Pops* had seen to that, but most times the cameras had been incidental to the performance, not something they had to keep stopping for, readjustments and repeats and the constant tweaking of light and sound. Even the kids in the audience looked as though they couldn't get into it; just as pale and anonymous as Joss remembered them.

He settled himself behind his drum kit, painfully aware of the camera gliding around them, its operator perched on the mount like some twiggy, pasty jockey, his eye glued to the sight. The lens flared under the lights; its glare made Joss wince. To his right, Charlie started to complain about being blocked by the stack.

"Yeah," Damon put in. "That's how you know God hates

bassists, yeah? You have to stand next to the drummer."

Joss pulled a face. Cheap shot and not even funny. The kind of jokes Damon made when he wasn't thinking, when something had him rattled. Leon still didn't look right. He kept glancing all around the place, at the petulant, bored teens and the gawky TV people, and his mouth moved on and off, as if he kept articulating something under his breath. Mantra? Prayer? Joss, not so lapsed from his childhood Catholicism as he might have been, wondered, but then he saw the glassy cast to Leon's eyes and made out the word-shape 'kaboom'.

The floor manager gave the count, the host did his bit of spiel, and Joss took a deep breath. He didn't have to think about this part. He knew the song like the back of his hand, and his bandmates were easier to read than *The Beano*. Two-four on the hi hat, double stroke roll and into the eight beat rhythm on the snare with a ghost strike on the third count... and in went a wailing lick from Day's Strat. Joss glanced at him over the cymbals, pouting for the camera, showing off. The kids loved it, of course. Loved him.

Them. Joss tried to prod himself with that thought because, even now, it didn't quite seem real. It had once—before the make-up got thicker and the fights grew more regular and they seemed to spend eight weeks out of twelve carping at each other like old women—but not now. And he would have thought other people would've noticed.

He went for a big cymbal roll, the tongue of the music slinking up beneath them, lifting everything from the floor up in one great shapeless swirl that smoothed the creases out of everything—

What the fuck?

—and, with a huge electrical *glurp* and a fairly impressive shower of sparks, the entire house grid went out.

Lights, sound, everything; all dismissed in a shattered dimness and the ear-itching, sucking pop of shorting fuses. Assorted screams erupted from the audience, Teutonic curses from the TV people and, in the middle of it, Joss saw Leon's dim silhouette. He backed away from the microphone, shaking his head.

"I told you!" he yelled, virtually unheard in the chaos. "I *said*! You didn't listen.... Nobody ever *listens*, man! I said it would! I *said*!" He wrapped his arms around his Les Paul and clutched it to his chest like a security blanket. "I said, and now look! Oh, God....'"

Charlie had abandoned his bass and got into an arm-waving, language-barrier-laden argument with the gaffer, while the German host flounced offset to his canvas chair. Joss glanced across the floor at Day.

"I tried to tell ya! I *said* it would! This is what happens, man... this is how it goes, all right? I *told* you.... I'm not doing this anymore! I won't! I'm gettin' shpilkes over here, man! I mean it! I can't—"

Damon nodded and set his guitar down. Joss stood and, wordlessly, they grabbed Leon under the elbows. He was still yelling when they marched him back into the dressing room.

Chapter Ten

Slightly less than one week later, I stood in a leafy country track, the tangs of overlaying manures on the air. A neatly painted sign poked out of the hedge before me:

OLD WALLOW FARM : ORGANIC FRUIT & VEG : RARE BREEDS
PLEASE DON'T FEED THE GEESE

A lifelong townie, I'd been half-expecting a mud hole with a couple of wooden barns and a tractor parked next to a cattle grid, or at least something vaguely redolent of a Stella Gibbons novel. Instead, as I walked into the tarmac and concrete arrivals yard, I saw a long, low, grey stone building to one side, flanked by a small timbered structure too big to really be called a shed and, to the other side of the yard, the corner of a larger building in the same clean-lined, grey masonry. I guessed it must be the farmhouse, though from what I could see it looked tall and square, more like a Georgian parsonage than one of those higgledy-piggledy homesteads that grows out of the land. I reached up to tuck my hair behind my ear, and my fingers brushed against Mum's sapphire stud. It seemed very quiet. I couldn't hear any of the sounds I associated with farms. Nothing was going 'moo' or 'oink' or even making any of those drawn-out, strangulated 'rrrrrggggrrrrgggghhh' noises that always so surprise young children brought up on Old MacDonald and fuzzy picture books.

Starlings perched on the roof of the house; unlike the ones that frequented my building, they weren't impersonating crying babies or mobile phones or anything except, perhaps, other starlings.

I looked around for some kind of sign or indication of where I should go. A young woman with a smart ponytail and a gilet apparently made from recycled mattress quilting appeared at the door of the long, low building, and waved to me.

"Miss Ross? Hello! Taxi found us all right, then? Lovely. Do come in."

I did so and found a cosy, comfortable office that held a large L-shaped desk covered with paperwork and supporting an elderly PC and printer. Underneath it, an equally elderly tricolour collie overflowed from a well-chewed wicker basket. The dog looked up, turning extremely intelligent liquid brown eyes on me, and then it thumped its tail half-heartedly on the faded blue carpet. Corkboards covered two of the walls, peppered with coloured pins and patches of paper. A scattering of ribbons and rosettes—red, blue, white, and green—with gold lettering on them, and photographs, had all been pinned up at eye level. Dogs, but also horses, sheep, and cows. I had no idea how you told the breeds apart, but I assumed that they were all excellent examples of what they were supposed to be.

I had spoken to Christy Brooks, the owner of the smart ponytail and squashed-mattress gilet, on the phone. In person, she seemed just as cheerful and clean-scrubbed as I'd imagined her.

She offered me a seat in a comfortable office chair and brought me a cup of tea from the little staff kitchenette. Then she picked up a radio and paged my arrival through to Joss Napier, explaining that they couldn't use mobile phones because the farm nestled neatly in a black spot with utterly dreadful reception. A voice crackled through over the radio, telling her to take me into the morning room. I hadn't been intimidated up until that point.

"Righto, will do. Come along," she said to me, all bright and chipper, and I headed meekly after her, out of the farm office by a back door.

The collie got up arthritically and followed us out onto a patch of beautifully manicured green lawn, where the dog squatted to relieve—ah—*her*self. The lawn, frilled with lavender beds and speckled with the browning leaves of daffodils and glossy blooms of tulips, hugged a brick paved path that led down to a set of french doors. Ms. Brooks took a key from her pocket, opened the doors, and led me into a small room with a tiled floor. Modern panelled doors led off to the left and right, while a rack of boots and wellies lay straight ahead of me, a knobbly, extremely muddy rug and a coir mat on the floor, and a washer-dryer rumbled to itself in the corner. The collie waddled over to a metal dish full of water and took a few gulps as Ms. Brooks opened the door on the left.

"This way."

After the muddy utility of the boot room and the well-organised informality of the office, I wasn't expecting such an impressive hallway. We'd come into the main house from the side—what would have been the servants' quarters—and entered the hall from the back. The floor was waxed pine, the walls a pale blue with soft cream paintwork, and tall, beautifully proportioned windows let in streaming yellow light. To our right, a panelled staircase with ornate spindles rose, a cupboard underneath it marked with wrought iron latch and hinges. A pair of dark wood occasional tables straddled the front door—a large, well polished affair with stained glass panels—and each held a big china vase full of fresh flowers, welcome profusions of colour, albeit still impeccably tasteful. It felt like walking through a three-dimensional jigsaw puzzle made from old copies of *Country Life*.

Ms. Brooks ushered me into the morning room, which was fairly small, but beautifully formed. Picture windows pierced the pale green walls to, I supposed, the south and east, because that way you would get the most early daylight. They overlooked, to one side, another well-kept garden and, to the other, the arrivals yard I'd first entered. Long curtains and deep windowsills framed a large, attractive fireplace. One or two oil paintings—farmyard scenes and studies of yet more flowers—graced the walls, but not in any way that might clash with the paintwork. The furniture was of the big, heavy variety, the chairs and sofas thickly upholstered with damask fabric, strewn with needlepoint cushions far better executed than my gran's efforts. At Ms. Brooks' invitation, I sat down in a chair between the fireplace and a sideboard laden with another vase of fresh flowers and a set of crystal decanters.

"Right, I'll leave you then," said Ms. Brooks, beaming at me. "He won't be a minute."

"Er. Thanks," I said.

The elderly collie bitch watched her go, then shuffled around, sniffing at things imperceptible to the human eye before coming and sitting heavily next to my feet. She tipped her head back and looked at me expectantly, her ears flopping out like wings, so I reached out and stroked her. After a few moments, I heard a car pull up outside, then the crunch of feet on gravel and the sound of the front door opening and closing. The collie got up and shambled to the door, wagging her tail expectantly.

Joss Napier came into the morning room tracking mud, one dark green welly already in his hand. He wore a pair of grubby jeans and a thick, navy blue cable-knit jumper of the bulletproof variety favoured by trawlermen, from under which came the suggestion of a checked twill shirt. A gold wedding band glinted on his left hand. He still stood on the tall side of average, not too generously padded, but if it hadn't been for the long, thin nose with the slightly crooked tip and the pale blue eyes, I wouldn't have recognised him. His hair was short, almost entirely grey, and his face had thickened and dropped considerably since all those photos I'd seen. He smiled at me as he toed off his other welly and bent to pat the collie bitch firmly on the flank.

"Good girl, Francie…. Hello. Miss Ross, right? Joss Napier. Pleased to meet you."

He shook my hand and flung himself into the other armchair. The big toe of his left foot had started to poke through his thick black sock.

"Do hope you don't mind," he said, "bit of a rush job, I know, and I'm afraid we are pretty informal. Someone ought to be along with some coffee and tea and that in a minute, and there'll be lunch in the kitchen for, oh, about half one. I do hope you'll join me."

"Of course. Um. Thank you," I said, trying to get my footing.

He seemed very pleasant—broad of smile and warm of tone—but I had the feeling that he held the conversation firmly in his grasp. I supposed I could expect nothing less; I'd come here posing as only one up from a journalist, after all. Not usually the object of much unguarded trust. Before I could blink, he'd started to tell me all about the farm, about the extremely rare chickens, and the cattle, and the sheep, and about how important the organic ethos and the preservation of heritage stock were in the age of intensive farming and, of course, in the wake of foot and mouth, not to mention the fresh threat of bluetongue disease. So few people really understood how their food got from field to table, he said, and the statistics regarding organophosphates and cancer incidence were truly terrifying; something of which, as a woman, he felt sure I was aware. I had barely formulated a cogent reply when, abruptly, he switched it all around.

"So, you're writing a biography of Damon Brent? I was amazed, I must say. It's a name I haven't heard in a very long time."

Clever, I thought. Not quite asking me why, but raising the issue. Letting me know he's thought about it.

"Yes," I said. "But it's important that heritage isn't

forgotten, isn't it, Mr. Napier?"

"Oh, very good." He chuckled. "And, please... Joss. Just Joss."

I nodded. The ever-efficient Ms. Brooks brought in tea and coffee and exchanged a few words with Just-Joss about a phone call that had come through regarding two hundred day weight prices. It went over my head.

"Sorry," he said after she retreated. "You know, I only bought this place eight years ago, though I saw it for the first time back in, oh, it would have been about '79. When I was still on the road, with Kaleidoscope Green... no one remembers them, of course. With good reason; we didn't last very long."

I wasn't sure how tactful it would be to agree with him at this point; we'd Googled and YouTubed his brief stint in that ill-fated prog outfit to within an inch of its life and it had been painful. Poe-faced, pretentiously painful. It didn't seem right to say that, of course, and it would hardly be the way to stroke the ego of my interviewee, so I grappled for something polite to contribute. Luckily for me, Joss had glanced out of the window rather than wait for my response, allowing me to get away with a non-committal but sympathetic noise.

"Back then," he said, "if you came up on the A-road, to the west, you could see all over the fields. There's a housing estate in the way now, but I remember noticing this, just, incredible place. Growing out of the ground, almost. Really... not just tumble-down. Actually already *tumbled*, you know?" He paused, one arm still half-outstretched, outlining the pattern of since-changed roads. "The same family farmed here for nearly two hundred years. The last owner was the only one left, and of course as he got older he couldn't manage, so it all just decayed around him. Poor old chap. All that heritage," he added with a smile. "Just waiting for someone to come along and save it. I was very lucky it was me... very lucky I was in the position to do so. Well, *we* were. My wife's at least half responsible," he explained. "A lot of this is her work."

His gesture to the wall behind me encompassed the fresh flowers, the carefully chosen artwork, and the tasteful paint job. I wasn't entirely surprised.

"It's lovely," I said. "And so full of character."

"Oh, it's definitely got that. Far too much character for Jessie's original plan, actually." He smiled. "She wanted to run a riding school. You know, she thought it would be nice...finally move out of London and get ourselves one of those rural idylls. Good for the girls. We have two daughters," he added with the beaming digression of a proud dad. "Lesley and Antonia. Both grown up now, or as good as. Lesley's at uni, reading law, and Toni's been working in London, at the Oxfam offices. I'm sure they'd both have loved to grow up with horses, but I'm afraid it never really got off the ground. This has always been a farm, and that's what it was crying out to be again. I thought I'd install a farm manager and not get my hands dirty. As it is, I seem to get more hands-on every year."

He grinned, and I could see that he didn't regret a minute of it.

"But, you're here to talk about the good old days. God, it's," he widened his eyes, "more than thirty years ago now. Frightening. Of course, we were all so young."

"Hm? Ah, yes." I checked my notepad, briefly wrong-footed by the fluid ease with which he directed things... made it easy for me. "You joined the band in '72, is that right? So, you were how old?"

"Oh, don't…. I was barely twenty-three. I'd been getting a bit of session work up 'til then, and I'd played with a few guys I knew from the Marquee fairly regularly, but we didn't do anything really fixed. I'd met Cris McIlroy at The Nottingham Boat Club… I suppose it would have been in the spring of that year. Probably about May, I'd think. He said he had these chaps who were going to be very big, but they needed a good, solid backbeat. Bit more of an… well, an edge, I suppose. So he invited me along to play, and it was decided, after we'd all messed around for a while, that I ought to come in full-time and see how it went. Of course, it went very well, and then *Saturday Loving* hit the charts… that was my fate sealed, as it were."

Joss took a sip of his tea and cleared his throat. He avoided my eye for a moment, as if wondering whether he'd just made himself sound like an egotistical arse or not. I smiled encouragingly.

"So that was first time you met them? The others?"

"Oh. Oh, yes." He nodded. "Well, I'd seen Charlie at Studio 51 and the Crawdaddy Club… the other two were more of an unknown quantity, though I had seen them about." Joss cleared his throat again, like he had some kind of irritable tickle. "You have to remember, Ellis, there was a thriving circuit in those days. It seemed like you rubbed up against everyone eventually, because everyone seemed to end up in the same places. It wasn't until a year or so later I actually realised I'd met Damon before, too, up at Eel Pie Island. Must have been, oh, '67, I suppose, just before it closed and the squatters moved in. I'd gone to see the Bluesbreakers. Incredible day."

He set his cup down and craned over in the chair, just

enough to scratch Francie's belly while he continued to talk. Reluctant though I was to admit it, I thought Damon might have had a point about cleavage. At his suggestion, I'd gone with a pale green V-neck jumper and the only padded bra I owned. As I leaned forward to put my empty cup on the low table, I noticed the very subtle, very brief peek that Joss took down my top.

"So I suppose Leon was the only one who was really an entirely unknown quantity for me. It was funny, 'cos we were all introduced for the first time at about two o'clock in the morning at a motorway services on the way to Leeds."

The collie thumped her tail and made a small noise in her throat as he rubbed her ears. Then she lumbered to the door and looked back at him with a little whine. As Joss got up to let the dog out for a wee, he explained that she was nearly fifteen and had a very weak bladder these days, though he'd had her from eight weeks old and couldn't bear the thought of being without her. He veered off into the day-to-day minutiae of running the farm, and every utterance made it so obvious how much he loved this place. This life.

Suddenly, I felt uncomfortable. Though it had been easy to make the idea of suspects and motives an abstract one, it quickly grew real. Where, with Fielding, I'd felt like I was walking on private memories, it seemed clear that, for Joss, it was his life *now* that was sacrosanct. The work he'd done to get here, and the future that followed.

And yet, even if I still didn't feel entirely comfortable thinking about it, I'd come here with the thought, somehow, that this man could—just maybe—have done something terrible. I thought of Damon on the prom, talking about his own death. The bleeding, the pain. I thought of all the cuttings in Mum's book, all the repeated tragedy and disbelief. *Someone* had been responsible. If he'd fallen, been lying there on that floor, someone had taken that moment of opportunity and... as the thoughts twisted around in my head, evading capture and control, I couldn't help but think that even Bill Sykes had adored his dog.

Francie's ablutions finished, Joss invited me through to the kitchen for lunch, pointing out an interesting original feature here, or a framed photo of one of his prize-winning bulls there. British White Cattle, he said, had been on the Rare Breeds Survival Trust's lists for years, though things were slowly improving. I looked at the picture of him in a white show coat, standing next to an enormously muscular walking lump of beef with huge, dark eyes, a wide, black nose and an immense expanse of beautiful, creamy-pale coat. An utterly thrilled Joss was holding up a ribbon for the camera, the bull's halter in his other hand. The bull, its hide gleaming in the light, appeared ambivalent.

The kitchen was large, blessed with an abundance of waxed pine, soft red quarry tiles, and original diamond leaded windows. The table had been laid with a glamorously informal repast of fresh bread, farmhouse cheeses, herb and Niçoise salads, fresh fruit, and a bottle of Bruno Paillard Brut Première Cuvée. As we ate, Joss told me—with just enough detail to make the comparison gently self-deprecating—about how he'd grown up in Kennington.

"Forgive me if I'm wrong," I put in, "but didn't all the promo material say that the entire band came from Bermondsey?"

"Ah. It was a bit like the old Hollywood studios, I'm afraid," Joss said with a smile. "The minute you sign, you find yourself reshaped, refigured, and repackaged, just like poor old Norma Jean. Who you were before didn't matter, you see. Kennington, Walworth... it's all South London so, for the press boys, suddenly all four of us came from Bermondsey. It wasn't true—only Damon did, really. He grew up in one of those Guinness Trust houses, I think... you know, like the Peabody Estates? Social housing," he added, with something that sounded—just for a second—like a sneer. "Very grim, I expect."

I said nothing and tried not to let my encouraging smile waver.

"Leon's people were from a little bit further west, Elephant and Castle sort of way, though of course he'd grown up in the States, and Charlie was a Walworth boy. But, as I said, that wasn't really relevant for the press chaps. And you quickly learn how important spin is. As true then as it is now."

He went on to talk about his own youth. The family had lived within a stone's throw of the Oval, he said, and for a long time he had wanted to be a cricketer. He still played, he was keen to tell me. He could often to be found at the Failand ground, with the cream of the sporting elite gleaned from the regulars at The Fox and Hounds, or donating a few hours to coaching for the youth league. There was a thriving set of knock-out cups, he said, and he wished there had been so many opportunities available when he was a boy. I heard, watching the slightly grim light of memory in his eyes, how Kennington had been in the late Fifties and Sixties. How, as a child, he'd been sent up to Bob White's for a pint of cockles or prawns, or for the Friday night fish supper from Ruby's. How, when he was a little older, errands gave way to weekends spent trying to convince girls to go to the Odeon with him, and how he'd seen *A Hard Day's Night* on that very silver screen and found it a revelation.

"I went back, not long ago," he said as Francie laid her head on his knee, hoping for an olive. "I was up in London and I had the car, so I thought, why not? Just to see it. My parents retired to Eastbourne in the Eighties, you see, so I hadn't.... Nostalgia, I suppose. It was very strange. It's... smaller. Definitely smaller than I remember. I parked up in Kennington Cross and went walkabout. They were knocking down the old Odeon." Joss tickled the dog's ears absently and slipped her a titbit of buttered bread. "And of course Bob White's hasn't been there for years," he said glumly. "I went right off the idea of cockles. You know, I'd sort of fancied picking some up, for old times' sake, but they wouldn't have tasted the same from anywhere else. And when I got back from my little stroll down memory lane, some bugger'd pinched my hub caps." He gave Francie a final pat and reached for his wine. "Things change, I suppose. Don't they?"

The kitchen windows faced out to the front and the gravel drive that approached the house. Through the leaded glass I saw another Land Rover pull up, tyres crunching on the stones. Joss' attention flicked to the window, but only briefly, identifying the vehicle and classifying its importance.

"So... what else is there you'd like to know? I mean, I don't know who else you've spoken to. Probably infra dig to ask, isn't it? Not sure, I haven't really done this before."

Another self-mocking chuckle, another sip of wine. I smiled.

"I've, um, been trying to get in touch with a lot of people. I've spoken to Leon Fielding, though."

"Leon? My God."

Joss rocked back in his chair, glass of champagne still in his hand. I wasn't sure if that could be genuine surprise. Did it shock him that Leon had consented to see me? Or maybe that I seemed further along in this enterprise than he'd expected. Outside, footsteps crunched on the gravel. A moment later, a gate slammed. Francie looked up expectantly at the door and wagged her tail, but no one came in. Joss cleared his throat.

"So how's he doing these days? Touring again, I know that. Hah… wouldn't catch me doing that. Younger man's game, I can tell you, Ellis. The, er, the albums have been very good, I must admit. Very… different to what he used to write."

I inclined my head—not quite a nod, not quite an admission of or agreement with anything—and chased the last olive around my plate.

"Yes. They worked pretty closely together, didn't they? Leon and Damon?"

"Well, they went way back, of course. But yes, they did. Though a lot of our earliest material was written independently." Joss smiled. "I'm sure you know how it goes. The label's interested in maintaining a consistent product, wanted us to sound just so. You know. I mean, that had to change in relation to the market, not what we wanted to record, but…."

"There was a bit of resistance to that?" I prompted. I knew damn well there had been. That all four of them had clamoured to get their own songs used, and that *Saturday Loving,* the band's first big hit, had been co-written by Leon and Day. I waited with interest to see Joss' take on that.

He drained his glass, paused with an inward-focused expression that suggested the bubbles had gone up the back of his nose, and then threw me a disarmingly artless grin.

"Hell, yes. You have no idea how frustrating that can be. We didn't want to be bubblegum, y'know? And when you think of some of the utter crap that gets pushed through.... I mean, of the releases in '72, *Angela* and *Lonely Evening* were both independents. Staff writers. So when Damon and Leon co-wrote *Saturday Loving* and it smashed into the charts, I was delighted. We all were. At the success, of course, but also to see a few noses out of joint. Prove that we could do it ourselves." He chuckled. "Obviously, then Damon got cocky. Pushed for his first royalty renegotiation in '73, which raised a few hackles."

"With the label?" I asked innocently. I found it difficult to believe either Joss or Charlie would have been entirely insouciant.

He shrugged.

"Thing is, Ellis, back then, writing his own material if really helped an artist see a profit."

I frowned. "Sorry... how do you mean?"

Joss leaned forward in his chair, arms propped on his knees, and fingers interlinked, as if patiently explaining something to a small child.

"Well, let's say you record an album full of songs you've written yourself. Legally, you're entitled to two types of royalties. Firstly, there's artist royalties, which can be anywhere from ten to twenty percent, depending on a number of things. You know... credibility, your contract, how good previous sales have been. Let's say you only get twelve points. It's not really that much, right?"

I shook my head.

"Well, then you've got mechanical royalties, which you're entitled to as the songwriter. Now, these don't add up to much either, but you still see around eight percent on the dealer price. So, if you've written, say, twelve songs to the album, you can vastly increase your royalty income, compared to the position you'd be in if you were just getting artist royalties. D'you see?"

I did. It was a giant game of double your money. And, as such, very probably rigged.

"Ah," I said. "So it's not just about artistic freedom and integrity?"

Joss curled his lip sheepishly.

"Not entirely. It's survival... I mean, signing the contract in the first place is only half, or less, of the battle. A very small number of signed acts will go on to actually see a reasonable outcome of all that work, especially given the recoupment obligations you're lumbered with."

He smiled, seeing my ignorance, and I wished I'd got Damon to explain this stuff to me more clearly. I felt like a complete idiot, so wrapped up in trying to work out all the motives-and-alibis stuff I'd picked up from Agatha Christie novels, I'd forgotten I was supposed to be posing as a music biographer. At least I'd said it was the thesis to a creative writing course; no one would expect me to be word-perfect.

"A lot of people think it's easy to make money in music, once you have a deal," Joss said. "It isn't. You see, the label acts sort of like a bank. Signing a record contract is rather like taking out an enormous loan on your future. You're expected to recompense the label for everything they invest in you, and usually you pay that back through royalties. Of course, if you're seeing less than twenty percent of the gross sales in the first place, that tends to take a while."

He paused to refill his glass, and mine, and I could sense the bitter rant begging to emerge from beneath the surface. I poked and prodded a little bit to see if I could help it along but, to his credit, Joss kept everything calm and professional. I relented.

"So, you'd find yourself in debt to the label, and obligated to—what?—produce more material? Or a certain kind of material?"

"It would depend on your contract," he said, a touch evasively.

"But is that what happened with Brother Rush? You had a pretty high output. There were…." I checked my notepad, the details of Damon's careful dictation a few nights before. "Twelve Top Forty singles between '72 and '76, and five studio albums. Plus touring."

"We were worked hard," Joss conceded. "And, yes, we were inexperienced to begin with. If I was shown today the contract we all signed back in '72…! But, at that point, we had a manager and a solicitor, and we thought we were already rich. And that it would last forever." He smiled wistfully. "We signed for six albums. By the middle of '73, I think we were already something like nine grand in the hole, on paper. Oh, there are other ways to get money, of course." His gaze flicked to the recorder I'd set, with his permission, on the tabletop. If it worried him, he covered it well. "But that obligation still remains," Joss finished smoothly. He gestured with his fork. "With The Mamas and The Papas, for example… they had to get back together in '71 to record *People Like Us*, even after breaking up in '68, because Dunhill Records wouldn't let them opt out of their deal. They owed one more album, so they had to do it. It was pretty much the same thing for us... we were contracted for six albums. That's why Damon's death coming when it did was such a blow. We'd started work on what would have been the sixth—never named it—late spring and summer of '76, but without him...."

He tore at a hunk of bread, not meeting my eye. A half-frown crossed his forehead as if, though he knew we would have to talk about Damon, he really didn't want to... as if any preparation he'd done for this part of the conversation hadn't been enough.

"That must have been very difficult," I prompted gently.

"It was. I mean, it was tragic, of course. And so utterly bloody stupid. Ridiculous. He never deserved it. And it was a very distressing time for all of us. Obviously, it could never have been the same without him. He was—I mean, of course he was extremely talented—but he had a great drive, as well. Very ambitious, you know. We fell apart, without him... all agreed to go our separate ways that November. Cris, our manager, he was very good. We got away with bringing out the *Live at the Carousel* LP in time for Christmas, with some tribute notes on it, then a greatest hits collection early in '77. Probably better for everyone that way. Commitments fulfilled, and no more expectations."

"I see." I nodded sympathetically. "So—and I hope you don't mind my asking—but would you say Damon Brent was a driving creative presence? It seems a lot of material was written by various members of the band, and—"

"Oh, yes." Joss smiled, but it wasn't an entirely happy face.

"Yes, he was. Of course. And I think he was always very determined to do things, you know, right up to the nth degree of his ability."

He glanced at the recorder again. Only very briefly, but I saw it.

"I think that's why he found the market we were in so frustrating. I mean, to be honest, it was hardly challenging, musically speaking. You'd really only see Damon light up when we played live. He didn't have the, um, the discipline or the patience for sustained creativity in the studio. Not to suggest that he really *lacked*...." Joss curled his fingers in the air. A half-smile lingered diffidently on his face. "He got bored easily, you know? Didn't like going over and over the same material... and he *really* didn't like being told he couldn't use something because it wasn't commercial, or the label didn't think it was suitable." He chuckled. "If he could see the way things are now!"

I bit my tongue. My mind had already been wandering too much, trying to picture Damon in middle age, saggy and greying. Would he have put on weight or stayed trim? Looked back at the past fondly or moved forward with hope and optimism? And would he have cut his hair? I blamed the warm, full flavours of the champagne and the way the bubbles went to my head. While they were there, they bumped up against other, harder thoughts. *I was talkin' to people at Decca, Universal... they were gonna offer me blind terms, more cash....*

Damon had protested, when I pushed him, that he hadn't really meant to leave the band in the lurch. He wouldn't have done it, he swore. They hadn't known, he said. But what if someone *had*? I dragged myself back to the here and now, not quite ready to put those questions to Napier. Not yet. Not and reveal my hand.

"It must," I said diplomatically, that sense of the surreal creeping back upon me like a panic attack, "have been very difficult for all of you. I mean, it's a very intense environment, and there must have been a lot of pressure, especially at the beginning."

"Yes. Yes, there was," he agreed. "This... um. This is a drugs question, isn't it?"

I laughed and nodded. If only I could ask him straight out. *I have it on excellent authority that it was, in fact, murder. Whose authority, you ask? Well now, that's the funny thing....*

"As I understand it," I said instead, "there was a certain degree of—"

"Ah." He patted Francie thoughtfully. "Yes, well, no point denying it. A certain degree. I take it you've read all those interviews Charlie gave a few years back?"

"Yes, I have."

"Hm." Joss nodded. "Then you realise that he'd be the one to talk to about that side of things. I can't speak for the others, though a fair amount of that stuff went on, that's true. And Damon definitely.... Well, I know he smoked grass. Popped a few pills—mostly amphetamines, I suppose—did some coke, a few hallucinogenics, and of course there was the booze. That, more than anything. I'd certainly never have called him an addict. Not at all. I mean, I don't think he ever really over-indulged or did anything too spectacular. There was that one time, when we were in Amsterdam.... You get very bored," he added in a tone of gentle self-justification, "what with all that travelling and, when you come off after a show, the last thing you wanna do is get back on the bus. It was one of the first tours we did, back in '74, I think. We partied, after the gig. Heavily, I'll admit. Poor old Charlie was heading up to his worst point around then. I remember Damon—completely off his face—trying to buy drinks for an entire, um, private club. Y'know, a, er...."

"Brothel?" I supplemented.

Joss turned ever so slightly pink and tried manfully to change the subject.

"Um. Well, as I said, we were all young guys. You know. First time abroad, practically. Of course, when we got back—"

"Amsterdam was a sort of safe haven, though, would you say?" I prompted, pushing gently. I was in charge, I told myself. "Out of sight of the British press... almost." I did my very best smile. "Do tell."

Joss looked shifty.

"We-ell... as I said, we partied quite heavily over there. And no one was going to forego de Wallen, or the head shops. In '74, I think we were still new enough to the whole thing to take it as an opportunity to... well, to misbehave a bit, to be honest. Maybe a bit too much. I mean, we only stayed two and a half days but, between us, I think we got into just about everything. There were some very... *interesting* places."

I watched the battle of the blush wage around Joss' face. Retrospective embarrassment fought cat and mouse with enjoyable memories, under the sniper fire of a now-married man's randomised guilt, and the guerrilla attacks of panic at whether or not he wanted to see this in print.

"Mm?" I said, leaning forward a little in my chair.

"It was... something that could be immensely relaxing." A

tide of pink washed about his jawline. "Y'know. Not... not just the, er, ladies, but... the whole nature of the place. The freedom. And—you're right—kind of a *discreet* environment. Or, at least, it seemed so at the time. You had to be careful, naturally. Getting snapped going into a brothel wasn't considered quite *de rigueur* in publicity terms... but we were young, so we did it anyway. I remember," he smiled into the mid-distance, "Damon buying drinks for the whole club, running up this enormous tab... just this... *huge* party. Major all-nighter, you know. Women, wine, song... a lot of grass. And stuff. It was great. Of course, he got carried away. He always did. Disappeared with a magnum of champagne and the blonde and the brunette he couldn't decide between, as I recall." Joss used his fork to fiddle with a piece of rocket. "We gave him a lot of stick afterwards, but it was, you know, sort of expected... in those days. Condemned man's last fling and all that, right? You know, with the wedding."

He gave an embarrassed little chuckle.

"Of course." I glanced at my notepad. "So, he and Inez... they met in '73?"

"Yeah. But I don't think I ever really knew the details. He introduced her, brought her along to a few studio sessions. I think we all thought he was going to pull that unforgivable betrayal, you know?"

Joss winked at me, grinning encouragingly, like I should know the joke. I must have looked as blank as clean paper. He cleared his throat.

"'My girlfriend does great backing vocals'. Y'know. About number three in the list of things you never want to hear in a studio. She wasn't really musical, though, Inez. Actually, I'm ashamed to say I didn't realise she was a tennis player at first. Of course, she didn't really look like one. Not off court. Very glamorous. They were a great match, really. Set a date for a summer wedding in '74, though I'm afraid I don't remember when. Must have been July, or maybe June... we definitely gave Day one hell of a stag do. Lasted most of that tour and, of course, um, there was Amsterdam."

Unspoken references to that sort of thing not being at all on these days, of course, wouldn't dream of it, total respect for women et cetera, hung in the air.

I smiled.

"Utter profligacy, of course," Joss added. "And it came back to haunt us. I swear I was hungover for a week. We lost Leon somewhere around the canal, complete panic 'til we found him again. Charlie got crabs. And we were in *serious* shit with management. I think it was really the last time we ever did anything like that, where we were culpable as a group, kind of thing."

I arched an eyebrow. How disappointing.

"What about separately?"

Joss flashed me a grin. "Miss Ross... you're not muckraking, are you?"

I tried to look innocent, and probably failed.

"No, not as such," I said, guessing that apparent honesty might be the best way to go. "But... there seems to have been something of a consensus that drugs and alcohol played a role in Damon's death. I suppose what I'm asking is how much of a role those patterns played in his life."

I swallowed, surprised to find myself nervous. I kept thinking of Day on the prom... and I kept thinking that, in taking this road, I was asking for trouble. Like, somehow, someone would find out what I was looking for. And then where would I be?

"In the life of the band," I added, trying to soften the question.

Joss nodded slowly. "Mm. Yeah, he... well, like I said, Day drank, more than anything. Me too. I was never that much into the harder side of things. It's—well, it's frankly scary, seeing how out of it you can get. And I don't like to lose control. Not that much. I drank... admittedly more than I should have, for a while. I think we all did."

I looked at the glass of Paillard beside his plate. *We all did.* The justification of the mob again. Still, if Joss had drunk, it wasn't as much as he could have done. He could still afford to have one drink, and that's one drink more than the seriously rehabilitated boozer.

"Of course," he added brightly, "no one had introduced any guidelines for alcohol consumption back then. Units per week and so on. Would've been laughed out of court if they'd tried, of course... but it does catch up with you, I'll admit. Personally speaking, I cut back a lot after Jess and I got married, and kicked the fags. Like the majority of my generation, I suppose." He smiled dryly. "You put in all those years of rebellion against postwar conformity, and you still end up packing in the booze and the fags and taking up jogging because you're terrified of your family losing you to a heart attack at fifty. We got middle-aged," he said with more than a touch of irony to his sadness. "They were good times, though."

He sliced a piece of farmhouse cheddar onto a cracker. After a pause to let Francie out for another loo break, we talked some more about the band's salad days, about the personalities and the egos and the anecdotes. I got the distinct impression that—although Joss had loosened up considerably—most of what he said had been cleaned up for his, rather than my, benefit. Still, plenty of interest there. I took notes and started to fill in more of the gaps my conventional education had left me with; what it felt like to skinny dip in the Thames off Grove Park and why it had never been a good idea; the many uses of toupee tape even before the phrase 'wardrobe malfunction' had been coined; smart-aleck responses to most musicians' top five favourite drummer jokes. Eventually, I succeeded in nudging him towards that night.

We were drinking coffee now. Joss dumped a teaspoon of sugar into his cup (proper cups. With saucers. Not like my odd collection of chipped builder's mugs and mismatched three for two IKEA specials), stirring far longer than could be necessary to get it to dissolve. He frowned at the little bubbles that bobbed and eddied on the surface of the liquid and tapped his spoon on the rim of the cup.

"Damon did throw parties a lot. He liked the attention, of course, and, to be honest, I think he needed to feel important. They were *good* parties, don't get me wrong," Joss added quickly. "And the right people were always there, but it never felt too staged, you know? Even that night, when the place was full of—well, there were actors, models, a lot of influential people from the industry."

He reeled off a list of names, some familiar to me, most totally unknown. However, the experience of talking to Leon already had provided me with a lot of background, so I managed to cover fairly well. Once Joss explained the connections—business, personal, and strictly under the table—between people, I began to see how it worked. Like a living flow diagram and, I supposed, rather like he'd described Amsterdam. Damon's place had been out in the country; not London, not town. Somewhere that rules could be suspended, pressure released. A weekend out of time, Joss called it.

"I-I have to admit that there are parts of that night I don't remember." He sipped his coffee. "I mean, I remember thinking there was something going on, because Damon was absolutely hyper. I thought either coke or amphetamines, but I remember he was drinking very heavily as well. Of course, pretty much everybody was. I saw him—can't remember what time, I'm afraid—arguing, I thought, with Cris. Vince Dexler was there too; all looked a bit animated."

"D'you know what it could have been about?"

I suspected I knew all too well. *Blind terms, more cash—Vince had it all lined up....* Day hadn't mentioned it all coming out that night, or a fight with Cris. I wondered why.

Joss shrugged. "No idea. Whatever it was, they sorted it out amicably enough, I think. Damon seemed fine. Hyper, like I said, but fine. I saw him on and off throughout the party, playing the good host. You know. Plying everybody with booze and... whatever else. At one point, I think he was trying to make a wax sculpture in the pool. The, um, the last time I remember seeing him was about three a.m., probably. Again, he was fine... he said he wanted to take a nightcap, then get some sleep. He, um, he gave me a key to one of the bedrooms. Winked at me, and that was it. I went upstairs with my girlfriend and the next time I saw him, he was...."

Joss trailed off, the coffee cup halfway to his mouth. There was something surreal about the image; cup and saucer poised delicately against the coarse blue sweater, the farmer's trousers and the house party memories. For a moment, his expression seemed indescribably sad. Then, just as quickly, he recovered himself. Coffee sipped, cup and saucer replaced on the table. He cleared his throat, reached out to nudge the cup with his thumb and straighten the handle.

"I, uh, I was still in bed when Leon found him, so the first I heard was the yelling. Got up, pulled on some clothes. I didn't know what was going on, but I knew something had happened. Went downstairs, and there were just people all over the place, it had just kicked off, you know? Girls screaming, and... then there was the ambulance, and the police arrived. No one knew exactly what had happened and, of course, as soon as they heard a siren people were trying to leg it... with very good reason, as it turned out," he added with a slightly bitter tone. "I should have taken the opportunity."

"I understand that a lot of drug charges were brought," I said, feeling about as subtle as a half-brick in a wet sock.

Joss seemed either not to notice or not to mind, because he just nodded.

"Yeah. I was charged with possession... it didn't stick, because all I was wearing at the time was a pair of jeans, and there was nothing in the pockets. There was hash in the bedroom, with the rest of my stuff, but.... Of course, worrying about that wasn't my first thought. I just remember seeing Leon. He was coming out of the lobby—that was this big split-level hallway, you know, connected the east and west wings. Damon had put in this great big partition, all glass blocks, glass door.... The door was open, and I could see Leon had come down the stairs in the west wing." He exhaled, long and low, through his teeth. "I'd never seen anything like it. His face.... He was white, you know? Not just pale. *White*. And shaking. There was blood on his shirt, on his face.... It was terrible."

I pricked up my ears. Joss stared at the tabletop and rubbed one thumb along its varnished edge.

"I've never seen anyone in a state like that. He just kept saying 'he's dead', then he started freaking out. I went to him, hugged him, tried to calm him down, get him to tell me what was going on. He just crumbled. It was awful. Seemed like just minutes after that, the place started crawling with police. Complete bloody mess. The whole day, just taken up with all this bullshit, you know... piss tests and questioning and statements. After all that, when we finally found out what had happened, and they said he'd fallen, hit his head. Terrible. I mean, he could have been up there for hours and no one knew. It was just so, so wrong."

Joss lapsed into silence, sudden and abrupt. My mouth felt dry, and I couldn't think of a single thing to say. Luckily for me, I didn't have to. His silence was as brief as it had been intense. He cleared his throat again.

"Of course, it all descended into farce after that. A complete circus. We were all shuttled off to the local nick to get... well, processed, I suppose they'd say. The whole place was absolutely chocka with people's managers and PR teams, trying to sort out the mess. Of course, it would have been handled completely differently in London. You know. These were a load of country coppers, sticking their size twelves in and really not knowing what on earth to do with all these long-haired, half-naked people." He smiled. "If Damon could have seen it, he'd have loved that. I mean, it was complete chaos. And the press started circling... the weeks after that were fairly horrible, I can tell you. Not just the funeral, though that was dreadful. Made it all real, somehow. But... what they did to him, in the papers. I hope that's not something you're not going to focus on."

"No," I said, my mouth operating without the rest of me, which was still some thirty years away. "No. I'm, um, I'm really much more interested in... before. Before that. It's so sad, so much potential—the potential you had as a group—to be cut short like that. As you said, it must have been virtually impossible to carry on in the same way, afterwards."

I thought I saw a look of... something in his face when I said that. Anger? Distaste? Whatever it was, it faded, replaced with a solemn nod. Yes, he said, it had been difficult, and they had all felt there was really no way they could continue, especially when the press started to drag out sordid details.

"And, of course, it was hard on Inez. There was a period, up to the funeral, when some of the hacks were very unkind."

I remembered Fielding's words: *I... may have said things I later regretted.* The press hadn't been the only ones to blame Inez.

"She, uh, she wasn't there at the party, was she?"

"No. No, they kept a flat in London. Used to stay there when she went down to shop... to be totally honest, I think she needed the occasional break from the whole scene. Though it was odd she wasn't there, when that party was such a big do.... I guess they must have had some kind of tiff."

I studied Joss' face carefully. If he'd intentionally lied, he'd done it well. Totally artless, as if he'd had no suspicion Inez had been playing away. Maybe he hadn't. Maybe the skewed dynamic had only ever been between Day, Inez and... Leon? It still didn't seem right.

"What would you say their relationship was like?" I popped back, hoping to strike while the proverbial iron was hot.

I wasn't quite quick enough.

"Really not for me to say." Joss smiled. "I know he did love her. She certainly wasn't his Yoko, though. Inez was more interested in the celebrity cachet than the music. I don't mean that nastily, just that that's the part of it she was used to. I suppose losing that, with the injury and everything, then losing Damon... must have been hard."

He moved on quickly, and I had to admire the way he'd sneaked out of it. I wanted to ask him more about Inez, but Joss was busy getting in references to the two decades he'd spent, since the demise both of Damon and of Brother Rush, producing a string of moderately successful bands and writing a raft of almost-classic songs.

He seemed to want to close by leaving me in no doubt whatsoever that not all the band's talent had died with Damon. I played along, taking details and feigning a more intimate knowledge of his pet projects than I'd really bothered with. I assured him that I would include the info where I could, and he seemed happy.

"And do pass on my regards to the others. You know, when you speak to them." He smiled sadly. "We've really lost touch over the years. It's a shame."

"I will," I promised, packing up my stuff. "And thanks so much for your time. It's been a real pleasure, and a great help."

"Pleasure's all mine, my dear," he smarmed.

We stood and shook hands. I thanked him once more for

his time, and he said I wasn't to hesitate to get in touch again, and he'd look forward to reading the book sometime soon. I smiled and said, of course, and he insisted on having Ms. Brooks drive me back to the station. He wouldn't let me wriggle out of it, so we went out of the beautifully proportioned Georgian front door, through the side gate, and into the arrival yard and—after he'd summoned her from the office—I obediently slipped into Ms. Brooks' Land Rover.

He waited to wave us off and, just before the car pulled out onto the road, a woman came out of the long, low farm office. Her long bob of strawberry blonde hair framed her face, her figure flattered by a pale blue sweater, battered but well-cut jeans, and dark green Hunters. Yet, in that fleeting moment, I could only think of her expression as anxious. She slid snugly up to Joss, one hand on his chest, and his arm dropped around her shoulders. She said something to him, and he looked at her and smiled. Then we turned the corner, and I saw no more in the rearview mirror except hedges and the occasional squashed badger.

Chapter Eleven
May 14th 1976

The party was already in full swing when the car drew up, cleaving the thick, soft night. The air smelled like gardenias and leather, and the strains of *Houses of the Holy* filtered down through the limestone wedding cake architecture and black iron railings of Chepstow Villas.

"How long do we have to be here?"

"It's a party, baby. There's no have to." Damon sighed and tipped the driver. "Thanks, Freddie. Look, baby, just try'n have a good time, yeah?"

Inez said nothing. She rearranged the neckline of her frock and waited for Damon to come around and open her door. He offered her his hand as she got out of the car.

"Come on, darlin'. You hear that? Remember that song? You love that song. Come have a dance with me, yeah? Maybe," he purred into her ear, arm sliding around her waist, "I can make your garden grow."

She smiled, despite herself. So bloody typical; he'd spend the whole day pissing her off, as if he actually had some kind of a death wish, then he'd pull something like that out of the hat. Pick up her favourite ice cream, sneak back to a shop to buy a bracelet she'd said she liked... make her laugh. Inez let him kiss her neck.

"All right."

"There, see? Good girl. And," Damon steered her towards the steps, "if you really can't stick it, we can always leave early, yeah?"

She didn't reply. He wouldn't leave. He never left anything early; he'd probably live to a hundred and twelve on pure stubbornness. His hand had already slipped south, and Inez reached back to remove it from her buttock. A piercing whistle cut the air, coinciding with an increase in the volume of the music and the party noise. They looked up. Charlie was leaning out of one of the sash windows upstairs, waving down at them, perilously close to falling out.

"Brilliant! You're here! Day, you gotta come up, man. Dino an' Steve are here... an' Ade and Rob... everybody's here, man! You have to get up. Back your mamacita up, too, she lookin' good. You lookin' good, Inez!" he added and scrabbled at the sill in an attempt to right himself. "Whoo... shit! Yeah, you come up, right? I-I'll come and... yeah."

The arms of unseen donors pulled him back in, and Charlie closed the window, still semaphoring suggestively. Inez shot a look at Damon. His hand tightened on the small of her back, and a muscle twitched in his jaw.

"He doesn't—"

"I know. It's all right." Inez planted a quick kiss on his cheek. She moved off, up the steps to the building's front door, and glanced back over her shoulder. "Well? Come on, baby."

Charlie's flat always presented a kind of a mystery. Though large—sprawling over the top floor of the villa, with a small but lush roof garden at the back—it still managed to give off a flophouse vibe. No matter how many modern pictures hung on the walls, between the gold discs and the framed photos of favoured idols, something about the place still gave off the feeling that, somewhere under foot, the carpet might be rotting.

Tonight the joint was packed. Charlie met them at the door, expansive and dramatic in stonewashed denim and polyester.

"You look beautiful," he told Inez, pushing the friendly kiss on the cheek in greeting right to the limits of acceptability before dragging them both inside.

A gaggle of lanky young things Inez had last seen on *Top of the Pops* loitered beside a large cheese plant, wreathed in giggles and heavy smoke. They hadn't looked quite so stoned when they'd been dancing for the camera in matching gauze pixie skirts.

In the middle of the room, a tall black woman in Zandra Rhodes and luminescent paint was dancing on a teak coffee table, striking angular poses against the beat. Most of Charlie's furniture had been pushed back, making space for the heaving press of people who were dancing, necking, and otherwise entertaining themselves on the floor.

"I know she was right here." Charlie waved a hand vaguely. "You have to meet her. You'll love her. Future! Future, where the hell'd you go? Oh, there she is. There's my girl! Day, Inez, this is The Future Mrs. Davies. Say hi, baby."

Inez stared at the creature in front of her. A dark blonde, with soft grey eyes and fair skin, her small and pointed face lent an affectation of elegance to her otherwise skinny frame. It took a few moments, but Inez realised that she recognised the girl; she was a model, familiar from a handful of hoardings between here and Piccadilly. As Inez looked over the extremely long, extremely slim, honey-tanned legs, the raw bones of elbows and knees, she recalled that the last place she'd seen this chick was buck-naked on the walls at Biba. She looked different without the thick, dark lipstick.

"Hello," said Inez, sticking the smile she knew she was going to need onto her face. "How lovely! Congratulations."

The girl held out a hand, all long fingers with large joints, short nails, and nicotine stains, and her limp, cool handshake lasted a little too long. Leaning forward, her voice barely audible under the pumping noise of the room, she looked earnestly at Inez.

"You hear the music, too, right?" she said, her eyes glassy but so very serious. "All bright, like a church in the sky."

Inez felt the smile turn into a rictus. She turned her head, looking for Damon, but Charlie had already dragged him off, intent on introducing him to some hot new local talent, great guys, sounded kinda like the Sex Pistols, that was where the scene was going, man, everything else was just so much corporate crap, right, and as a matter of fact, these guys said they were gonna be supporting the Pistols at the 100 Club, wasn't that just fuckin' brilliant?

Inez gently removed her hand from The Future's clammy grasp.

"So, tell me, sweetheart," she said, edging them both

carefully towards the kitchen, "what did you say your name was?"

* * *

Charlie cracked open another bottle of scotch.

"Th-thing is," he said, topping up Damon's glass, "it's all changing, man. It's all—y'know what I mean?"

"Everything changes," Damon said uncertainly.

"Fucki— Yeah, but... but this is *changing*, man. Can't you feel it?"

Damon looked from the two inches of liquid amber in his hand to the rooftops of Ladbroke and Notting Hill, stretching away before and beneath him. Funny, really. He'd thought about coming here once, when it was all distant and paved with... stuff. After Leon had lent him his copy of *Absolute Beginners*, and he'd read it and they'd got stoned and talked about how shitty at least half of life was, and all the crap that people did to each other and in the names of people that didn't want the shit done, and wasn't it about time the norms all got freaked up a little bit? Yeah, 'cos that's what they oughta do. 'Cos it wasn't guns that changed the world, man. It was people, and ideas.

Only... they'd never quite got here. And now it would all be different, wouldn't it? He supposed so. Maybe it had always been different. Maybe it had always been angry. He wouldn't know, not really, and that made him kinda feel like a fraud. Beneath his hand, mica glittered in the stonework. On the street below, an evening breeze ruffled the uncollected rubbish banked up on the pavement. That was different, too... the strikes, and all the poisonous resentment there was these days.

Damon shifted position on the balustrade, hooked one foot around the rise of the ledge, and let the other dangle out into the open air, his body poised halfway between the party and the coolness of the night. Charlie's collection of plants—mostly sickly or half-dead, excepting the more exotic seven-leaved ferns, which were thriving, as always—whispered dryly in the breeze. Charlie was right. Things *were* changing.

"You're stoned, man," he muttered, taking a mouthful of his drink.

"No. I swear, I'm straight, all right? I'm tellin' you, man, we gotta get in this. This is where it starts, y'know what I'm sayin'?"

Damon took a drag on his cigarette and squinted at Charlie through the smoke and the gloom. Sweat gleamed on his face, his breathing shallow. Yeah, he was straight. Straight-edge like a beach ball. Damon shook his head.

"Nah, I don't think so, Charlie. It's not.... This punk thing, it ain't gonna last. It's not where we are, anyway. If it's startin', y'know, it's startin' without us, yeah? And it don't need us. We don't need it."

"Shit, man, you sound fuckin'— Don't you want it no more?"

Damon slugged back the last of his scotch.

"It's not... nah, it's not that," he said, wondering if he meant it.

True, he wasn't hungry for it—the money—like he used to be. But then it had never just been about money. Not entirely. Not the fame, either; that was... beautiful, frightening, powerful... but incidental. No. It had been four years, near enough. He'd paid off the house, he had cash set aside, a name he could still bank roll. Inez had what she made from contracts, appearances, plus winnings. Politics didn't concern him, not really, but he wasn't ready to quit. Not yet, not by a long chalk.

How did you quit your own bones?

"It's not that," he said again, pretty sure he meant it, and stared at his empty glass. "I just... I don't dig the way this scene's goin', man. Y'know?"

Charlie huffed irritably.

"What if I said I did? What if I said—"

"What?"

"Forget it."

Charlie leaned over and sloshed more scotch into both their glasses. Damon frowned. From inside, there came a loud crash, followed by a ragged cheer. Neither of them looked around.

"Charlie, you're not thinkin' about quittin'?"

"No! Nah, man." Charlie took a mouthful of scotch. "Why, are you?"

"No." Damon shook his head. "Look, I know nobody wants to do Holland. But we're... wossname. Obligated, innit? It's only a few weeks. Won't be long 'til we can get back in the studio, work on the new stuff."

He swigged his drink and watched the night deepen beneath his feet. Somewhere, down below, dark figures moved through the blacked out street. Laughter drifted on the air. For all the union crap, all the strikes, all the ill will, you still had to love the power cuts, man.

Charlie grunted. "Oh. Yeah. *Your* stuff."

"No, man... well, yeah. Maybe. Yeah, I mean, sure I got some ideas, but—"

"You know what?" Charlie snapped, suddenly aggressive

and suddenly, it seemed, much closer than he had been a moment ago. "You don't get it. You don't fucking *get* it, do you?"

He lurched forward, half-lunge, half-stumble, and struck Damon's shoulder with his own as he caught himself on the balustrade, sagging at the knees and swearing. Just a clumsy, chaotic moment, all over in a few seconds, but they were long ones. Damon wobbled, grabbed at the rough stonework, and grazed his hand in the bid to stop himself falling. The glass slid from his fingers and disappeared into the soft, perilous night. In the ragged quiet between them, torn by the noises of revelry from inside the flat and the sound of a car door slamming below, they heard the tumbler smash. Somewhere distant... pavement, maybe. Maybe someone else's window ledge.

Damon raised his left hand and squinted at it. Blood oozed from a series of small scrapes on his fingertips and palm. He looked up. Charlie stared at him, eyes pale in the half-light. Slowly, they both pealed into dry, hoarse laughter. Charlie grabbed at Damon's shoulder, fingers clenched on the nap of his velvet jacket.

"You're a lucky fucker, you know that, man? I.... I gotta get back."

"Sure." Damon swung his leg over the balustrade and dropped to the terrace. He wiped the bloody hand on his flares. It barely stung. His brow furrowed. "Hey... Charlie?"

"Yeah?"

"You really gonna marry that chick?"

Charlie paused, his hand already on the handle of the half-glazed door.

"Huh? What, Future? No. Yes. Fuck knows, man." He

turned, backing off the terrace, his arms outstretched, his body backlit for a moment against the open door, the noise and the music flowing around him in a thick haze. He raised his voice: "Everything's fucking changing, baby!"

* * *

Inez clutched her Pernod and lemonade like a talisman as she inched through the crush. Some of the Grove's biggest stars were holding court here tonight, fresh back from Abbey Road, and it put her teeth on edge. Charlie, coming in from the roof garden, almost backed into her.

"Inez!" he exclaimed, turning to her, grinning. "He's just out—"

"I don't want Damon, I wan— I was looking for you."

"Whassa matter, babe?"

Inez grabbed at the sleeve of his shirt, pulling herself closer to his ear. She could have shouted and still had complete privacy—the kind of isolation generated by a room full of people all totally absorbed in their own universes.

But that wasn't the point.

"I'm late. *Late*. D'you…?"

Charlie looked confused, and she knew saying anything else would be useless. Not when he was like this… not here. Better just to leave him to that chalk-faced, junk-thin thing in the kitchen. She knocked back the rest of her drink in one swallow and pushed the empty glass into his unresisting fingers.

Of all the bloody *stupid….*

"Huh?" he said, squinting at her.

"I-It doesn't matter," she said, fighting the sting behind her eyes.

Across the room, Damon came in from the terrace and drifted seamlessly into a knot of people. A black woman with a mass of pomaded hair and a high, carrying voice had already draped herself around him by the time Inez got there. She glared at the bitch until she disengaged herself and floated off, leaving Damon beaming happily at her.

"Hey, baby! I don't think you know… this is Paul and—Joe, yeah?—this is my wife, Inez. Inez, honey—"

"I didn't get my dance," she said, nodding a cursory greeting to the young men he'd indicated. "I want to dance. Are you gonna dance with me or not?"

He smiled that lazy, blissed-out smile that made her want to hit him, and held out his hand.

"Sure, baby. Come on."

The throbbing intro of a rock track Inez didn't recognise wrapped itself about them, and Damon's hands slid around her waist, pulling her close.

"Who's this?"

"Aerosmith," he said, his breath grazing her ear. "*Lick and a Promise.* Nice, yeah?"

Inez tried to think of a reply, but she had Day's hair in her face—dry curls crisp with cigarette smoke—the scent of his body heat, and the YSL cologne he liked so much caught in the back of her throat. He ground against her, all hands and horn, and the hot waves of a blush rose to her cheeks. She loathed the fact he could do this to her—that he *would* do it—in front of all these people. His arrogance astonished her. His fingers tugged at the fastening of her dress, a wisp of chiffon concealing the zip below her shoulder blades.

"Not a chance, sunshine," she muttered, twisting away.

Inez raised her arms above her head, let the music take her out of herself, higher and wilder. Day's mouth curled into a predatory grin. Somewhere on the fringes of the thing, out of the sweat-haze and the crush of bodies, Inez made out the shape of Charlie introducing The Future around the room. She dangled off his arm like an expensive cufflink.

Inez returned her attention to her husband, his sinuous gyrations, and his apparent current obsession with her breasts. Oh yes. She'd take the lick *and* the promise, thank you very much.

Chapter Twelve

Getting back from Bristol took over three hours. It irked me that travelling by road would have been quicker, quite probably more comfortable, and not laced with the slight miasma of panic that trains had held for me since Uncle Duncan's accident, but I couldn't complain. I had no way of running a car *and* the flat on a student's budget, and what I might have been able to spend on a rental I'd already blown on wining and dining Leon Fielding.

The relief at being home was immense, though, even if my flat wasn't totally my own anymore. In the sitting room, the piles of paperwork had been cleared off the coffee table. In their place sat an artistic arrangement of scented candles on a copper tray, with an incense stick smouldering in a silver ash catcher that I didn't recognise.

Jefferson Airplane's *Bless Its Pointed Little Head* played

softly on the stereo, which seemed strange because—although I knew it—I didn't own the album. In the corner, my computer had been left on. The printer was flashing a combination of lights and making sad little noises suggestive of terminal indigestion. Balls of scrunched up paper littered the floor.

I padded into the kitchen, which was empty, but clean. A frying pan sat soaking in the sink. From there, I noticed that the bathroom door stood open and, on closer inspection, I found the bathroom itself still wreathed with the traces of recent steam. Mist streaked the mirror, a wet towel left crumpled on the floor. An open bottle of expensive salon shampoo stood on the side of the bath, and I decided not to contemplate the contents of the plughole. There appeared to be razor scrapings in the sink.

I sighed, because I'd quite fancied the idea of a hot bath, and now I suspected I could never feel the same way about my bathroom again. I'd had a long day. I didn't need to see this. After a moment, unwilling but unable to resist the temptation, I picked up the bottle of shampoo and gave it a sniff. It smelled of coconuts or, at least, that pleasingly sweet but synthetic coconut milk perfume. Nice, all the same.

"Hey, baby."

I *really* wished he wouldn't do that. Shampoo still in hand, I turned. Damon was leaning decorously against the doorjamb. A beautifully tailored jacket—a slick of silk shot through with reds, oranges and golds—hung unbuttoned over a purple Peter Pan shirt. A skinny black fur boa swaddled his neck, ends trailing down to his slim hips. His bare toes protruded from under the hems of a pair of denim flares heavily patched through style rather than hard wear, a dazzling collage of brightly coloured velvets, paisleys, chintzes, and gaudy striped fabrics. His skin had that pink, clean-scrubbed look to it, his eyes freshly made up and his hair damp, coils springing out at strange angles, all gold and dark honey. He beamed at me, and I wondered where the hell (or wherever) he'd sprung from, where he went when he wasn't terrifying the living daylights out of me, and why—though I'd probably regret asking the question—he needed to use the bathroom at all....

"How'd it all go? What was he like?" Day passed behind me, an impish grin on his face. "You don't smell like cows. That's gotta be good, right?"

"How the heck would you know what I smell like?"

Damn. I hadn't intended to sound quite so accusatory. He shrugged in dismissal, and the fur boa (was it real? I wondered, then the irony made me smile) slid across his throat. It gave him, for a moment, just a hint of the Forties starlet.

I didn't intend to let that one go; it seemed, on top of everything, indescribably unfair to think that he could perceive the physical world in a way that I couldn't perceive him, but it really had been a long day.

"So you trashed my bathroom?"

He frowned and peered at the chaos. "Oh, yeah. Oops."

Raising his left hand, Damon snapped his fingers and, when the horrible sense of pressure lifted from my sinuses and I opened my eyes again, the bathroom was clean. The wet towels had landed in the laundry basket, the sink and bath shone, and the chrome sparkled. I detected a vague scent of lemon. He looked smug and, though I now felt the need to sit down, preferably in a darkened room with a packet of frozen peas on my head, I had to admit he'd impressed me.

"Nice," I said, proud of my measured tones and lack of excitement or, indeed, expletives.

"I have my uses."

"I'll bet. Um. I'm going to go and put the kettle on."

I stood the shampoo back on the side of the bath and headed off to make the coffee. It just seemed like the safest thing to do. In the kitchen, I felt him behind me, like a shiver outside of the body.

"Listen, I was thinking.... Why don't I take you out, baby?"

I turned, and he slunk around me, smile on his face.

"Whaddya say? Hmm?"

Hand on the fridge door, ready to fetch milk, I frowned. "Out?"

"Yeah. You deserve a break. And... well, y'know." Day gave me one of those semi-shrugs that affected complete nonchalance, though he couldn't quite meet my eye. He reached past me—ice on the shoreline and cold weather chills—and plucked the little blue leaflet off the front of the fridge. "I sorta thought it might be fun. Y'know?"

With darkly sinking dread, I looked at the bad block printing and exclamation marks on the flyer. I'd forgotten about Open Mic Night at The Crown.

"You want to play at my local? Tonight?"

"Well, if you don't wanna go, baby," he said with the hint of a pout. "I just thought maybe you'd like to come. Y'know. I'll buy you dinner an' everything. Show you how much I appreciate what you're doing. But if you're not in the mood...."

He folded the leaflet up and tucked it into his pocket, a picture of wounded feelings. I shook my head in something that didn't make it quite all the way to disbelief. So little left I found hard to believe, after all. Day gave me a sly look and raised his eyebrows.

"Well?"

I was tempted to poke fun. Oh, in an amiable way, of course... but to poke fun all the same. Did he really need it that much? Or did he just miss it? Either way, I knew I wouldn't refuse; I couldn't help but think of Mum. Dinner and a Damon Brent gig, all in the company of the man himself....

When I thought about it like that—thought about what he'd been, to her, and to Auntie Jan, Auntie Gail and all those other girls who should probably have known better—it seemed so ridiculous that I started to feel dizzy.

"All right," I said.

"Cosmic!" He shot me a disarming grin. "Well, 'course, I *say* buy... ain't got any bread, babe, so technically you'll be paying. But it's the thought that counts, right?"

I rolled my eyes.

* * *

Dinner turned out to be fish and chips on the prom, eaten out of oil-smudged paper as we idled away a few minutes en route to the pub. Day had given me time to take a hot bath and change. He'd been waiting at the door for me, a pair of cherry red platform boots added to his outfit and a guitar case slung over his shoulder. I looked quizzically at the latter, but he just smiled and started to question me about my interview with Joss.

I let him get away with it for a while but eventually I crumbled and, as we walked, I had to ask. The streetlights painted orange smears against the tarmac, and the occasional souped-up speedster throbbed past on the road. The salt smell of the sea seemed strong tonight.

"So, where'd you get that? The guitar, I mean."

Damon shot me a guilty look. "Does it matter?"

"I just wondered," I said as we side-stepped a knot of bright young things having life-changing emotional crises via their mobile phones. Shrieks of laughter and wails of tears rent the night. "I wondered how—"

He cleared his throat. I closed my eyes.

"You didn't nick it, did you?"

"No! Well, nah, not really."

"Oh, God…."

"Nah, babe, it's not like that. Chip?"

He offered me dibs from the greasy packet we were sharing. It wasn't exactly the sit-down dinner he'd promised me, but I couldn't afford that, especially if I was off up to London again at the end of the week. Turned out I'd had an email from Charlie Davies while I'd been out. Damon had been proud of himself for playing secretary and dealing with the computer (despite whatever he'd done to my printer… I suspected it would never work again), and I gathered from how snide he'd been about the string of letters after Charlie's name that he'd been at least a little bit impressed. Charlie had used his work address, from the clinic in Northwick Park, and seemed cautiously eager to meet me.

That in itself worried me.

"Thanks." I took a chip and bit into it thoughtfully. "So what is it like? If you didn't nick it?"

Damon wrinkled his nose. "Temp'ry liberation. I'm gonna take it back. Was only sitting in some dealer's back room, y'know. All padded up and not bein' played. Ain't right." He broke off a piece of battered plaice and offered the packet to me again. "And then, y'know, you see all these mass-produced things up on the wall, all plywood glued together…. I got talkin' to the bloke in the shop, and he says these days a '74 Deluxe goes for thousands." He scoffed and gesticulated with the bit of fish. "He *says*, right, girl: 'The music might've been shit, mate, but the guitars are well sought after.' Huh."

I winced. "Ouch."

"Yeah, well. What's that, uh… 'decade that taste forgot', yeah?"

I reached over and took another chip. Perhaps surprisingly, they were still warm. Walking beside him was still reminiscent of a bracing stroll on a tarn, but I supposed I'd been getting used to that.

"Taste is subjective," I said. "And we'll probably grow out of post-modernism soon. I wouldn't worry."

"Post-what?"

"Culturally sanctioned historical sarcasm," I said and reached in for a bit of fish. "Y'know. The ability to see how absolutely everything refers to everything else, but still fail to either declare your allegiance to something, or come up with anything truly original."

"Oh. Right."

Damon looked at me with that expression of faint… well, admiration. I wasn't used to it. I took another chip.

"Anyway," I said, chewing. "It wasn't all shit. The music."

He gave me a withering look and took the chips away.

"You're gonna pay for that, baby. I mean it! No… get off."

"Oh, come on. I'm hungry!"

He laughed. Not really thinking about it, I stuck out my foot and caught the back of his leg with my ankle. A split-second of cold, slimy fire slid up my spine and it felt a little bit like standing in semi-congealed jelly. I smelled something sweet, heavy and woody, and there was the solid shape of him, somewhere beneath the acreage of his patched flares. It was over quickly. Damon righted himself with barely a stumble, offered me a conciliatory chip, and we walked on, him chuckling and me pretending I hadn't felt slightly queasy.

"Nah," he said, after a minute. "I know what they mean. But they're wrong... it wasn't taste, y'know? It was forgettin' to stand up for anything. I mean, there was so much crap... a lot of black days, right? The strikes, and the unemployment. Inflation, the oil crisis. People were comin' into that, coming into knowing that you can't take the Man down, yeah? 'Cos even if you do, you become him. And when you got all that shit together, yeah, people wanted to forget about it. Escape. Music can do that."

I shot a sideways look at him, saw the complete faith in his face when he said that. It scared me.

"Thing is," he continued, "it's never just been about that. Y'know? Not just escaping, not just bein' something different. It's... it's everything. All the shit you can't put in words. And," he smiled at some distant memory, "fuck it, y'know, Leon was actually right... it shouldn't be an industry. But it is, and as soon as you're in it baby, y'know, they got their claws in. S'all about giving people what they want, makin' a buck, getting so bloody competitive, y'know? You lose perspective. Hah. Y'know, *that's* how David Bowie ended up with that song about the laughin' gnome, right? At least I never did anythin' like that."

"Fair point," I admitted.

We turned the corner, and The Crown loomed ahead, neon and laughter in the gloom. Ron and Jeremy were among the first faces I saw when we entered the pub. They descended on us with ruthless alacrity, which didn't surprise me; I knew I'd be in for a bollocking. What did get me was the way, quick as a blink, Damon Brent—in his Paradise Garage finery, with all his memories and all his tattered dreams—slid away somewhere, and Jack Yorke stood next to me, talking cheerfully to my neighbours.

"Oh, I didn't know you were a musician." Ron beamed.

Damon tipped a nonchalant little uni-shrug. "I dabble a bit."

I groaned inwardly. It just seemed like the sort of statement to come before a night I'd live to regret. Ron nodded encouragingly and, while he ran interference, Jerry slipped his hand through my arm and drew me aside.

"You all right now, are you, Ell?"

I grinned. "Um. Yes. Look, about the other day...."

He wrinkled his nose. "It doesn't matter. Did it help? The info? With your... book."

It wasn't so much how he said it, or what he said, but the unspoken dimension to it. The look in his eye in the dim electric light, the sound of his voice against the mediocre pub rock standard a local band had started flogging away at. I had an absurd flash of panic. Did he know?

No, he was just still pissed off with me. I *knew* that. Pissed off and a touch jealous. Jeremy and Ron had been friends of mine since I moved into the area, and Jerry could get territorial about relationships like ours. Freud might well have had a field day with it. I followed him to the table they'd already bagged, not far from the stage. The local band—fronted by an acne-speckled, red-headed kid of about eighteen—were groaning laboriously about a metaphorical train that never arrived at its destination. Ron got the beers in; I supposed Damon had gone to find knobs to twiddle and wiring to play with backstage, or whatever one had to do in these situations. I usually gave Open Mic Night as wide a berth as I did the monthly Karaoke Bonanza.

Jerry still kept trying to pump me for info. I tried to get by with the bare minimum of details; yes, it had been going well, yes, he'd helped immensely. No, we didn't have anything he could read yet. Yes, I'd share when we did. Of course I would. No, I hadn't known that... *Jack*... played the guitar. I gritted my teeth and went along with it, though my head was still spinning with motives and maybes, and all the things that Damon hadn't bothered to tell me; things that echoed, shapeless, in the shadows.

Who else had known he was courting other contracts? Was it enough to kill over? And what about Inez? Leon Fielding's words kept coming back to me:

All she got was the house and the money.

Had she? Could she have done it, when she hadn't arrived back at the house until so much later? And, if what Day had said was true, why had she come back? Had she wanted reconciliation, or just her suitcases? Suddenly, all my suspicions were overtaken by a single thought, one I should have had before now. Damn, I was a fucking idiot!

I couldn't stop seeing, nestled behind my eyes, the picture

from *The Mail*, pasted into Mum's scrapbook. My mother, Auntie Gail, and Auntie Jan, three pale faces behind a cordon. In front of them, Inez Blackman, the grief-stricken and newly widowed…what had Auntie Jan said? *There we were, and she shows up.*

I was an idiot. I hadn't even thought—how had Inez *known* to come back? Had she heard the news on the radio, had somebody called her? And why was it Charlie Davies holding her up?

Slowly, I became aware of Ron and Jeremy, both looking at me, waiting for some kind of response to something.

"Um," I said. "Yes?"

Jeremy elbowed me in the ribs. "You're hopeless," he chided. "Hopeless. Come *on*, we both want to know where you met—"

"Shh!" Ron hissed. "Look."

As the dutiful applause for the local band died away and Big Eric did his mein host thing on the dodgy microphone usually reserved for pub quiz night, I realised that Day was taking the stage and that, although the patrons probably didn't realise it themselves, every eye in the place was on him.

The 'temporarily liberated' guitar, now slung around his neck, drew lustful glances from the local band. Not surprising, as it was an early Seventies Gibson, probably promised to some yearning buyer who wanted it for long-term investment potential.

I watched the way he touched it as, picking through the muddle of cables, he strolled nonchalantly up to the mic.

"Hello," said Damon Brent, into the polite smattering of applause.

The wedding-disco spotlights, blue and yellow, glinted off the coils of his perm and the silk of his jacket. I couldn't help but glance around the room and marvel at the fact no one else seemed to be seeing what I did.

"You all right?" he said conversationally to the pub at large, picking across the first few notes of a Cmaj7 chord.

I shot a sly look at Jeremy and Ron, but got no clue as to what they saw, what they thought. They laughed along with his warm-up banter, just two in a sea of faces fixed on that coruscating figure. The insanity—the sheer ridiculous impossibility—of it started to shake me, and I wanted to laugh, but then Day began to play. I recognised the first song: *Likely Too Much*. It had been the B-side to *Darby & Joan*, one of Mum's favourite Brother Rush EPs, and I buried my nose in my beer, trying to pretend I couldn't hear every bright, jangly chord ringing out from my childhood.

> *I like to think it's likely that*
> *It's all a world we're dreamin'*
> *With purple spires and last chance hires*
> *And all things real are seemin'*
> *I like to think it likely that*
> *It's heaven when we touch*
> *But you know, honey, I think it's likely that*
> *I likely like it all too much!*

I'd not heard it played this way before, though. Well, obviously not, as I'd only ever heard Mum's copy, but I'd never heard *him* play like— I shook my head and sunk back into my drink. Oh, I'd been prepared for him to be good… and he was.

Very good, and he hit the kind of form that made the air sparkle. His voice, agile and more than easy on the ear, sought out all the cracks and corners of the room, spinning out into something solid and real.

All that I could have managed... I just hadn't been expecting him to be funny. But he had this sharp, self-deprecating humour in his delivery, the way he engaged his audience. And they *were* his. From the minute Damon started playing to the minute that he stopped—after two Eric Clapton covers, a rearrangement of Humble Pie's *79th Street Blues*, another Brother Rush B-side, and something I'd never heard before but which he winked at me during—the entire room belonged in the pocket of that eye-wateringly flashy jacket. He knew it, too. I could tell by the way he smiled as, chin tilted, he slid side-on up to the mic and purred:

"Thank you very much. G'night."

* * *

We left The Crown some substantial time later and wove through the gentle pools of the streetlights.

"I don't believe you!" I protested. "'Oh, just hit me up on MySpace'? You haven't even got a M— You haven't got a MySpace page, have you?"

Damon giggled. While Ron and Jeremy quizzed me on just how 'closely involved' we were, he'd joined the local band for a few drinks. Well, several drinks. He'd never seen jelly shooters before.

"I could have."

"No, you c— Look," I said with the intense seriousness of

someone who shouldn't really have had that third pint. "You can't have a comeback. Not now. I mean, c'mon, man... not even Lazarus pushed it that far!"

He looked at me for a minute before dissolving into sniggers, and I realised I'd called him 'man'. A tricked out Ford Escort with running lights and spinning hubcaps roared past us, and Damon wrinkled his nose, getting a grip on his giggles.

"Ain't no need gettin' all bliblical at me, babe."

"Blibical, eh?"

He snorted. "F— Y'know what I mean, darlin'. S'all.... Hey, Ellis?"

"Hm?"

He smiled lazily, digging his hands deep into his pockets as we rounded the corner. He didn't have the guitar anymore; he'd looked sad about it, but he'd reluctantly let it go. Hardest thing about the corporeal universe, he'd said. I had my hand in my pocket, too, already on my door key. Ordinarily, I wouldn't have walked home alone at this time of night; Ron and Jeremy would have fussed and made sure I didn't. Technically, I supposed— and so they had assumed—I wasn't alone. Damon did a little quickstep dance up the tiled path to my building; I smiled and wondered what good he'd be in a fight.

He turned to look at me, comfortably dishevelled and bright-eyed in the gloom. "You're all right. Y'know? You're... you're solid, baby. Somethin' else. You know what I mean? You are."

I laughed. I almost didn't notice the front door was open, either. My keys already clasped in my hand, we went in cautiously. Maybe it was the fact I'd been drinking and my reaction times weren't what they could have been, but my heart leapt in my throat, very nearly hand-in-hand with my dinner. I gasped and felt stupid about it when the dim, guttering bulb in the stairwell revealed the shape of the man who had the flat beneath mine. We knew each other to nod to, and occasionally pass the time of day, though I tended to try and avoid it.

Mr. Downstairs loitered on the bottom stair, one hand extended and resting on the newel post, the other held curled in the air in front of his face, forming a sort of telescope that he looked at us through. His beard, coarsely wispy and ginger, with hints of abandoned cornflake, reached the middle of his chest, although his head was completely shaved. A nicely executed tattoo of an ohm symbol had been inked over the shiny pink dome, and his ensemble, as usual, displayed curiously mixed influences. Tonight, there was a checked tweed jacket, a *Rocky Horror* t-shirt, and a pair of ripped blue jeans with a neon green belt and a pair of mismatched canvas deck shoes, in slightly different sizes. Mr. Downstairs was in the habit of wearing wristbands for several charities, extending between four and six deep up each arm. If he felt talkative and you couldn't get away fast enough, he would tell you why each of them needed to be supported and you would have to agree that, yes, they were all very worthy causes. I had heard that Mrs. Shah, in the garden flat, had once told him she only donated to animal charities, whereupon Mr. Downstairs had become distressed and thrown a flowerpot through her window.

Now, he lowered the telescope-hand, and his watery, boiled-gooseberry eyes were wide, his mouth half-open.

"You shouldn't be here," he said.

"Just going in," I said briskly. "Straight upstairs, that's me. Are you going out? I'll hold the front door for you."

"You shouldn't be here," he repeated, and I realised with rising dread that he wasn't looking at me.

"Ellis...."

I glanced over my shoulder. If Damon had sounded worried, he looked terrified. And, I realised, not just that. Not just scared, but somehow... paler, as if, in the right light, you could start to see through him. No, that was completely ridic— I stopped.

Oh, *shit*.

"Ellis," Day murmured again, "say somethin' to the man, girl. Yeah? Somethin', like, *nice*.... 'K?"

I swallowed. Mr. Downstairs wasn't moving, and he still blocked our path.

"We're, um, we're just going through," I said, struggling to keep the shake out of my voice. "Just going upstairs. I, er... I have the flat above you, don't I? It's nice to see you again. Don't think I've seen you for a few weeks, have I? Been keeping busy?"

As I spoke, I walked—with far more nonchalance than I thought I'd manage—up to the stairs, Damon following so close behind I was convinced my spine would end up freeze-dried. Mr. Downstairs still gazed at us with that look of pallid focus, but he moved aside a little, taking his hand from the newel post and leaning back against the wall. We edged up onto the first step, me still talking brightly, incessantly, trying to ignore the stale hash, beer, and sweat smell that rolled off my neighbour. Mr. Downstairs stood, silent and motionless, until we were almost past.

"You can't stay," he said with a terrible, quiet certainty. "Can't stay here. S'not your place."

Damon whimpered. We picked up the pace, all but legged it

up the stairs and piled into my flat, slamming the door behind us. My hand shook a little as I slid the chain on.

"It doesn't have to mean...." I began.

Finishing the sentence seemed irrelevant. Day had flung himself against the wall, lighting a cigarette like he was clutching at a life preserver in a stormy sea.

"Are you all right?"

He didn't look it. His cheeks hollowed, and the ciggie flared.

"That's not s'posed to happen," he said, pointing to the door. "That... that's dangerous, that's what that is."

I frowned. "What d'you mean? How can—hang on. What, if people see you for what you are, then...? It's like if someone says 'I don't believe in fairies', and somewhere Fairy Bluebell or whatever drops down with a massive coronary?"

Day shook his head. "Forget it. Don't matter. I can't...." He dredged up a smile for me. "You did bloody good though, girl. Stone cold mama, ain't ya?"

Despite myself, I had to fight down a blush. I should have known he wouldn't explain it. That made a certain sort of sense, though, when I thought about it; people like Mr. Downstairs, who patrolled the boundaries of a different reality than everyone else, would... *see*. And the observation of a thing not only changes it, but changes all reality.

My head snapped round at a noise in the other room. It took a moment before I traced it to the fire escape. Mr. Tibbs padded through, ignoring both of us, his tail raised high with the end kinked like a question mark.

Damon exhaled, the smoke spooled odourlessly around him, and he leaned his head back against the wall, shooting me a smile and a roll of his kohl-rimmed eyes.

"Bleedin' 'ell. Any gin left, baby?"

"Yes," I said, "But I'm making coffee. Some of us still have liver functions to be concerned about."

Chapter Thirteen

My interview date with Charlie Davies came round quicker than I'd hoped. I'd had to spend more time on campus, dropping into a few seminars and putting in some library time, trying to catch up on my work. Also, and most importantly, dodging Helena, my supervisor, who wanted to know where I'd been and where that chapter of my thesis she expected to be reviewing had got to. It all just felt so unreal now, that was the trouble. The fact that Damon took off for another day or so should have helped matters, but it didn't. It left me in a constant state of anticipation, always waiting to hear him, see him. Thinking didn't help, either. I found it hard to write cogent academic prose with all those questions about the nature of reality flitting around inside my head.

I'd tried calling Inez again. She hung up on me. Still, at least she hadn't threatened to phone the police or block my number. I supposed it could have been worse. I was still wondering how to phrase the questions I needed to ask about her when I got off the tube at Kensal Green station. I found a cab to get me to Charlie Davies' place and put up with listening to the driver's opinions about immigration, congestion charging, and everything in between until we arrived at what, for all the world, looked like the overgrown entrance to some kind of secret garden.

Kensal Green Moorings, tucked in at the top end of Ladbroke Grove and at the far end of the Grand Union Canal, held eight residential berths and, frankly, wasn't the sort of place I was used to finding hidden away in London. I picked my way around the gate and found myself on a narrow walkway, cracked paving stones underfoot and a mellow brick wall to one side. Abandoned clay flowerpots, crops of dandelions, and stray sweepings of gravel littered the path. The air was richer, with that slight hint of ozone and bilge that spoke of the river, growing stronger as I reached the end of the walkway and came out onto the moorings proper.

Damon had tried to explain about places like this. How the city had its hidden corners, its villages, and its enclaves within enclaves. He'd said I ought to get it, living in Kemp Town; same kind of thing, he assured me, just on a bigger scale. Standing with my back to the bridge, the noise of the traffic echoing above me, I wondered which boat belonged to Charlie. His last email, confirming our appointment, had said I would find him aboard *Curly Sue* but, right now, that didn't really help. I passed two boats that were what I thought of as the conventional thing to find on a canal—long and vaguely rectangular, with all that brightly coloured curlicue artwork— and noticed that they each had mini gardens on the mooring.

Here, two white plastic chairs and a coloured glass lantern on a white plastic table. There, terracotta troughs stuffed with a selection of herbs and salad leaves. Further along the mooring, I spotted something that looked suspiciously like a pergola.

Berthed beside the pergola was a long, low boat that didn't look anything like the barges. A simple black and white paint job kept it—*her*—looking clean, and she had a somehow more streamlined profile than her neighbours. As I got closer, I noticed a figure bent over her midsection, presumably doing something esoteric with knots. All I could see of him was a broad back clad in a striped blue and grey hoodie, a scuffed and muddy pair of black wellies and, between the two, an elderly, baggy pair of blue jeans.

"Mr. Davies?" I enquired tentatively, picking my way past a mosaic bistro table with a cardboard box full of empty wine bottles on it and four wrought iron chairs stacked nearby.

Charlie straightened up and turned to look at me, wiping his hands on his jeans. A half-smoked cigarette dangled from his lips. As his staff photo from the clinic had shown, he'd aged, but he was still a big man. I put him at around six foot three and, though most of his bulk had dropped to a paunch and the outline of his face had slackened, he still cut an imposing figure.

"Miss Ross," he said, coming up to me with something a little like a slow swagger. "Nice to meet you at last."

His handshake was solid, firm, the hand itself dry and rough. His face, as he looked me over, showed wary scepticism, for which I supposed I couldn't blame him.

"Blimey," he said, cracking a smile around the ciggie, "I know you said you were a student, but I didn't expect you to be quite so young."

"Flattery gets you everywhere," I said with a grin, and he chuckled.

"Yeah? Well, in that case, you'd better come in. Like I said," he added, flicking the ciggie into the river, "I hope you don't mind me dragging you up here, only I really couldn't see any other time we were going to be able to meet. I have a pretty heavy week at the clinic and, to be honest, I don't really like shoutin' my past around up there anyway, d'you know what I mean?"

I took that one with a pinch of salt. Charlie stepped easily aboard *Curly Sue* and, seeing as I must have looked rather uncomfortable, offered me his hand. I took it and let him ease me onto the... deck? It was hardly that, just a narrow ledge that led down to a low doorway and, to my surprise, a very comfortable living area.

"She's a Lee & Stort widebeam tug," he explained. "Built in the Twenties, converted in the Nineties. Doesn't look bad for her age, eh? 'Course, she was liveable when I bought her, a couple of years back, but I've been doing a full refurb, so I'm pretty much here all the time at the weekends. Just seemed the easiest way to do this. So... welcome to the humble abode," he said, gesturing tangentially to the thick-varnished woodwork and cream walls of the boat's interior.

Bijou but comfortable, it smelled of fresh paint and cigarette smoke. Two well-loved, two-seater leather sofas were arranged around a glass-topped coffee table, which had a glass ashtray and a glossy book about Thai cookery on it. Up against one wall, there was a small TV, a stereo, and a narrow bookshelf which held—on the most cursory examination—some medical and psychological volumes, a few box files, and a couple of cheap thrillers. A potted spider plant hung from the ceiling and, on the walls, I noticed some framed black-and-white photos and... yes, at least one gold disc. Somehow, I wasn't surprised.

A little wood burning stove stood in one corner and, beyond that, what apparently served as the galley, at least for the duration of *Sue*'s aforementioned refit. A mini-fridge and mini-oven supported a short length of off-cut melamine worktop. Above it, a wooden spice rack bulged with whole-wheat rice and pasta, cellophane noodles, and all the other things that would normally live in cupboards. A selection of steel pots and pans hung from a rack, while a brass-faced clock ticked softly from the wall.

"Thank you," I said, impressed, despite the nagging sensation of claustrophobia.

The living space was open-plan and well-equipped, if a little unfinished. Charlie said he had a fixed double bedroom, a study, and a second berth further aft, plus more space in the old engine room, leftover from *Sue*'s days as a working tug. Together with the cosy little space in which we now sat, plus the brick terrace and the garden on shore, he reckoned *Sue* held more than enough space for him, plus being a neat circumvention of the London property market.

"You're not married?" I asked casually.

"Divorced," he said, filling the kettle. "Twice, actually. One grown-up daughter, one son... not so grown-up. Grandkid, too, now." He laughed, took a pack of cigarettes from the pocket of his jeans, and came to sit back down. "Mental, isn't it? And here you are, talking about—Christ!—thirty-odd years ago. Long time. D'you mind, Miss Ross," he added, a gesture of not-quite-respect, as he put a fresh cigarette to his lips, "if I ask why? I mean, seriously, what on earth made you want to write about Damon Brent? You couldn't even have been born."

I laughed politely and tossed out the spiel I felt glad I'd been getting used to—the imaginary thesis, the interest in celebrity and public reactions to death—and watched his face while I did it. Oh, he was good, I didn't doubt that. On the surface, he listened, responded, made the right social noises and the right expressions but, beneath that, those green eyes clocked everything I did and said. Voice, body language... I was being analysed, and it started to shake me.

"Well," Charlie said eventually, leaning forward to pull a glass ashtray across the table. "That's very laudable. Very interesting. My daughter, Mel, she went to Keele. Spent three years doing an English degree and still ended up working as a data entry clerk in some poxy office."

I smiled, set up my recorder, and tried not to get irate. The way he did it—the way he never quite used phrases such like 'pretty little head', even if he seemed to be thinking them— infuriated me, yes, but more than that.... It was as if he *knew* it irritated me and he used that to keep me off balance.

I'd always hated those kinds of games.

"I hoped," I said, deciding to take charge of the thing, however much that seemed to amuse him, "that you'd be able to fill in some of the background for me. To start with, anyway. I understand you once played at the Crawdaddy Club?"

"Blimey... yeah, I did. Briefly. Late in '64, not long before it closed. Eel Pie Island too. Yeah," he said again, took a pull on his cigarette, and nodded.

He had, Charlie was keen to tell me, played with the greats. He'd gigged at iconic venues with a succession of bands that had never really come to much, but he'd *been* there. He'd jammed with Keith, Rod, Eric... he'd been places, known faces, made connections, but never quite seemed to find himself in the right place at the right time.

"I met Cris McIlroy," he said, bringing in thick ceramic mugs full of the kind of orange tea that normally requires a poorly cleaned urn and a couple of weeks to brew, "in, uh, prob'ly about September, 1970. I was in a band called Roman's Handle at the time; you won't have heard of us. Broke up after Christmas... we really weren't going anywhere. Cris had seen us at a gig, though, come up and said to me, y'know, nice job. He called me, after the thing had split, said was I interested in cutting a couple of demos? Of course, I said yes... ended up spending the weekend at his place in Chelsea. We recorded the whole thing in his bathroom—for the acoustics, yeah?—him running this deck in on an extension cord, all this stuff banked up. Eccentric wasn't the word, right? Very effective, though. I still got the tapes around somewhere. Of course, nothing ever came of it."

"So, wait, you were originally a solo artist?"

Charlie looked at me, a faintly sarcastic smile on his face, as if he'd expected absolutely nothing less than that I wouldn't know. I could have kicked myself.

"That's right. Never really took off, though. I mean, maybe a few years earlier, even a few years later I'd have done better, but...." He chuckled dryly. "What I'm saying is, Nick Drake never shifted more than a couple of thousand copies of *Pink Moon* in his lifetime, and I wasn't any kind of Nick Drake. Y'know what I mean? No, when Cris said he wanted me to meet with Damon and Leon, I was more than happy to give it a shot."

He told me about those early sessions as we drank the tea, and he seemed to relax tremendously. I found that confusing—Charlie Davies looked to me to be a man totally at ease in his own skin—until I realised that what he'd relaxed about was me. I'd done something, said something... whatever it had been, he regarded me with a less calculated kind of consideration. I had been, I felt, assessed and judged harmless. My first thought was to be slightly pissed off by that, until I realised that it gave me the upper hand and a potential element of surprise.

The pictures that Charlie painted were vivid, and beautiful, in a lot of ways. They'd all been young, he said, though him perhaps not quite so much; he'd had a couple of years on the other three. They'd all been talented. He talked theory for several minutes, for the benefit of my book, about the harmonics, the range of Damon's voice, Leon's impeccable timing and cluster chords, and how he'd always thought Joss could have been a drum prodigy of Jerry Shirley proportions, given the right gentle guidance. Those early days, rehearsing at the place near Grove Park, not far from the river, feeling the whole thing coming together, the elation of that sudden clarity, that 'oh, so *that's* what it's meant to sound like' moment... he made that time sound halcyon.

It jarred me when Charlie told the same skinny-dipping anecdote that Joss had shared. How, one summer evening, finishing up late at the rehearsal studio, when everyone had been complaining about the heat and the stuffiness of the room, Damon had said it would be nice to go swimming. How he'd bet that they wouldn't have the balls and how—howling with laughter and hot-footing it like schoolboys—they'd leapt into the river, naked in the soft air.

It had, unfortunately, been before the concerted campaign to clean up the Thames, but it had still been one of those memories that stuck with you. A bit like the more unsavoury floating things did, but hey, they'd been young, immortal, and maybe a little bit stoned… and they hadn't got caught.

"We did feel invincible," Charlie said, knocking ash off his cigarette and clearing his throat. I heard the smoker's rattle deep in his chest. "We signed the contract with Garten Records, we had Maxwell Vost on board, producing *Rush Hour*, our first LP. We spent the whole summer of 1971 playing festivals, gigging a couple of times a week at clubs we prob'ly couldn't even have got into before, y'know what I mean? Of course, the direction did change a bit between then and '72."

I raised an eyebrow. "Do you mean for the band, or in the sense of the music scene in general?" I asked, slowly crossing my legs.

"Oh, generally," Charlie said, glancing at my face instead of my knees for a moment. "Well, no. Yes. Both, really. We reacted to external circumstances, I mean. Well, the label did. Y'know when T. Rex did *Ride a White Swan* on *Top of the Pops* and Marc had th-the glitter?"

He gestured vaguely to his eyes before reaching for the cigarette he'd left smouldering in the ashtray. I nodded. Of course I knew that performance; as a child, Mum had also made me sit through the entirety of her *Born to Boogie* video. It had been excruciating.

"Well," Charlie continued, "it was weird, in a way. Just opened some sort of repressed pop culture flood gate. I swear, next thing you know, we'd somehow ended up with bands like Angel and The Sweet. Sweet were massive in the Midlands, y'know, long before anybody even *mentioned* Mike Chapman. We underwent a pretty similar repackaging, I suppose you'd say." He smiled and pulled back on whatever tirade had been on his lips. "But at least nobody ever suggested getting us dressed up like Native American chiefs."

I chuckled, and he appeared happy to let it pass off as a joke. When I tried to push it further, he resisted.

"So, would you say you were dumbed down?"

"Hmmnn…." Charlie pulled a face. "Not exactly. Not in those words. We—well, we were musical Luddites, in a way. D'you know what I mean?"

"Luddites?"

I struggled to keep the snigger from my voice as he nodded, all intense honesty and carefully considered responses. That seemed to be the thing with Charlie: he spoke easily, fluidly and —I suspected—with all the paper sincerity of a televangelist. I hoped I was wrong.

"Oh, yeah. I mean, that's what glam was, Miss Ross. Deconstruction, demystifying the form. You strip it all back, it's just a simple four on the floor, everything forward in the rhythm, no pretences and just let it all go. Good, honest rock 'n' roll," he said—the very words I'd heard Mum use more than once.

It felt, for a moment, as if *Curly Sue* rocked gently in her moorings. I'd been prepared for it—I knew about the movements of boats and I didn't have a problem with them— but it still took me by surprise, as if we'd moved in time and space. That trivial little lurch, a tiny listing of the world that, just for a moment, made me catch my breath.

"You don't get seasick, do you, love?" Charlie asked with

that smug, slightly slimy smile.

I shook my head and prodded him gently back to where we'd been. Charlie happily carried on, talking about how, sure, glam might have meant what Brother Rush had done was take an easier route, and how—in retrospect—it probably had held a generation of talented musicians back at least a couple of years.

"Take Leon, for example," he said, sipping the last of his tea. "Now, we haven't seen each other in God knows how long, but I've heard some of the stuff he's done recently, and it's great. Y'know? It is. But he's had to do a hell of a lot of growing up to get there. I mean, when we were playing together, if you'd handed him a sheet with 'ad lib Ionian' on it, he'd have taken it as 'spend ten minutes playin' out of tune'. Y'know what I mean?"

He inclined his head a little to the side, encouraging me to nod and say, yes, I did; encouraging me to believe that, by default, if the young Leon Fielding had been musically naïve, then Charlie had known everything from the get-go. I wasn't sure I liked where this looked headed.

"Thirty years is quite a lot of practice time, though," I said, and Charlie looked—for a very brief moment—piqued.

"Well, that's my point," he said, a trifle brusquely. "Back then, we weren't even remotely encouraged to grow as artists. It was simply a case of sticking to the formula… certainly as far as the management was concerned, yeah? It was the whole attitude. Makes you lazy. Lazy and frustrated. I mean, and this is very relevant for you, I know Damon certainly was. Frustrated, I mean."

"Oh?"

I sipped my tea. Outside, a light rain had begun to patter

against the reclaimed brick terrace. It misted on the window, fine as needles. Charlie crushed his cigarette out in the glass ashtray and cleared his throat.

"Yeah. I mean, the first eighteen months we were together, y'know, when we were gigging, it was either covers or staff writers' stuff, then *Saturday Loving* charted high, and—"

"He co-wrote that with Leon Fielding, yes."

"That's right, and it was a real confidence boost," Charlie said, a little too kindly. "Only, 'course, I think Damon believed that meant there'd be more autonomy. Like, all of a sudden, they were Lennon and McCartney in loon pants, yeah? He got pissed off when he realised success didn't equal freedom and then... y'know, early in '73 we landed a hit with *Dance Me Down*, and that was such a bloody *dog*, that record. But it sold, because it was what the kids wanted. Bubblegum music, y'know what I mean? We, huh," he laughed bitterly, "we were still playing that bloody song the year he died, and we all hated the damn thing. Cheap music," he added dismissively, reminding me of Noël Coward's sentiments on the subject.

Cheap, but potent; Brother Rush had, I remembered, had a run of songs like that between '73 and '75. Three minute sweaty-palmed electric boogies, effervescent but not exactly cerebral. The surprises usually lurked on the B-sides—tautly quivering pop torches like *Only a Woman (Does It That Way)*, raunchy all-out blues standards like *Alone With Me*, and even the occasional ballad—and Mum'd had the lot on vinyl, treasuring every bend and lick.

"Thing was," Charlie said, "it's a difficult position to be in. Knowing that, potentially, all you've really got to do is put your name on something and you can ride it all the way to the bank.

Anybody'd be taken the same way," he added magnanimously. "'Cos, however much you wanna be a serious musician, you still have to pay the bills. D'you know what I mean?"

I nodded.

"And," I said, silently thanking Joss Napier for explaining to me how contractual recoupment worked, "you were obligated to recoup out of the royalties, of course."

"Exactly." Charlie grimaced. "So... lazy, 'cos you want the cash. Frustrated, 'cos you know you can do better. You know you can do more. That, uh... that hunger you have when you're still trying to make it. That never really goes away, you know. Of course, it was all a bit of a dichotomy for Damon, once we started chipping away at the big time."

"A dichotomy?" I echoed. "Wh—"

"We-eeell... Damon had a tendency to believe his own hype. Y'know. How many lead singers does it take to change a lightbulb?" Charlie asked rhetorically, raising a thick index finger. "One. But he can't screw it in. No, he just holds it up and waits for the fitting to revolve around him."

That raised a smile, and then I felt guilty about tittering.

But why shouldn't I laugh? After all, Charlie had a point. Day *was* a bit of an egotistical prick, and he'd probably been worse when he was alive. I listened to the sound of that in my head and blinked. Concentrate. That was the thing. Just keep concentrating.... Outside, the wind had started getting up, and water slapped against the boat's hull.

"So," I said, "it was an ego thing?"

Charlie shrugged. "After '75—well, perhaps it started earlier—it's no secret, we did start to find there was more tension in the ranks. It came to a head after the *Rush On Love*

LP came out, December that year. I'm not saying, before that, we never had disagreements, never got pulled in different directions—we wouldn't have been normal if we hadn't—but that last album.... Well, I'm sure you'll agree the sound's changed, yeah?"

I nodded. Fair point. A harder, rockier drive, moving away from so many catchy riffs and bouncy beats. The re-issued, extended disc I'd bought Mum had a compendium of live cuts on it, too, full of pulsing bass lines and searing guitar work, with vocals that blistered the air. Some of the last live recordings they'd ever done.

"Well, Damon pushed for royalty re-negotiations off the back of that. And he got 'em. Made him cocky. Had him thinkin' he held all our futures in his hand, for a while. Not that he was ever one for rocking the boat, so to speak. Not so long as we were still making money and he was still getting his rocks off to an audience, y'know what I mean? Obviously, Leon wouldn't have said a word against it.... Let's face it, if Damon had told him to jump off a cliff, the only thing he'd've said was 'where d'you want me to land?', but I know they did squabble a bit with material." He leaned back against the leather sofa, spread his arms along its length, and fixed me with a coyly conspiratorial gaze. "You are aware that a lot of their jointly credited material came mostly from Leon, right? Songs like, oh, *Love You (Like a Brother)*, *You Don't Say*, *One More Night*... they were all almost entirely his. Yet he never got a straight split with Day on the rights."

I tried not to show that he'd surprised me. All the same, I felt Charlie watching me, scouting out a reaction, any hint of a fractured or fallen idol. If he knew the truth, I suspected he'd be a damn sight less confident in his little exposé. Still, he seemed to be enjoying himself.

"*Come On Back*, that was Leon's too," he added with a slight trace of triumph. "Of course, Joss and I had input on everything at some stage or other, and then there was all the production process, but in terms of actual writing output—"

"But you wrote as well?" I cut across him, because I was having trouble putting up with this smug, smarmy performance. And, if I was honest with myself, also because I had trouble with the fact that, when I had spoken with Fielding, he'd never mentioned any of this. "I believe, um, the *Smoke Gardens* LP of '74, that was largely your work?"

A low blow, I knew. Damon had told me about how badly that disc had bombed, how much backbiting, sniping, and general bitching there had been in its making. I'd even had to look hard to find it in Mum's collection.

"The British public really weren't ready for a conceptual album," Charlie said airily. "Not of that nature. And, to be honest, I should have realised it wouldn't fit with the market we had at the time. But you live and learn. Can I offer you another cup of tea, Miss Ross?"

His arrogance astonished me. Not, I thought, for its depth, its breadth, or any simple distinguishing feature, but for the way it blossomed from him so fluidly. I decided that this was the right time.

"Please," I said and then, just as he got up: "Of course, I believe you did have some personal problems at the time you were working on that project. Problems you had to face very publicly, in the end. That must have been difficult."

He halted, mid-rise, and I saw the look on his face: part

irritation, part acceptance. He'd known we'd talk about this, of course he had. With the work he did now, all the things he'd said in the past, how could we not? He still didn't look happy about it.

"I mean, it really must have been hard," I pressed. "That level of scrutiny. To be constantly under that kind of pressure, that kind of unfair judgement."

Charlie laughed. It sounded forced. He dusted his hand against his jeans and, taking my mug, went to make more tea.

"Oh, Christ. You're very thorough, aren't you? I thought we were just here to talk about Damon," he said, gently reproachful from the galley.

"Well, you went on record," I said, making pretence of glancing at my notepad, "as saying you believed his death was basically a direct result of drug abuse. W—"

"It was," Charlie said. "Definitely."

For once, I didn't so much mind being interrupted. The hollowness in his voice caught my attention. He turned to look at me, leaned against the rocky melamine worktop, and pulled out his pack of cigarettes. He put a fresh one in his mouth where, unlit, it drooped archly against his lip.

"I mean, he was wasted, and he fell and he hit his head." Charlie counted off on his fingers. "It's pretty basic reasoning, excuse me for saying so, that if he hadn't been stoned, he wouldn't have smacked his head. Right? As far as I can see, Miss Ross, that's pretty cut and dried."

He took a translucent purple lighter from his pocket and struck a flame, then sucked on the cigarette. I looked at him for a long moment, as if I could somehow see inside him, see whether he really did believe that. It sounded as if he did, but that wasn't an effective guide. I thought I saw something... desperate, perhaps, in his eyes. Like Charlie kept himself sane by clinging to a carefully constructed, carefully nurtured truth.

"It's fair enough, I s'pose," he said. "You asking about that. Have.... I mean, I don't know how far you are into this, who you've spoken to already. I'm not about to start listing off who took what with who or anything, but obviously, yeah, there was a lot of it about."

I kept my face blank as he made hard drugs sound like a bad head cold and thanked him for the tea he set down on the table.

"I'd started getting into coke by the beginning of '73. Before that, I used to mainly take amphetamines... you gotta remember, there was a different culture around it. I mean, up into the Sixties, doctors were still doling 'em out like sweeties for everything up to and including weight loss for teenage girls. The odd pep pill wasn't really.... Well, it's what we'd call a gateway drug today. Y'know what I mean? It's much easier to internally normalise the use of things like uppers and downers as an extension of licit drug use... just the same as you might say, 'oh, y'know, it's been a really bad day, I'll have a glass of wine' or 'I'm really tense, I need a cigarette'. You're not, like, setting out to score in the same way as you do with high tariff drugs like coke or heroin, but the very fact you're internalising it *as* normal makes moving into that side of things that bit easier."

I nodded and had to admit that I liked his candour. No hedging around it, no self-justification. The professional in today's Charlie came out to play, a determined set to his face.

"Y'know," he said, taking a drag on his cigarette, "you start looking for a bigger hit, you start getting sucked into the world. With me, the fact I'd regularly used stimulants increased my addictive liability, though for a while it was purely recreational. Y'know. I wasn't, like, thinking about it all the time, always needing to— Not at first."

He glanced out of the window, avoiding my eye. The brass clock ticked into the stillness and, somewhere, rainwater gurgled as it trickled through guttering.

"So, you're saying it tied in with the band's success?" I prompted.

"In a way, yeah. It's always been that aspect of human nature that gets people in that world, I think.... You know, you find yourself in this bubble, and it's very hard to keep grounded, so you start to do things just because you can."

"Like a loss of perspective?"

"Yeah." He nodded fervently. "Yes, that's very much it. And then, once you lose that, it starts taking over. An' it's not just recreational anymore. You're thinking about it more and more, 'til there's nothing else in your head, and nothing else is that important. Even when you're not actually using, you're doing the next best thing, 'cos you're thinking about when and how you're gonna score, what it's gonna be like...."

"So, you mean, a sort of distortion of your motivational processes?"

I cringed inwardly as I threw his own jargon back at him, though I wasn't sure he even recognised it as jargon anymore. Before this week, I hadn't even known there was such a thing as addiction studies. Mentally, I thanked my university library for its many foundation-level texts. Charlie looked at me with a new light in his eyes; the joy of realising he had someone here with whom he could not only talk shop, but see his opinions in print.

"Exactly! 'Cos, y'know, physical and psychological addiction are two totally distinct things… even if your body can take the downs, and withdrawal isn't an issue in why you use, you can still have that subjective awareness of the compulsion to do it. I mean, sure, there's a huge range of inter- and intra-personal factors involved in addiction liability; you can be using in a purely hedonistic way over the long-term and still not really have what's classed as an *addictive* problem…. Like Damon. Y'know? He dabbled, but he never really got hooked on anything, though he definitely used drugs as a crutch. Pretty much for as long as I knew him."

I thought of what Day had said to me: *You had to keep up, be amped, all the time, so you pop a couple of hearts here, a bomber there….* I thought of the way he'd talked about how pills segued into coke, and how easy it was for coke to segue into heroin and how, once that happened, you were seriously fucked.

I found him passed out with a needle in his bleedin' arm.

Something I couldn't quite identify loitered in Charlie's expression as he sipped his tea. It might have been the careful blankness, the studied calm that I could so easily picture him applying to his clients.

"The culture was certainly endemic," I ventured.

"It was worse than that," Charlie popped back. "It was fashionable."

He took a pull on his cigarette, and I actually found the way the smell of the smoke enveloped us comforting. Sort of a relief to see physics behaving as it should, though I had to suppress a cough. Charlie leaned over and levered open one of the windows. Outside, rain beat against the bricks, slipping down to the water like a scattered glissando. The traffic noise, cars swishing on the damp road, seemed more distant than it should do, knowing how close to the centre of Notting Hill we really were.

"I mean," Charlie said, frowning into the depths of some memory or other, "that song Damon wrote—don't know if you know it, it was never released—*Tuesday Afternoon Swoon*, that was all about injecting heroin."

I blinked, because I had to admit I hadn't seen that one coming, and Charlie saw me. He thought he'd shocked me, and a little smile twisted his mouth.

"'Brown-eyed girls make me weak / Make it so I just can't sleep,'" he quoted, leaning forward to knock ash off his cigarette. "'Slipping and sliding away / I just swoon the whole of Tuesday afternoon'. I think that was how it went."

I raised an eyebrow, and he shrugged, apparently amused.

"Well, Damon was never exactly subtle. Brown-eyed girl... 'cos heroin works on the brain pretty much like sex does, chemically speaking, and it came as China brown, y'know, powder. Slipping and sliding, that's the way the needle— Well, it's all pretty self-explanatory, really," he finished, returning to his cigarette. "And, like I say, hardly subtle. Cris went ballistic, wouldn't let us put it out."

I sipped my tea, found an appropriate, non-committal response to make, let him think he'd scandalized me at least a little bit, and listened to the obligatory anecdotes of decadent self-destruction. Talking about 1974, the year he felt his use had turned to serious abuse, Charlie got almost wistful. It was interesting to hear him talk about it. Far from the saccharine drivel he'd spouted in the papers, he seemed calm now. Relaxed, in a strange sort of way.

I only caught a flash of his anger once, when he talked about how Damon had—as he put it—got him into rehab for the first time.

"It was at that point I think everyone realised I had a problem. Y'know. 'Cos when I was on the junk, I didn't function as well as I could just using coke, or pills... and I was using it more. We.... On the tour that year, the first time we did Holland... we all went a little bit crazy. D'you know what I mean?"

I wondered if I should tell him I'd heard about Amsterdam, but part of me wanted to hear it from Charlie's side.

"Well, there must have been temptations," I said, re-crossing my legs.

He gave a bitter chuckle. "Yeah, and I don't remember most of 'em. I know I came back with crabs, though. We, uh, yeah.... Damon and me scored some shit and had ourselves a little party at the hotel. Thought we were really big men, I s'pose.... Of course, I was the only one that went on using regularly. The only one who ended up in rehab. No, 'cos *he* never—"

I jumped in quickly, taking a gamble while he still choked down that mistake, that little burst of ire.

"He found you, didn't he? In '74, at your flat."

Charlie stared at me. Shock, guilt, and a thick, dark anger danced over his face in one cloudy instant. I thought I'd screwed up massively, using that, but I'd wanted to catch him, trip him up, make him—

"How'd you know about that?" he demanded, his voice a little hoarse, even when he cleared his throat. "You, uh, you been talkin' to Inez?"

"I can't really reveal sources," I said and smiled, trying to look compassionate and understanding.

I wasn't sure it worked, because he started giving me real daggers, but I didn't care. *You've been talking to Inez*. Now, why would he assume that?

"All we ever released about that was that I decided to go into the clinic. For my own good," Charlie said flatly. "Didn't work. Not in the long run. It took years…. You see, Miss Ross, people will tell you it's about wanting to stop, but it's not. It's the day you wake up and you realise you don't want to be like this anymore—you don't want to be high, or pissed, or reliant on something just to get through—but you can't stop on your own. You *can't* change. To be brutally honest, it's the day it isn't fun anymore. D'you see what I mean?"

He took a drag on the cigarette and exhaled slowly, pausing to give a low cough. He glanced at me, then the ciggie in his fingers. I realised, with slight alarm, that I couldn't stop the sardonic upwards creep of my eyebrow, but Charlie smiled at me.

"Yeah, I know… I know." He cleared his throat again, heaving with that gut-deep rattle. "See, the point is, I was losing control. And, yes, I prob'ly do owe my life to the fact that Damon stepped in like he did. I mean, I wasn't OD'ing or anything." He glanced at my recorder, and I thought—just for a second—toted a deep, sour resentment in his voice. "But he came round, found me shooting up, saw the state of the place, decided it all had to stop. Made it a bit of a project. Very bleeding heart. Ironic, really, that it was him that ended up dead, isn't it?"

He leaned forward and knocked the ash off his cigarette, the spiteful cynicism that dripped from his words rapidly replaced by that cool, professional tone. As if it had never happened.

"Anyway, that's one way of looking at it."

"So, you don't think that your work was affec—" I began, aware that possibly now wasn't the best time to challenge him, but thinking of what Damon had said about Charlie's long absences, failures to show up for rehearsals and recordings.

He cut across me, hotly dismissive, green eyes anthracite hard.

"Y'know what, Miss Ross? I've done all the justifying and the confessing and the penance and every-fucking-thing, excuse me, and I'm not going to keep doing it."

Okay, so that put me in my place. Charlie sat back and took a long drag on his cigarette. He exhaled, and smoke wreathed his head. I cleared my throat, reaching around for some sort of conciliatory response, but he spoke again before I got there, back to that calm, considered monologue that I couldn't help but wonder if he'd rehearsed.

"I mean, to be frank, I was never more focused than when I was doing speedballs. Psychomotor stimulants'll do that to you. But, like I said, that kind of use is very different to the place I ended up in. And it was true, what I said in those interviews. It was what happened to Damon that really cleaned me up, in the end. I mean, I didn't just get up the next day and swear never to take another line... it took time, and I tried a lot of stuff. Cold turkey, twelve step, even lofexidine and all that crap. I'm not going to say it wasn't a fight, and there were a hell of a lot of casualties along the way. My first wife left me, I lost a lot of friends...."

Had Inez been among them? I searched for a way to turn the conversation to her as subtly as I could. Rain thudded dully against the window, jagged rivulets streaking the glass. After a moment, Charlie sniffed philosophically.

"I mean, the other week, my daughter was asking me about *Top of the Pops*. You know, they have all those archive footage programmes and... well, Melanie's got a little girl of her own now. Amy. She's five, and Mel was watching one with her, wanted to show her," he laughed dryly, "what ol' Granddad used to get up to. Sad thing is, there's parts I really don't remember. I mean, when Mel was born, in '82, I was still on the junk, off and on. I only really finally got my act cleaned up when she was about the age Amy is now. What she wanted to know about, the performance they'd seen, I just couldn't pin any details to it. In the end, we had to look it up on the bloody internet."

I nodded, sympathetic and understanding. He talked, for a brief, vulnerable minute, about how different everything got when you had a child, how the burden of a little bundle of responsibilities outside of yourself changed every piece of perspective you thought you had. I genuinely felt for him, but it didn't stop me having an idea.

"So, um," I said as we drifted back to the matter in hand, the alleged reason for my presence. "You were saying about how you felt things were in '74... it was the summer of that year Damon married Inez Blackman, right? How did that impact the band?"

I wanted to see his reaction, but he didn't give me a damn thing. Just a quick blink, a half second's pause before he answered.

"Oh, Inez...? She was great. I mean, Damon always had a pretty girl on his, uh, arm... but *she* was a real class act. I think he liked the challenge too, y'know?"

"You mean he had to pursue her?"

Charlie smiled and shook his head. "No, not.... Well, just that, y'know, you have a certain kind of woman you normally find yourself taking a pick from. Especially the way things were then. We were spending a fair amount of time on the road, there was a lot of stuff happening... you didn't meet a lot of very balanced people, you know what I mean? And Inez wasn't like those girls. She was a serious athlete, for one thing."

He took a long drag on his cigarette. His gaze drifted over the tape recorder again, and I wondered where to play my trump card.

"It was still tough to be a woman player, I guess," Charlie said after a minute. "You know? Billie Jean might have won the battle of the sexes, but it was still girls like Chris Evert that caught the public imagination. Well, Inez just never had that kind of press. Until she and Damon got hitched, of course."

I nodded, choosing my tone and my moment with care.

"And how would you say their relationship was?"

Charlie looked at me carefully, that cautious expression I'd got depressingly used to seeing these days. If only people would just hide their own secrets, instead of trying to keep a lid on everybody else's.

"Well, fine. Obviously. It was good."

Liar liar, pants on fire....

"It couldn't have been easy, though," I said. "Got to be hard on any marriage. The pressure of touring, of...." The look on his face told me I was losing him. Shit. I decided to bring my big guns forward. "I mean, it must've intensified everything. For example, when Inez had her miscarriage in May of '76. That must have been very hard, and then, of course, the injury, coming so soon after...."

I let my words hang in the air, digesting what I'd just seen. On the word 'miscarriage', Charlie's cigarette dropped in his lips. He blanched and blinked rapidly before he answered. I fought down the urge to clap my hands.

He hadn't known.

"I, uh," he started, thoroughly wrong-footed. "I mean, that's a very personal thing for anybody. I wouldn't like to... y'know, it must have been tough. I actually didn't know she—just before the injury? God. Poor Inez."

I'd been ready for him, watching and waiting. And now I had him. It felt great, for all the pain I saw in his eyes. The pain, and the... loss? It was all over—literally as quick as a blink—and then Charlie had his defences back up, but it had been a precious moment.

I was certain of it then. Yes, he'd loved her. And maybe more than that. Maybe... maybe, all of a sudden, I didn't feel so clever anymore.

"Have, um, have you spoken to her yet?" Charlie asked me, for the second time that day.

I still wasn't sure how to respond. Outright lying would probably come back to bite me in the arse—there could be a chance he was still in touch with her, after all—but neither did I want to let him think he had a complete advantage. I settled on something close enough to the truth to seem sensible.

"Yes. We, er, we have spoken. Though I've, um, mainly had

to rely on third party information. It was hard trying to track her down."

He nodded slowly. "Yeah, well, it would be. She took the whole thing pretty hard, and there was a bit of backlash in the press, too, which wasn't fair."

"I did hear a rumour she was having an affair at the time of Damon's death," I said, slipping it in with all the subtlety I could muster.

Charlie didn't twitch a muscle, and his very lack of reaction betrayed him. He shook his head.

"Nah," he said, and pulled too heavily on the last sorry inch of his cigarette. "That's crap."

If I'd learned nothing else in the past few weeks, I'd learned how to spot the cigarette tell. He coughed again, a real wheezy tar-rattle, and leaned forward to crush the ciggie out.

"I mean, sure, they had their ups and downs." Charlie dusted his hand against his jeans. "But they were happy, those two. Even if Inez *had* played away, it wouldn't have meant anything, d'you see what I mean? Not in the long run. Not anything worth digging up, anyway."

He flashed me a very quick, very hard look as he sat back, and I supposed he'd given me the closest thing I would get to an admission unless—*until*—I spoke to Inez herself.

It was loyalty, of a kind.

Getting Charlie to talk about the night of Damon's death proved next to impossible, though. The afternoon plodded steadily on, with my welcome wearing increasingly thin. The rain faded out, but the light grew heavy and grey.

"Not a lot," Charlie said, in response to my asking what he remembered. "Not in any real coherent order... it was a pretty wild bash."

Privately convinced I'd just been bullshitted, I nodded, smiled sweetly and threw in the names of a few people I'd been told were there, was that really true? Had he seen Vince Dexler? I wheedled from him—in what seemed, to my limited experience of Charlie Davies, to be his classic form—a roll call of influential, well-known figures and how he'd known them, but he didn't admit to having seen Dexler, or knowing anything about what might have passed between him, Damon, and McIlroy.

"I'd, uh, heard they might have had a few words," I prompted.

"I wouldn't know, but Day was in a bit of a mood, part of that night. Flew right off the handle at me."

"Oh?"

"All I did was ask where Inez was. I mean, she didn't always stick around for Damon's parties. Y'know, she wasn't supposed to drink when she was in training, and it can't have been fun to have to be the only sober person in the room with all of that going on... but he didn't like me asking. 'Course... he was pissed, I was high. I don't even remember what I said; something about her not being around, he oughta keep her on a tighter leash, and he just went for me. 'You sayin' I don't know how to keep my woman happy?' then bam, right in the kisser. Struck a nerve, I suppose. Figured they'd had some kind of argy before she left." He cleared his throat, hunched forward on the sofa to light another cigarette. "I remember that morning, when it all kicked off. I was in the kitchen, cooking some eggs, heard the commotion. Stuck my head round the door and I saw Leon coming down from upstairs. Blood on him. I thought he'd cut himself or something—he normally managed to do something stupid when he was off his face—but he was really freaking out. Joss was there, tryin' to calm him down, then some chick started screaming. Next thing I know, we're making a sortie up there, me and Joss and a couple of other guys."

Charlie looked away, staring down at the glass tabletop and the fag ash for a moment. Somewhere, a car horn blared.

"Joss called the ambulance. I—well, I was gonna check for a pulse, but there wasn't much point. Not with all that blood, and his head all.... 'Course, after that, it was sodding pandemonium. Cops turning up, along with the ambulance. Total chaos. We knew it wouldn't be long 'til someone tipped the press the wink, either. I called Inez, up at the flat. She always went there when they had one of their periodic scraps, but... couldn't have had her finding out on the radio or something like that. She came straight back, like a bat out of— I mean, it was a shock, but she did take it hard, poor girl. It was just so... not that it was sudden, though that was part of it, but it was, like, *wrong*. You know? His own house, his own place, and then, of all the times to— Like I say, maybe if he hadn't been wasted...."

Charlie shook his head. The rain that seemed to dog me these days—harbinger of the British summer, perhaps—danced on the brickwork outside. I thought I heard footsteps, the sound of another boat owner going to their berth, the creak of moorings, and the thump of shoe on deck. I hadn't expected to get the full picture from Charlie, but what he had said didn't sound fake. I wasn't sure why I wanted to believe him; the thought of Day's death—*murder*—being at the hands I now watched stubbing out a Woodbine, or the thought of everything that seemed to have fractured since.

Poor girl.

Just how much had Inez really suffered?

We drew to a close not long after. I thanked Charlie for his time; he assured me it had been a pleasure, that he'd be happy to offer any further assistance. He gave me his mobile number and watched me until I was off the moorings and walking back up to the bridge. When I looked back for the last time, he'd gone.

* * *

I felt bone tired by the time I got on the train. Railway station coffee and a microwaved bacon roll that probably tasted marginally worse than its polystyrene box hadn't helped.

Charlie Davies had left me with mixed feelings. All right, so I was now convinced he had been Inez's dirty secret, not—as I had first thought—Fielding, or even Cooper, the coach whom Damon had suspected. And, for all his careful understatement, I'd seen Charlie covering for her. He'd skirted around talking about Inez and Damon's relationship, avoided talking of the details he was happy to share when it came to his own past.... *I won't speak for anyone who can still speak for themselves*, he'd said, even as he seemed to take inordinate pleasure in describing how Damon Brent had shot up in a grimy Dutch bordello.

Maybe that was why I couldn't see him in that bathroom, doing the deed. Charlie still seemed angry, resentful... bitter. I could understand it, based on what he'd said. He was right: Damon had, as he'd seen it, led a charmed life. He'd had the chances Charlie hadn't, the luck, the breaks. He'd had Inez, whatever that had meant between the three of them.

But if Charlie had done it, I reasoned, it would have been cathartic; he wouldn't still be so full of acrimony more than thirty years later. Would he? Unless the fact that it hadn't helped, that it hadn't made anything better, or got him what he wanted, fuelled his anger. If that was true, it would be easy to keep hating someone like that. Perhaps life could become the kind of existence where hatred kept you going. I shuddered at that, at the thought of a soul so twisted, and wished I had the luxury of choosing to presume everybody innocent.

Instead I thought about Inez and wondered what Charlie had said to her when he called that morning to break the news. A pale dread swum in my mind: what if they'd talked about it? Not planned it as such, but... what if she'd always meant to be away that weekend—the perfect alibi—and he'd always meant to.... No. One thing I felt as sure of as I could without access to the police and pathology reports—a reasonable request, I thought, which Gloucestershire Police had so far chosen to ignore—was that Day's murder had been an act of opportunity.

If Charlie had taken that opportunity, too high to think clearly, and lost everything on that one risk, maybe she'd never forgiven him.

Just maybe Inez really had loved her husband.

I thought of Fielding, blood-stained, hysterical... and screwed over? I needed to know if what Charlie had said about the Brent/Fielding material was true, if Damon had taken credit for Leon's work. It didn't seem like something that he'd— I stopped myself, sharply reminded that I didn't know the man. Not then, and not now, however it had started to feel.

It didn't sit right, though. If Damon had done that, then

surely Fielding would have challenged for his dues by now. All right, maybe not at first, but time had passed, and if the money had been the key.... Damn it, money was always the key. I needed details on the management of Brent's estate, and I didn't have a clue where to find them.

I thought about contacting Joss Napier again; he'd been clear, focused, and lucid when it came to the business side of things, and I had the feeling that, if anyone could give me a simple snapshot of the whole deal, it might be him. Not that I felt any more comforted by that than I had by Charlie's psychotherapy jargon, or Leon's schmoozy charm.

When my phone rang, I just assumed it was Damon. Perhaps I'd grown too used to his habit of encroaching on my contemplations. I fumbled the phone out of my bag and snapped irritably:

"Yes?"

"Hello, Ellis, love. You all right?"

I closed my eyes, trying to ignore the juddering of the train as it rattled through an overgrown cutting.

"Hello, Auntie Jan. I'm fine, thanks. How are you?"

"Can't complain, darling. I tried you at home, but you weren't there, so I thought I'd ring this number."

She sounded slightly distracted, and my mind raced with a dozen potential disasters.

"Well," I said, determinedly bright, "you found me. Is everything all right?"

"Oh, yes. Well... yes. Yes, I suppose so," she said, not sounding quite convinced. "I've just had a letter from the solicitor. Something about a proposed settlement. I don't really...."

"Would you like me to pop round?"

"Ooh, I know how busy you are, love. I don't—"

"It's not a problem. I'm only on campus," I lied, glancing first at my watch and then out of the carriage window. Not long before we got into Brighton. "Nearly finished. Just a couple of bits I need to do in the library, then I'll be on my way, if that suits you."

A small, grateful pause, then, "All right, love. If you like. Be lovely to see you," she said, because not exactly asking for help was the way we handled things.

"All right, then. I'll see you in a bit. Bye."

I wanted to get her off the line before she realised I was on a train. The horn blared as I broke the connection, and I leaned my head back against my seat, listening to the rhythm of the track.

Chapter Fourteen

Auntie Jan already had the kettle on when I arrived. Uncle Duncan was, she said, fractious, and she sent me in to talk to him, impossible to argue with in her crisp efficiency and brand new lowlights. When I said her hair looked nice, she put a hand to it for a moment, as if she'd forgotten she'd had it done.

In the front room, Duncan stared sullenly out of the bay window. The last fingers of sunlight caught the framed photos that lined the walls and—just for a moment—reminded me of Charlie's boat, filled with those glossy black-and-white pictures of him with The Stones, with George Harrison, Steve Marriott... each shot somehow more pretentious for the fact that he wasn't posing, per se, but just caught in moments of casual movement. Smoking, drinking, talking... as if they were just the kind of informal shots he had albums filled with. Maybe he did, I supposed, but then surely he didn't need them blown up and hung on the walls.

I shook the thought… for now.

"Hello, Uncle Dunc," I said, pulling up a chair.

He looked at me, his upper lip drawn tight across his teeth and his lower lip jutting out, tongue flexing as he tried to frame what was probably a rude word.

"'llcks," he said, eventually, the first in a series of tortuous word-shapes, mostly referring to the unappealing qualities of solicitors.

"Well," I said, having waited patiently for him to finish, "I don't know about that, Unc. I mean, they must have, if you think about it. Otherwise, who would accountants look down on?"

Uncle Duncan laughed and lifted his hand, hooking onto my arm with his hard fingers. I patted the hand, traced figures of eight on his reddened knuckles, and considered his warm, clammy skin. As a child, I'd known his hands well. They'd picked me up when I fell over, patched up scrapes and grazed knees… shared ice creams and Cornish pasties with me during family holidays.

Mum had split up with my sister, Becky's, father approximately four months before my birth for reasons that, with that timing, should be obvious. Becky had only been three and, as her dad never really seemed to show much inclination to stay in touch, neither of us remembered him well. He and Mum hadn't been married—an institution she'd appalled her own mother by expressing intense distaste for—and she'd not maintained many long-term relationships while we were young. I remembered a few transiently affectionate 'friends' of hers who'd been around, but Becky and I had been her priority and, once we were grown, I often wondered if Mum had forgotten how to let people into her life. Maybe she just decided not to, or maybe she'd decided it wasn't worth it. I never knew—never talked about it with her—because she'd have taken it as a challenge, an affront. As if I was questioning how she'd lived her life, judging her success at it.

I couldn't have hurt her like that.

So, she'd had Becky and I spend time with Jan and Duncan, and Uncle Dunc had been the non-threatening, confidence-inspiring, loving figure of my childhood that I supposed fathers were meant to be. Later, as I grew up, I would wonder about the whole Freudian concept of women's relationships with their fathers dictating their taste in men, but then Becky had married Mark, a sandy-haired would-be art student she'd met at sixth form college. He'd failed as an artist, but succeeded in fathering her two boys, Ian and Grant, and now they lived near Cheshunt, where Mark worked as an IT consultant.

We had less and less in common as time passed and, every year, there seemed to be something more pallid and stiff about Becky's Christmas letter. She was a lot like Mum, really. I had no idea whether her life fulfilled her, or why what she thought of as normal—the school fetes and the nativities and the PTA—filled me with a cold dread, but I knew I could never ask her.

I had been talking to Duncan about the everyday minutiae of what I had, supposedly, been doing on campus, and he'd been asking me questions, taking an interest just like he always had. He might not have a clue what it was all for, but he'd want to hear about it, and he'd listen, proudly and dutifully, with a slight sense of confusion, if not exactly disapproval.

Very fatherly, I always thought.

"What's that, then?" Jan came into the room bearing a tray

of tea and biscuits. "Not going to have a tantrum for Ellis, are you? Oh, no. All nice for your niece. Old bugger."

I smiled, despite the tone of bitterness in her voice, and tried to be the peacemaker. She caught herself, and she let me do it, sitting down by the window and trying to pretend everything was fine. She gave me the solicitor's letter to look at, and we talked over the implications of an out-of-court settlement, as opposed to carrying on with the case. I saw what she'd had to put up with all day when Duncan started to get agitated, frustrated at not being able to keep up, not being able to shape or hold on to what he wanted to say.

"Sshh, love, steady on," Jan said, reaching out to pat his arm. "Just take it slowly and y—"

He wrenched his wrist away from her, starting to get loud and—even I could tell—abusive. Jan just sighed and shook her head.

"Oh, sort yourself out," she muttered, crossing her legs and looking out of the window.

I cleared my throat, loud in the awkward quiet. I wished I could have gone straight home and sunk into a hot bath, but such little luxuries had never seemed further away. Though already awash with the stuff, I drank my tea and suggested that maybe it would be a good idea to talk to some of the support group members and see whether anyone had experience of or opinions on the sort of offer being made.

It boiled down to a fairly simple choice: Jan had never wanted to go to court, but recognised that they needed the payment, because there was only so far disability benefits would stretch. Duncan, among other victims of the crash, wanted to take the case to its fullest legal extreme, up to and including charges of corporate manslaughter. It made for a strained half-hour's discussion.

"You could take that holiday too," I said, stretching out for some last-gasp conciliatory effort. "Cotswolds, or something similar. You know, you were talking about that, with the adapted...."

Uncle Duncan glowered at me, his mouth crooked, and I thought for a moment I'd really stuck my foot in it, but then his face softened, and he turned his gaze to Jan. She was staring out of the window again, pale and tight-lipped, her chin resting on one hand. There was an awful silence, endless and shifting, around which unspoken things moved like tides.

"'An," he said eventually. "Sso'y."

Auntie Jan looked at the pale dusk and the tarmac for a moment longer, pressing her lips together. Then she turned, dusting unseen biscuit crumbs from the front of her pink sweater.

"Oh, you haven't got anything to be sorry about, love," she said. Then, briskly, she turned to me and smiled. "Coo, I don't know. Look at the time. Did you want to stay for dinner, Ellis, love?"

I shook my head. "I'd like to, but I really ought to get moving. I, um, I said I'd meet a friend."

It wasn't entirely a lie. I had realised, satisfying as it was in its insanity, that Damon would be wondering where I'd got to. *Sorry, can't do dinner tonight... dead rock star waiting at home.* Disappointed in myself, I also realised I wanted to get back and talk to him about all the stuff I'd heard from Charlie. My two worlds, I thought, were eliding. Not as dramatic as a collision, but an insidious, silent thing.

"Oh. All right, then, darling," said Auntie Jan and, as I bent to kiss Uncle Duncan goodbye, she caught me quite by surprise.

"Not your Seventies man, is it?"

"Erk," I squeaked. "Um…."

"Y'know, the one who wanted Caro's scrapbook," she continued blithely, fetching my jacket from the hall and smiling at me from the doorway. "I thought you was dressed nice today."

I opened and shut my mouth, then decided I was getting too good at lying as I watched the words troop off my tongue.

"Actually, yes, but it's really not, um…. It's a working thing, really. We're looking at an editorial collaboration. The copies I took from the scrapbook have been incredibly useful. It's proving to, er, be a really interesting project."

Jan smiled—far too knowingly, I thought—and slipped the jacket over my shoulders.

"Well, I'm glad it helped, darling. I have to say, I wondered how he was getting on… certainly got me thinking about it all! You know, all the things you don't really think about remembering. Fondue, and staypress trousers." The smile broadened into a delicate, soft laugh, and I was so glad to hear it from her. "Those silly men with great big moustaches and polyester shirts, all reeking of Brut and YSL. Terrible, really… but we thought it was so sophisticated!"

I blinked. "YSL?"

"Yves Saint Laurent aftershave, love," Jan said absently as we moved down to the front door. "Smelled like, oh, I don't know… quite heavy. Sort of like soggy nutmeg and carnations, I suppose. Mind you, they have those people who're actually employed for all the different smells, don't they? You know, picking them out. Like with wine. I don't know. Gail took me shopping for perfume last Christmas, wanted me to pick out something I liked for a present. A lot of it just smells like toilet cleaner to me. All them years on wards, I suppose. You lose your sense of smell. It was nice, though, that YSL."

Tracking the flow of her thoughts could sometimes be like following jetsam on the waves. I kissed her on the cheek and said, if there were any problems or she wanted a break, she knew where I was and she only had to ask. She hugged me very tight and, if I hadn't been concentrating on not hearing it, I might have caught the sound of a tiny sniffle.

"Bye bye, darling," she said, loitering in the porch to watch me walk down to the bus stop.

The air smelled sweet, overflowing with the perfume of night-scented stocks and sun-warmed earth. My heels clicked on the pavement and, for a little while, nothing in life seemed in the least bit fair.

* * *

It was getting late by the time I got in. I met Mrs. Shah in the hallway, with her son Vik, and Omid, the boy she still insisted on referring to as his cousin. They were filthy; she'd obviously had them cleaning out the brick-built barbecue and, quite possibly, the little lock-up shed at the bottom of the garden. Omid took his hand out of Vik's back pocket long enough to wave at me, and I stopped to exchange a few words and say, of course, yes, I'd be around next weekend and how lovely, thank you, I'd love to pop down for a halal barbie and a Virgin Mary.

It took a few moments of feeling like there was an itch in the middle of my back that I couldn't scratch before I glanced over my shoulder and realised that Mr. Downstairs was standing at the other end of the hallway, sorting through the post in the pigeonholes.

At exactly that moment, he looked up at me and smiled glassily. There was nothing about it that should have been eerie —it was just a big, bald, tattooed guy with a ginger beard, wearing Doc Martens, yellow canvas trousers, and a striped t-shirt—but I suddenly wanted to take my skin off and scrub it from the inside. *You can't stay here.* I smiled back.

"Well," I said, "I really ought to, um…. See you next weekend. Give me a shout if you want me to bring anything, or you, y'know."

Mrs. Shah and the kissing cousins said of course they would, and wished me a pleasant evening. I did likewise and promised myself I wouldn't run up the stairs.

The door opened before I'd quite finished taking out my key, and I suppressed a shiver at the chill. Damon, in a diaphanous paisley tunic and red velvet loon pants, looked at me with wide-eyed relief.

"What bleedin' time d'you call this, then?"

I muttered something explanatory about Jan's thing with the solicitor and left it at that. Mr. Tibbs rolled sybaritically on the carpet, and a half-finished mug of tea stood on the coffee table, next to a copy of *The Times*, open at the easy crossword. A well-chewed biro lay on top of the semi-completed puzzle, and Janis Joplin was crying her heart out to her *Dear Landlord* on the CD player.

I heard Damon slide the chain on the door and I sniffed,

picking up the smell of something in the oven. Something that smelled good.

"I thought you'd be hungry," Day said and brushed past me like a winter morning, "so I did a casserole."

"Thanks," I said, after a moment of adjustment.

"Go on, baby," he called. "Sit down, take a load off. Tell me how it went."

The comforting *glug* of wine being poured gurgled from the kitchen and, sure enough, he came in carrying two full glasses, the open bottle cradled in the crook of his arm and a half-smoked cigarette in his fingers. I wasn't about to argue. I took the wine, barely thinking anymore about the way the glass seemed to crawl under my fingers, realigning itself to some new reality. I had kicked off my shoes and flung myself on the sofa, pulling one of Gran's dodgy needlepoint cushions onto my lap. Damon passed behind me and absently touched my hair. Just a little gesture, but it gave me goose bumps... the broken central heating or creepy psychological thriller kind. I tried not to let him see me shiver, but watched him pad over to the armchair and curl into it, tucking his bare, pale feet up under him. I almost didn't want to talk about it, but there has to come a time for everything, and the time for letting him get away with keeping me in the dark was well and truly over.

"You never told me you did smack," I said.

Damon glanced up at me, lips clamped around his cigarette. He shot me a dismissive mini-shrug.

"Once or twice, yeah. With Charlie. He tell you about that?"

I shook my head in disbelief.

"And you never thought that's why he was pissed off with you? That you did that... and you didn't have a problem, while he couldn't kick the junk?"

That incredulous look again, like I'd just suggested boiled baby's kidneys for dinner. I sipped my wine; he'd opened one of my half-decent bottles of Shiraz. The worst thing was that he managed to make me feel bad. I'd wanted to come home and demand answers—about the drugs, the money, the credit split with Fielding—and I'd probably wanted to take how I felt after going to Jan's out on him too. And the bastard had made me a casserole.

I leaned over to root through my bag, pulled out my recorder, and tossed it to him.

"There you go. That's pretty much the lot. It's a nice boat."

"Yeah?" Damon weighed the recorder in his hand and looked warily at it. "Always said Charlie wouldn't leave the Grove. Found a place that fitted him, there."

I took another swallow of wine, let its warmth wash through me.

"Mm. Have I got time for a bath?"

"All the time in the world, darlin'," he said, still looking at the recorder.

"Right, then." I rose and snagged my shoes from the rug. "I'll nip and do that. Still feel like I'm wearing London."

Damon didn't say anything until I was halfway across the floor, and I almost thought I'd made it.

"Ellis?"

I turned, shoes dangling from one hand, wine glass lifted in the other.

"Hm?"

He looked at me and, but for the dull anger in his eyes, his expression would have been close to pleading.

"Was he balling my wife?"

I leaned against the doorframe, expected to have some easy, non-committal, mollifying response lined up, but found my mouth oddly empty. Instead, I lifted a shoulder, a mirror of all those little mini-shrugs he threw at me when he didn't want to answer.

"See what you think. I'd say yes, but—"

I would have expected more of a reaction, but I supposed he'd already worked through it. He'd had time to. His mouth tightened a little, and he nodded, once. I slid quietly into the bathroom and shut the door behind me.

I made my bath last as long as I could, wanting to give him time to… well, to have his tantrum, if he was going to have it. To make his own judgements, his own decisions. I didn't want to wait around while he did that, so I sank into the bubbles, lulled by the low sound of voices, mine and Charlie's, playing on in the background, along with Janis. I tried to picture Damon's face, wondered how he'd take it.

It was a little bit like knowing there was a wasp in the room and not being quite able to relax until you'd found it.

Eventually, I emerged, steamed pink and towel-swaddled, and found everything suspiciously quiet. The recorder had been shut off, the sitting room empty. I sighed.

"This is classic avoidance, you know," I said to the ether. "You can't just sulk your way around it."

There was no response, at least not one audible on my current astral plane.

I shook my head, about to go in search of that casserole, when the intercom buzzed. I cursed, being neither clad for nor expecting company, but I trundled over to the door anyway. If it was Jehovah's Witnesses, I could tell them I was a Mormon, and vice versa.

"Hello?"

"Miss Ross? I've got the right place, haven't I?"

Oh. My. Effing. God.

I closed my eyes and silently banged my forehead against the wall. Leon Fielding. On my doorstep. No mistaking the voice, even through the fuzzy blur of the intercom. I bit my tongue.

"Ou— Mr. Fielding! This is a... surprise. Um."

"Yeah, I'm sorry to just show up like this, but I'm in town for a few days and I had some stuff I thought might be useful to you. I hope that's okay."

I looked frantically around the room, at the discarded coffee cups, the screwed up balls of paper on the floor, the untrammelled dust bunnies prowling the lower reaches of the skirting boards....

Oh, *shit.*

"Y-Yes. Oh, that's... really.... Um. Thank you. I'll just buzz you in. Er, top floor. Sorry. On the left. I'll, uh, put the kettle on." I took my finger from the button, swore profusely, and then—suddenly remembering I was only wearing a towel—slammed it back on again. "Um. I, er, I just got out of the bath," I blurted, releasing the intercom again.

Damn.

Damn, damn, bloody damn and bugger! Still, with no time to think, I did a quick circuit of the room, flung open windows, grabbed cups, ashtray, loose paperwork, and anything else that couldn't run away fast enough in a frenetic pretence at tidying. I re-knotted my towel just as the knock at the door sounded and wished fervently that I had some sort of bathrobe that didn't look—with good reason—as if Mr. Tibbs had variously slept on it, clawed it and chewed it. I opened the door.

Fielding, in dark slacks and an off-white self-stripe shirt, still managed to exude Pierre Cardin charisma. He held a cardboard archive box in his arms and, as he looked me up and —mainly—down, a grin slid over his face.

"Wow... bad timing, huh?"

"Not at all," I squeaked. "Please, come in. Um. Make yourself, er…. If you can just give me a minute."

I dashed for the bedroom, threw on the first available clothes, and flicked my wet hair out of my collar, carrying on a low-grade internal mumble of ire as I did so. How the hell had he even found my addre— business card. Of course. Damn it, I hadn't even expected him to keep the bloody thing, much less *use* it.

As I stepped back into my sitting room, I was close to shaking and furious that he'd got me so rattled.

"Something smells good," Fielding remarked. He stood just far enough away from my desk to not possibly have been taking sneaky peeks at anything.

"Casserole," I said. "You're welcome to—"

"Oh, I've inconvenienced you enough. I really am sorry. It's just that I was in Brighton, like I say, and it was probably the most opportune moment to…." He gestured to the archive box, which he'd put on the table. "It's, uh, just some odds and ends. A few photos, some old, um, notes of Damon's. Y'know, sentimental stuff, more than anything. I took some copies, thought you might, uh…."

He dried up again and looked faintly embarrassed. I did a

surreptitious check of my shirt buttons to make sure I wasn't exposing myself, but then I realised what bringing me this stuff must have meant to Leon. Even if he hadn't had the courtesy to phone me first. I smiled, thanked him, and he managed a strangulated grin.

"So, uh.... How's it coming on? The book?"

"Oh, er, yes. Not bad. Pretty well," I lied, acutely aware of how easy it would have been for him to have checked me out far more thoroughly than via my home-printed business card. "Your input was really...."

"Yeah," he said, too quickly. He seemed puzzled.

Puzzle... shit! I realised I hadn't moved the crossword Damon had been doing. Had he noticed it? All right, I'd moved the ashtray, but what about the cooking smells from the kitchen, his handwriting on the newspaper, his choice of music on the CD player... as if on cue, the whir of a new disc slotting into place leached into the awkward silence. It was a T. Rex album, and I licked my lips self-consciously as the opening riff from a live cut of *Cadillac* burst crisply through the speakers.

Leon grinned. "Thorough researcher, aren't you?"

"So, um... what did you say you were in Brighton for?" I asked, subtle as a brick in a wet sock, but desperate to change the subject... and desperate to get rid of him, although, I had to admit, if he'd wanted to, he could have struck me over the head a dozen times already.

Even so, this was my place. My own home. I'd barely got used to Damon dropping in and out; what was next? The rest of the band, plus groupies, make-up artist, and four roadies manhandling a hundred watt Marshall stack? Because, if so, there was no way they'd get it up the stairs.

"Oh," Leon said dismissively, shifting his weight onto his back foot. "I'm at the Brighton Centre. Four days, starting Monday."

I cringed inwardly. Once again, damn.... Foot, meet mouth. How had I missed that? Why hadn't I even *checked*?

"Got in today, did a signing this afternoon, but, uh, I have tonight off, so...."

"I didn't know," I was already running off at the mouth. "Or I would have come along."

"You want tickets? Like I say, it's up 'til Thursday. I'd be happy to—"

"Oh, well, I— Thank you."

"Sure. It's the least I can do, seeing as—"

"Oh, no, not at—"

"Well, y'know, I didn't call, and I got you out of your bath and everything."

We lapsed over the end of each other's sentences like a ropey Nineties sitcom, and then we both laughed the tight, slightly awkward laughs of people who've just realised how stupid they sound.

"Um. Actually, if you really don't mind," said Leon, looking hopeful, "I'd kinda like to take you up on that casserole."

"No problem," I said, firmly convinced that my life couldn't get any stranger without at least one alien abduction and a talking vegetable.

I went through to the kitchen and, aware of him propping up the doorframe and watching me, I served the food. It was excruciatingly strange; catching sight of him from the corner of my eye, he looked just like Damon. An older, dark-haired version, but.... So much of the way he stood, his mannerisms, all seemed the same. Yet, the differences—aside from the obvious not-being-dead one—were huge. His whole body language was tighter, more defensive. His looks, roughened with time and hewn into character rather than prettiness, still lent him a certain glamour, but there was something hidden, something unpredictable about him. Also, I could hardly dispute his physicality. Everything that had thrown me off with Damon by its absence, with Leon, mixed me up by its reality. There was that slight but pervasive hint of vetivert and oranges, the sound of his breathing, the movement of his body, his clothes. He was, I realised, a disconcertingly attractive man, despite pushing sixty.

We sat at my rickety kitchen table, and I served the casserole. It should have been weird. The day I'd first met him at Dulwich, I'd been left in no doubt that he didn't want to be there. Tonight, he'd turned up purely of his volition, so what had brought about the change of heart? I tried to work it out, read the hidden things on his face.

Maybe he felt he owed it to Damon. Maybe he wanted to make sure I wasn't screwing up the biography... or maybe he was worried about what I might uncover. Either way, showing up out of the blue like this had to be his style of experimentation. How would I take it? Where did I live, and what kind of person was I? What did I know?

We picked and talked our way through the casserole. It tasted good—very good, as a matter of fact—heavy on the onion and black pepper, with lots of rough chopped fresh veggies. As he ate, Leon looked slightly startled, slightly dislocated in time and space.

"You ever make this with green beans?" he asked, and I was

nearly paralysed with the strangest sense of terror that he knew.

He knows everything. Ridiculous, I told myself, and I forced out some generic, TV-chefs-made-me-do-it reply. He smiled. My open bottle of Shiraz was a far cry from the pricey Sauvignon we'd drunk together before, but Leon had way too much class to comment on it. Bastard. We chatted about his show at the Brighton Centre, his forthcoming album... my apocryphal book, once again. Nervous catatonia aside, with the electrically ethereal strains of *Life's A Gas* curling lazily around us from the CD player, I decided that I liked Leon Fielding a lot better like this. He seemed at ease, not putting on the charm like he had in Dulwich, not pulling the moody and intense act. He'd started to throw in a few anecdotes about local characters and crazy people he'd met backstage; he was overlapping, just, with the nationwide tour of a TV talent show, and it made, he said, for more drama than he'd seen in the wings since being with Brother Rush. I laughed, cleared the plates, and wondered again exactly why he'd come here.

"Freaked the crap out of me, actually," he said with a smile. "There's a girl group—I think they made the final twelve on the show—doin' a cover of *Come On Back.*"

"Oh?" I put the kettle on. Charlie had mentioned that song... one of the things he said Day caught credit for. I fought the urge to punch the air. "You, um, co-wrote that with Damon, right?"

Leon nodded. "Uh-huh. It's, I dunno, kinda nice to see some of our stuff still out there. And the girls are sweet. They mobbed me in the green room, made me sign... things."

I quirked an eyebrow. "Oh, yeah?"

"Mm." He chuckled. "Day woulda liked that."

"Yeah," I said, adding casually, as if it had just reminded me of something in passing, "So, you still get a split on the Brother Rush material, royalty-wise? Because, as I understand it, *you* wrote a lot of the—well, I suppose you'd say classic—songs, didn't you?"

Leon looked surprised, so before he could disagree I tossed out the song titles Charlie had given me.

"*Love You (Like A Brother), One More Night, You Don't Say*...."

He shook his head, faintly suggestive of mild irritation.

"Nah, I-I thought I explained. We co-wrote all of that, me and Day."

"You wouldn't say that your input—"

"What? W—look."

Setting down his glass, Leon went to the archive box he'd brought me. After a few seconds' rustling, he brought out a thin sheaf of photocopied manuscript paper, held together with a treasury tag.

"Take a look at that, tell me it's one person," he said, tossing it at me with a little of the same belligerent defiance he'd had in Dulwich. "Tell me you can split points on that. Huh... y'know, there have been times I wished I'd just let Inez have the lot."

I stared at the paperwork. The pages were covered in two different hands. It should probably have worried me that I could recognise Damon's rounded, florid script, which meant that the spidery scrawl was Leon's. The first page contained rough draft work for *Sit Tight, Baby*, and I had a brief moment of feeling star-struck. I held in my hand the first inception of a song that I'd heard played more times than I could count, a song that—

for Mum—had been iconic and, for me, had been as much a part of my childhood as watching *Thundercats* on TV or buying virulently coloured pick 'n' mix sweets from Woolworth's.

Assorted doodlings covered the edges of the page, and about a third of the lyrics had been crossed out, some more heavily than others, with occasional abusive marginalia. Damon had annotated one line with an arrow and a cheerful 'what the fuck??? I don't think so!', to which Leon had scribbled back 'sez you' and rewritten the chord, in big, black letters. It reminded me of schoolboys passing notes on coach journeys but, in the middle of it, there were lines I recognised:

> *She got a face like Mona Lisa (Sit tight, baby)*
> *But she ain't smilin' (Sit tight, baby)*
> *And I can't see her.*
> *Sit tight, baby / She said and then she walked away*
> *Sit tight, baby / Now, what did she mean to say?*

Leon was right; no line could be drawn between one and the other. There were plenty of tab diagrams, little notes and asides... the chords were all there, along with a fluent mix of opinions. I looked at the other pages. He had similar drafts for *Only A Woman (Does It That Way)*, which still popped up on the odd TV advert these days, and *Darby & Joan*, another of Mum's favourites. I tried hard not to be shaken. Only as I finished flicking through the pages did my brain catch up with my ears. I looked up sharply at Leon.

"Sorry... what d'you mean, 'let Inez have the lot'?"

He peered at me over the rim of his wineglass—perhaps realising he couldn't pretend he hadn't said it—and swallowed.

A wine stain bloomed on his lower lip.

"Well, she did make, um.... See, after *Saturday Loving* charted—that was the first thing of mine and Day's that we recorded, right? The two of us got a fifty-fifty split on the mechanical royalties, though it was still a pretty shitty deal. He pushed for a renegotiated package in late '73, and we got it in '74, then he kicked up again in '75, after *Rush On Love* came out... mainly because she kept telling him to. Of course, squeaky wheel gets the grease. We got more points on artistic royalties as a band, plus the two of *us* got a bump on mechanical royalties. Um. Actually, Day got more than me. Which didn't bother me," Leon added quickly.

I wasn't sure I believed him, but I said nothing.

"Y'know, like I said, I really didn't feel my material had a lot in the way of form until Day got to it. I'd just start throwing things in, but it didn't come together 'til we— Thing was, everybody had an opinion, y'know?"

I wished I knew the right way to go; to keep quiet and let him talk, or to try and prompt, draw him out. He'd reached back into the box, pulled out an envelope full of photographs. They were black-and-white eight by tens, a lot like Charlie's glossy private collection, but not proving so much of a point.

Leon emptied his glass in one large swig. "Yeah. I mean, Charlie always thought Day was arrogant." He smiled, but showed no inclination of sharing the joke. "He thought he took credit for my stuff where he shouldn't have, that he was too— what?—autocratic about the way we did things, I suppose. Hmm. Joss was much more laid-back about it, happy to let everybody get on with their own way of doing things, so long as he could get on with his."

He reached out for the wine bottle, topped us both up without asking if I wanted a refill. I hoped he wasn't driving and found myself wondering if he'd called a cab, or if he had some luckless driver sitting down on the street.

"Joss did kinda think we were all peasants, though. Y'know, because I didn't know to use a raised seventh in a minor scale over some particular chord change, or 'cos Charlie'd be popping notes all the time…. Of course," Leon continued, stifled a belch, "after Inez came on the scene, like, seriously… well, *she* always said Day deserved more money. But, y'know, she would've said that. You speak to Inez yet?"

"I'm working on it," I said truthfully.

As a matter of fact I was aching for the opportunity, sick and tired of hearing the bloody woman's name. Leon nodded consideringly, twisting the corner of his mouth.

"Last I heard," he said, fingering the edge of the envelope full of photos, "she sold Westleve and went back to London. Moved around a bit… I think she ended up out Cheltenham way, but I'm not sure. 'Course, that was still well over twenty years ago. I got no idea if…. She never played again, I know that. Not professionally."

"That's… sad," I said, aware that there had been—for the briefest of moments—something in his voice which suggested he felt quite the opposite.

Maybe I'd imagined it. I was certainly enervated from the oddities of the day. I still couldn't work out what the hell Fielding was playing at here, or why I couldn't convince myself that he didn't have some kind of ulterior motive.

"It's awful, really," he said, this time sounding as if he believed it. "When…. Y'know. With losing the baby and everything else. That wasn't fair."

I glanced up, a little nervous. I'd never relayed that to Damon, not after what he'd said about Inez's protestations of Harley Street doctors. If he hadn't known back then, dangling the child in front of him now seemed unnecessarily cruel.

Realisation struck me like a knife then. *Cruel.*

What else had I been when I let him listen to the interview with Charlie? We'd talked about it on the boat; I'd watched with glee as I sprung his former lover's lost child on him from the pits of the past.

Oh, *fuck.*

I blinked rapidly, not wanting Leon to notice my disarray. I needn't have worried—he wasn't paying me any attention at all, deep frown on his face, his mouth crumpled up and his eyes darkened.

"I went down to Westleve one weekend. Guess it was late May, early June… just before she hurt her leg. Found her in his studio. She was messed up, y'know? Drunk, cryin'… pawing all through his records and stuff. I said he'd get really pissed if he found her messing about with it, and she kept bawling, said he loved all that shit more than her." He shook his head. "I gave her a cuddle, calmed her down. It all just slipped out. She was furious with herself for telling me. Made me promise not to squeal. Her words."

"Damon never knew?"

Leon's lip curled. "I wanted to tell him. I mean, it'd have hurt him real bad that she wanted to keep it to herself, but she was some kinda strong woman. She really was. And it wasn't my place to say anything. I could never do that. Y'know. Put myself between 'em like that."

The silence stacked up quickly when he stopped talking. If I had a window to take back control, it was tiny, and I missed it. Leon smiled brightly—a tinge of that falseness back in his face —and slapped his hands against his thighs.

"Anyway, listen... you've been really hospitable, Ellis. But I ought to get going. I hope this stuff, uh... well, y'know, if it gets some use."

"Of course," I said. "Are you sure you don't mind—"

"Oh, no." He waved a hand dismissively. "They're all copies. Um. Maybe, I don't know, sometime... if it's useful, you wanna come by and take a look at some other stuff? I got a pile of pictures and junk at home. Somewhere. Y'know. Day never had any family, after his parents died. Didn't make much of a will, either. Inez just boxed everything up and.... Yeah. So. Um."

He smiled awkwardly. I had a sudden, painful image of years and years of photographs—memories, childhood snaps and moments caught in time—dumped into archive boxes like the one now on my coffee table. No care for chronology, sentiment, or meaning. I thought I smelled cigarette smoke too. An odd light passed across Leon's eyes, and he smiled again, this time brittle and uncertain.

"Thanks," I said. "That's really kind. And... really useful. Opportunity. Uh."

"Mm. So, um, yeah. Well, we'll fix.... We'll fix somethin'. So keep in touch, all right? Maybe I can read something soon."

He said it with a cheeky little grin and an actual wink. I chuckled, well and truly disarmed, but not really minding it that much.

"I'll get those tickets over to you too," Leon said as we got to the door. "For the show. Is there, uh, anybody particular you'd like to bring along?"

I blinked. Was he just checking how many, or asking if I was single?

"Er...." I thought immediately of Auntie Jan and then tried not to. It was just too complicated. "Possibly."

Leon grinned. "I'll just send a bunch, okay?"

"Right. Um. Thanks again, I—"

"No problem."

"Bye, then."

I'd opened the door, not expecting him to go all Continental on me and kiss my cheek. His hand still cupping the back of my elbow, Leon smiled at me.

"By the way... you have really nice towels."

My mouth hung open, and he jogged off down the stairs, chortling to himself. It wasn't that I couldn't think of a comeback, just that too many crowded on my tongue and—as Charlie Davies had mentioned earlier that day—the man really did have good timing.

Chapter Fifteen
April 5th 1976

"…and hoooo-ooold it there. Sorry, boys, I wasn't full on." Damon's Telecaster made a sad, metallic gurgle as his fingers left the strings. "Can we try it again, only not so fast, right? And Leon, man, you've gotta— You know, you're not feelin' it, man? All right? So let's try to concentrate. All right. Once more."

He counted off into the grim, irritable disquiet, apparently oblivious to the face Leon pulled behind his back. Joss tossed off a big double roll and struck up the rhythm, his muttered comment about human metronomes almost lost under the drawl of Charlie sliding into the bass riff. Leon wrinkled his nose and concentrated on his Les Paul. He knew how to play the damn song. He'd written it. Or had Day forgotten about that? Seemed like he managed to forget a lot of shit when he tried. Leon frowned and made the awkward chord change Day had wanted to include. Maybe it didn't matter, the forgetting. Y'know. 'Cos… if the past was only something you remembered —like how you remembered being that person at that time, even if you weren't anymore—who could say whether it had really been real or not?

Yeah. So maybe nothin' mattered. Maybe nothin' was real.

He hit a duff note on the D string and stared down at his hands like they had nothing to do with him. *Dream It Better* ground to a crunching, uncomfortable halt for the eighth time in almost as many bars, and it took Leon a while to realise Damon had started yelling at him.

"…sake, y'know? I can't always be, like, checking it, y'know, man? 'Cos, when I'm singing I can't, like, telepathically… fuckin'…. Y'know?"

Leon shook his head, still gazing at the Les Paul's neck. A variety of dings and scratches marked the mahogany, and the binding looked a little whacked these days. He loved this guitar.

"Yeah," he mumbled. "S'easy to blow it, I know. Sorry."

"Well, that ain't the point, man. I mean…."

Damon drew a breath, preparing to really let rip. Not fair, Leon thought vaguely. He heard Charlie scoff, set his bass down, and reach for the bottle of scotch that stood by his foot.

"Tin hats on, lads," Charlie said cheerfully. "I think the lovebirds are gonna have a tiff."

Leon glared at him. He turned to glare at Day as well, but he wasn't paying attention, distracted into a general complaint —directed at the glass wall—that the tone didn't sound punchy enough. They intended to do something about that, right? Cris took his cigarette out of his mouth and waved in wordless assurance, but Day had already hit his flow. The sound engineer rolled his eyes. Leon's gaze fell to Joss instead, and softened a bit. Joss gave him a small, tucked-up smile.

"I thought it was all right, actually," he volunteered.

Charlie's snort of laughter wasn't quite stifled by the scotch bottle. Leon curled his fingers back on the fretboard, back where everything made sense, and moved a shape further up the neck. Doors opened, on and off: Cris coming in to calm Day down, Joss pushing away from his kit and going out for a smoke... behind the glass, Inez got up and excused herself. Leon popped a couple of strings, and the partial chord echoed sweetly through the scuffle of voices.

"Inez?" Damon leaned past Cris and called after her even as the studio door swung shut. "Inez? Where you goin', girl?"

Leon tried another partial version of the same shape; it sounded better. The melody, they'd had for years. Used to play it as an eight bar blues back when they were still gigging pubs down Jamaica Road. Everything was different now: the time signature, at least half the lyrics, the goddamn key... but the tune itself had stayed unchanged.

Day dumped his Telecaster off on Cris and left, abrupt and hot on Inez's trail. Leon didn't know why he kept dragging her down here. She didn't care about the music. Cris put the guitar aside, clapped his hands, and looked around the room with a glassy and slightly desperate optimism.

"Let's take a lunch break, huh? What do we say, boys? Who feels like Chinese?"

A half-hearted murmur of assent sounded from the remaining bits of the band, and the sound engineer cleared his throat, a crackle across the com.

"Uh... 'scuse me? I'm still on the clock, right? 'Cos, y'know, it's an hourly rate, man, and—"

"Yes," Cris snapped. "Fine. You can wear a party hat and order triple prawn balls for all I care. Just…. God. Play me back that last take, will ya?"

Leon sighed and slipped out, glad to leave the clunking drumbeat and the mistimed riffs behind him, discordant reminders of failure and stubborn pride. Charlie started to hold forth about how much better it would be if they did it his way, or even better dropped the song altogether, because it just didn't have the character the new album deserved and, incidentally, had anyone heard what he'd been working on at the weekend? Leon grabbed an abandoned soda on his way out into the corridor and rummaged in his pocket. He'd been necking Tueys on and off since before the session started and he thought twice about swallowing the last one. It nestled comfortably in his palm, its little blue and red jacket cheerful, like a child's sweet. He knocked it back with the dregs of flat soda and tried not to listen to Damon's voice, faintly strained and out of tune on the tape.

Sometimes I dream about it baby
I dream dream dream it better
Better better better than it ever was with you….

The door closed on the sound.

Voices. Funny things, when you thought about it. He could hear two of them now, echoing along the corridor. Day and Inez. Leon realised, with slight concern, that he was about to walk into one of those marital… thingies. He loitered at the corner, stuck somewhere between forward and back.

"I don't know why you even bothered to ask me!"

Inez sounded angry, her voice rising in pitch. From Damon's tone, Leon guessed he'd have his hands up in that semi-innocent, soothe-the-beast pose.

"Baby, I'm doing what you wanted, ain't I? I'm working. All the new material, the... commercial stuff. We done *Supersonic*, *Pops*—we're doing this German crap next month. I thought you cared about that. You said—"

"I said you should be pushing yourself more, not pimping yourself! Have you even *seen* what you look like?"

Leon winced. This didn't sound like it would end well. Also, the Tueys were kicking in harder. He took a last swig from the soda can.

"What's that supposed to mean?"

"How much of my eyeshadow are you wearing?"

"What?"

"You heard. Anyway, I was there when you were putting it on this morning. You look like a complete—"

"Hey, hey... all this shit is an allusion, baby. I—"

Inez loosed an exasperated sigh.

"It's an *il*-lusion, you prat! Christ, Damon.... You look like an idiot, you *sound* like an idiot, and I don't want to waste one more minute of my day listening to the four of you having a pissing contest over some stupid song that's still going to sound bloody awful when you're done!"

Leon closed his eyes at the sound of a slap on flesh.

You stupid bastard....

He ventured a peep around the corner. Inez stood on the opposite side of the corridor from Day, tight-lipped but wide-eyed, her hand clasped to her jaw. Close-fitting green cord flares accentuated the length of her legs and the slimness of her hips. The top half of her body quivered with righteous indignation, emphasized by the sheer fabric and fripperous bow of her high-necked secretary blouse. Her dark hair had started to escape from its elegant chignon. Damon reached out to her, but she backed away.

"I didn't mean that, babe. I'm sorry, I—"

"You do that again, I'll kill you. I mean it."

Leon held his breath. Stars seeped around the edge of his vision for a moment. Inez looked furious. She took the hand away from her face; no red mark, though she glanced at her fingertips like she expected somehow to see blood. Damon shifted awkwardly from foot to foot.

"I'm sorry."

"Yes."

"Inez...."

She sighed deeply. Leon wasn't close enough to see her eyes, but from the texture of that breath, he guessed her mascara had probably started to run.

"Look, baby, it's just all this... y'know? It's gonna be over soon. I promise."

Leon frowned. What did that mean? They'd barely started the new album. He *knew* that. Piles of work to do. Then they had meetings coming up in the summer for the contract renewal. Cris said it was gonna be great—cool terms, bumps in all their perks—but... Inez was smart enough to know that, wasn't she? Did Day really think he could bullshit her?

Inez sniffled. Damon drew her into a hug, stroked the lost wisps of hair, bound his arms tight around her.

"I just miss you." Inez's words sounded choked and hoarse.

She put her hands on his shoulders and levered herself backwards. "*You*, not... this."

Day nodded. Leon wished he could see his face.

"You shouldn't have to put up with all the shit that goes into it, love. You don't.... Look, d'you want me to take you back to the flat?"

"I'll manage. You're busy."

"All right. I won't be long. Promise."

He kissed her; soft at first, but not chaste for long. Leon rocked back around the corner and took a couple of steps away from the... stuff... before he swayed into the wall. *Ow.* The soda can fell from his grasp and clattered to the floor.

"All right, mate?"

He jumped at the sound of Joss' voice, coming as it did through cotton wool and the comforting Tuinal blindfold.

"Wh— Yeah. Yeah, I'm just... um. Yeah."

"Feelin' no pain?" Joss smirked.

"Uh." Leon curled his lip. "Hey, c'n I bum a smoke?"

"Sure."

Joss flipped him pack and lighter and smiled, a look of slight enquiry on his face. Leon lit up and took a long, thoughtful pull.

It's gonna be over soon.

Damon wouldn't do that. Would he?

* * *

He took longer than he said he would, obviously. He always did.

By the time Damon rolled in, Inez had not only gone back

317

to the flat, she'd made some phone calls, done a spot of shopping, and cooked dinner. *Played the good little wifey*. The thought made her feel slightly queasy as she slopped pasta with mushrooms, scampi, and a cheese sauce onto two plates. She left his to desiccate in the oven and took hers over to the orange chenille sofa.

The flat wasn't much more than a comfortably appointed crash pad. Avocado walls, chocolate paintwork... thick shag pile carpet, and a purple rug in front of the fire. He kept two black-and-white photos from their wedding on the mantel; perfect couple in silver frames, accusatory stares boring into the dim room. She turned them to the wall when... well, it was silly. Not as if they could really *watch*.

Inez ate her dinner and washed up the plate. She could have gone out to eat, she supposed. She just didn't like going alone. More eyes, probing and questioning. More... awkwardness. She flopped back down on the sofa and found an episode of *Thriller* to stare mindlessly at. Her cheek still stung when she remembered to think about it.

His key scraped in the lock. On the TV, footsteps echoed against dark streets, and a woman screamed in the gloom.

"All right, darlin'?"

Inez lifted a hand above the back of the sofa and wriggled her fingers in greeting. "I'm over here. Dinner in the oven."

Damon crossed to her, hands descending to her shoulders for a conciliatory backrub, and planted a kiss in her hair.

"You all right, though?" he asked again.

She smelled the liquor on him, beneath the heavy scent of his aftershave.

"Mm."

"You wanna go out anywhere? Wanna—"

"No."

"'K."

He sloped off, leaving the air cold behind him. Inez burrowed down into the itchy, musty fabric of the cushions. Day clattered about in the kitchenette, then came to sit beside her with the plate balanced on one knee. She pretended the TV held more of her attention that it really did. He ate quickly, like he'd not seen solid food all day. He probably hadn't. She recalled grilled grapefruit served to her in bed this morning, and toast, with lashings of the hot, sweet tea he made, almost strong enough to hold the spoon vertical. After that... who knew? She'd seen him go for days on nothing but cigarettes, tea, and digestive biscuits before. He said he couldn't afford to get fat.

She cleared her throat as he went to rinse the plate.

"When are you seeing Vince again?"

"Monday. D'you want a brew?"

"Mm."

He put the kettle on. More tea. Inez bit her thumbnail thoughtfully.

"What are you going to tell them? The others."

Day set the cups on the Ercol coffee table and sat down once more beside her, arm along the back of the sofa. He'd shed his velvet jacket, clad now in just his jeans and a dark blue skinny rib crewneck, the fabric worn to softness and impregnated with the overlapping scents of his day. His hair had turned frizzy and bedraggled... he looked tired, she realised.

"Nothin', not yet. Not 'til I know for certain. You know how these blokes are, yeah? Won't know for sure. Not yet. Could all go south still. You won't mention it, will ya?"

"No. 'Course not."

He raised his hand, played idly with her hair. "Good girl."

"They won't take it well."

He stifled a yawn. "Mmn."

"Leon won't, especially."

"They'll unnerstan'," Day mumbled after a while. Even he didn't sound convinced. "For the best, yeah?"

Inez stared at the TV. His fingers stilled in her hair.

"Day?"

There was no reply. Inez looked over at her husband. His head had lolled back, turned a little towards her; his eyes drooped closed, and his breathing grew soft. He looked peaceful like that, as if the constant churning drive that kept him going had dropped down a gear, some internal motor room slackened off for the weekend. His chest rose and fell with a deepening, regular rhythm. Inez watched it—watched *him*—for longer than she meant to.

After a while, she shunted along the sofa and, quietly and gently, so as not to wake him, she laid her head next to his, close enough for his breath to warm her face. Inez rested her arm across his chest and stayed there, in this strange parody of an embrace, until cramp screamed in her neck.

Chapter Sixteen

The tickets turned up in the post on Monday morning, delivered by hand. Seeing the Brighton Centre's logo on the envelope, I opened it up right there in the hallway and tipped four tickets and four VIP passes into my hand.

Oh boy....

I knew I'd never be able to live with myself if I didn't take Auntie Jan. I'd certainly never be able to look her in the eye again. But how did I explain it to her? Maybe I could just give her a ticket and not a p— no. No, that wasn't fair. *Damn.* This meant I was going to have to introduce her to Fielding, and that left me with no option but to tell her at least a little bit of the truth.

I trudged back upstairs and shut the flat door. Damon wasn't in evidence; I didn't like to speculate where he'd got to. Mr. Tibbs sat on the coffee table, washing his bum. I wrinkled my nose and tucked the tickets and passes back into the envelope before setting it carefully on the mantelpiece.

The need to go into the university campus—to force further excuses under my supervisor's door and make a quick trip to the library, hopefully before anyone caught me—loomed. I'd have to explain myself up there one day, maybe even try to patch up the damage I'd already done to my academic prospects, but....

I stopped off at Auntie Jan's place on my way. It made me feel both slightly better and a lot worse about things.

Golden light sliced thickly through the kitchen window, like summer had started without us. The creamy pink shrub rose outside the back door had just come into its first blooms, and its scent wafted through the open window.

"So, what was it you wanted to tell me, love?" Auntie Jan asked, pouring us both a cup of tea.

She'd left Uncle Duncan napping in the front room. I picked a custard cream off the plate Jan put on the kitchen table and looked at it, as if it might be of some kind of use.

"Well, um, I brought your CDs back." I took them out of my bag and slid them over to her. "Thanks for those. Um. He's on at the Brighton Centre, actually, at the minute."

"What, Leon Fielding? Really?"

"Yes. W— Uh, would you like to go?" I asked, counting the pressed curlicues on my custard cream, just so I didn't have to look at her. "Um. Sort of, celebration, if you like. You know, with the settlement and everything."

The mugs chinked as Jan set them down on the varnished wood of the table. She blinked owlishly at me from behind her round glasses and sat down, neatly folded in on herself, pink lips pressed together.

"Oh, darling, that's nice, but I—"

"It's just that I've got tickets," I blurted. "And, um, well...."

I pushed the VIP pass across the table, looking up at the sound of her shrill squeak. Jan put a hand to her mouth, eyes impossibly wide behind her glasses.

"Ohhh, you *never*...! Ellis, where did you—? Did you win a competition or something?"

I bit into the custard cream. I'd thought about telling her that, but it wouldn't have washed. Not if Leon started talking to me, which I had every suspicion he would, and I could hardly spend the whole night hiding from him just in case. I took a sip of tea to wash down the biscuit which, suddenly, might as well have been a lump of concrete in my throat.

"Not, um, exactly... no. Y'know I said I was doing an editorial collaboration with," I hated myself for doing this, I really did, "Jack Yorke, the guy from uni? Well, the project, it's a, er, a biography of Damon Brent. So, I've sort of been in touch with...."

Auntie Jan inhaled so deeply that I thought she'd physically inflate.

"Ohhhh," she breathed. "Oh, Ellis, love... you never said! Ohh, you mean you— Oh, your Mum would be proud of you. She would, though, darling...."

I said nothing. She seized my hand, squeezed it, and then abandoned it in favour of the pass. Jan looked at it in wonder, traced the plastic edges, and turned it in the light. The corner of her mouth curled in a dreamy little smile.

"Oh," she said softly. "Thank you, darling. This is lovely of you. In a minute, sweetheart," she added, raising her voice as, from the other room, we heard Duncan waking up.

She was still smiling... and still looking at the pass.

* * *

The afternoon got swallowed up with writing. I pushed all the thoughts of Leon Fielding and his show, his past—and everything else eating away at the inside of my head—into a dark corner and wrote up two sets of notes. Stuff for my thesis and my other book. The more I looked at it, the more apparent it became we still needed Inez. I made myself a coffee, poured a G&T, and dialled her number once again.

She picked up the phone on the eighth ring, sounding a little out of breath. I pictured a big garden, with roses and herb patch. A willow trug and a quintessentially English floppy-brimmed hat. Secateurs clasped in one elegantly manicured hand. How wide of the mark was I?

"Hello?"

"Ms. Shawcross, this is Ellis Ross. Had you thought any more about—"

"Who?"

"Ellis Ross. I've called before. I'm writing a book about Damon Brent and I'd really appreciate it if you'd—"

"Oh, for Christ's sake." Her terse exhalation rattled against my ear. "Look, this is bordering on bloody harassment. If you think—"

"I've already spoken to Charlie Davies." I pushed the words in fast, rough, gave her no time to consider them. "Also Joss Napier, Leon Fielding... a lot of people who were there."

"What?"

Her whole tone changed in that one small word. Had what I

said sounded like a threat to her? I didn't know, but I pushed on anyway.

"It would be wonderful if you could give me just a little bit of your time, Ms. Shawcross. I'd really appreciate your point of view. Just a short interview. We could do it over the phone if you prefer."

I held my breath. She seemed to be thinking. I hoped she'd care; I hadn't realised how much I wanted to see her, face to face.

"Ms. Shawcross?"

Inez cleared her throat. "How far are you from Stroud?"

I bit back a broad grin. "I can travel, that's not a problem. Thank you very much for agreeing to…. Um, when did you have in mind?"

"Well, it's really no difference to me. How are you fixed for Wednesday?"

That surprised me. For all the long-suffering laissez-faire she tried to inject into her words, we had her. I could feel it, like a ripple of excitement under my skin. I'd been so slow, so bloody slow.

If all I'd ever had to do was mention Charlie….

I wondered, as I said my goodbyes and hung up, if they were still in touch, if he could have forewarned her. No, surely not. They hadn't stayed, or got, together—whichever way you wanted to put it—after Day's death. She'd remarried, more than once, I believed. There had been no hint of her in anything Charlie had said… not like that. And I couldn't picture either of them as the sort of people to have what they wanted in their grasp, yet leave it unclaimed. No, if my suspicions were correct, then something had kept them apart. The word lingered at the back of my mind, bitter-tasting like a late winter apple.

Guilt?

I wished Damon was here. Unfortunately, there appeared to be neither hide nor hair of him around the flat. I'd seen nothing of him since I left him with my digital recorder; the half-finished crossword still lay on the coffee table, chewed biro and all. I swore at the empty air and drank the rest of my G&T while taking a look through the envelopes of copied photographs Leon had left me. Choice morsels from however many hundreds of memories he had, I supposed. All the things he thought the world should remember about Damon Brent.

It reminded me of Mum's scrapbook. The same face, over and over, though at least he wasn't wearing quite so much slap in most of these. Leon's version of Damon looked more or less like the one I'd encountered, although... different. Younger? Maybe. Not a callowness of youth, but an irrepressible energy, and a sort of self-conscious grin at the camera, as if he couldn't quite believe it was still pointing at him. I cracked when I got to a black-and-white profile shot of Day, all frizzed-out curls and tight-lipped mouth, staring out at the Thames in the dark. Behind him, a string of electric lights twinkled, blurry points caught in the camera's eye—a party, by the looks of it—and the obligatory cigarette smoke wreathed him in translucent coils. He was leaning on a railing, maybe a balcony of some kind, overlooking the wide, dark snake of the river below while, on the right-hand side of the frame, stretching away into infinity, the city spread out like a map.

So much possibility, so much potential.

I dropped the photos to the table, grabbed my jacket, and left the flat. Air. Outside. Walk. Those sorts of things suddenly became concepts I needed, the past weeks bunching up on me like the seat of an ill-fitting swimsuit.

So I walked: feet on pavement with regular rhythm, no need to really think about where I was headed. The smells and hubbub of my favourite coffee house calmed me—even the time spent interminably queuing seemed to be moments I could feel normal again—until, fumbling for change, I pricked my finger on something sharp in the bottom of my purse.

"Ow!"

The girl on the cash register arched her eyebrows, breaking long enough in her conversation with the barista to admit to my presence. I handed over the right change, smiled, and took my cappuccino to the nearest table. Blood oozed from the tip of my left index finger, a glossy little egg of red. Another careful dip into my bag revealed the weapon.

Red and gold.

I put the tacky brooch down on the table, frowned at the smiley face in chocolate powder the barista had shaken onto my coffee, and then, with a certain lack of surprise, looked across the table.

"Hey, baby."

I glanced around us. The Roaster wasn't exactly a luxury coffee haunt—best blend in the city, by general consensus, but not somewhere you went to chill out for long periods of time. Certainly, most of the people here were strictly drink 'n' go, and maybe that explained why no one was paying any attention to a man in dark green velvet flares, matching jacket, and a black polyester crewneck with a burst of pink sequins across the chest. A string of huge cobalt blue ceramic beads hung at his neck, spaced with dark blue enamel and Lucite stars. He reached out and swiped a finger through the foam atop my coffee, making the smiley face wink. Then he sucked the digit clean, far more slowly than necessary, and peeped coquettishly at me from behind his perm.

I raised an eyebrow. The finger left his lips and crooked in the air.

"So… I didn't mean to leave you in the lurch, babe."

Probably the nearest Damon-bloody-Brent ever got to apologies.

I sighed.

"No, I'm sorry. About the… thing. You'd have heard, on the tape, from when I spoke to Charlie. About the—"

"Baby?" He tilted his head. Kohl-rimmed eyes met mine. "Yeah."

Ouch.

"I'm sorry. I should have thought."

Damon pulled a little mini-shrug and snitched the paper napkin from beside my cup. He frowned down at it while his fingers worked on ragging the edges. I took another surreptitious peek around the coffee shop. Nobody was staring at me like I'd started talking to myself, but I still felt uncomfortable. Exposed. My coffee had cooled considerably, as well.

Bastard.

"I dunno which one's worse, yeah? Her… shaftin' another bloke, or havin' his kid. Or that she lied. I mean, did she say that just so I wouldn't think it was me? That I was… y'know. Or 'cos she didn't *want*—" His mouth crumpled into a not-quite-smile, an inverse little expression of… what? Acceptance? He bit the inside of one cheek, lips twisted. Shredded wisps of paper scattered the table. "Who'd you find out from? Leon?"

I eyed the ever-winding queue that knotted somewhere around the door, stragglers on the pavement outside. A girl with a tie-dyed headband and a green calico pinafore dress left, clutching a small bag of take-home blend. All the enjoyment of Brighton's best coffee in the comfort of your own sitting room, none of the waiting. To one side of the menu board, hessian coffee sacks hung from the ceiling, livid with the bright reds and greens of African-inspired tribal masks printed on them. Local artwork.

"Inez made him promise not to tell you. I don't know why he told *me*."

Damon glanced up. "Same reason he come to your flat."

I frowned. "You w—"

"I seen what he left." He chuckled. "Always was soft in the head. Daft bugger. I didn't know he kept…."

I sipped my coffee and pulled a face. The milk tasted musty, and it had gone almost entirely cold. *What a waste.* Day had finished wrecking the napkin and started digging his forefinger into the pad of his thumb.

"D'you think he feels guilty?"

"No." He shook his head. "We went through this, girl. Out of everyone, Leon was… he wouldn't have."

"So who would? Charlie?"

He flinched. A terse little breath slid across my lower lip. "All right, then. Inez? I mean, what if she didn't leave? What if she decided inheriting a hundred percent of your assets as a widow was better than less than half as a divorcée?"

Day scowled, his gaze slipping over my shoulder, away to the occupants of other tables. I wondered how he saw them;

how they saw him. Brighton's bright young things, trendy middle-classers with baby sick stains on their Ben Sherman shirts. His perm wavered a little as he shook his head.

"Come on," I said, my voice hardening. "She pushed you for the money. You said so yourself. Always wanted you to work harder, do more. Wanted you to take the solo deal."

"That was busted anyway, baby. Vince let me down. And I couldn't'a done anything until the contract was completed. It… nah. Y'know what? She wasn't like that. She…."

I cleared my throat, swept together some of the scraps of napkin on the tabletop and moulded them into a wad in my palm.

"I'm seeing her, the day after tomorrow."

"Yeah?"

"Mm-hm."

"Oh."

I'd expected something a little more than that. Suddenly, Day looked up and flashed me his centrefold smile, with dimples. It didn't quite reach his eyes. A strong scent itched under my nose… nutmeg and soggy carnations? YSL. Of course. And fag ash, with undertones of something dust-rimed and electrical, like sun-warmed leather.

Behind the counter, one of the baristas dropped a cup. A general muttering and shuffling occurred, with a ripple of applause, and I blinked. The scent—the imagining, whatever it had been—lifted, and Damon eyed the remnants of my cappuccino.

"Ain't you gonna drink that, baby?"

* * *

The prospect of meeting Inez had me far more nervous than I'd been in a while. I wasn't sure why. Possibly because the journey to her semi-rural home not far from Stroud—and really not that far, as Damon pointed out to me, from the old place in Westbury—gave me too much time to think. As usual, I had to go up to London, mess around with the Underground, and spend far longer than I could ever have wanted on another train, taking me out to the far reaches of Gloucestershire.

Finally, an exorbitantly priced taxi ride took me to the end of the lane at which I would apparently find Little Cleve Cottage. Fine rain misted on the overgrown hedges, and my kitten heels slipped and crunched on muddy gravel. I cursed royally under my breath. Damon had wanted to come too; the first time he'd suggested it. He started coming up with hare-brained schemes in the Roaster; we could hire a car, make it a road trip. He wouldn't come in, but he'd be there, he'd get to *see*....

I hated to tell him no. He'd looked so crestfallen, so genuinely hurt. I reminded him that he'd thrown four star wobblies when I asked him if he'd wanted to come to Bristol, or Dulwich. That he'd said—his very words—it was better if he laid low than risk freaking up the whole deal. He said this was different. I'd raised my eyebrows, pointed out he could have picked a better time to start with the Hardy Boy thing. He shut up, but he sulked. And, oh, how the man could sulk.

Privately, I had to admit that I'd always wanted to see Inez on my own, to judge her for myself. I headed on up the track, the dank air thick like a veil. Eerie, to say the least. The cottage was part of a terrace of lopsided little houses hidden away in the trees, well-manicured and built of neat, mellow stone. Little

Cleve was easily identified by the twee painted nameplate hung on its white wooden gate. The gate led into a narrow front garden, in which hostas featured prominently. Hm. Not the quintessential English roses I'd imagined. White-framed UPVC windows glowered down at me as I plucked up the courage to go and knock on the door. I ran a hand over my soggy hair, wiped the thin film of rain off my face, and hoped that my make-up hadn't run too badly.

The door opened, and Eileen I. Shawcross, as she was these days, looked me up and down. She'd not changed that much since the photographs I'd seen of her had been taken. She stood around five feet nine in her canvas pumps, her hair cut softly to flatter a face that couldn't exactly be called beautiful. Her jaw line, heavier now than it had been, was a little too determined, her chin a little too broad, and her nose a little too long, but she had razor-sharp cheekbones and deep-set, strikingly dark blue eyes. Her mouth, thinner and now framed by heavy lines, had retained its shape, but her hair had lost its chestnut lustre, skilfully dyed ash blonde to blend out the grey.

She was slim… well, thin, really. The willowy quality of her figure, combined with the way she held herself—ramrod straight, but halting, as if she always had something kept back in reserve—made her seem incredibly elegant. Far more so than the wide-leg black yoga pants and blue-and-white striped polo shirt really merited, I thought.

"Oh," she said. "You're Ms. Ross."

More than a touch of the frosty schoolmarm in her voice. I fought the urge to polish one shoe on the back of my other leg and say 'Yes, Miss, sorry Miss, won't do it again'. Though, no… *Ms.* You could hear the effortless sibilance of an old women's libber in the way she said the word. I smiled.

"Yes. Hello. Thank you for—"

"Come in. This way."

"Um. Right."

I followed meekly. Somehow, she was so very different from anything I'd thought she'd be. We went inside, making uncomfortable small talk about the state of the weather, and I realised why. I had thought of Inez—imagined Inez—as Damon Brent's wife, and never anything else.

"Do come through," she said, leading me down the hallway.

Going by the outside, I'd assumed the cottage would be full of period features—wonky walls, beams, and crooked floors. In fact, it looked like a modern, perhaps recent, renovation job. The floors were all cherry wood, polished to a warm shine, the walls and ceilings all a terrifyingly uniform soft cream. Downlighters glinted in the ceiling like little carbuncles, and the paintwork glistened a pristine white. There were pictures on the walls; I'd expected memorabilia of her career, but on closer inspection, I was disappointed. Plein-air prints, mostly seascapes and storm scenes.

Stairs led up to the first floor on the right, but I could see nothing more than a glimpse of beige carpet and a flower arrangement on the landing. Down here, all the immaculate white doors had been firmly shut.

Inez led me straight through to the conservatory, a bright, airy space furnished with a wicker and rubberwood suite and a small, square coffee table. A copy of *Country Life* had been placed artfully on its surface, along with yesterday's *Financial Times* and this morning's *Guardian*. In one corner, a small wrought iron étagère held numerous pots of Asiatic lilies, glossy stems dark green and tight-furled buds fading to bright-coloured tips. Some blooms had already opened, splayed stars of spangled white or shocking pink, and reticulated Turk's caps in rich shades of orange and yellow. Their fragrances muddled in the air, sweet and heavy.

"Please sit down."

Inez pointed rather than gestured to one of the generously upholstered chairs, and I obeyed. She asked me if tea was all right and went to fetch a pot, making sure the door was shut on her way.

"Can't have the cats getting out here. Pollen's bad for them. Won't be a tick."

I sat still and quiet, not sure if I was allowed to peer out of the window. The back garden looked nothing like I'd imagined; fairly easy maintenance, like the front, but small. Lush and green, though it didn't seem she spent that much time out there.

I glanced up guiltily when she brought in a tray of tea and biscuits. She walked with a hint of care on her right leg which I pretended not to notice, though privately wondered about. The legacy of the weakened Achilles tendon, perhaps.

"Well," she said, once we were both equipped with tea and biccies and I'd set up my recorder, though not yet turned it on. "I never expected to be doing this again. It's been a very long time since I even heard Damon's name."

"I appreciate it must be difficult. Thank you for—"

"Oh, let's just get on with it, shall we?"

Inez shivered lightly and dug her shoulders back into the pillowy upholstery of her chair, pale cream with printed sprigs of wildflowers speckled across the fabric. It threw me off a little bit. Even Leon, that first time in Dulwich, had at least pretended to be polite.

"Um. Okay. So, you met in '73, yes? You were the UK Ladies' number seven seed at the time, is that right?"

"Yes." A nostalgic look passed briefly over Inez's face. "Did... did you want to know about that?"

"Please."

I wondered if this could be a hook I could get into her. It seemed to open her up a bit. I leaned forward, clicked my recorder on, and we talked for a while about her career, up to the point she'd met Day. It was classic girls' storybook stuff: a grammar school scholarship, a keen and sympathetic sports mistress who'd spotted her potential, encouraged her... there had been hot-housing, hours of training, followed by match after match, competition after competition, school colours and captaincies. By sixteen, Inez had been so well inured to the sport it felt like she'd been born with the racquet in her hand. Or so she said, with a small, lingering smile. Success at the local and county level—her native Buckinghamshire—led into greater things, and she'd turned pro at twenty.

At twenty-three she'd married Damon Brent and, a little over eighteen months later, her career had been finished. I blinked at the connection she drew, but she sped past it before the words had fully left her lips.

"I met him at some club or other," she said, popping a low calorie sweetener into her second cup of tea. "I think it was Zinc, but frankly I'm not really sure anymore. Check the old interviews, I'm sure he came up with some poetic version of events to spread around."

I felt slightly foolish for thinking she might see their past through rose-tinted glasses, thinking there might have been some moment that stayed clear, even while the years blurred everything else. Inez tapped the spoon on the side of her cup and smiled fondly.

"He was high as a kite. Totally uninhibited... like a child, really. Though, of course, I suppose there was always something of that about Damon."

It wasn't exactly the kind of fondness I'd been expecting, though I had to admit that she did have a point.

"It didn't even bother him that I was there with another man. He did that cute act of his... like a kid pushing the envelope? Kept on at me to dance with him. Harry—my date—got very annoyed, and we ended up leaving. I gave him the elbow not long after that, and the next thing I know, Damon's sending me flowers... sending round cars to take me places. I sent him a note, said if he thought he could just snap his fingers like that, he had another think coming. He was very apologetic, but he didn't let up until I went out with him." She smiled again, the cup pausing on its route to her caramel lips. "Huh.... No, he could be very sweet, really. Theatrical, moody, self-centred, obsessive—" Inez sipped her tea. "—but sweet. And funny. He was very different, away from that whole music scene. D'you know what I mean?"

I nodded and made an innocuous little comment in concurrence, even as I privately disagreed with her. He wasn't that different. None of them were.

"So, you got married in June of '74?"

"Mm. He proposed on New Year's Eve. We were at a party in Ladbroke Grove. Some record producer or other.... Day took me out on the balcony at five minutes to midnight, asked me if I'd make the New Year the best one of his life. I asked what he meant; he dropped to one knee and whipped out the biggest sparkler I'd ever seen, in a Cartier box. 'Marry me, baby'." She chuckled wistfully. "I said yes, and fireworks went off over the Thames."

Outside, a bedraggled grey Persian made its way across the lawn, bellying low to the ground. It glanced at the sparrows flitting in the shrubbery with a decidedly disparaging expression and slunk on, ears flat to its head. I blinked. I could imagine the scene of the proposal all too well. Damon really saw —*had seen*—the world like that, a place full of big gestures, cartoon motion, and simplicities that defied belief.

Inez smiled. It softened her face immeasurably.

"We got married in Bucks... my home turf. My family were, huh, flabbergasted. It was nice, though. He made such an effort with them—my dad, especially. He wasn't keen on it at all, to start with, but Damon won them round. We had flowers, and ribbons on a big white Rolls Royce. Whole village turned out to see us. Leon was his best man, of course, and Day had all his A-list friends turn out."

She gave me a roll call of names; some I knew, some not. A few were bigger than I'd expected.

"Really?"

Inez shrugged. "Well, it was a much smaller world back then, in a lot of ways. We honeymooned in Portugal. Three weeks. He took the penthouse at this hotel by the sea. He said he liked the s—"

Sound it made.

I so nearly said it, so nearly finished the sentence for her. I had to bite back hard on the words. Inez didn't seem to notice.

"He used to sit on the balcony with a guitar. Write songs."

She crossed her legs, right over left, gently flexing the tendon she'd once so badly injured. I bet it gave her gyp in the damp. "He sang for me. He *was* talented, you know. Beautiful voice."

I agreed with her and tried to put from my mind the memories of Day at The Crown's Open Mic Night... the way he winked at me when he'd played that song I'd never heard before.

> *Like the rainbows in a pool of gasoline*
> *Takes a special kinda lady / Show me truth*
> *Behind the things I might have been.*

Inez uncrossed her legs, put down her cup, and brushed invisible lint from her knee.

"That's what used to make me angry," she said after a moment. "I suppose. Seeing him like that, then.... Well, we got back to England, I'm back in training, he's fussing around and getting the house at Westbury fixed up how he wanted it. I turn on the television, I see him on *Tiswas*, getting pelted with green shaving foam flans. Kids' TV, light entertainment shows. They did everything. All about placement, apparently," she added bitterly. "Exposure. Charlie used to say they'd have done much better concentrating on live gigs and producing quality output —that would have been far more beneficial than turning up on *The Cilla Black Show*, miming their feather boas off."

The rain had hardened from fine mist to fat drops, pattering against the glass. The conservatory darkened with the drawing in of lowering grey clouds. I calculated how to angle this one; I hadn't expected Inez to be the first one to mention Charlie's name. Neither did I expect to have to battle down a sneaking thought that didn't feel like it was entirely mine.

Hey... little bit of lip-synching paid for your home tennis court, baby.

I blinked, and my cup rattled in its saucer. What the...? No. No way. I cleared my throat. "Um. You, uh, did you have a role in a lot of those sorts of creative discussions?"

She stiffened. Perhaps she regretted mentioning lover-boy.

"Well, I could hardly avoid it. All the band were in and out. At the flat, and even more so once we moved to Westbury. Everyone flocked there. You know, it was out of London... creative space. A retreat. All those weekend parties. Damon used to enjoy playing the country squire. Surprised me, really. City boy like him."

"And you and Charlie, you got on well?"

Her gaze shifted; she didn't quite look me in the eye. "We all did. Not that I really had much to do with anything. Strictly sidelines, really. I mean, I was just Mrs. Damon." A weak joke. I didn't believe her for a minute. Not someone like her, who'd had such an identity, such a presence of her own. It must have been so hard to see it slipping away. Inez's mouth twisted. "At least, he always gave me to understand that's what I was... y'know."

She looked away. The wind rustled through the verdant undergrowth of the cottage's small garden, caught raindrops in its grasp and flung them against the conservatory windows. I realised what she was trying to hide. It *had* been hard, letting go. Her whole life, first marginalised and then taken away. I'd not appreciated it before, too busy wondering about who she'd been screwing, how interested she'd been in the money... but who'd been interested in *her*? Inez raised one slim hand and bit her thumbnail thoughtfully as she glanced out at the garden. The air seemed to smell dusty, almost melancholy, and I—or the me that wasn't entirely me, or whatever was trying to happen inside my head—felt a sudden urge to hug her. It was strange, and over quickly, for which I couldn't have been more grateful.

I cleared my throat. "I appreciate it must have been very difficult, living in the shadow of, um, everything that Damon... was."

A pretty stupid thing to say. I should have realised that. She shot me a derisive glance.

"Well, if you believed Day's own opinion of himself, then yes."

Ouch. That put me in my place. I flapped my mouth a couple of times, and I assume Inez thought I was a wounded fan, because she rolled her eyes skywards and sighed deeply.

"Look, let's be perfectly honest, shall we? Damon Brent was far from perfect. And I... I loved him. I really did. But I didn't always like him very much, Ms. Ross."

Fair enough. She didn't look or sound in the least apologetic; also fair enough. A lot of water under the bridge since then. I pulled back, and for a while we talked about what had happened next, couched in the human interest language she'd expect me to use in my book. Most of my assumptions— and some of Damon's—had been right. She still went by Shawcross, though she'd divorced her third husband two years before. Her second marriage had been to Graham Cooper, her former coach.

"He was the only one who truly understood what I'd lost," she explained. "Really. With the injury coming when it did and then Day…. I needed a friend."

I didn't push it; not then. She went on, elucidating the switch from Inez to Eileen. Using her middle name, she said, helped put the death hounds off the trail.

"It was disgusting, just after he died. Press and people—fans—all coming to the house, all wanting to… I don't know. See it, smell it, touch it. Like, this… aura of him still clung to the place."

Strange choice of words for such a clearly practical woman, I thought, reminded again of Day's words: *My own old lady, and she just throws a plate at me, then swears blind she never saw anythin'*. Had she been afraid of losing her mind? Fingers of sympathy stalked through me as she talked about those eerie, ugly days.

"It was… exploitation," Inez went on, her voice cold. "You know? If he'd died in a car, they'd all have wanted to photograph it or nick the wing mirrors. If…." She rubbed a hand up her arm, her face signalling both discomfort and distaste. "Well, it sounds strange to say it, but I think I was actually glad he died naked on the bathroom floor. No blood-stained rags. No obvious trophies."

I wondered if she knew about the bathroom tiles hitting eBay, but declined to comment.

"You, um, you weren't there when he was found, were you?"

She glanced sharply at me; not so lost in memory as all that. "I didn't always go to Damon's parties."

"But you left Westbury," I made a pretence of looking at my notepad, though I knew the story well enough not to need it now, "on Friday afternoon, after Leon arrived."

"He tell you that?" Inez snorted. "Surprised he can remember anything prior to 1982. Yes, all right, fine. If he filled you in, I might as well get *my* version down too." Her gaze lingered for a moment on my recorder. "We had a fight, Damon and I. It was stupid. He was getting very... stressed. About the party, and with me, and... I got short-tempered. It was just one of those silly things. I left, went to our Chelsea flat. Wish to God I'd never gone, but that doesn't do much good, does it?"

She was flustered. That surprised me, though the lie didn't.

Inez pressed her lips together and looked down at her knees, long fingers crooked over the bare, tanned skin of her arm, sliding up and down repeatedly. I'd have given anything to know what she thought, what she saw, in that moment, though I hated the images that jockeyed behind my eyes, the way they made me view people... and judge them.

"Charlie called you, on the Saturday morning, didn't he?"

She nodded, avoiding my gaze.

"Did he know you'd be there?"

I didn't know what I wanted from her; some twitch of a lip, flicker of an eyelid... some ounce of hesitation. She just shook her head, her face pinched and weary.

"Someone must've said. I used it whenever I was... in town. It was our place—Damon and me," she added hurriedly. "When we were in London. When we got together, I gave up my place in Merton, he moved out of that rat-pad he shared with Leon in Kentish Town. Everyone was in and out. Good days. I-I'd've been happy never to go to bloody Westbury! But it was this stupid dream of his, y'know? What he thought he should have, what he thought he wanted."

"Children?" I asked softly.

She glared at me. "We never—"

"No, but...." I cleared my throat. The woman put my back up, but I couldn't relish what I was about to do. "You lost a baby, didn't you? The year he died."

The irritation slipped out of her eyes, replaced with a much colder fury.

"How did—oh. I suppose *he* told you? Leon-poxy-bloody-Fielding? He was the only one who knew. Little s— Always so bloody *understanding*. Used to drive me bonkers." She sniffed, hard. "Yes. Yes, I did."

Composure back in place, she straightened up, uncrossed her legs, and stared evenly at me. I tucked my feet further under my chair and fidgeted a bit, tugging at the hem of my skirt. *Bugger*. I hadn't noticed the run in my tights, either. Clearing my throat didn't help dispel the tension in the air. For a moment the insanity of it all gripped me like the urge to cough in the middle of a funeral; irresistible and all-consuming. Here we sat, me wondering what she knew I knew, her probably thinking the same. Cats and mice and comedies of errors. In any self-respecting film noir, we'd either have shot each other or gone out for cocktails by now.

"It wasn't Damon's, was it?"

I expected her to swear, to get angry, demolish me with viciously measured words. Instead, tears welled, she blinked rapidly, and the tip of her nose reddened. Her hand clenched on the arm of her chair, and she glared at me with... I could only think of it as murder in her face.

"Think you're clever now, do you? Big exposé?"

I leaned forward and switched off the recorder. I didn't feel clever at all.

"No."

"How—" She sighed, pinched her lower lip between her thumb and the knuckle of her forefinger. "I don't suppose that matters, does it? All right. No, it wasn't."

I lowered my gaze, turned my attention to the glossy magazine on the coffee table, the pattern on the melamine tray she'd brought the tea in on... anything to avoid looking at her.

"Stupid, really," she blurted with sudden venom. "I tried to be kind, would you believe? I mean, I'd have had the pregnancy terminated, even if it hadn't.... Obviously, I had my career to think about. Plus, I'd already told Damon I saw a consultant in Harley Street, that I couldn't—you see, I didn't want him to think it was *his* fault. Wanted to spare his delicate little male ego. Ha!" She wiped her eyes. "He wanted it so much, but the whole time Mr. Sex-in-Satin-Pants was firing blanks. It would be ironic if it wasn't so bloody funny."

My jaw tightened. "How long? You and... Charlie?"

Inez looked at me like I'd just been scraped off the bottom of her canvas pump. Again, I waited for the outburst, but nothing came. The tension between us shifted slightly; a form of acceptance rather than glacial bullishness.

"Not that long, really," she said with a slight shrug. "Maybe a little more than a year, intermittently, all told. He was kind to me."

"And your husband wasn't?"

I sounded waspish, but I couldn't help it. She got on my nerves, even when I didn't think of Damon and how much he'd clearly loved her.

"Charlie treated me like a-a *person*, not some kind of porcelain princess. We didn't mean for anything to.... Look. I don't expect you to understand it, and I don't expect forgiveness." Inez burrowed herself further back in the chair and glared at me, all that artless grace a little punctured by defiance. "I suppose all this'll be in your bloody book, will it? Guilty consciences and dirty laundry?"

Ignoble though it might have been, I got a kick out of seeing her like this, ruffled and laying herself open.

"Because what you don't know, you people.... I mean, all right, our marriage was short, but Damon never got to know me at all. All the attention, all the presents in the world, but it was never about *me*! He was so bloody self-obsessed!"

Had she still been in her twenties, the edge Inez's voice had taken on would have been that petulant, husky tone that, for mid-Sixties minxes, used to be deemed sexy. My fingers itched. Outside, the clouds split and deposited rain in a thick, hazy sheet that hit the conservatory glass like an open-palmed slap. I caught my breath, feeling momentarily light-headed. I cleared my throat, pulled myself back on it, pushed one more time to see what she knew—what she suspected.

"Charlie had a temper, though. Didn't he?"

Inez gave me a look of pure disgust. "What's that supposed to mean?"

"They fought over you, the night he died," I said, though it was a petty retribution.

"What? Charlie and Day?" She stared, nonplussed. It pleased me to see the wind knocked out of her sails. "I don't understand. He never knew. We were... so careful."

Not bloody careful enough, lady.

"It wasn't about whether you were careful," I said, hearing the low fury in my voice, "it was about whether you were happy."

I tried to choke it back, remember that I shouldn't be so pissed off, so emotionally involved, but the damage had already been done.

"Well I can't see it's got anything to do with...." She sniffed. "Oh, God. You're suggesting...? Look, I don't know. I wasn't there," she added quickly, though I'd already seen that quirk of fear in her eyes.

No. Poor cow. Inez hadn't known. She hadn't planned a thing. But she'd had her suspicions, that much seemed clear. I couldn't imagine what that must be like... carrying that around for thirty years. Always wondering, always suspecting, but too scared of the truth to ever voice it.

"I told you, Damon and I fought, on the Friday. You might as well— I-It was about that. Not Charlie, he didn't know." She stifled a laugh. "He thought it was *Graham*. See? Day never understood me, not even then. Um." She wiped at her reddening eyes. "So... I went up to London. Spent a lot of Damon's money and wondered why it didn't make me feel any better."

Inez blinked, worked the inside of her lip against her teeth. My irritation and irrational dislike were subsumed by a sudden and quite unexpected wave of pity. She really did believe it was her fault. That perhaps if she hadn't gone, if she'd been there....

"Charlie didn't have anything to do with what happened," she said—and she sounded convinced of it. Woodenly, determinedly convinced. "If you thought there was bad blood, or they.... I mean, you'd need to speak to him about it. Y-You said you had."

I nodded, aware of Inez studying me in intense detail. "Yes.

Yes, I have."

She almost squirmed in her chair when I gave her nothing more than that.

"Well, I hope you won't be suggesting in this book of yours that he in any way contributed to.... I mean, we all know it was a stupid accident. It's a very long time ago, anyway," she added, hard on the tail of another sniff. "There's no reason to... rake through it all."

The anger, the urge I'd had to slap her one receded, cat claws into pads.

"I won't be," I assured her. If she only knew.

Charlie could still have done it, though. Couldn't he? The motive, the means, the opportunity, and even Inez still believed.... I felt dirty. Didn't these people ever just *talk* to each other?

She gave a bitter chuckle. "It would be nice to think that. Frankly, I should never have said—"

"I really appreciate you deciding to speak to me," I said quickly, convinced the next thing past her lips would be a demand that I leave. "It's great to be able to balance things up. I mean, of everybody, you probably knew Damon best."

Desperation, pure and simple. I knew—if I'd been her—I'd have wanted me out of my house. Inez laughed, an ugly little noise, and pressed her fingers again to her red-rimmed eyes.

"God... if you think *that*...!"

"You saw him away from the rest of it, though. You said yourself he was different. When he bought Westleve, he must have—"

"What?"

She looked at me like she really did expect me to answer,

like she really wanted to hear... I wasn't sure. Some kind of truth? I swallowed, the last traces of tea on my tongue bitter and cold.

"He said it would be a 'Garden of Eden'."

Her expression tautened. She knew who I'd heard that from.

"Leon?"

I flexed one shoulder; not quite a shrug, but neither dismissal nor admission. Inez scoffed.

"Thought he knew... huh. Jealous little— I don't know what baggage he's carting around these days, but...." She stopped, pulling her lips in, and I suspected I knew what she wanted to say. I just didn't intend to give her the satisfaction of my asking. Inez tilted her head, a self-righteous little sneer. "He hated that we went to Gloucestershire! I mean, it's like I told you... I didn't mind London. I liked it. But Damon had all these plans, these dreams—yes, he did talk to me about them. He never bloody shut up! But it was pie in the sky. To hear him talk, they were going to be big in the States, they were gonna do this, do that...."

"Did he ever talk about leaving Brother Rush?"

Inez stared at me. "How—? No, not really. Well, a few months before he... he did *talk* about what kind of deal he said he could get, on a solo contract. The, um, there was some man from the label... or used to be with the label."

"Vince Dexler?"

"That's right. Day said he could get him good terms, but we had to keep it quiet, because of the fuss it'd cause. If... the others found out. But I don't think he was ever serious about it. Oh, I mean he promised me all sorts of stuff. More money, more cachet, like he was the next Clapton or something, but it would never have come to anything. He'd never have left them... not like that." She looked away, out at the rain, like his loyalty had been a betrayal. I wondered whose idea it had really been, that new deal. "The contracts were a bust anyway—he never had anything concrete. I spoke to Vince Dexler after it was all over. He said he had to duke it out with Cris that night at the party... Cris was furious."

Inez glanced back up at me, fingers half-curled again on her arm.

"He would never have let Damon walk away. If you want to talk to anyone, talk to him."

That coldness I'd heard before touched her voice again now. She watched me with the same kind of caution as a cat sitting on a high shelf. It reminded me of Mr. Tibbs; that moment of contemplating how badly he really wanted to get down as opposed to how pissed off I'd be if he jumped on my head. I weighed up my own pros and cons; what I really wanted to ask her lingered sluggishly on my tongue. There had been too much of this. Too many games and too many circles I felt I'd been led in, like a well-worn path dragging me through some box-hedged maze.

"I plan to," I said shortly. "But... just how angry d'you really think he was?"

She looked blankly at me, or tried to.

"I don't understand."

Sure, it wasn't the greatest idea to leave myself open for this, but I'd made the decision. I had to voice it, at last.

"Look," I said, "what if—I mean, just conjecture. But what if, whatever happened that night, it wasn't an accident?"

Inez stared at me, and any dislike of her I'd harboured melted at the edges.

"What?" she croaked, a very real fear written on her face. She'd known... or *thought* she'd known. "He hit his head. I don't understand what—"

"Someone could have helped him fall. Someone there, that night, who had reason to be that angry with him. All it would have taken—"

"Stop it!" The poor cow actually sounded as horrified as she looked. "No. No, if there had been anything like that, the police would have.... I can't believe you're actually suggesting anything of the kind. Nobody who was there at that party would have— It's just ridiculous. I suppose next you'll be saying it was me? I wanted his money?"

I said nothing. They weren't my words. She glared at me, and all I could think was *you poor bitch*. What must that be like, spending three decades believing you'd been right at the centre of that?

I suspected she really was arrogant enough to believe it could have been over her.

"His royalty share did go to you, though, and you did push him to renegotiate the split with Leon. I'm not saying that—"

"You better bloody not be!"

Rain dimpled the conservatory glass, the world beyond blurred and misty. It had got a whole lot colder than it had been this morning, and I couldn't shake the notion that he was somehow here, a conventional ghost at last. My gaze darted to shadowed corners, reflections in the windows, expecting... what? Inez's fingers worried at the hem of her shirt, knuckles paling as her glare got steeper.

"What happened to Damon was an accident," she said. "I-I really don't have the time for any... sensationalist crap you want to try and peddle, Ms. Ross, and I doubt anyone else will either. You might work yourself up some standing among the dregs of the band's fanbase, you might even make a tabloid or two. But that man was only ever a superstar in his own mind, so there's no point in trying to build a career on Damon Brent."

Her eyes were icy, and I couldn't help the feeling she spoke from personal experience. Her next words certainly didn't surprise me:

"And now I think I'd like you to leave."

No argument from me. I left my card with her, saw the expression of distaste she gave it, and found myself ushered briskly and firmly to the door. It shut behind me with a *clunk* that brooked neither resistance nor dispute. I exhaled through puffed-out lips and started the walk back down the muddy lane.

Chapter Seventeen

He'd sat in for me. When I got back from Inez's the flat gleamed, dinner awaited me in the oven, and he'd arranged candles and soft music. His music, admittedly, but still a nice gesture. I felt guilty for my lingering irritation, the bad taste the day had left in my mouth. As we ate, he watched me so intently I was convinced he could pull the thoughts right out of my head.

Damon didn't ask half the questions I'd thought he would. He seemed distracted, which I didn't understand until I took our empty plates out into the kitchen and noticed Mum's scrapbook laying open on the table. He'd left it at the page showing Inez in front of the gates, swooning in the arms of Charlie and a young policewoman. A chipped saucer stood beside the book, two squashed cigarette butts and a small pyramid of ash in its centre. I dumped the plates in the sink, put the kettle on and, unable to help myself, stuck a digit into the ash and drew a short, grey line on the table. The ash ground into my skin like the inking preparatory to a fingerprint and smelled... well, ashy. The pages of the scrapbook rustled in a breeze that wasn't there.

"What were you looking at?" I asked before he could do that looming-up-behind-me thing. "Her?"

Cold pooled at my left shoulder. "Nah."

I turned my head. Day was lighting up again, squinting down at the scrapbook. He took a drag on the cigarette, exhaled a lazy spool of smoke, and I lost myself in wondering when it transmuted from that wraithlike wisp of nothing to the cold, gritty ash in the saucer. When he stopped concentrating? Or was there some kind of ectoplasmic half-life I wasn't aware of?

Day shook his head. "I dunno. She.... I can't see why she'd've been there, y'know? Not then."

"Who?"

I looked from him to the picture: Inez, Charlie, and the young policewoman. The three white faces behind the police cordon—Mum, Jan, and Gail—and the sea of other people milling about in the general chaos of the scene. Photographers, staff, hangers-on, and mourners... some girl with a gym bag, in the far right of the picture. I supposed a lot of people must have gone there ready to camp out all night.

Damon flipped the book closed. "It don't matter."

I got no more out of him, though he remained distant and vaguely petulant all evening, poking through everything I told him about Inez like a child with a bucket of pond mud. If he'd been alive, I might well have strangled him. Instead, I gave up and went to bed, protesting that I'd have a long day tomorrow. He nodded, stared moodily off into space.

"Night, babe," he said, like he so frequently did, and I left him sitting on my sofa, smoking and looking pensive.

He'd gone when I got up—again, so often the case—and I wasn't sure I liked the way we'd fallen into these routines. But I had no time to contemplate it; I had that long day stretching out ahead of me.

* * *

After spending the morning skating on thin ice up at the uni, I had errands to run and actually had to buy a new top for tonight's foray to the Brighton Centre with Auntie Jan—and Auntie Gail. She'd dropped everything in one squeal-ridden phone call, thrilled and delighted and furious with me for not saying I'd been doing a book about Damon Brent.

"She's the other one, right?" Day asked as I was checking myself over one last time in the mirror. "The one you told me about."

"Hm?"

I glanced over my shoulder. Half past six on an ordinary weekday evening, but it might as well have New Year's Eve for all the anticipation going into it.

Jan and Gail would flay me alive if I showed up late.

"The ones that brought me flowers."

Damon lounged against the fireplace, navy blue velvet jacket open over a pale yellow polyester shirt patterned with eye-watering golden brown sunbursts. The skinny fur boa dangled from his throat, and he'd matched black patent loafers with dark blue velvet loon pants and lime green socks.

"Yeah, that's right. Gail's coming down from Manchester, so it'll be her, me, and Jan. Are you sure you don't want—"

He shook his head, like I'd known he would, and fiddled with the photos on the mantel. The fourth ticket and VIP pass I'd been sent remained there, propped up just where I'd left them, next to my graduation picture. Mum and Auntie Jan either side of me, grinning madly. Me, with the wind blowing up under my gown, clutching the stupid mortarboard to my head.

"Nah. Anyway, it's not like I ain't never heard Leon sing."

I smiled. He always dropped double negatives when he was down.

"So, you... you have fun, all right?"

"Okay."

A polite beep in the street below heralded the arrival of my taxi. I looked back before I shut the door, and he was a silent portrait against the coving, a frown on his face and an unlit cigarette halfway to his mouth. Day glanced up at me and winked.

"Go on. Bugger off."

So I did.

Auntie Jan had moved heaven and earth to get someone to keep an eye on Uncle Duncan. She didn't like to do it, she said, because he got fretful with people he didn't know well, and because she didn't like to let him feel like a burden. If it had just been the tickets, she might not have come. If it had just been tickets, Auntie Gail probably wouldn't have rescheduled her week to come down from Manchester—something she only usually did a couple of times a year—and join us.

She worked for a pharmaceutical supplies company, lived in a newly-built executive home, and was now on her second marriage to a newly-built executive (well, newer built than the first one) called Aron. Childless but fulfilled, she said, alluding to their regular extended holidays in his native Mumbai.

"Elly-Welly!" she cried when we all met up outside the Brighton Centre.

I cringed at the cold-blooded use of my childhood nickname, and she laughed heartily, hugged me tight, and rocked from foot to foot as she squeezed. She'd dressed her black business suit up for evening wear with a glittery top and a tiny handbag, her dyed ash-blonde hair glossy and her make-up heavy. Auntie Jan had gone for a similar look, discarding the glasses in favour of her contact lenses, seldom worn because they made her eyes itch, and a trouser suit that would have looked more at home at a funeral than in the boardroom. All the same, it was good to see her out of those bloody leggings.

"Mrs. Constantine's with him," she said of Duncan. "You know? Pam, from the support group. I left all the numbers, but… I don't know. Do you think I should call? Just check?"

Gail rolled her eyes and glanced over at me. Wordlessly instructed, I took one of Jan's arms, she took the other, and we marched her inside.

Behind its squarely modernist, squarely grey concrete façade—considered the height of progressive architecture when it opened in 1977—the Brighton Centre was a great local venue. It hosted more conferences and civic functions than landmark concerts and sporting events these days, but still offered just over five thousand seated capacity. Leon Fielding seemed to have comfortably managed to draw over two-thirds of that, even on a mid-week night. I wondered how many people he played to regularly on this tour, how well it was all really doing… and how much he still coined in royalties.

My thoughts hushed, however, when the show started.

He looked good, sounded great, and of course there was all that honed, fluent charm. Spread out across the whole audience instead of directed at me like a laser, it felt much more natural than it had the first time I'd met him and, to my eye, Leon appeared more relaxed than he had done that day. Yes, he was working—something a little businesslike and slick lingered in his presentation—but the banter, the enjoyment of it, didn't seem forced. And, when he played, he had an energy, a total involvement that put me in mind of Damon at The Crown although, with Leon, I saw something different. Not just stylistically—though admittedly I hadn't heard Day do anything with gospel-influenced backing vocals and esoteric altered tunings—it was more fundamental than that.

It fell into place for me halfway through the intricate, lilting break of *Love, Justice & Dust*. He *performed*. You could see, on closer examination—easy enough, with our seats right down in the stalls—that somewhere behind his eyes he was clicking away and noting everything down, making lists and checking marks. Beautifully done, but not what I'd seen Damon do. From the moment he'd picked up the guitar and swanned up to that rickety pub microphone, he'd just *been*, as if he only had to flick a switch somewhere and magnify himself, open himself up to all those people.

Terrifying thought.

Leon was good, though—no, better than good. Rousing, moving, inspiring... I could see all those words popping up in notices before my eyes. When, closing the set, he did *Only the Rain*, I came very close to crying without quite knowing why.

In the still husk of the night
I do nothing but count your name
Don't know why it feels like every drop's the same
Whiskey or water I know it's
Only the rain.

He finished to rapturous applause and two curtain calls. By the end of the second he looked knackered, with good reason. It had been two hours; not exactly the scattergun approach to twenty-five minutes and a handful of songs that bands like Brother Rush used to get away with.

We extricated ourselves from the crowds and hustled along to the VIP lounge, which wasn't quite what I'd expected. It was large, with a lot of very low chairs and sofas upholstered in scratchy blue fabric and floor-length, depressingly brown curtains drawn tight over all the windows. A rank of mid-height cupboards ran along one wall, apparently ensuring that the VIPs were well-equipped with Twiglets and fizzy water. Though pretty busy, the place wasn't exactly heaving, most of the bodies being local press, reviewers, staff or—in the case of the largest gaggle of people—the friends and family of the youngest backing vocalist, who was not only on his very first tour, but also celebrating his nineteenth birthday. There was a cake, and quite a lot of high-pitched gushing. I spotted Leon in the middle of it as we came in and grew suddenly aware of Jan and Gail pressed up behind me like tugs on a stricken tanker.

The applause died down, the cake got cut, and with dismay I realised Leon had spotted me. Disengaging himself, he bore down on us, smiling cheerfully.

"Ellis! I'm so glad you made it."

Behind me, Jan squeaked.

"Wouldn't have missed it," I said smoothly. "Great show. Had a wonderful time."

"Bless you." Hand on my elbow, he dipped in to kiss my cheek. "You can definitely come again."

I laughed dutifully, stepping aside a little to introduce my guests.

"Um. This is my aunt, Jan Saunderton, and my friend, Gail Jyothis."

"Ladies. It's a pleasure."

He did that same elbow-cupping, cheek-kissing thing that he had down so well, and I was reminded—briefly but cruelly—of Regency ladies carrying smelling salts to the ball; Gail melted a little bit at the edges, Jan went breathy, and they both fawned and giggled something chronic. My smile stiffened. Though I was glad to give them both this night—especially Jan—and pleased they were both so lit up by meeting Leon, since seeing Damon slope around my flat in the small hours of the night, I'd started to find the whole concept of celebrity far less rarefied than I might once have done.

"We didn't even know Ellis was doing a book," Jan said, "so it's all a bit of a surprise, though it's a very nice one…."

I pricked up my ears, looking for a way to jump in and derail her before she said anything I'd regret, but I wasn't quick enough. Not by a long chalk.

"Just a shame your friend Jack couldn't make it, isn't it, love?"

She turned to me, and I felt the icy inevitability of a world about to go horribly pear-shaped inch over me. I should have told her not to mention it; I should have explicitly *said…* it had just been one little lie. A lie I hadn't even thought she'd remember, but she'd latched on to it, sure enough.

"You know. Jack Yorke. Ellis' editorial collaborator," she added, smiling, proud of the phrase.

I saw Leon's expression lock. He did it well, I thought. Extremely well. Seamless recovery, really. The tightness around his eyes, the flicker at his mouth… it all just seemed like a little blip of concentration, as if he hadn't really been listening.

"Well, these things can't be helped, and it was real short notice," he said suavely. "And it does mean there's more champagne for us. You'll join me in a glass, won't you, ladies? It's Nick's birthday, y'know… did you see Nick? Isn't he great? Look, why don't you…. Oh, this is more like it. Yeah, one on each arm, thank you… okay, come meet some people."

I watched him palm Gail and Jan off into the birthday festivities, and I allowed myself to eddy along in their wake. With a glass of champagne lifted to my lips, I almost didn't expect it when I felt a hand grab my upper arm—a polite but firm pressure—and pull me out through a side door.

I found myself in a strip-lit, pallid corridor of the linoleum warren kind that permeate all backstage areas, echoing and populated only by lonely cleaners and internal tannoy boxes announcing two minute calls to the empty hallways.

The door closed with barely a sound. I couldn't help but feel it would have been less menacing if Leon had slammed it. My back pressed against the paintwork, he leaned over me, face dark and his eyes hot with anger, confusion and, in the main, fear.

"All right," he said. "What the fuck?"

I swallowed. Oh, *shit*….

"Um."

Not exactly a helpful response. All I could think was that he couldn't kill me here. Not in that clean white shirt. He'd never get away with it.

"I mean, th-the book, sure." Leon pushed away from the wall, pacing the few feet in front of me, one hand running over the back of his hair. "I figured you'd just done your homework. Even, on Saturday night, the music… the pen. 'Cos a-a lot of people do that, right? He was like that. He could never, never write anything without chewing the goddamn pen…. Th-the fucking casserole. I mean, that was *weird*, but…."

He spun round abruptly, palm hitting the wall just above my head. I flinched, and his eyes narrowed.

"*Jack Yorke*? You've gotta be kidding me. He only ever used that when he was gonna be incognito, like that time he wanted to take Inez up to Ambleside for the weekend and…. Why would you even—?"

I licked my lips nervously and stammered.

"L-look, I don't—"

Leon rocked back on his heels, shaking his head, his face still dark with fury.

"It's… this isn't— This isn't fair!" he spat. "It's not— I *told* Gavin I didn't wanna do this. You even *know* how long I was in therapy? Huh? D'you know what I…?"

He ran a hand over his hair again, backing away. Overhead, the strip lighting guttered a little, flickering on the white eggshell walls. Leon stared at me, the shadows painting hollow planes on his face.

"I used to see him," he said hoarsely. "Like, he was just sitting there, talking to me. Watching me. Standing by the window, or the end of the bed or something. Just for a second. He'd be there, talking, but I c— I could never hear him, y'know?"

Something crumbled a little inside me. He'd *seen...*? I shook my head, desperate to say something, but how did I even start? Leon leaned back against the opposite wall, still looking at me like I'd sprung straight from the pages of Revelations.

"Then I'd look, I'd blink, and he'd be gone. They said it was grieving, that it was... *normal.* It wasn't fucking normal, okay? It took me eight years to get off the Valium. I did.... God, I did fucking Buddhist retreats! You're not gonna drive me crazy, whatever you're trying to do, I-I don't know what you're...."

He came at me like he really did want to hit me and, for a split-second, I thought he would. I tried to work out whether a knee to the groin, ducking, or a combination of both would be the most effective defence. The lights blinked, odd metallic popping noises pinging from the fittings.

"I couldn't hold down a relationship, a job...." Leon's voice took on a higher, sharper note, but his hand met the wall again instead of my cheek. "I even got fucking *married*, and that didn't work either. I screwed up too many people's lives— I can't do this again! I can't—"

"Leave her alone, man."

Leon kept looking at me, but the colour drained from him as if someone had pulled a plug. His eyes searched mine, pupils dilated into saucers of terror, his mouth turning slack.

"I... I can't," he murmured plaintively. "Please... no."

Slowly, I reached out and put my hand on his shoulder.

"It's all right," I said, and looked towards the end of the corridor. "It's all right."

Damon stood by the fire doors, one hand in the pocket of his blue velvet loon pants, the other flicking ash off a half-smoked cigarette. He exhaled, a muscle clenching briefly in his jaw as smoke spooled around his head. I glanced first at him, then Leon. He was dead white, his breathing shallow, but he straightened up, my hand slipping from his jacket, and I knew he was seeing just what I was. And the sky didn't appear to have cracked in two.

"Wh—" he began, but stopped, shaking his head.

Damon took a last drag on the cigarette, then tossed it to the floor and crushed it out under the toe of one patent loafer.

"I'm sorry, man. I didn't know. Really. If I'd known that you—"

"Day?"

"—then I wouldn't of—"

Leon glanced at me. "You can...?"

A short breath broke from him, and he was blinking too fast, too hard. Then he turned, going to Day, tentative but determined. I wanted to warn him, tell him about the coldness and the whole iced jelly sensation thing, but he wouldn't have listened even if I had.

Damon stood there, kohl-rimmed eyes guarded and his mouth crumpled as, disbelieving frown on his face, Leon reached out and touched the lapel of his velvet jacket. The frown melted into breathless incomprehension.

"*Day...?*"

For one strange, woozy moment, a strong taint of tobacco, rich and bitter, warred with that sweet, woody fragrance... carnations and nutmeg. And more. A whole mesh of things, tied up with one another, the ghosts of laughter and loss in my ears.

The corridor seemed to flex against my eyes, the walls bending a little. Leon stared over his shoulder at me, searching out explanations I didn't have.

"Wh…. How? How does—"

I shook my head, watching Damon step back, just out of his reach, Leon's fingers slipping from the velvet as his head snapped round, looking desperately for him.

"Don't go!"

"I'm not." Day held up his hands. I could have sworn I heard his loafers echo on the floor. "I ain't going anywhere. It's all right."

There was something very serious in those Theda Bara eyes.

"This is insane," Leon murmured.

He looked down for a moment, staring at his fingers. I wondered if they hurt. He clenched and unclenched his hand, and Damon spoke to him, his voice carefully measured, deftly coaxing, every word a steady beat.

"Leon? Leon, man, you need to listen, all right? This is important. You with me?"

"I— Day, you're…."

"Shut up. Shut up and listen, okay? It's cool. Everything's cool, all right? You ain't crazy. Ellis is gonna look after you, yeah?"

News to me. I opened my mouth, but he shot me a viper-sharp glare over Leon's shoulder, and I leaned back against the wall, my arms folded across my chest.

"And what you're gonna do," Day continued, in that placid, no-nonsense tone that seemed to be working, "is go back in there and make nice, all right? 'Cos you done real good, baby.

There's all them people in there come to see ya. Yeah? You're *on*, man. It's all lit up, just for you. And there ain't nothin' wrong. Nothin' that can't be fixed later, all right?"

"But you're—" Leon raised his head, half-curled hand dropping to his side.

"Shh. Whatcha gonna do, man?"

"Go back in," Leon said, almost automatically, his voice hollow.

"That's it, man. Maintain, yeah?"

I was impressed, though reminded of Charlie's words: *If Damon had told him to jump off a cliff, the only thing he'd've said was 'where d'you want me to land?'*

Leon turned distractedly to me: still pale, lost, like a child. His lips moved, trying to frame questions that couldn't really be spoken. I nodded, wanting to comfort him, wanting to help, even if I didn't understand for a second what the hell Damon had just done.

"It's all right," I said. "We'll, um, well... we can explain, right?"

"Yeah," Day said encouragingly, slipping around Leon so that he stood between us. "Only not now. You come by Ellis' place later, okay?"

I shot him a look, but it was water off plastic. Why my place? I needed time to get rid of Gail and Jan, and I wasn't sure that I wanted whatever scene Damon had planned to happen in my home. Leon frowned, as if trying to shake a stubborn song out of his head.

"Wait. Why.... You were really there, weren't you? All those times when I thought I saw.... All those—"

"I'm sorry." Damon seemed genuinely diffident, though it

passed quickly. "I never meant to—"

"No, hold on. I was in therapy for the best part of fifteen years, and it was *real*?" Dull horror struck Leon's face. "You *bastard*! You complete, utter *bastard*...."

"Hey, if I'd known—"

"Well, what did you want? What did I have to know? Tell me."

"I—"

"Now! Tell me, or I'm not moving."

Damon glanced at me, fleetingly rattled. I suppressed a smile. Evidently, he hadn't been expecting Leon to grow a backbone over the past few decades.

"Was there something you didn't do? Something you wanted to... somethin' that had to be done?"

Leon would get there on his own before too long. Damon glanced desperately at me again, as if I could be the one to tell him. I shook my head, and those Theda Bara eyes folded into a heartfelt wince.

"All right. Look, it.... It wasn't an accident, man. What happened that night. When I—"

"No!" Leon stepped back, shaking his head. "Oh, n-no.... You mean...?"

"Seriously, man. Don't freak out."

"I'm not freaking out," he snapped. "I just... oh, God. Da— Wait a minute. *That's* why you're doing this?"

Leon slipped me a wide-eyed glare that pinned me to the wall. I gulped and nodded, not quite daring to speak. I hoped Damon knew what he was doing. After everything he'd said about rules and guidelines.... Leon shook his head, mouth bending around empty words. After a moment, he blinked and turned to Damon.

"What can I do?"

Day smiled, a split-second of pride and warmth.

"See?" he said to me, jerking his head in Leon's direction. "That's why I love this guy. Go back in, man. Yeah? We'll talk later. Promise."

Leon stared at him for a long, complicated moment. I heard a burst of cheers erupt from the VIP lounge and, further up the corridor, the sound of one of the double doors swinging. Leon jumped at the noise.

"What are you doing?" I murmured to Damon. "How can... I mean, I thought that—"

"Be still, baby," he said in the same undertone, his glance darting between me and Leon. "S'all right. Just... keep an eye on him, yeah?"

My jaw tightened. Leon—pacing the corridor down to the fire doors and back and muttering to himself—was not the only problem I had to handle.

"All right," I said grudgingly.

"Good girl." Damon almost reached out to me. He winked, hand clenched on empty air at his side.

I narrowed my eyes. "You are on *such* thin ice. You know that, right?"

He grinned. I grabbed Leon and, him still glancing anxiously behind us, we went back into the lounge. Some of the longest hours of my life followed.

Auntie Jan had been getting tipsy on the champagne, and Gail kept derailing her from sentences that started with 'Caro would have loved...', because no one wanted her to dwell on Mum. Not now. I had a fresh glass of bubbly pressed into my hand, my previous drink having been abandoned on the way out of the room and—as is the way of these things—long since appropriated.

Gavin Malpas, Leon's PA, buttonholed me to talk about the book for a while. He didn't appear to be more than thirty; dark-haired, round-cheeked, and scrubbed to the point of oiliness before being poured into his suit. I guessed, from the brittle quality of his friendliness and his pointed questions, that he'd noticed us slip out of the room. Great, I thought. He was either cross with me for trying to cadge illicit interviews or... oh, good grief, no. He surely didn't think....

On the other side of the room, Leon glided through everything on autopilot, a fixed, hazy smile on his face. He kept looking over at me, and I couldn't quench the itchy, uncomfortable feeling I got from his eyes. It must have hurt him so badly that it should be me, not him. I'd have guessed that from our meeting in Dulwich, but not until tonight had I really seen how much....

I wondered if Damon knew. If he'd ever known, come to that.

"Can I get you another drink?" asked Gavin, in tones that suggested he planned to slip strychnine into it.

"Yes, please," I said. "That would be really nice."

* * *

It was almost one-thirty by the time I got back to the flat, Gail and Jan poured into a taxi, all hugs, kisses, and ecstatic effusions, and I'd barely closed my door behind me before the intercom buzzed. I closed my eyes and depressed the button, already knowing who it would be. Leon's voice was hoarse and over-eager.

"Ellis?"

"I'll buzz you in."

"Hey," he said weakly, when I opened the door.

He looked like crap warmed over. I stepped back to let him in, wondering how closely he'd followed me home. People would be talking before long.

"Is he—?" Leon looked quizzically around the flat.

"No, he's—well, I don't know," I admitted after a moment's thought. "I haven't seen him. But it's, um, complicated."

"You're telling me! How did…. I mean, when—"

Leon sagged visibly, not quite managing to get the words out. I gestured to the sofa, suggesting we sit down. I did my best to explain things, recounting what had happened; everything from that first night, through Damon's revelations, to the phoney biography and the follow-up work I'd been doing ever since. Leon slumped dull-eyed against the cushions, listening with only the occasional murmur and shake of his head. I gave him what I could, not mentioning that much of what we'd learned, or who I'd talked to, because I still wasn't sure exactly how far to trust him. He'd lied to me more than once, after all.

"I just can't believe that anybody would…. God," he muttered, fingers kneading his lower lip as he stared into space. "It's horrible. You don't—I mean, you don't have any idea…." Realisation slowly skirted his face. "Oh, God, you thought *I*— Oh, Jesus, no! No, I—"

I decided to chance my arm.

"You knew what he and Inez fought about that night, though. Didn't you? At Dulwich, you said you didn't, but you still dropped her right in it. You told me she lost the baby. Did you know she was having an affair?"

"I wanted her punished." Leon shot me a cold, harsh look. "What she did...." He scowled down at my carpet, clawing back a little of that flawless composure. "I suspected. It was Charlie, was it?"

"You knew?"

"Maybe a little." He shrugged. "He used to flirt with her somethin' awful. Woulda all been fun and games but, that morning, I saw the way he held her when she cried. I thought it was just me. But Day was... laying on the floor up there, and there were cop cars all over the place and *they*.... They made me so mad, y'know?" A thought appeared to strike him. "Oh, God. You don't mean...? You think *Charlie*—?"

"I don't know." I sighed, leaning my head into my hands, pushing my fingers deep into my hair. "I've gone so far through crazy I've come out the other side, and still nothing makes sense."

A clatter sounded from the other room; Leon nearly jumped out of his skin, though I didn't move a muscle.

"That's Mr. Tibbs," I said from behind my hands. "The cat."

"What, like *Call Me Mr. Tibbs*?"

I peered at Leon between my fingers. "Mm-hm."

"I love Sidney Poitier."

Mr. Tibbs took that opportunity to stalk haughtily into the room, where he leapt up onto the window seat and began to wash his ears.

"You put the kettle on yet, babe?" Damon asked. "I'm bloody parched."

Leon almost fell off the sofa, turning wildly against the needlepoint cushions. After the initial spine-stiffening moment of surprise, I had simply got up and started to meander towards the kitchen, aware of the changes in the texture of the air, the dimension of space that meant he was here; the changes that *were*, I supposed, Damon.

He stood by the fireplace, ratty moccasins on his feet, ancient drainpipe Levis worn with a heavily embroidered cheesecloth shirt and a hip-skimming, belted, black leather waistcoat. Leon stared, and I thought I heard him whimper.

I padded out to the kitchen and left them to it. I boiled the kettle and pretended not to listen to Leon trying to put words to it all, still just missing the only question he really wanted answered.

"No, she was telling me…. I just don't believe it. I can't—I mean, it's really…. God, this is incredible! This is—I, y'know, I never needed to—'cos it really was you, yeah? I wasn't crazy. God, I'm sorry, Day. I just—why now, man? Wh-why *her*?"

I smiled to myself. He'd lowered his voice a bit for that last part. I didn't mind, though. Maybe it was the sleep deprivation, but I just felt so happy to know I wasn't alone, that even if I'd gone crazy, it was someone else's kind of crazy. I didn't care in the slightest that I could hear Leon getting indignant.

"…I mean, she wasn't even born, right? And I—well, it's not fair. After everything I… I mean, why couldn't I? Huh? Why not…. 'Cos I just don't get it, man. Y'know?"

"There's nothin' to get," I could hear Damon saying, as I warmed the teapot and reached down the decent loose-leaf tea. "It just is, all right?"

"But—"

"Hey, c'mon… don't you remember what you used to say to me? 'Not everything has to have a reason. That's what makes life fun.' Remember that?"

"It's hardly the same fucking thing!"

"Yeah, but look, man…. You can't blow your mind on it when there's nothing you can do. All right? So just be cool. It's not—"

"Well, it sucks!"

I bit back another smile and took the tea in. Damon was perched on the window seat, arm draped carelessly across his raised knee, the way I'd first seen him. Leon, calmly collected *distingué* forgotten, sprawled back on one elbow on the sofa, his classy shoes toed off under the coffee table. I put down the tray, and he glanced apologetically at me.

"Sorry. We were just—"

"It's okay," I said. "I can imagine it's… difficult."

Damon frowned, looking faintly confused. Leon cleared his throat.

"So, uh, how far have you gotten? I mean—"

I opened my mouth, glancing at Damon, because I wasn't sure how we were supposed to play this, but he got there first.

"D'you know how to find Cris? I know he used to say he'd retire to California, but…."

"Yeah, I remember that. I don't know if he did, though. I never saw him after the band split. Not really. I took some, um, some time out," Leon added diplomatically.

Day looked slightly guilty and reached for his cigarettes.

"Toby could find out," Leon said after a moment's thought, glancing at his watch. "I'll call him t— well, later this morning."

"Who's Toby?" Damon struck a flame from his lighter.

"My son. He lives in Sacramento. He's a sound engineer," Leon added with a touch of paternal pride.

I folded into my armchair, enjoying the sight of Damon almost choking on the cigarette.

"You've got a *what*? Christ!"

"Yeah, I know." Leon smiled. "He'll be thirty next year. His mom and I didn't really last. You'd have liked Judy, though. Hair like Grace Slick, body like Sheryl Goddard... married her in Mexico, in '78. Divorced just after Toby was born. She said I was too difficult to live with, and it all got kinda messy. I wanted to do right by the kid, though. He's turned out great, despite it all."

He stopped, perhaps a little embarrassed at having laid bare so much, so quickly. Damon shook his head, taking a deep pull on the cigarette. I could see Leon slowly realising that he couldn't smell the smoke and, when he reached out to take his tea, I noted the blistering on the hand with which, earlier tonight, he'd touched Day's jacket. I wondered, idly, what he'd tell the ever-efficient Gavin he'd done, and hoped it wouldn't impact too badly on his playing. At least it wasn't his fretting hand.

"So," Leon glanced at me for the first time, "you think Cris knows something?"

"It's possible," I said quickly, knowing I sounded cagey and feeling the disapproval in Damon's look. "But it's really a matter of talking to everybody. The money may well have been a key factor."

Leon furrowed his brow. "Money?"

"The royalty splits." Day took another drag on his cigarette.

Leon watched it very carefully; I wondered how long it had

been since he quit smoking. He shook his head.

"I already told Ellis. That never bothered me. I never— Yeah, everybody bitched. But we bitched about everything. You know Charlie was jealous of you, man… and that whole thing with Inez."

Damon's expression tightened. "Did you know about that, man? Did you?"

"No!" Leon winced. "Well, not as such. I mean, you know how he was with her, but…."

"Don't shit me, man."

"Well, all right, so I wasn't sure. But I told you— remember?—you oughta take more care over that thing. And, if I'm bein' honest, man… I wouldn't have blamed her."

Damon scowled on an impressive, and possibly Olympic, level. "Fuck, man…!"

"Day… c'mon, Day. You know she wasn't happy."

I got up discreetly and excused myself to the kitchen. Boy talk. I boiled the kettle again and listened in, the he-said-she-said dissolving into the impotence of retrospection. Leon cleared his throat, lowered his voice, and the sofa creaked beneath his shifting pose.

"I… I'm sorry, all right? Y'know? About all of it. We coulda done so much different. Couldn't we?"

A long, drawn-out moment wound into the dimness. The tinny noise of an American talk show—studio whooping and applause—punctured the floorboards. Mr. Downstairs, in his usual form. There was a crash, something like a falling bookcase. I reached for the biscuit tin.

"It don't matter," Damon said softly. "Y'know? We had a good run. I mean, it would've changed anyway. Somehow.

Everythin' does. But I'm glad you was there, man. Always."

Leon said nothing, though I heard a sniff. A familiar chuckle followed it.

"Soft bugger. 'Ere, Ell? Where's the tea?"

Mr. Tibbs, sitting on the kitchen table, looked at me and switched his tail.

"Quite," I said.

They talked long into the morning. After a while, I just wasn't involved anymore, relegated to keeping up a steady supply of tea and stifling my yawns. I couldn't understand how Leon could show no sign of tiredness; I was knackered, and a man of his... age.... I backed away from that thought and just stood, propping up the doorframe. How old exactly was he? Fifty-five? Sixty? He didn't look it. Certainly not now, stretched out on my sofa, disbelief and fear replaced with laughter and streams of memories that waltzed around the room, drenched in nostalgic affection and that faint scent of YSL.

I was sure that wasn't just me.

I didn't like to mention it, though. And I'd never seen Damon so cheerful, so... alive. However obviously erroneous, it was true. I left them to it and sneaked off to bed, barely stepping out of my brogues before I hit the pillow and began to snore.

* * *

When I woke, golden sunlight filled the room, with strong overtones of bacon and coffee. I blinked, mumbled, and turned over, pulling the duvet over my head.

"Ahem."

The throat-clearing noise issued from an unfamiliar

mouth. In my dim, eider-filled cocoon, my eyes opened wide and my brain kicked into gear.

Bollocks.

I peeked cautiously over the top of the duvet. Leon stood at the end of my bed, a mug in one hand and a grin on his face.

"Oggoddurgh," I said.

"Good morning. Are you, uh, decent under there?"

I frowned and peered beneath the covers. It appeared so; last night's clothes were in place, though rumpled and none too fresh.

"Urr," I admitted and levered myself upright.

He put the mug down on my bedside table. I wasn't sure why it surprised me that he was still here. He looked very much at home; dishevelled and a bit worn at the edges, but coursing with an intense vibrancy, a barely contained glee. Too bloody cheerful by half, in other words.

"This is just.... This is amazing, y'know?" He lingered by the foot of my bed, looking for all the world like a kid on Christmas morning. "I can't—well, I can't even begin to... to thank you, I guess."

I reached for the mug. Coffee. That would help. I took a sip. "S'not me. It's *him.*"

Leon shot me a sad little smile. "Yeah. It always is." He cleared his throat. "Hey, there's... uh, breakfast. When you're ready. I'll, um...."

"Mm."

He backed out and left me to the tender mercy of my coffee. I heard voices in the other room.

He's still here?

I followed the gut-rumbling smells to the kitchen and

found Damon Brent—still clad in moccasin and cheesecloth ensemble and looking somewhat rumpled and unshaven—chatting away as he plated up piles of bacon, scrambled egg, and fried bread. The coffee machine I rarely bothered to use had been dusted off and was bubbling quietly to itself. Leon poured me a cup and pushed it into my unresisting fingers with a cheerful little smile.

"So that'd be the best thing to do, right? Mornin', babe," Day added, acknowledging me with a wink. "'Cos he'd know about that, wouldn't he? And if Vince dropped off his perch, then Cris is the only one who—"

"What?" I asked, the second cup of coffee finally prodding sluggish synapses into gear.

Leon opened his mouth. "Um. We were just—"

"You ever go to California?"

Damon beamed at me, affecting an expression of artless innocence, which wasn't one of his strengths. I raised an eyebrow.

"California?"

"I, um.... I mean, if it'll help. I, er...." Leon looked embarrassed. "I offered to, uh, y'know. I can get you out there, get Toby to dig up Cris McIlroy. I spoke to him about a half hour ago—he's looking now. So if you wanted to... um."

I looked between the two pleading faces, one framed by fuzzy wisps of gold and the other weighted down with a brand new, burning crusade.

"What? Oh, hell.... Really?" I shook my head, and sighed wearily. "All right. Fine. Saddle up the Mystery Machine. It's road trip time."

I'd have to ask Ron and Jeremy to pop in and feed the cat.

Chapter Eighteen

Leon was as good as his word. Or Damon's word. Hard to be sure which. Either way, the following Monday morning I boarded a transatlantic flight, business class, and he sat next to me, reading through Mum's scrapbook as I tried to concentrate on us not falling out of the sky. We talked for part of the flight like we'd done at my flat; him not really listening to me, hedging around the enormity of his own incredulity, yet somehow managing to comfort me all the same. I liked the solidity of Leon's presence, his expansiveness, and that faint hint of vetivert. I liked the way those expensive clothes hung off a kid who, after all these years, still couldn't believe he got paid to do what he loved best in the whole world.

"Your mom was some kinda fan, huh?"

He'd flicked back to the early pages, brightening himself up after the pale, quiet moments of 'Death House Horror'.

I nodded. "She was. Well, all three of them were."

"They ever...? I mean, I don't recall—"

I smiled. "She was never a groupie."

"Oh." Leon looked relieved. "Right."

I turned my laughter to the window and watched the darkness stream past.

The flight wasn't that bad, not counting the recycled air and my general distrust of all forms of communal transport, but I could have done without the six-hour stopover in Minneapolis. I hated the hanging around, the altered time zones, and the way everything seemed to catch up with me like a brick wall travelling at speed. Leon remained irritatingly unruffled, even smiling graciously when the first of several well-preserved women *d'une certain âge* shimmied over in her biscuit-coloured business suit and asked if he was really Leon Fielding. He chatted her up for five minutes, gave her an autograph, and nodded like he really cared what she'd thought of the gig she'd caught in Illinois six weeks ago. Perhaps he did. I melted into the background and inspected the toes of my shoes until she buggered off.

Leon shot me an embarrassed grin. "Sorry."

"Oh, no. Must be nice."

"Drives Toby crazy," he confided, and I noticed how he seemed a little tighter wound than he had done. Paternal anticipation?

I didn't get chance to probe; there were more autograph hunters.

Early evening, local time, we stumbled into the arrivals lounge at Sacramento Metropolitan with me feeling—and probably looking—a complete wreck. The fruit of my companion's loins arrived to pick us up, eschewing any notion we could simply have caught the shuttle to the hotel. Leon grinned and waved, and I stared at the figure bearing down upon us through the gushing sunshine and the square, white corners of everything. Talk about your mirror of years.

"Dad! You have a good flight? Great. Yeah, I'm fine. You're Miss Ross, right? Toby Fielding. Hi."

Broad voice, broad accent, broad palm: virtually Leon's carbon copy. Same cheekbones, same nose, same chin. Same hair—or as Leon's had once been, anyway. Toby wore his short and fashionably tousled, and he had a slightly different build. Taller, longer, and lankier than his father, with a narrower jaw line and, I assumed, his mother's blue eyes. Great dentistry, though. He pumped my hand and smiled Leon's smile at me, asked how the flight had been, were we ready to go to the hotel, did we want to grab a bite to eat first... he even sounded like Leon, albeit without the mangled Anglo-American vowels.

"Um. Thanks," I said, a pale and vaguely English response.

Leon grinned and dripped with pride, his hand on Toby's shoulder as we walked to his Toyota hybrid, making the small talk of people unaccustomed to each other, but too polite to show it.

Toby had booked us a hotel not far from the airport, all pseudo-Spanish arches and bright geometric print furnishings, which reminded me a little of the trendy Dulwich restaurant in which I'd first met his father. He apologised to me for not being able to offer his own place, but it was apparently nothing more than a rat-hole and, in any case, currently stacked to the ceiling with flight cases full of equipment from a party he'd run at the weekend.

"Oh, yeah." Leon beamed. "I remembered you said you

were doin' that. How'd it go? Hey… wait a minute, this is the place in Meadowview? You're not still living there, are you?"

Toby rolled his eyes. "It's safe, Dad. Honestly. It's not even really Meadowview, and—"

"You said you were going to look for somewhere else! Hell, your mother'll kill me if she finds out…."

I excused myself and went to freshen up. We segued from the hotel to dinner at a nearby seafood place where they piped Californian indie pop through paper-thin wall speakers linked to LCD displays perpetually morphing in patterns of hot pink and acid green. Possibly because of the jet lag, barely having time to have a pee and dump my flight bag, or simply due to the fact I'd never been an enthusiastic traveller, I couldn't help but think it looked like someone's lava lamp had exploded in an IKEA store.

Toby asked pertinent questions about my apocryphal book, gently ribbed his father over days lost in lurex and sequins, and turned a little more respectful at the full mention of Damon's name. I wondered how much the shadow of Day's life—and death—had touched Toby's early years; whether he knew his dad hadn't been around that much because he'd been busy falling to pieces, or falling in and out of different retreats and shrinks' offices. They seemed close, nonetheless. Toby looked genuinely worried when, talking about the trip to see Cris tomorrow, he prodded Leon with a gentle caveat.

"Yeah, so it's, um… assisted living. Nursing care."

Leon's thick brows arched. I'd stuck with sea bream and a salad; he was addressing a mixed platter that contained hints of tentacle. I wanted very little more than to go to bed. Around us, well-heeled patrons chatted and laughed, and the melodiously bland indie pop tinkled on.

"I didn't know he was sick."

The corner of Toby's mouth furled around a dubious smile. "Mm. I don't know what it is, but the place is… well, it looks good, on the website. I just thought I oughta say. I mean, I know you guys haven't seen each other in a long time, and if you're going to—"

"Only if Ellis doesn't mind me tagging along. I don't know how much, uh, company she's planning on having," Leon added with a glance at me.

He meant Damon. He'd tried to word around it on the plane and, ever since we'd landed, I'd seen him taking nervous peeks into dark corners. To tell the truth, I didn't know when or where Day would pop up. Before we left, I asked him how he wanted to play it. Teased him about running water and whether or not he could cross it. He'd pouted at me and asked precisely what I thought sewers and water supply pipes were. I judged his current absence to be more to do with making it easy on Leon— maybe avoiding meeting Toby—but I doubted he'd keep away for too long. I had the tacky red brooch in my luggage, anyway.

"You're more than welcome," I said. "Both of you, of course, if you…."

They both smiled at me, and it seemed settled. In stereo.

The home wasn't terribly far away, considering the size of the state. The English find it deceptively easy to think of Americans as insular, defined and corralled by their localities— but what we neglect to realise is how much more landmass there is over there. Where, just a few weeks ago, I'd been spending hours swapping trains and sodding about on the Tube just to get to Bristol, it seemed that, here, a longer journey would actually take less time. Toby and Leon chatted away about it, in any case, and I decided—perhaps uncharitably— that my comment about a road trip in the Mystery Machine hadn't been that far wrong.

We got back to the hotel rather late for someone still working on Greenwich Mean Time. Leon wanted to stand me a nightcap in the hotel bar—terrible wallpaper and walnut veneer, with baseball on the TV and soft complimentary peanuts—and I didn't feel I could refuse.

So, his kid waved off into the night, we sat there shoulder to shoulder drinking vodka and tonic, and he stopped being a dad again. The news about Cris had got to him, though he was trying not to show it. Chilly winds of mortality blew for us all, I supposed, even if they seemed to come from a rather different direction these days.

"I still can't believe—" Leon began, out of nowhere. He shook his head. "Huh. *Any* of it."

I swigged my drink. "Mm."

"Poor Cris. What d'you think it is?"

"I have no idea. But I hope he remembers everything."

I picked at the soft peanuts. The bartender had started taking second looks at Leon. A lot of people did, when they realised they recognised him. Some got it instantly, and I found the red-faced stares or falsely familiar smiles thrown his way much more unsettling than he apparently did. I wasn't sure he always noticed them anymore. Cheers erupted from the TV, a commentator put in his two cents, and the baseball game went to commercial.

"There's no one else left who'd know about the negotiations Vince Dexler had been doing with... other labels," I finished diplomatically, taking a sidelong look at Leon.

He chuckled. "Day was scouting for a solo deal, wasn't he?"

I'd not said as much and weaselled away from answering.

"Don't really know. But I think that, if anything—"

"I wondered back then." Leon looked mournfully at the slice of lemon in his drink. "Inez always pushed him to it. Said he could do better. He coulda, prob'ly. I just never thought he'd sell out from under us. Though, if Cris did find out what he'd been planning, that night...."

He took a swig, not voicing the thing we both wanted to avoid. I remembered the words Inez had used. *Dexler said he had to duke it out with Cris that night at the party... Cris was furious.* Whether Damon would have signed anything or not— whether Vince had ever truly had a chance of nailing a deal or not—might almost have been irrelevant. Charlie wasn't the only one who'd been angry with Day.

"It, um...." I cleared my throat, regretting having said anything when he glanced at me. "It must have hurt, though. Thinking that he'd been considering—"

"Huh." Leon snorted dryly. "Not really. I got over being hurt by Damon Brent a *very* long time ago. I'd never have hung around if I hadn't."

He drained the rest of his glass. When he looked at me, I tried not to make it obvious that I knew—that I'd always known —what he meant, but perhaps I'd been living in Brighton too long. He folded his lips in and drew a short, tight breath, suddenly interested in the walnut veneer of the counter top.

"Yeah. Well, it wasn't like I was pining away, y'know? I mean, Damon... he never swung that way. So nothin' like that was ever—it wasn't going to be an option. I knew that. And it was fine. It really was. I dug girls too, so...." Leon weighed the glass in his fingers, and tapped it rhythmically against the bar. "After a while, y'know, I prob'ly wouldn't even have *wanted* to. It would just have felt wrong. But I still— He was my friend."

Those last words hung in the air, resolute and incorruptible. I nodded.

"I know."

Leon gave me a terse little smile. "Mm. I know you know. Goddamn smartass, you are."

I laughed. After a while we migrated upstairs and, at the door of my room, he kissed me goodnight. Or I kissed him. I wasn't entirely sure which way round it was, but it was nice.

* * *

Toby turned up bright and early in the morning, a dutiful chauffeur. If Leon regretted anything from the night before, he didn't make it obvious. He smiled and slipped back a little into Dad Mode. The... facility, as everybody seemed to insist on calling it—making it sound like some sort of nuclear containment installation—wasn't far, really. Not with Toby driving. The highways slipped by, the radio bubbling with cheery pop tunes, and this strange sense of a jaunty excursion settled over the car, like we were all headed off on some kind of Victorian picnic with wickerwork baskets, thick plaid rugs, and real china plates. Weird.

We found it easily enough, though. High gates and clean walls; the place played on the sense of rural tranquillity it got from its manicured grounds. Very American. We processed up the leafless, shadeless, sunny path, and I felt a twinge of nostalgic homesickness for discarded chip wrappers and empty beer cans. The place did look nice, I had to admit. Not like the sort of nursing home I'd been terrified of putting Mum in—endless beige corridors and an all-pervading smell of piss.

No. *These* people had a fish pond.

A little red wooden bridge crossed it. Two men in sweats stood on it, one with a cane and the other holding a neat little crocheted sling that I didn't realise, until we got closer, had a colostomy bag in it. The sun glimmered on the low roofs, red-tiled and gabled, and the sun-warmed fullness of new-mown grass and pond water perfumed the air. The men waved at us, we smiled and nodded back, and perhaps the three of us bunched a little tighter together as we walked.

I gave our names at the reception, and a Filipina woman—small, dark, and birdlike, efficient and graceful of movement in white nurse's shoes, slacks and shirt, with a green cardigan draped around her shoulders—said she'd take us straight down to see Mr. McIlroy. She led us through to another bright, sunny room. A TV had been mounted on the wall in one corner, a big flat-screen job flashing up commercials and cable news, the distinction between the two never entirely clear. The view from the window stretched out across the valley, endless blue sky and green, leafy slopes.

Cris McIlroy sat in a chair not far from the TV, and for a few seconds I didn't even see him. He looked sunken into himself, as if he barely took up any space at all. He'd be tall if he stood up, but I realised when he turned to greet us that wasn't likely. What I'd taken for a seat was a wheelchair, and what I'd thought to be the hum of some distant machine actually came from a squat grey box, about three feet high, that stood in the corner by the curtain. It was attached to Cris by a nasal canula and a long length of clear pipe, which pooled at his feet. A selection of green and amber lights blinked on the upper part of the machine and, every few seconds, it gave a long, hissing heave, rather like a mechanised fart.

"Please," Cris said, by way of greeting, "excuse the thing. I can't take a breath without it. Emphysema."

There was something of the late, great Vincent Price in his delivery, but only because he found it so hard to breathe. His voice sounded light, thin, the way the rest of him looked—attenuated, boneless and gaunt—but he put everything into it. His appearance still mattered to him; crisply pressed tan chinos, polo shirt in muted blue. His hair had greyed and turned very sparse, but what he had left had been neatly slicked down. Pale eyes seemed enlarged behind over-sized glasses, which he wore pushed high on his long, sharp nose. His thin-lipped mouth never quite closed. With sinking horror, I saw the way he used his whole body to pump in air, trying to supplement the pure oxygen forced into him through the pipe.

He peered up at Leon and smiled, lips pulled back over even, creamy teeth not his own.

"Leon." He held out a hand, blue veins proud on the back of it, skin nearly translucent. "It's been a very long time."

"Yeah. Yeah, it has. Too long." Leon went to him, took the hand and shook it, awkward as I'd ever seen him. "I, um...."

"Ah," Cris patted his knuckles, "everybody loses touch eventually. How... how would we ever move on if we didn't? Miss Ross. Forgive me."

He relinquished Leon and reached out to me; more clasping of hard, faintly damp fingers that reminded me of

Uncle Duncan's. I suppressed a wince and, behind him, Cris' farting Dalek wheezed and creaked. Leon introduced Toby, who seemed less discombobulated than either of us—or might just have been a better liar—and Cris dispatched the pleasantries with fluid ease. The four of us chatted for a few minutes... or, rather, we chatted and Cris made patient contributions between which he kept having to pause for breath. The discomfiture of it was of the kind experienced when going to see an elderly relative whose Sunday afternoon visits have been so long postponed that, when the eventual obligatory tea is had, neither the visitors nor the visitee can remember the slightest detail about each others' lives. A shared background, a mutual obligation lingers, but is cobwebbed and stilted by guilt and general foot-shuffling embarrassment.

It was like that, only thirty years worse.

"Well, we'll, um... we'll leave you to it," Leon said cheerfully.

I thought I saw a touch of relief in Cris' face.

"There's a cafeteria down the hall. Third right. Stay away from the egg rolls. It's... it's very good to see you."

"Yeah." Leon lingered, weight on his back foot, hands in pockets. "Yeah. Um. Not so long next time, that's for sure! Uh... now I know you're here, I guess—"

"Yes. That'd be nice. And... nice to meet you, Toby."

"Same here, Mr. McIlroy. You take care."

Cris kept his smile in place almost as long as it took them to go. The machine whirred, and I suspected that, if he could have heaved a deep sigh, he would have done. I ferreted in my bag for my recorder, checked with him he didn't mind its use, and set myself up while, all the time, the breath rattled in him like a cavernous echo, tearing and sucking at every scrap of quiet. I found myself talking just to fill it, just to avoid having to hear that sound. We skirted the preamble quickly enough; I wanted Cris to save his words for the things that really mattered.

"So, um, you managed Brother Rush from the start? Vince Dexler introduced you, I believe."

He nodded. "Yes. Vince had a nose for talent. Would have made a great career for himself if he'd stayed off of the blow. Impairs your judgement... can't hear the difference between 6/8 and 12/8 anymore. He OD'd, of course. Sad."

"Indeed." I hadn't expected such a swift demolition job; did he still bear a grudge? "Mr. Dexler, in '75 and '76, he worked for some larger labels, didn't he?"

The Dalek bubbled; it had, I noticed, a tank of water recessed into its body, presumably to hydrate the gas Cris breathed. The curtains were long, floor-length, and a particularly unattractive shade of mustard. Outside, birds dipped in the cloudless sky and rattled against the acid greens of the trees. The TV news loop cycled around again. Cris shifted position in his chair and winced, reaching up to adjust the canula where it hooked over his ears.

"Mm," he said, at length. "Briefly. I... wouldn't read too much into it, though. You're referring, I assume, to Damon's abortive attempt to switch and run?"

"Er." I glanced down at my notepad, annoyed that he'd caught me out. I'd thought I had the upper hand, that he wouldn't mention it right off the bat.

But then I'd thought that about Inez and Charlie. Did people always pull their secrets out into the open, waving them at me like armour? Maybe Day just hadn't been as subtle as he'd thought.

"So you'd say there was never a concerted effort at his negotiating another contract?"

Cris turned those pale, ghostly eyes on me and smiled. "Vince rarely had the kind of influence he thought he did with anyone, least of all in business. Sure, he... he talked a good game. It was people like him, people like Inez Blackman, who got behind Damon and pushed. Whispered, told him to do one thing or the other, told him to go for this or go for that. D'you see what I mean? The... the most powerful man on the council is the one who had the king's ear last."

"The king?" I raised an eyebrow.

"Figuratively." Cris twisted his mouth into a dismissive curl. "I think the point you'll grasp, Miss Ross, is that it was a difficult world. A *different* world, but.... Damon had talent. Real talent, and that's easy for people to feed off. They swarm to it. And it's easy to crush, hard to nurture. He was lazy, of course. Coasted on it."

"I'm sorry?"

"What he could do. Connect with the fans, play the game, the... music. Turn out the crowd-pleasers. But Damon had more to him than that. It's why he'd get frustrated, every now and then. Act out, push boundaries."

I nodded, thinking of the song Charlie had told me about, the studied misbehaviour of Amsterdam. The way he'd played at The Crown. Behind us, the Filipina nurse (manager? I wasn't sure what kind of pretences they kept up here) passed through, ostensibly en route to another communal room. Cris raised a hand at her—gave a quick, tight flicker of a smile—and I wondered which he found worse. Being checked up on every ten minutes, or being physically tied to the machine.

"He'd... you know, he'd do things just to prove he could, or because someone told him it'd be a good idea. Like with the royalty splits, the... deal Vince promised him."

"So you knew about that, at the time?"

A melancholy look crossed Cris' face. "I did. It got back to me, what Vince was doing. He'd... been talking to a lot of Garten's big sellers, making... approaches. That night, the night Damon— There were a lot of people there from Decca, EMI... no one with half the brass Vince said. Like saying you've invited the Pope, then having some local deacon show up. I... I said to Damon, he's playing you for a fool. And you're acting it, if you think—well, you-you get the idea."

He stopped, pale and stiff with the effort of prolonged speech, and gestured to a jug of water on the table beside him. I helped him pour a glass, which he sipped carefully. Horrible choice to have to make, I thought: talk or breathe.

"You argued?" I prompted. He nodded. "And it got, um, heated?"

"Yeah. I... regret that. Last time I saw him alive."

Again, he'd thrown me off track. I cursed inwardly. Of all people, I should be able to see beyond the present frailties of his flesh, to imagine him a younger man, wound up with frustration and anger. They'd argued—Day had said Cris always seemed highly strung—so how hard would it have been to follow him upstairs, take the opportunity as it came?

Oblivious to my internal meanderings, Cris drank more water in those halting, delicate sips. He had to work up to talking again afterwards. I wondered how the hell he ever managed to eat anything.

"Last time, and I told him he didn't have the flair to make it. That he'd be nothing on his own. Ah, he'd embarrassed me. Standing there with Vince, like they were on the shore of a brave new world." He shook his head, face a mask of pensive repentance. "Like I was the old guard. He really was naïve sometimes, that boy. But I shouldn't have said—he *could* have done it, you see. I mean, he wasn't the only one. Charlie did some great work, early on. Dream to work with, in those days. We've all seen how Leon's matured. And Joss! He had talent *and* sticking power. Just look at what he achieved. But Damon.... Hell, if he'd stuck to his guns, done his own thing, and stopped trying to... to chase the money, just gone with his best ideas... people would have remembered his *name*. He—hah—*he* might even have... have won that damn Novello!"

Cris gave a sticky, bubbling laugh, but he'd lost me.

"Novello?"

"Like... the one Joss picked up for that, uh, that song he wrote. *Morning Light*. That, you know, that boy band sang it? '91, '93. Something like that. I remember when I first heard it. Thinking what a damn long way he'd come. Learned to have the courage of his own convictions... you see? 'Course, there's a difference between that and sheer pig-headed, which is what he *used* to be. They all were. Young guys, you know.... Times I tried to tell those boys anything. It was like with Charlie's trouble, or-or Joss and that damn girl."

He took a moment, obviously in some discomfort. I waited as patiently as I could, topped up his water, and tried not to bounce impatiently in my seat. The nurse padded back through and watched us while she pretended to be busy adjusting the volume on the TV set.

"What, um… who d'you mean? The girl?"

I struck lucky. Cris wasn't thinking fully about what he said, his concentration still partially taken up with the need to keep breathing. The Dalek creaked away to itself, and the phlegm gurgled inside him.

"Jessica," Cris said, hauling in for another few seconds' fruitless breath. "Minute he got involved with her… I told him to leave her alone. Vicious little bitch, and if Max had found out…."

"Max?" Tiny little bells started to ping in my head. "Not Maxwe—"

He wheezed, gut flexing against the effort of it, eyes fixed on me. "Vost. Yes. She was Maxwell Vost's niece. I… I saw that kid in freckles and pigtails in '69. Apple of his eye. I told Joss— leave her alone, I said. He thought I was this crusty old fart… didn't know what it was like. Huh."

Another rippling, sucking pull of air. The machine rasped. A cold sweat broke out at the base of my spine as Cris' face seemed to pull tight, skull-like and pallid. He coughed, and sputum rattled in what little lung capacity he had left.

"Are you—?"

He held up a hand. The moment drew out, thick with the bellows of the machine and the sound of his gasps gnawing at the air.

"Fine. She was… young, y'see. God, she didn't look it. But he was almost twenty-six. If the papers had ever—damn, if the *police* had found out! Only takes one… screw-up."

I bit down on all the reactions I wanted to have—the surprise, the prurient curiosity—and all the judgements I wanted to make, keeping my tone measured and my interviewee safely in his stride.

"How young?"

"F... fourteen, back in '74."

Damn near gagging on my own tongue, I tried to channel my shock into innocent throat-clearing. Cris folded back into his chair, looking tired.

"Attitudes were different then, I suppose," he said. "They broke up, anyway. I saw her, the last tour the boys did. Holland. She... tagged along. He'd worked out what was good for him by then, I think. She went back to LA, I believe. Max had a place down there at the time. Horses and such. You... I'm sure you know how... how young girls are... with horses."

Those pale eyes closed and, for a moment he sat eerily still, not even his stomach moving. Such a strange thing to have said, I thought. A weird, incongruous statement. As if I could reconcile my mental image of Joss Napier—drinking tea from a bone china cup with holes in his socks and wellies by the door— with that of an underage groupie who just happened to be his producer's niece? And as if this girl would have been happy to turn her back on clubland for the nearest Pony Club gymkhana?

That didn't seem right for a second.

The farting Dalek jerked me from my reverie, and I smiled nervously, aware that Cris had probably reached his limits. The limit of all coherent discussion, anyway. I thanked him for his time, and he nodded graciously, murmured something about what good days they'd been, despite it all, how good it was to see Leon again and how I should drop in any time. It all came across rather garbled, and I doubted he still remembered my name by the time we said goodbye. I knew one thing for sure:

I'd never been happier to leave a place behind me.

I found Toby and Leon waiting out by the car and nodded my readiness to go. *So* ready.

"He's only nine years older than me," Leon said, by way of greeting, a slight wail of panic in his voice.

Toby poked him in the middle of his back. "And you're healthy, Dad. So count your blessings and get in the car. I thought he was all right. You ought to try to stay in touch, huh?"

I let their conversation—Toby's sense of mischief and Leon's thrashing around on the shores of uncertainty—wash over me and wondered how I was supposed to prove a thing. Cris had given me little of concrete value, all things considered. He and Inez had both known about the business with Vince Dexler, though from slightly different angles. Cris could, just like Charlie, have been furious enough with Day to kill him… but I just couldn't see it. It brought me back, over and over, to those original problems. The only person anyone had seen with blood on their clothes was Leon and—as I hastily reminded myself—he'd found the body. So our murderer must either have had the opportunity to change their clothes, or to slip away unnoticed. That would take some presence of mind. Luck, too. It didn't fit with my conviction that the act must have been born of some moment of fury, the snap of blind rage. And there were plenty of people I could like for it. Day might have thought he'd been on the verge of something wonderful, but Leon had suspected the gist of his plans.

Currently, the best-friend-betrayed was fiddling with the radio and nagging his son about the local crime rate in his district. It made me slightly nauseous to think of him with his hands on Damon's head, the crack of skull on sink... no. Okay, so what about the publicly embarrassed manager? Day had thought Cris highly strung. But he'd have to have cleaned up, dealt logically with the aftermath of the crime. Cris had the brain to do it, yes, and he'd likely not been as smashed off his face as most of my other suspects, but did I believe he'd done it? My mind drifted back to the cheating spouse and her grudge-bearing lover. I grimaced, reminded of Cris' revelation about Joss and his fourteen-year-old groupie. Yet another can of worms. Who else had known her real age? Maybe, if—*if*. That was the problem. I had nothing but ifs. How did I prove a thing? Go back, say, to Charlie's boat and ask him if, incidentally, he remembered stoving anyone's head in, circa the mid-Seventies?

Maybe I could get them all together, try to grandstand the truth out of them. *All right, here's one. Take a drink if you've never... committed pre-meditated murder! Ha! Gotcha....*

No. Probably not.

I slumped in the back of the Toyota and let the majestic Californian highways zip by me. Sheets of blue sky and wide spaces, so different to the sludgy greens and browns of English roads, and without the cheery red-and-white signs and promised mushroom pancakes of Little Chef outlets, which for some reason I suddenly missed.

The good-natured bickering about the necessity of Toby finding an apartment in a slightly safer, more respectable part of the city cheered me up a bit. Amused me, too, given what I'd heard about the flat Leon and Day had gone halves on in Kentish Town: massive weekenders, shared girlfriends, and rats the size of pygmy goats, if Damon was to be believed. I hid my smiles in the back of my hand. It would have been nice to lay my problems out to Leon, but he worried me now more than ever. For one thing, I found it far too easy to forget he was old enough to be my father. Secondly, I wasn't sure what—or who —either of us might be trying to catch hold of, but I'd felt it lingering there last night. Like at least one of us was reaching out for some kind of pretence at sanity, maybe, or the lost threads of the past, the last whisper of something, some*one*, so badly missed.

We got back to the hotel in good time, effusive hugs and affectionate goodbyes between Leon and Toby, handshakes and warm wishes on my part. He didn't do the cheek-kissing thing his father did; different generation, I supposed, born into concepts of personal space and women not necessarily welcoming the gesture. The Toyota pulled away, and I mumbled something about going to freshen up, battling up to my room through a growing sense of unease.

I showered, hot as the water would go, pulled on jeans and a shirt and rubbed my hair halfway dry with a fluffy white hotel towel. Feeling slightly better scrubbed, if no cleaner, I leaned on the wrought iron railing of my room's tiny balcony. Inhaling the dry air, I watched the sun turn to soft dusk light over the crowded sky and tried to pretend I couldn't still hear Cris McIlroy breathing in my ear.

"You all right, babe?"

I didn't bother to turn around. He barely surprised me now.

"Not really."

Damon came forward and leaned on the rail beside me, the whisper of a chill and maybe a waft of cigarette smoke. Maybe I imagined that. I wasn't sure how to tell anymore.

"You saw Cris."

"Yes." I glanced sidelong at Day. He looked rather like he had in that photo of Leon's: contemplative profile surveying the river. The dying sun flared off his curls and picked patterns on the oily sheen of his silk dupion jacket, shot through with threads of gold and orange. "It gave me the creeps."

He turned, leaning back with his elbows on the railing and studying me with his head on one side, mouth tugged around a small, mirthless smile.

"Sorry, baby."

"Yeah." I picked at a flake of paint on the iron. "Well, it's...."

I wasn't sure what to say. It's nothing? That would have been a lie. I shivered, momentarily dizzy, and glanced up. Damon's hand dropped from my hair. He'd been trying to brush it back off my forehead, unthinking, forgetting that he couldn't... well. I cleared my throat, and my fingers completed the gesture, smoothing down the damp, fuzzy strands. He said nothing, but a muscle in his jaw jumped like a frog. Cigarettes and lighter were pulled from the pockets of dark brown corduroy flares, and he made that familiar, complex arrangement of hands in front of his face as he lit up, head bent over the flame.

"I just don't ever want to be like that," I blurted. "Stuck in your own body while it dies off around you. Like a-a flesh prison. It's... horrible."

Damon exhaled. The smoke danced around him, and he squinted at me through it, his face at once blank as a cover shoot pose and yet full of sympathy, and the most terrible understanding I could have asked for. I tried to make myself believe I wasn't thinking of Uncle Duncan. That it didn't scare me every time I thought about it, that—

"You'll be all right, babe. Promise."

It could have pissed me off, his saying that. I wanted to know what right, what grounds he had to say so, yet I also wanted to hear it again, unconditionally and repeatedly, until I could stick myself to the lie like glue. Beyond the railing, the orange flickers of streetlamps and the far-off prickles of buildings had begun to light up the dimness. The world had turned that grainy, greyish blue that precedes proper dark. Day loosed an attempt at a smoke ring, and it dissolved in a fat blotch, a stain sluicing through the air. He appeared to be about to say something, but a knock at my hotel room door distracted us both.

The room wasn't much. It had the air of commercial business travel about it, as if everything had been designed for bland anonymity. White bedding, dark cream curtains, beige carpet, lampshade and armchair. Beech veneer desk with electrical sockets and broadband access, TV and coffee making facilities, and a pokey en suite with limescale on the shower screen. Somehow, Leon made the room seem smaller, even as he came in sideways, uncertain weight on his back foot and shifty glances all around us.

"Did you get... I mean, did Cris—?"

A splash of lamplight illuminated his face, shadowed every wrinkle. He looked up and tried to wrap a hundred different things around that first moment of unexpectedly seeing Damon. I knew the feeling well, though it had paled for me by now. I pushed the door shut behind Leon.

"Not sure how it helps. It's.... I don't know. Did either of you two ever know a girl called Jessica?"

Leon was still staring. Day frowned, exhaled a thin stream of smoke, and moved away from the lamp and its pool of low wattage light.

"Dunno," he said. "There were a lot of birds."

I let that slide by with only a small barb. "Well, this one was Joss'."

Leon finally moved, like someone had turned a key in his back. Day nodded at him, and he gave a little smile of greeting.

"Jessica?" He lurched to the beige chair by the window, attention still fixed on Damon, and dropped into it. "I... oh, I don't know. When was this?"

"'74, '75ish. Cris said she was around on the last tour you did, too, spring of '76."

Day leaned back against the cheap desk and wrinkled his nose. "Holland? Nah, there w—"

"Wait. Yes!" Leon slapped the arm of the chair. "'75... that summer! Joss 'n' Jess. Don't you remember? She was the one with the hair right down to her— Redhead," he amended with a compunctious glance at me. "Pretty, but... he never really introduced her, showed her off. Except for that one time at Charlie's place. Don't you remember that, man? You gotta remember *that*! At that party... she was the girl who didn't recognise Ringo!"

The cigarette drooped against Damon's lip. "F... you're right. Yeah. Twiggy little thing, with them big eyes. Dreamy look on her face."

"You called her a dozy mare!" Leon cried, hitting his stride. "And Joss got really ticked off! Remember? He never used to come out with us so much after that... then she was off the scene again. He never talked about it."

I tried to get in between them, catch either one before they both went so far down memory lane I couldn't keep up. "You didn't know anything about her?"

Day shook his head. "No, not as such. Not that I—"

"Joss liked his private life private," Leon put in. "He'd trot out girls from time to time. We all did, but... they were—I mean, they weren't—"

"Permanent fixtures?"

He gave me an apologetic wince. More like moveable furniture with attractive wobbly bits, I suspected.

"Apart from Inez. And Charlie dated that model for a while... that was almost serious. But...." He frowned. "No, I don't think I recall Joss ever making like that girl was a big thing. I just remember her 'cos of the hair, and—"

"She was underage." I folded my arms across my chest. "And she was Maxwell Vost's niece. Neither of you knew?"

"Bloody 'ell." Damon took a drag on his cigarette and shook his head. "Dangerous water, that is. How old—"

"Fourteen, apparently."

He cringed. Leon uttered a strangled expletive and rocked back in the chair. "You're kidding? She was never.... Shit, man!"

I chewed my bottom lip. "If neither of you knew, then—oh, damn it."

Another perfectly good hypothesis straight out of the window. Something still nagged at the back of my mind, though. Tasteful floral art and farmyard scenes.

All my wife's work.

"Son of a— I want to go back to Bristol," I said, the tinkling pieces of my own blind stupidity falling into place behind my eyes. "Got some pertinent questions for Mr. Novello Award Winner."

"Eh?" Damon appeared nonplussed.

"Joss. He won an award," Leon said, with what might have been a small hint of bitterness, "for that song of his... whatsit... *Morning Light*. That crappy boy band sang it—what was it? '92? '93? Judy loved 'em." He shot me a rueful glance. "We're much better friends now we're not married. But, yeah, Day... it's true. The guy churned out a bucket of stuff after he quit Kaleidoscope Green."

Damon held his cigarette up by his cheekbone, mouth set thin and eyes guarded. "He won an Ivor? *Joss*?"

"Yeah." Leon sounded slightly less confident. "The... the song's really not bad." He looked over at me, like I wouldn't mind being a human shield. "You remember it, Ellis? It was at Number One for weeks. Real catchy."

I muttered non-committally, less worried at that moment about Napier's writing credits than his legal infractions, but Leon had started tapping out a rhythm with his foot. He swiped his tongue over his lower lip and hummed under his breath. I knew the tune. Even now I had to walk out of shops when it started playing in case it got stuck in my head for another thirty-two weeks. The song had been hugely popular, though the boy band had faded into relative obscurity. Some of their members still popped up in solo efforts and television careers, all built on the fact that *Morning Light* had been one of the ultimate couples' songs of the decade.

Seeing your face in the morning light
I know you're the only thing

I've ever done right.

Yes, I'd had it strummed at me on a badly-tuned acoustic once or twice. I opened my mouth, prepared to own up to knowing the song, if not the bit about the acoustic, but I didn't get a chance.

"Fucking bastard!"

Leon stopped abruptly in his humming. Damon pushed away from the desk, scowling blackly.

"I'll fucking kill him!"

I blinked. "Wh—?"

He ignored me, the full force of his temper directed at Leon.

"How could you? How could you think he wrote that? How did you not— That fucking talentless little twerp? You were always so bloody cosy, the pair of you, and you never once thought—"

"Hey! Now, that's not fair and you know it, man!"

If it surprised Damon to see Leon standing up to him, it only served to piss him off further. He crossed the floor in two jerky, stop-motion strides, and static sparks jumped off the coffee making facilities. The curtains whispered in a non-existent breeze.

"Bugger fair! That tune—that's my fucking tune. E minor, right? Minor third, major sixth and seventh, syncopated run... that little blues hook on the bridge? I dubbed two acoustic parts, put in a 'lectric lead, went like...."

He snapped his fingers, pulling a rhythm out of the air, cloaking it with the same melody Leon had just sketched, but sweeter, cleaner—not like he had to work to remember how it went. Leon fumbled his phone from his pocket, got up and started edging around the room, looking for decent enough reception to find and download the track.

"Y'know?" Day relinquished the tune and turned to face me. For the first time, he really seemed unearthly, eyes raw behind the kohl, his skin bleached by the seeping lamplight. His hair flamed gold, and cigarette smoke kissed his cheeks. "That was… that was brand new, baby. I ain't never…. Shit!"

"Got it!" Leon flicked up the volume on his phone and set it on the cheap desk. "This is it."

The music filtered out in sweeping style, a string quartet giving way to an acoustic part, moody and languorously melancholy. Damon cut across the intro just before the first harmonies of the four clean-cut, teen idol boys hit the air.

"It's too bleedin' slow! S'meant to be a love song, not a bloody funeral!"

He stared all the way through the first verse, lip curled and eyes narrowed, but it appeared to be the chord shift on the bridge that finally did it for him. He let out a long line of curses with way more vowels in them than they really ought to have, and his hand flexed like he wanted something to throw put into it.

"What'd he do to the bleedin' *lyric*? What the f—those ain't my fuckin' *words*! He killed it! He bleedin' *killed* it!"

Leon snatched up the phone; he obviously knew these tantrums of old. "I think that's enough," he said and blipped it off. "Day, really, I didn't— I swear I didn't know. How—"

"I *tole* you I heard someone!" Damon moaned, his voice a hollow wail, cigarette hand pointing at me. "I said! Din't I say? My tapes. My fucking *tapes*…."

"What? What tapes?" Leon looked to me for explanation. "No, 'cos when I... I cleared out the studio at Westleve, it was just the stuff we'd been working on for the new album. Some notes and a couple of demos for *those* songs, but nothing that related to—oh, God." He'd finally clicked. "You don't think—?"

I lifted one shoulder, wordlessly apologetic. Right now, we could only guess, though they seemed like pretty safe bets.

"My fucking *tapes*! Bastard!" Damon paced the beige carpet, fuming and pulling on his Camel. "That's the only way he could've had that... it was new. Brand new. I never even— I'll fucking kill him. I will. I'm gonna fuckin' *do* 'im...."

Leon, pale and horrified, bit his lip. "No, he could never have.... No... 'cos, 'cos when I found— He was trying to calm me down. He came upstairs with us—me and Charlie—an'... he never went close. Ran off to call the ambulance. Jesus, if he... oh, Day!"

"But why?" I said, thinking aloud more than anything. "This material, it was new stuff you'd been working on... nobody else knew about it, right?"

Damon shook his head, with only the briefest of guilty glances at Leon.

"Vince hadn't even heard the tapes. And he wouldn't have, not after what went down at the party, with Cris and everythin'." He shifted, a trifle embarrassed still, I supposed, by the pride that had always stopped him admitting he'd never really been headhunted by EMI. He shrugged. "Cris... well, he was right. The deal Vince had offered me—it wouldn't have gone through. He couldn't get me the terms he said he could, y'know? And I... I wouldn't have taken 'em, even if.... Not after he'd lied to me like that."

Leon gave him a warm little look, the smile of long-held faith vindicated. If we hadn't had more pressing concerns, it might have been a male bonding moment.

"So… maybe it didn't start off about that. Maybe," I said, running with the idea, "it was straight out jealousy. What if he just went nosing, found the paperwork, took the opportunity to bean you on the bonce while you weren't with it, then realised that he could take the tapes *and* the music without anyone knowing?"

"Fuck," Leon murmured, "that's cold."

Damon nodded slowly. A touch of the avenging angel dropped from his face as he started to calm down. "It'd take balls. I never thought he had 'em. He could've bought the stuff off of someone…. I mean, just havin' it don't mean he killed me for it."

I sighed, exasperated. Even now, and he was still making bloody excuses!

"It's enough to ask some very pointed questions," I snapped. "It's enough to go back to Bristol."

Chapter Nineteen

August 27th 1976

Damon ducked. The vase flew past his ear and shattered on the bank of cherry wood wardrobes behind him. He straightened up, shook out his curls, and glared at Inez.

"Yeah? Well you ain't such a great shot now, are ya baby? Either you're losin' it, mama, or you still love me, 'cos you ain't even *trying* to aim right."

Inez growled in frustration and looked for something else to throw, but her dressing table was devoid of anything except a bottle of Dior perfume, and she'd regret that later if she lobbed it now. He glowered at her, his white cotton tunic open to the top of his breastbone, garlands of embroidered scarlet flowers bright around the neckline and wrists. He'd had his hair done, and the ends of it just brushed against the slips of skin the tunic left bare.

Love him? She couldn't stand him.

The bed yawned between them, a king-size affair smothered in purple geometric prints. The box of rubbers he'd found lay where he'd flung them, on the covers, discreet packaging incongruous and full of blame. The doors of the centre wardrobe hung open, and the full-length mirrors on their interiors winked at Inez, doubling her image back at her, half-dressed and fully caught out. She should, she supposed, either have hidden the johnnies somewhere else, or not asked Damon to fetch her a fresh pair of stockings.

"D'you, then?"

His voice was low; his stillness scared her, the way he was staring and the depth of his eyes. She reached absently for the strap of her shift, tugging it back onto her shoulder. A quirk of her mouth, plum lipstick and the pretence of not understanding, but he wouldn't let her get away with that. He crossed the room, too close to her too fast, and seized her wrist.

"You tell me, baby! Yes or no?"

She wrenched out of his grip. "I thought I was just a whore."

His word. He flinched when she said it, and it gave Inez an ignoble pleasure. He hadn't asked who, she realised. Did he know? Certainty didn't appear to be one of the things boiling on his face. He'd left finger marks on her wrist. She rubbed them as he drew in a single, rigid breath.

"Look," he said softly, sounding beaten and sore. "It don't have to matter. I don't care who—it's Graham, is it? I know he helped you, he made it better, with the injury and that, but…. We can patch it up, babe, yeah?"

Inez bit down the urge to laugh. Sudden, terrible, and very tempting. Part of her still cried out for this simplicity of his, for that endless capacity to keep on trying, but it was a minority demand compared to the parts of her that couldn't believe his arrogance, his density, his general... *Damon-ness*. She hadn't even admitted to her fault, and he wanted to play a forgiveness scene.

Bloody typical.

"I think... I think it does matter," she said, as kindly as she could.

"Baby—"

"Look, I don't *want* to be your 'baby'. All right? I... I just don't wanna hear it anymore. I'm tired of it."

His face hardened. "And me?"

"I didn't say that. I—"

"You ain't denying it, either."

Inez sighed. She didn't want to laugh now. He was still staring, gaze like a knife, chin lifted and mouth set in that stony little line that usually presaged some kind of tantrum. But that look....

Who'd have thought he paid enough attention to her to be this hurt?

Unwanted tears prickled at the back of her eyes, soon subsumed in bitter anger at her own reaction. That he could *do* this, when she knew what she'd done was wrong, but when it had seemed like the lesser of two evils, like something she could justify. Sod it, neither of them had been perfect in the last two years! She wanted to shout that out, rationalise what had happened, all the things she'd never meant, but she couldn't make the words come. Not when he pulled all this humiliation, embarrassment, and shame out of her.

She tried to look away, but the mirrors mocked her from

across the room. Snared and trapped. As hot today as it had been all summer, yet her nipples still stood proud through her shift, her nose reddening and her hair unbrushed. She blinked, bent her head.

"I'm… I *am* sorry, you know."

He scoffed, just a small scrape of breath against the dusty air. "Yeah?"

"Look… I could go up to town, stay at the flat for a few days. If you want to talk, then—"

"No."

Inez glanced up, thinking for one foolish moment he'd ask her to stay, to put everything on hold and dig into the mess she'd made until he found out why. That he really wanted her here. She sniffed.

"No?"

"Nah… I need you here tonight." He said it matter-of-factly, the way he'd asked the caterers if they'd brought enough vol-au-vents. "The party. I need some moral support, baby. You gotta be here, you can't leave."

Inez watched him intently for a moment. The pulse at the base of his throat beat steadily. The summer had brought out the bridge of freckles across his nose, picked out natural highlights in his hair. The air thrummed between them. She drew a careful breath.

"Well. Yes. Obviously it's about what *you* need."

His composure started to crack, narrowing eyes and fish-wife vowels. She pushed past him, back to the wardrobe and the inculpating mirrors.

"Yeah? Well, I ain't the one with the guilty conscience! H-How long you been playing this, eh? All the time he's been comin' up here... bleedin' *physiotherapy*. I know what that is now, yeah? You—whatcha doin'?"

Inez snatched a dress from its hanger and a flight bag from the bottom of the compartment in which she kept her shoes.

"I think it's best if I go for a day or so. Just... we both need a break."

Bag tossed on the bed, she grabbed clothes at random. Overnight stuff. That frock with the high collar, slippery fabric and psychedelic print. Maybe she wouldn't even be at the flat. Maybe she wouldn't even come back. She threw the clothes at the bag, and Day threw them out again, petulant and finally— yes, thank God, finally—letting rip. Somewhere through the mists of it all, Inez felt grateful for that. It made it easier to stay angry with him.

"What the fuck d'you think you're doing? You ain't goin' nowhere, baby! You—Inez, stop it! Fuckin'.... Look, you go, mama, you don't need to bother comin' back, you know what I'm sayin'? You ain't—will you stop doin' that?"

She faced him down, baby blue negligee in her hand. "Or what?"

Outside, tyres whisked on the gravel drive. Inez didn't have to look out of the window to know it would be Leon's black Mini joining the rank of cars parked out front. The bedroom windows were all open in deference to the scorching drought heat, and the sound of a car door slamming, the jangle of keys, and that familiar jaunty whistle drifted up clear and bright on the thick sunlit haze. It distracted Damon, however briefly, and Inez's anger surged anew. Already, his attention was split. She hadn't lost him; she'd never had him. Not fully. Not enough for.... She supposed she'd relent, if he asked. If he just looked at her now and said 'please', she'd stay. She'd do all he wanted, and they could work out the screw-ups later, like sane people.

Instead, he scowled.

"Or you can sling your hook, yeah? And you won't get a penny."

She curled her lip. "I don't want your bloody money."

"I mean it!" The pitch of his voice rose like a desperate child trying to cling to a confiscated toy. "That'll be it, yeah? Over. You go now, an'—"

Inez moved to the bed, folded the negligee into the bag, and shook her head. She picked up the clothes he'd pulled out, folded those too, oddly calm beside his taut fury. His hand clenched and unclenched at his side.

"Inez...."

"I'll see you after the weekend. You have your party. Have fun."

She didn't look at him. She didn't need to, and there didn't seem to be much point in anything anyway. It had never been so easy to just close down, just shut everything off. And the relief seemed immense... she wouldn't have to spend tonight dangling between uncertainties, lying with her face and ignoring her head. No more staring at what she couldn't have, no more blinding herself on the sharp edges of it, running and running and never moving an inch.

Downstairs, more doors slammed, and Leon—he wasn't capable of doing anything quietly—called out, incessantly cheerful. He'd come jogging up the stairs any minute, Inez knew. Because there were never any bloody boundaries. Not between anything. She zipped up her bag.

Damon muttered something about a nicotine fix and

turned away, sweeping out of the room and changing the texture of it behind him. No more cloud of fag smoke and YSL. No more moods, no more arrogant, insensitive demands, no more... assumptions. Inez pressed the back of her finger to each eye in turn, trying to mop up without smudging her mascara. Her mouth buckled, and the efforts were all in vain, because the tears came anyway.

She pulled herself together after a few gasping, luxuriant minutes. Bit late for all that, really. And she still wasn't dressed. Voices drifted up the stairs, low and unintelligible, and the record player went on. Hendrix. Leon had probably brought Lenny Bruce EPs too. Inez pulled a tissue from the box on her dressing table. Cherry wood, matching the rest of the room. Small, plush-seated chair in faux Louis XV style, and what did it all add up to? She wiped her eyes, blew her nose, and took one last look around her. Clothes first. Then she needed to make a phone call.

She dressed quickly, but not in the frock Damon had picked out for her to wear tonight. Yellow skirt and short sleeved blouse, sunglasses in hand ready to shade her puffy eyes. She'd slip out through the kitchen, take the car as far as the station. He could pick it up from there later. When he'd sobered up, probably. She stifled another sniffle and sat on her side of the bed, phone clamped to her ear, waiting for an answer.

"Yeah?"

Charlie sounded sleepy, like he'd just rolled out of bed or something... or someone, she supposed. Inez took a deep breath.

"Darling, it's me. Bit of a pickle."

He seemed to wake up at that. "Shit. What?"

She guessed he'd been stoking up on rest before tonight. He cleared his throat, the rattle of it harsh on the line.

"Are-are you all right?" he asked, a little more with it now. "D'you need—"

"I'm fine," she lied. "But I'm not going to be here tonight. I'm going up to the flat."

"Aw, fuck... he hasn't—?"

"No. Well, yes. Sort of. He thinks it's Graham. Anyway, we — Look, I have to go. Just watch your back, won't you?"

"Yeah. Yeah, I will. Can I... d'you want me to come over? I could meet you there, before I leave town. Won't take me long to—"

"I don't know... no. No, don't. Call me there, maybe. Tomorrow morning. We'll—well, we'll sort something out. He was talking about divorce, so... I don't know. It's probably going to blow over. Just sit tight, okay? I'll speak to you tomorrow."

"All right, sweetheart. Take care."

"Mm. Bye."

She hung up, eyes damp again. At least she could trust Charlie to keep his mouth shut. He was good at that. Inez stood, picked up her flight bag, and headed downstairs. At the foot of the stairs, the house split into two. To one side, the glass partition, the bubble of voices and music, preparation and anticipation. To the other side the corridor, burgundy walls leaning in on each other, lined with their photos. Engagement party, wedding, Portugal.... She made her way past them, not looking. She'd barely set foot into the kitchen before a voice called out behind her.

"Inez!"

She closed her eyes, exhaled slowly. Not him. She couldn't put up with it now. The kitchen clock ticked away to itself and she turned, regarding Leon with a weary glare.

"What?"

He looked coolly tousled in navy blue and cream. Print shirt and sharp tailoring, a move away from all the hippie hangover clothes she'd got used to seeing him wear. With one hand at the back of his waist, the other scratching his head, he didn't quite pull off suave, but he was getting there.

"Uh. Is it true? You guys have a... like, a tiff?"

Inez weighed the flight bag in her hand. What else, precisely, did it look like? An impromptu picnic?

"I'm, um, I'm going to swing out for a couple of days," she said. "That's all."

Leon frowned. "Well, he's really—I mean, d'you have to go tonight?"

She ran her tongue over her teeth. "Is it really any business of yours?"

He turned his mouth down, disguising an obvious anger with the charade of ambivalence. "It's just... it doesn't look good. Y'know? And he's... he does seem really cut. He wouldn't tell me what—"

"There you are, then." Inez glanced up at the clock. She'd have to go soon if she wanted to catch that train. "Perhaps it isn't your business after all."

"Ouch! That... that's not... I mean, c'mon, Inez. I'm just tryin' to help."

It could have been the way he stood there, wavering a little, all self-righteous anxiety and well-meaning interference, or it could have been the memory of the spring and the way he'd held her, smoothed down her hair when she cried. The day he'd found her in Damon's studio, caught her off-guard enough to spill it all, and she'd told him about the baby... how he'd listened and looked after her. The way he'd never, to the best of her knowledge, breathed a word about the miscarriage to anyone—but not because he was her friend. No. It was never that, was it?

Not when telling would have hurt Day.

"Yeah," she muttered. "Well, you can help him now, can't you? Go and be a shoulder to cry on. How long have you been waiting for that, hmm?"

Leon's frown deepened. "What?"

Inez loosed a short, dry wrinkle of laughter. "Don't think I don't know."

"Know what?" The corner of his mouth twitched. "You sure you're okay?"

"You mean am I drunk?" She snorted. "No. Some of us don't start knockin' 'em back with our cornflakes."

"Uh-huh." His stance grew stiffer, irritation in his eyes. "Well, I think you need to go back in there and talk to him. He's —"

"I don't give a stuff! I told you, I'm going for a day or so. I'll be at the flat."

He scratched his head again, dry coils of dark hair ruffled and fuzzy. "Look, I don't know what this is about, but you can't do this. You need to be here tonight. He's gonna look.... Well, what'll people think? And whatever he said to you, he doesn't mean it. You know that."

Inez shook her head. "D'you ever listen to yourself? How

long have you been apologising for him? Mopping up his mistakes, throwing yourself over the puddles? I *know* you don't get anything in return."

"I'm his friend." Leon shifted on his back foot, cleared his throat. "I'm tryin' to be yours too, yeah? So don't do this."

"Oh, come on!" The smile pulled at her lips, an ugly, insidious movement. "I know all about you, you know."

Leon's expression tightened. She could really start to enjoy this, Inez decided. She stepped forward, inserted herself between him and the door, put her red-tipped hand to the mellow wood, tilted her head to the side.

"D'you *really* think I don't see how you look at him? Those little moments, when you think no one could possibly notice? *I* see. I've seen the way you—"

"You don't know what you're talkin' about, Inez."

"The fuck I don't," she spat back. "I'm still his wife."

Leon winced. It gave her a sharp little thrill, and she bit hard on the heels of that, chasing it down.

"He thinks you're pathetic, you know."

"Shut up."

"He does! He *knows*, and he thinks it's pathetic."

"Shut up!" Leon pulled away from her, stumbling over everything, his own words included. "Fuckin'... who needs this, man? All right? Just— listen, you wanna screw this up, Inez? You go ahead!"

"Poofter."

He lunged, pushed her hard, swung her away from him and sent her cannoning into the Deal table. She caught the back of her leg—still weak from the injury—against the wood and cried out, hoarse and guttural. The flight bag dropped from her fingers and scudded on the tiles. Aghast, Leon backed away, shaking his head.

"I—aw, shit. I-I didn't mean to—"

He blinked, stared… then turned and ran, footsteps on the tiled corridor followed by the rattle of the glazed doors as he tried to open them, disappearing into the muddle of music and chatter. Inez leaned on the edge of the table and tipped her head back.

Ouch.

Definitely time to make a move.

* * *

The party kicked off properly sometime around ten-thirty, when the last veins of daylight were still bleeding through the dusk and the heat that had shimmered right into the evening finally gave way to a grimy coolness. Things pumped from there onwards; what had been leisurely grew frenetic, what had been chilled grew hot and, for Leon, the whole deal just melded into something bigger and more complicated. It had been several hours since he'd gone back in to tell Day that Inez had left, and he couldn't stop seeing the look of disappointment he'd gotten for failing to make her stay.

Day wouldn't say what they'd fought about, though Leon could guess. He tried to wash away the suspicions the same way he thought he could wipe the sadness off Day's face, but the 'ludes didn't seem to help. Oh, they blanketed crap out… but they made Day sleepy, and *he* just ended up with slightly dodgy co-ordination and half an erection that wouldn't go away.

But, after that, people started showing up. Day bummed a

bunch of reds from him and got kinda hyper, throwing his arms around the shoulders of strangers and laughing a lot. Leon tried to pretend it was good to see him laugh—even though it wasn't, at least not like that—and turned his attention to the cute blonde who kept tugging on his elbow and giggling. She'd turned up with somebody, he was sure, but eventually he took her outside and let her suck him off behind the conservatory. Party lights twinkled in coloured glass jars all around the pool, and he was still sober enough for the prospect of getting caught to be mildly exciting.

Probably time to do something about that.

So he did.

By midnight, the girl had long since disappeared back into the throng with a glint in her eye and a spring in her step, and Leon had talked to a bunch of people who all looked the same. Charlie arrived—late, breathless and sans obligatory chick. Said the traffic had been a nightmare. Joss was around some place, last seen being real serious and talking about sales figures with Cris, who hadn't stopped smoking those weird stinky clove cigarettes he'd picked up in Holland a couple of months back.

It had been up to the minute modern music all night, but now someone had dug out another one of Day's old Hendrix albums, and *Foxy Lady* pulsed through the heart of the room, touching the edge of the air and tingeing it purple. Whole place smelled like the Isle of Wight tonight, Leon decided. Grass, booze, and women. God, women smelled good. Didn't they, though?

And *this...* this had always been *her* song.

He wasn't sure if Day had ever told her that. He shoulda done, 'cos it fitted her perfectly. Fox. Big bushy tail, neat little paws and sharp teeth. Leon lounged by the glass partition and brought the next glass of bourbon to his lips. They were numb, but that was a good sign. It meant other crap would be, too, sooner or later.

'Cos… who did need it, y'know? It w-wasn't *fair*. It wasn't.

No.

Not at all.

Uh-huh.

'Cos Inez… she was just a bitch. Yeah.

Big ol' foxy bitch. Lady fox. Vix—vixen?

Yes.

He slumped back against the wall like he meant it and drained the glass.

Bitch.

And somethin' wasn't right, someplace. He knew that. Too much chit-chat in murky corners. People were having a good time—joint jumpin', jive swingin', cute little dishes of coke doin' the rounds—but it was froth on the water, bubbles over undercurrents. Leon peeled himself away from the wall, stumbled on the step down into the room, and caught someone laugh in his general direction.

"Yeah, yeah," he muttered, waving a hand and making for the french doors.

Long, long way through the crowd. He made it out, scent and sight and sound sticking to him, and spooled into the night, letting it all close over him. Out here, the candles had burned down in their glass jars, colours melted and dimmed. Melting like time, like hours that burned down into years. Nothin' was real, man. Moonlight dappled the pool, butting up against strange and arcane shapes floating in it… brittle sculptures of wax, Leon realised, poured in hot and since turned cold. Huh. A naked brunette was swimming lengths at a leisurely crawl, flipping over like a mermaid each time she hit an end wall. Music still ripped through the night, every grain of the air vibrating with raw-edged chords, but not as loud once he got away from the doors.

The brunette hit the end of the pool closest to Leon, flipped over and rose half out of the water to wave and smile at him before she cut down again, just the rhythmic slap of stroke after stroke.

"Someone's nicked her clothes, y'know."

Leon didn't turn, aware of Charlie filling up the space behind him. A shadow over shadows, with a waft of Brut, fag ash and weed, touched with whisky.

"Yeah," he said.

"Wasn't me," Charlie added, an apparent afterthought.

Leon smiled. "Me neither."

Charlie sniffed. *One, two.* Then footsteps—*one, two*—and he stood beside Leon, knuckle of his right fist worrying at the region of his nose. Blood marked the back of his hand when he took it away, black-looking in the darkness, and Charlie squinted at it.

"Bollocks. You got a tissue?"

Leon patted his pockets and came up with something ragged and grey. It did the job.

"Y-You won't have a nose left, y'know," he observed, due mainly to the booze and the pills, because that kind of remark could hack Charlie off under normal circumstances.

But maybe normal had all corroded away now. Maybe— like Charlie kept saying—everything was gonna change. Maybe,

Leon reflected, that's what he could feel. Undercurrents. Ripples. The earthquake was coming.

Charlie grunted and took the wad of tissue away from his nostril.

"Yeah, don't talk to *me*. Talk to Captain Psycho in there."

"Huh?"

"Threw me a knuckle sandwich just 'cos I asked where Inez was. They have some kinda spat?"

"Oh." Leon shifted, not sure what to say. "Uh… I guess. I dunno."

The brunette had abandoned the predictable rhythm of lengths and now floated on her back in the middle of the pool, sculling in lazy drifts, body silvered by the moon. They watched her for a while, admiring the way water washed away gravity, and lapped at her boobs. Leon blinked.

"Wait, what? *Damon* hit you? Inna face?"

"I know! He's… he's fuckin' wasted, man. He was yelling at Cris earlier."

Leon frowned. That didn't sound like Day. Well… it *did*, but not tonight. He'd been so excited about the faces he had coming, the people he wanted to look good in front of—and he could still do that, even if Inez wasn't here, right? He burrowed his hands deeper into his pockets and bit the inside of his lip. Day had somethin' on his mind, that was for sure. Maybe something to do with the new album. He didn't have a lot of time for the material, Leon knew that much. He thought the songs—Charlie's songs—were too simplistic. *They sound like we're not trying anymore*. That's what he'd said. And… Charlie had taken offence at that, Leon recalled. Joss had arched an eyebrow and said 'well, are we?', as if it was a question they ought to seriously consider.

Charlie nudged his shoulder. "Hey—you think I could score that?"

"Huh?"

"Ophelia over there." Charlie nodded to the pool.

"Oh. Prob'ly."

"That's what I thought. Do me a favour, man, yeah?"

Leon hesitated, then clicked. "Ah. Right. Yeah. I-I'm a tree, baby. Leavin'."

He pivoted on one foot, inexplicably clumsy, and left Charlie to it, wondering vaguely why the flagstones were conspiring to trip him over. Sneaky. He didn't want to go straight back into the heart of the party either, so he paced out along the back of the house, down to the west wing, and went up the steps to the kitchen, pausing to run his fingers through the pots of thyme and mint by the door. The scent came up to greet him, and his stomach rumbled.

Hungry? Huh. Seemed so.

He ambled in and made himself a cheese sandwich, top slice of Wonderloaf carefully aligned and squelched down with a satisfying, mayonnaisey *thrrp*. Whole thing in hand, manna from heaven, Leon settled himself at the kitchen table, feet up. Yeah. Way better than those little pastry things that came in flavours of pink or grey and always fell apart before you actually got 'em into your mouth.

The moment of solitude and solace lasted only as long as the sandwich, however. A guy with a heavy-fringed cascade of baby blond hair came in, talking to Leon like an old friend. Whoa, it was good to see him, hadn't had a chance to catch up since the time they'd shared a dressing room on the set of

Supersonic. How the hell was he these days? And hey... did he still have that red hot connection?

Leon dug a bag of grass out of his pocket and turned it over with a smile, talked shop some, and struck the guy a light, still not entirely sure who the heck he was. He left Mr. Nobody to go to Dreamyland on his own and migrated back into the main drag of the party, in the mood for something with a little more buzz.

He found it.

Several hours and some really hot shit later, Leon realised he hadn't seen Day in a long while, and that seemed... odd. Even odder than odd. Like, spaceball crazy odd. He climbed out from under the girl on his lap, knocked knuckles with the dude on the couch, and said yeah, they were totally gonna catch up in LA in September, baby. Bitchin' to the max. The room had quietened a lot. Practically breakfast time, he realised. The party had splintered up into knots and slopes of people: the down before the up. Leon picked his way through them with care, heading back through the partition towards the private part of the house. Inner... thingy. Scro—*sanctum*. Whoops.

Sanctum. Yeah.

He bumped his way up the stairs, jiggling the bag of pills in his pocket. Funny how Day kept it like this. Cocoon out of time. As if smaller rooms were somehow safer than the big rooms downstairs. Being held in a careful, protective grasp. Buildings like tall fingers, black against the smoke-choked sky; tenements and gritty stone covings, blind eyes on busy streets. God, had they ever been so young?

Leon pulled the uppers from his pocket and tossed the bag in his palm. Young and bright and beautiful. Seemed a lifetime ago though only, what? Six years. Eight years. Ten years. Man, all those different stages, different landmarks, just slipped on by. Crazy. He remembered Damon Brent with short hair, baby. Fifteen and ageless. Vital. God, he'd been somethin'.

He still was.

Leon slid his hand along the warm wooden banister, and it purred under his touch, a tiger in the brush. Fine and silken, and the air parted around him like musty curtains. He saw all the things sheeting through it, the colours and the essences of everything. Like auras, they glittered, vapour trails overlapping and crossing. Damon was bright silver; he always had been. A comet. A burning flame... star. Thing.

Only the light looked all, like, fizzled up. The top stair wavered under Leon's foot for a moment. He frowned, filled his lungs with chocolatey, sticky-rich air.

"Hey! Day, you up here? I don't know if you're decent, man, but I brought ya somethin'. Trousers on, man, yeah?"

Something didn't feel right. Leon padded up onto the landing, hand lingering on the carved newel post.

Why'd he leave the bathroom door open?

It seemed... quiet.

"Day? W-Where you at, man? I-I got... got some stuff."

Is that a foot?

Leon stared at the bathroom door. More than slightly ajar, a band of light visible through it. Glimmers of it on the vinyl. Wet and... red.

"D-Damon? You all right?" His voice creaked with forced mirth, sweat breaking out on his back. "You havin' too much fun there, man? Told ya... that's some hot shit Steve brought, right? Y-You ain't, you ain't s'posed to pop the whole thing....

Day?"

Body contorted in messy awkwardness, vile puddles on the pale floor, and the plastic shower curtain like a half-shed skin across some mangled serpent.

It wasn't Day, 'cos it couldn't be. It just couldn't.

The bag of reds fell from Leon's hand, pills rolling across the landing. A strangled whimper left his throat, and he lurched into the small space. The blood... it oozed between his fingers where he touched the floor, tried to lift Day's head, and saw the wound that marred it. Bone winked through the ragged, detached edges. His fingers brushed across the shiny gloss of exposed muscle and blood, partly congealed, rusted beneath his touch. Leon pushed back the shower curtain, obsessed by the need to get rid of it, like if he wasn't shrouded then he wasn't dead and he might just wake up. Wet hair, slippery in his hand. Some of it came out as Leon cradled Day's head against his neck.

Weird feeling, decided the small part of Leon currently detached from whatever sick mockery of reality this might be. He knew—this awake part of him could tell—that his body still worked. He was still breathing, still intact, yet it felt like his chest had folded in two, crushed and broken, and it had taken the rest of him with it. Lifeless. Limp. Just... not working anymore.

Like Day.

Leon pawed a hand across his face and gagged at the stink of the blood. It filled his mouth, bitter copper and the aroma of shampoo. Yet Damon kept staring at him. *Eyes, mouth...* not Day's, not anymore. Not bright with some flash of something, or twisted in a smile. Not eager and awesome and ready for the whole fucking world. Leon let the head fall from his lap; harder to breathe now. And see. Vision blurred, with falling rain and broken world, sobs wracking out of him that he couldn't stop, and just the smell of it, tinny noise on his tongue.

Getting... getting help. Yes.

He wanted to call out, but there weren't words. No sounds to this. He didn't want to leave Day this way either, but.... Leon staggered out onto the landing, back down the stairs, ankles bowing beneath him and steps betraying him, the blood rushing in his ears and the garbled sounds of panic in his throat. Glass partition. Big ugly blocks... distorting the world. Faces of people, seen through them, looked twisted and strange. *Gotta not fall over the step.*

He's dead. Oh, God. He's dead.

They turned to look at him, one by one. Wide, inquisitive eyes, mouths frozen in half-relinquished traces of laughing chatter. Morning coffees and teas. Somewhere, someone was cooking breakfast.

Eyes and mouth. Slack. Cold. Dead. No....

Joss came to him through the alien crowd, bare-chested and level-headed. Warm hands on his shoulders; even, steady stare. Calm and collected. The shakes had gotten worse. Leon's teeth slammed together when he tried to talk.

"What's wrong?" the voice through the tunnel kept asking. "Did you hurt yourself?"

Joss shook him gently. Leon struggled with the words that, once they started, wouldn't stop. Same tattoo beating and beating, over and over.

"He's dead."

Evil words. They made it real, and he couldn't get the

bitter-copper taste out of his mouth, gunmetal grey and stinking.

Joss held him, and more tears came.

Chapter Twenty

The plane trip home seemed to take forever. We kept hitting turbulence; I suspected Damon... somehow. I almost wished he could have been there with us, in a way. He hadn't been doing much to leaven the atmosphere recently, but he'd have at least provided a buffer zone.

"What are you thinking about?" Leon asked me.

His breath scraped along the back of my neck. I suppressed a shiver, stopped staring out of the window, and turned to face him, finding him uncomfortably close, even though he'd paid for first class seats.

Stop it. He's old enough to be your father. Maybe even your grandfather, if two successive generations bred early.

I turned a moment over to doing the mental arithmetic of that, but it didn't prevent me from watching his lips when he spoke.

"Ellis? What are you thinking?"

My answer came without thought. "What if he's wrong?"

"Who, Day?"

"Yes. He could be. It could have been an accident. Even if Joss—"

"I know." Something darkened in Leon's expression. "I know. I-I guess I'm kinda hoping that, but...."

"Mm."

He smiled at me, a cautious gesture of faith. "Guess we'll find out, huh?"

I returned the smile, though there probably wasn't going to be much to be cheerful about. Especially when I got arrested for storming into the farmyard and making insane accusations against private citizens, as I undoubtedly would do.

"Looks that way," I said.

"Will, um, you want...? I mean, if— Y'know. You're not going to go alone, are you?"

He inclined his head, refusing to let me look away. The warmth of a blush threatened my neckline.

"I hadn't really decided what to—"

"'Cos if—it might not be a good idea to.... Jeez. Listen to me, huh?" He sighed. "I mean, this is *Joss*, for God's sake! I-I just wanted to be— I just want you to be safe."

Oh, crap. Blushing. I'm bloody well blushing....

"Um. I, er, I'll—"

"Yeah."

Leon patted my hand companionably, which didn't make me feel better about anything. I leaned my head against the window and watched the clouds.

For something so fast, we seemed to be going incredibly slowly. Once again, the layover only made it worse. We hung around in the glossy, neutral, well-lit terminal at Minneapolis St. Paul, edging through the minutes and hoping the hours would take care of themselves. I flicked through Mum's scrapbook while Leon went to get coffee. When he came back he cocked an eyebrow at me.

"You can't take time out, can you?"

I looked at the coffee—plastic foam and sticky flavoured syrups—and shook my head. "Nope. You never know. Might have missed something."

He folded into the seat next to mine. "You can't beat yourself up about it. What you've done, it's—"

"Nothing, if I can't prove it," I said, a trifle grumpier than I wanted to be with him.

Leon gave me a small, acerbic smile and sipped his coffee. "I see why he—man, that is foul!—why he likes you so much. Hey. What d'you think they do to the coffee here?"

My gaze skated over the scrapbook pages, those sorrowful last few leaves before the expanse of blank, unfilled paper. "I don't know."

"I haven't had coffee this bad since West Germany, I swear. Am I allowed to say that? You gotta be careful, 'cos the coffee police are everywhere. That and political correctness...."

I appreciated his efforts to make me smile—and his point about how bad the coffee was—but my attention lay elsewhere. I frowned down at the picture of Inez outside the gates, the police cordon and Mum, Gail, and Jan behind it. Leon fidgeted. I wondered whether the image or the headline made him more uncomfortable.

"D'you really need to—"

I stabbed my finger at the page. "There. Is that her?"

"Huh?"

"The girl with the gym bag. There. Bottom right corner. I know she's got shorter hair than you said, but...."

Leon's face tautened. "J—y'know, it could be. It's not a good picture, but it *looks*... yeah, it looks like her, I guess. I only met her a coupla times, I can't—"

I shut the book with the rustle of paper and a faint waft of white musk.

"Shit."

How had I been so dense? So bloody *slow*...! I glanced at my watch impatiently. Leon put his hand on my arm, pushed it gently back to the seat.

"Staring at the hands doesn't make them go faster. Trust me."

I bit the inside of my lip. "How can you be so patient?"

He took another sip of the appalling coffee and looked thoughtful, like a man about to impart a pearl of philosophical wisdom.

"You ever go to a place called Nijmegen?"

* * *

Coming home felt good, though time zones were not my friends. When we finally tottered out into the cool night breeze at Heathrow, even Leon had started to look ragged at the edges. He hailed a black cab, and we almost came to blows when he asked for his home address.

"No!" I protested. "We need to get to the station. Paddington, or-or maybe there's something that goes from here, from the bus terminal. It's only an hour straight through to Bristol. I need... I've got to—"

Leon pulled me down to the upholstery, synthetic leather and the smell of industrial disinfectant.

"...go to... to Bristol...."

"Sweetie, don't rush. Take a rest first, okay? It's still going to be there in the morning."

My behind thumped to the seat, and my mouth worked soundlessly.

Sweetie?

I was used to that kind of crap from Damon, but not him. Still, after eleven hours in total on board various planes, being buffeted by time changing around me and breathing second-hand air, I wasn't in too much of a position to argue, however much I itched to get started... finished. Whatever.

"All right. Fine," I mumbled, the heart and soul of all graciousness.

London rumbled past us in its comfortingly lumpy, greyed out shapes: brash hoardings, neon lights and Bengali takeaways, trees in cages and pavements lined with cracks. Leon's place turned out to be a stone's throw from Russell Square Tube station, just on the edge of Bloomsbury. Not the chic, hidden little enclave it had been once—back when it was the city's literary capital—but still very pretty, stippled with greenery and unchanged landmarks. Tall Art Deco townhouses and blocks of flats in broken red brick and creamy Portland stone, shallow steps, and a hot dog cart parked on the corner. The smell of boiled onions assailed me as Leon propelled me up to a shabby block with wooden sash windows and a front door that had less of a security system than my place in Brighton. An early Eighties renovation of a Thirties building, I realised, and not a great renovation at that. The hallway boasted truly atrocious pub carpet—a maroon and orange pattern that would have made my eyes water if they hadn't been so dry and gritty—and walls painted an institutional sort of yellowish-green. A doorman in a greasy black jumper loitered behind a dark wood desk.

Leon nodded at him. "All right, Terry?"

"Evenin', Mr. Fielding."

Terry gave us the kind of meaningful smirk that suggested Mr. Fielding didn't bring many young ladies back here. Young men, then? Or older ladies? I wondered briefly, but the fatigue hung too heavy on me to make it much of a pressing issue.

Leon trundled me into the lift, a black-caged, rattling thing, most likely the one the block had been built with, and I tried not to yawn because I didn't want to prove him right. I wanted to… to… to complain when he put his arm around my shoulders, for a start, rather than lean against him in all of that complicated, comforting warmth. He talked, planning out how we could approach dealing with Joss—*we*, not me, because it could be dangerous—and what the next step needed to be.

No police… no proof. Not yet.

The flat lay up on the eighth floor, overlooking treetops and the slated, heating-pipe-ridden Deco collations of other roofs, which made for weird shapes in the dark. Towards the blacked-out horizon, London glimmered in flickering yellow enormity, hidden and endless. Sirens wailed in the distance, which I found refreshing. At home, they frequently streaked under my window.

All in all, the place was small, but at the moment perfect: neutral colour palette, big sofa, and a guest bedroom. I noticed family photos on the walls, and on the wooden mantel over the fire, a gas-powered faux wood-burner set against exposed brickwork. Toby featured a lot, as did his mother, presumably; a woman with long, straight black hair and blue eyes. His grandparents—an elderly bespectacled couple—looking proud with Leon and Judy beside them, then Toby again, grinning madly in university graduation garb. Sweet. I had pictures like those, too, only mine were... different.

Leon dialled out for Chinese. I didn't think I could eat a thing, but I managed, shoes off and feet curled under me on his couch. He looked really, truly tired, at last. Smiling at me, he said he didn't jet set so well these days. We prodded our way through fried rice and chilli beef and tried to ignore what hung over everything, black and inevitable. He gave me the guest room—plain décor except for one strange, disturbing little painting in angularly minimalist red and white, broken pieces of colour bleeding like shattered rain. His Forrest Bess, I realised. A fluffy white robe with *Hyatt Hotel* emblazoned on the pocket hung behind the door.

We said an early, awkward goodnight, interrupted by a phone call he got from what sounded—judging by Leon's end of the conversation—like an incandescently furious Gavin Malpas. I wondered what commitments Leon had thrown over for Sacramento and hoped it was nothing too awful. I reflected that I should make an effort to call Ron and Jeremy, check everything was okay at home. In the general haste to get across the pond, I'd forgotten to pack my phone charger, and the battery had promptly flat-lined. Still, it wasn't like I couldn't sort it out in the morning.

I fell into Leon's spare bed, jet-lagged and feeling like there was nothing to me but pieces of unconnected skin and nerve endings. He had a point: after thirty-two years, it could afford to wait one more night. And sleep looked so good from here.

So why did I spend so long staring at the shadows on the ceiling?

* * *

Dawn came early. I'd already woken, slipped around the place—if not like a thief, then as quietly as I knew how, muffling the stubbed toes and 'oh bugger's of my morning— and dressed. A quick peek through Leon's bedroom door, left ajar, felt slightly prurient but confirmed he was still sleeping. I gathered my things and let myself out of his flat, out of his protective auspices and the vaguely cloying sense of Being Looked After Because, After All, I Was A Girl.

He didn't mean it that way, I knew, but… somehow, in the straw fingers of the morning light, I didn't trust him so much. Or I didn't *want* to. I wasn't sure. Maybe I'd just stopped thinking with what passed for the sensible part of my brain.

Morning light.

Bloody song.

I walked around the corner to Russell Square, bought myself a ticket to Paddington, and hopped into the grimy, greasy, and irrefutably grey world of the early Underground commute. If I hated ordinary trains, the Tube felt worse. Rattling like mad, mirror-black windows and claustrophobic, endless tunnels. Paddington Station's massive arches and throbbing concourses came as a relief. I found the right platform and hunched up on the uncomfortable metal seat, staring at the flickering orange digits on the departures board like that would somehow make the train come quicker. I wondered if Leon was awake yet. Probably. Probably a bit pissy with me too. At least I didn't have long to wait for the train to Bristol, and my rapidly dwindling reserves of carry-around money would get me the taxi fare to Old Wallow Farm. From there... well, I'd cross that bridge when I came to it.

On my own. That seemed suddenly very important to me, and I couldn't help the sneaking sensation that Mum would have been terribly proud.

And amused.

My train finally pulled in with a grinding rush of stale air, shrill wheels, and shrieking metal, and I fought against the momentary flip in my gut to get on board, battling jelly legs to a seat. Less than two hours. I'd be fine.

I counted off all the stops on the way. Sometimes we seemed to go so fast, yet other times to inch along at an excruciatingly slow pace that made me want to get out and push. I went over and over my previous meeting with Napier in my head, just like I'd been doing half the night, and played different versions of how today could go to myself, trying to plan for contingencies, crises, and varied outcomes. Somewhere around Reading, I started to wish I'd waited for Leon, but that only made me more determined to see things through alone.

Eventually, with bleak drizzle giving way to sunshine, smudgy strips of fields and embankments yielding to concrete and cities once more, the train pulled in at Bristol Temple Meads, and I managed to find a taxi willing to cart me out to Old Wallow Farm. My cab driver deposited me by the neatly painted sign I'd last stood before barely a month ago. Strange that so much should have changed, when everything here seemed exactly the same. The greenery looked a little more vibrant, perhaps, the hedges in the lane that led up to the gate more alive with the snails, hoverflies, and cow parsley of an English summer, but it all held weirdly patterned shadows for me.

I had no idea what I was doing, how I should go about this. Did one just announce one's intentions from the outset? March into the low, grey farm office, blunder up to the work-a-day chaos of Christy Brooks' desk and say 'Good morning, I'm here to accuse your boss of murder. Is he free?'

Not likely to get me far. In fact I was worried that, if I made my presence obvious, Joss might become suddenly absent. I hadn't called ahead, made an appointment…. If he *was* guilty—even if only of appropriating and recycling Day's notes—then my being here would alarm him, wouldn't it? Now, maybe I could turn that to my advantage, but only maybe. My recorder hung heavy in my pocket, ready to be switched on with the flick of a finger, its microphone settings jacked up all the way. My own little black box. I just had to hope there wouldn't be wreckage from which it needed to be salvaged.

Right. So, where exactly did one start looking for people on a farm?

I looked around me. Ahead lay the side gate and, as I recalled, its access to the front of the house, grey stone wall rising up above the tangles of honeysuckle foliage. On the right side of the yard, the farm office, flanked by its timber storage shed. A tarmac camber led behind it, presumably down into the working bowels of the place and—to the far left—stood a dilapidated row of brick sheds, with part of a tractor parked outside that hadn't been there when I last visited. Nowhere to go but past the office. Damn.

I straightened my shoulders and strode towards the office, pausing to knock at the half-open, panelled door. The same landslides of paperwork, photo-covered corkboards, and overflowing filing cabinets greeted me. Francie the collie, filling up her well-chewed wicker basket, rolled a liquid brown gaze at me and wagged her tail. Christy Brooks sat behind her desk, same businesslike ponytail and, I could have sworn, the same gilet apparently made out of pressed mattresses, worn over a short sleeved t-shirt in deference to the warmer, humid weather. She glanced up from her keyboard.

"Yes?"

"Hello. I'm Ellis Ross. You probably don't—"

The crinkle of confusion on her brow gave way to a bright, plasticky smile.

"Yes! The biographer. Of course. Um… we weren't expecting you today."

"No." I smiled, edged my way into the office. "Damnedest thing. Found myself just up the road, in Failand," I lied, surprised by my fluency, "and I thought I should drop in on my way through. I have a few chapters I've been working on, and Mr. Napier was so keen to see them. Is he around at all?"

Defeated by the cheery rhythms of her own speech, Ms. Brooks relented. It's hard to say no to someone being extremely, Englishly, polite.

"Um… actually, he went over to the barn not ten minutes ago. I'll just, um—hang on a sec."

She grabbed her radio and excused herself to the little staff kitchenette that lay at the back of the hut. Francie rolled in her basket, exposing a pudgy, hairy tummy and the pink insides of her ears, one leg elegantly extended towards me. I could just make out the sound of Ms. Brooks' voice, and could imagine the panic blurting through the airwaves: 'Mad journo out front! D'you want me to say you're indisposed?' I just prayed I'd be lucky.

I knew I hadn't been when she re-emerged looking apologetic.

"I'm ever so sorry, Miss Ross. I can't seem to get him."

Bull. Even if I couldn't make out the words, I'd heard the pauses she left for someone else to speak. I held the irritation down and just gave a little 'oh' instead.

"He's probably very busy," she assured me, the same way grown-ups used to say that Santa couldn't possibly be in all the department stores in the world at Christmas, so had to hire helpers.

It hadn't worked then, and it wasn't washing now.

"Of course," Ms. Brooks added, "if you'd like to leave the papers with me, I can pass them on."

Ah. Shit.

She smiled at me encouragingly. *Busted.*

I grinned back. "Ri-iight. Uh… oh, I can, um, I can email it along, actually. That'd be, er, better, wouldn't it? Thinking about it. No bother."

"If you like. Sorry I couldn't get him. Does tend to be all go here," she said, cut-glass tinkle of a laugh.

"I can imagine! I'll, um, see myself out. Got a… friend waiting."

More fluent lies. Where did they all come from? I backed out of the office, and my idiocy must have convinced Ms.

Brooks, because she returned to her desk. I stood in the yard, feeling like a complete pillock until I realised she couldn't see me from the door. I nipped around to the far side of the building, still undetected, heart pounding with a sudden and ridiculous thrill.

The part of the yard tarmac-laid for heavy vehicle access sloped away ahead of me, smeared with the traces of boggy straw and the varying browns of manure and mud, leading down to a large, bulky building further cordoned with tubular steel gates. Well, that looked as much like a barn as anything I'd ever seen. I set off in search of my quarry.

Wandering down past this side of Old Wallow, apparently more to do with extruded aluminium and concrete than pretty climbing plants and Georgian brickwork, I searched the dark corners for any sign of Joss. The metallic scrape of a shovel on solid ground drifted on the air, and I looked for its source. Mingled farmyard smells hung sharp all around me; my hand wavered to my pocket and the recorder within it. I passed the steel gates, found the open frontage of the part of the barn given over to temporary storage. Bales of straw stood stacked high next to the wicked, curved metal tines of things that looked like bits of ploughshare.

"Why, Ellis! What a surprise!"

I turned, heart ready to burst out of my ribs. Joss stood not four feet away on the concrete apron, straw and crap sticking to his wellies, shovel in hand, and a healthy glow on his face. Bullet-proof jumper knotted around his waist, he'd pushed the sleeves of his checked shirt up to the elbows. Mud streaked his arms, the beds of his fingernails were grubby, and one long, dark red scratch reached across the back of his hand. He blew out a breath, jetted the hair off his forehead, and grinned at me.

"Um. I w-was… I was passing," I began, mouth dry, courage faltering.

"Something I can help you with, or have you got something for me?"

I swallowed heavily, found my voice. "Just hoping I could ask you a quick couple of questions."

Joss propped the shovel against the barn wall, pulled a rag from his back pocket, and proceeded to wipe his hands on it. "Oh?"

"Y-Yes. About your wife, actually."

He tossed the rag aside as easily as his smile. "I thought your book was about Damon."

"It is. But—"

"Mm?" His gaze pushed me just that little bit further, challenged just a little more than someone with nothing to hide. "But what?"

"Her name's Jessica. You, um, you never mentioned when we spoke before that she was Maxwell Vost's niece, but she is, isn't she?"

The smallest hint of his smile returned. "Now, where on earth did you get that idea?"

"It's true, though." I stood my ground, didn't let him shake me. "I spoke to Cris McIlroy. He told me how… there was a bit of age gap between you."

"You spoke to Cris? Really?"

He'd not expected that. My turn to smile.

"Yes." My finger butted against the recorder's buttons. "Cleared up quite a lot. I didn't realise, for example, quite how much of an influence you must have had on a lot of Damon

Brent's writing. But the similarities between some of his projects and—oh, say, your song *Morning Light*—they're really quite marked."

The studied blankness of Joss' expression slipped, revealing a touch of contempt. "Excuse me?"

"Oh, I think so," I said airily, hoping to trip him with his own vanity.

It was a foolish hope. Joss flashed me yet another charming smile, though it didn't disguise the fact I'd rattled him. I could see that, feel it catch in the back of my throat like wood smoke.

"I'm thrilled you've been getting so deeply into the project," he said, sounding very genuine. "That's great. But I am rather busy right now. Why don't—"

Convinced I was about to get thrown out on my ear, I drew breath to argue. Joss put his hands together, rubbed one broad thumb over his palm and looked, just for a second, as if I'd really wrecked his day. He exhaled, his shoulders dropping a little.

"Why don't we go into the house? Give me a minute to clean up; we can have a proper chat… maybe a cup of tea. You've got time, have you?"

"Well, yes, I…. Thank you," I said with the deepening certainty that this might not have been a good idea.

Joss nodded, perhaps a trifle sadly. "Right, then."

He led me back up past the office—Ms. Brooks' shape glinted at the door for just a moment—and through the side gate. Seen from the front, the house almost glowed. Perfect proportions, immaculate window frames… red and pink geraniums spilled from terracotta troughs. Joss let me in, showed me into the light, tasteful morning room I'd interviewed him in before.

"Take a pew," he said. "Won't be a minute."

The door shut firmly in his wake.

Shit, shit, shit! What the hell was I doing? I grappled my phone out of my handbag, silently pleading with it to ignore its dead battery and work for me, but there were no signs of life. I stuffed it away again, remembering the radios they used to communicate here. Black spot for reception anyway.

Bollocks.

I breathed deeply and reminded myself that other people knew where I'd gone, other people knew what I knew—well, all right, that Leon did—but it wasn't much comfort.

The seconds lingered, reluctant to become full minutes. Eventually, the door opened, the movement of its shiny brass handle riveting my attention, and Joss came back in. He'd had a quick wash, changed his shirt... lost most of the pervasive poop and straw aroma, and combed his hair. His stance seemed diffident, oddly unbalanced.

"Um... d'you want to come through to the kitchen?" he said, eyebrows raised. "Kettle's on."

I followed on, through the *Country Life* jigsaw of a hallway, into the endless mellow pine and dusky red quarry tiles. No expansive lunch laid on today, no Paillard. The table was littered with paperwork at one end and, in the centre, newspaper spread out beneath a dismantled bridle, pot of saddle soap and cleaning cloth to one side, tarring the room with the strange mixed smells of leather and grime. I sat down where Joss gestured, and he dropped teabags into two chunky ceramic mugs that stood next to the kettle.

"So," he said, settling down opposite me, mugs between us.

"What's brought all this on?"

"Have I made a mistake?"

Joss looked at the tabletop, fingers of his right hand worrying at his wedding ring. "I suppose it was all easy enough to track down. Certificates and things. If Cris gave you the basics... we never tried to hide anything."

I doubted that, but I didn't say so.

"She was very young."

He frowned. "Initially, yes. I didn't know how— She *looked* a hell of a lot older. They all did. Those girls... you'd see 'em in clubs, hotels—it was almost a profession for some of them. Competitive, you know? Jessie was never like that, though she was on the edge of that life when we met. '74. In LA."

He spun the story for me: the Strip in its hedonistic, Technicolor glory days. His drinking bouts had grown larger, unwieldy and lonely, just something else that islanded him from the rest of the band. They were over there for a TV appearance and a series of recordings being done in Maxwell Vost's studio. She had been a breath of fresh air, an unfamiliar face in a too-familiar club, just a first name and a bar tab on an ID he later learned was fake. A hotel room, a weekend, a girl he couldn't forget. The way he said it made it sound like he believed in romance. Back in London, he'd tried to find her, locate anyone who could. Cris had put the dates and description together, grilled him for details... gone through the roof. Yet it hadn't stopped them. Late spring of '75, Jessica rolled up in Grove Park with dual nationality from an English father and the keys to a rented flat close to the river.

"I fell in love with her," Joss said without an ounce of regret. "More every day. We knew we had to be careful, take it easy until... well, her birthday. But it was worth it. You just *know* when you've met your other half. The one who fits you. And nothing else matters."

He glanced up, pale blue eyes gauging me for judgement, revulsion... the intent to publish.

"How about career-wise?" I asked softly.

"Huh?"

"It could have ruined you. All of you."

"Yes." A slow, deep breath slipped from him like a stale breeze through all those close-held secrets. "I was a selfish prat back then. And a good liar. Cris thought I finished with her, finally got off my case. We took what we could get. Counting days."

"And in '76? She turned up on the tour. Holland."

The corner of his mouth twitched. "Cris remembered that, eh? Yeah. We screwed up. He went ape. Had to lie low for a while after that."

"She was there at the party, though. The night Damon died."

That caught him out, punctured the roseate glow of his memory, and perhaps whatever assumption he'd had of my grasp on the truth. His eyes hardened.

"No. She wasn't. Not then."

I reached into my bag, pulled out Mum's scrapbook, and laid it on the table before him, flipping with ease to the right page—the nearest thing I had to proof. My nerves stiffened, coiled themselves into determined cords of bloody-minded, outraged anger. I pointed to the figure in the bottom right of the picture. The girl with the gym bag.

"What's this...?" Joss' amusement turned to denial. "Come

on, that could be anybody. What point are you trying to prove, precisely? I made a mistake? Yes. I did something wrong? Yes. But in the long run, I-I... I mean, no one got h—"

"Damon did."

"That was an accident!" He fell just shy of shouting it. His voice dropped fast, the nervous tic of lip and exposure of teeth less a smile than an admission of guilt. "An accident. Everyone.... You know about that."

I wanted to smack him in the face with the damn book, grind the page against him until the ink smeared his skin.

"See," I said, swivelling the scrapbook back around towards me. "Here's the thing. I don't think it *was*."

Joss gave a short, dry bark of laughter, hollow and unconvincing. "Oh dear... it's not going to be that sort of book, is it? I suppose next you'll be saying his millions all disappeared into an obscure Bahamian corporation with unidentified beneficiaries?"

The urge to fling myself at him—to scrape nails down bristled cheeks and gouge thumbs into eyes—grew stronger, but I kept my gaze steady and my tone calm.

"No. I was thinking more about his demo tapes."

Joss actually bottled up the nerve to sip his tea, though his grip shifted a few times, sweaty hands slick on the mug. Quick swallow, raised eyebrows, *what the devil are you talking about?* Oh, yes. Very nice. And all belied by the pallid, waxen cast his face assumed.

"Tapes? Hmm. All Damon was working on at the time of his death was the new album we were contracted for, and there weren't really any demos at that point. Charlie had some stuff roughed out—they were predominantly his songs, first time since *Smoke Gardens* he'd had that kind of input—but.... No, I'm afraid I don't know what you... I mean, really, Miss Ross." He put down the mug and looked at me with a very sober, disappointed expression. "If you're going to go down the conspiracy route, with absolutely no evidence that Damon's death was anything more than tragic misfortune, I really don't see how I can help. I don't think it's something you *need* to do," he added, catching my gaze with such a sudden intensity that I forgot how much I wanted to hit him.

His eyes cried out—quick glance to the back door—for me to shut up and sod off, widened in their desperation. He must have known I wouldn't let up.

Not after that.

"No," I said, wishing my recorder could have caught that little performance. "I don't need to, but I do plan on asking once more for the truth. There *were* tapes. I think you knew that, because I think you overheard the argument he had with Cris McIlroy and Vince Dexler about the solo deal he'd been promised. You virtually told me as much yourself."

"I never said—"

"There *were* tapes," I repeated. "New material. Different material. At least one song we both know. E minor, Dorian mode, syncopated rhythm... had a little blues hook on the bridge. Two acoustic parts and an electric lead? You made some changes, in the long run."

Where Joss' eyes had widened in warning, now shock dilated them. He licked his lips, mouth hanging loosely open. "H-How could you know that? This—no! No, this... all of this is utter speculation, and I don't like what you're implying. You think that—"

"I want to know what happened," I snapped.

"There's really nothing else to tell," he retorted, a harder, harsher edge to his voice, urging me to drop it, though I'd gone way past stopping.

"Did you go up there with the intention of killing him, or was it always about the music, the tapes?"

If there had been a Rubicon, I'd crossed it. I didn't see he'd left me anywhere else to go. Joss' face folded around a sick look of horror. I didn't break eye contact, ready for him to flat-out deny everything and tell me to leave, or to stammer some justification, some weak attempt at covering his—no, *their*—backs.

His silence spoke louder than anything I could have imagined.

"Look...." Sweat beaded on Joss' lip. He raised a hand as if to wipe it away, but left the gesture incomplete, fingers furled on nothing. "All right. So I heard when Cris—he was really furious, you know? Vince... Vince made it sound like Day was... well, all there bar the handshake. And I looked at the people there that night. And I thought... what's he done? What... what has he done to get *this*? I figured there must be stuff up in his studio. Pretentious little—and all behind our backs! You know? That was the worst thing. I figured it would do him good to share. I-I was only ever going to take a look. Just... just to see."

A shadow whispered on the kitchen wall, over by the back door. I leaned forward, aware I needed to push him now, hear it from his lips.

"So what went wrong? You went upstairs, and—"

"Not then. Not at first. I bottled... it was later. Jess—I told

449

Jessie what I'd heard. She said I should do it. She said she'd keep an eye out, make sure I didn't get caught rooting through his stuff. We didn't know he was up there!"

The door began to open, the softest murmur of movement.

"What happened?"

"I… I found his notebook. Papers. I-I'd have left it at that, but… she came in. She had… blood…." Joss' voice slumped to a thin whisper, and he stared at his hand, seeing some stain long since disguised. "He fell. Y'see? When I went out onto the landing, I saw the bathroom door was open. I saw…. I'd have got help. I would, but—"

"What?"

A shaft of light, straight-edged and bright gold, fell onto the quarry tiles from the back door, leavened with the sound of a footfall.

"He *moved*." Joss' breath came shorter now, his eyes damp. "You don't understand. I couldn't let… we couldn't have…. Jessie screamed. He was—Christ, it was awful—he tried to get up. Blood all over him, his head all… God, his head! He c—he couldn't move properly. Like something a cat's had. And he was tryin' to talk… he'd've *talked*, don't you see? I-I just… I finished it."

I had no words to put to his confession. No reaction to have through the strangled taste of bile in my mouth. Joss wiped a hand over his face, sniffed heavily.

"We took the tapes, the notes, booted it out of there. I wanted to go, but Jess… she realised how that would look. She —"

"Had to clean up," said a voice I didn't know. Smooth, gentle, well-spoken.

Jessica stood, framed in the gold light of the kitchen doorway, her hair shining. Dark green Hunters, well-cut jeans, a duck egg blue blouse, and a ten gauge shotgun in her beautifully manicured hands. I started back from the table, my chair squealing on the tiles, but she raised the gun just enough to stop me. Joss got up, shaking as he braced himself against the table, his attention on her and her alone.

"Jessie...."

"You really shouldn't have said anything, sweetheart. She doesn't have proof. If she had proof, there'd be police cars." Jessica slipped her husband a fond, reproachful look, like the kind one might give a naughty puppy. "You should just have denied everything."

"I can't. Jess, I can't keep—"

"Shh, it's all right. We can come to an arrangement, I'm sure. Can't we, Miss Ross?"

I stared. Mainly at the gun. I wasn't used to them. In this instance, particularly unused to the way the thing kept nudging up towards me, as if those narrow black barrels wanted to make friends.

"What, um, what sort of thing did you have in mind?"

My voice, pale and breathy, wavered. Joss moved closer to his wife, nervous glances between the two of us. I could only wish I'd taken the hint he'd tried to give me. *Get out.* That... or that I'd brought reinforcements.

Jessica nodded to the door. "Outside."

I did what I was told, which seemed sensible, squinting in the bright sun. There was a pleasant kitchen garden out here; raised beds with veggies, salad crops and herbs, pretty borders splashed with tea roses, and a set of white iron patio furniture.

Fresh, sweet scents of thyme, marjoram, and rose mottled the country air. The friendly sound of chickens emanated from a coop and run further off at the garden's rear, another path leading around to the side of the house. I could picture the pair of them enjoying a quiet glass of wine out here in the evenings, with Francie curled at Joss' feet.

There were worse places to die, I supposed. And it probably wouldn't hurt as much as Day's death had. After all, shooting would be quick, right? Unless Jessica was a bad shot. My lip kept quivering, so I bit it until I tasted blood.

"Stand there. Back a bit. Good."

I positioned myself where she directed, my back towards the path, like I'd happened unexpectedly upon them. Upon someone cleaning a gun, perhaps. I hoped I wouldn't wet myself and wished—fleetingly—that I'd worn knickers that matched my bra. That thought soon got overtaken by other regrets. The way Auntie Jan would find out, for a start.

"Jess… don't. Not here."

A note of desperation crept into Joss' voice. I thought I understood it; it was what I'd seen that first time we met. Whatever else he'd done, wherever else he'd been, this place was his home. *The only thing I've ever done right*. His Morning Light. The farm, the girl… the killer. I didn't believe for a second Damon had ever fallen. I doubted Joss believed it either. Had he, back then?

"Don't, love. Please."

Though his body shadowed every movement of hers, he hung back from her. The gun sat lightly in her grasp, as easy to shoot him as me, I supposed. Would she do that? She must have been a strikingly beautiful girl. Young, elegant… she still oozed class, even as she raised the shotgun, pointed it right at my chest, and closed one eye.

"Jessie, don't! No more—please? You can't cover this one up. Please. No more accidents. No more falls, no more bad brakes. Think of... think of the girls."

"I always have. And you. Bad brakes bought this place, didn't they?"

Joss looked desperately at me, terror and regret waging a last-minute stand-off on his face. In the chicken coop, a cock gave a gurgling, cheerful crow. Funny how they do that at weird times of the day. I'd never imagined Vost's car accident had been fixed. Stupid, really. I should have matched up the dates... should have done a lot of things, thinking about it.

Bugger.

"It'll all come out, Jessie." Joss licked his lips. "Whatever you do. People'll miss her. Questions. It's *time*. Let me take it, love. It was all me. I'll make them believe it. But you back out now. Now, and they won't be able to pin anything on you. Let this one go... let it all go, darling. Please."

Jessica's gaze slid away from me to her husband. She smiled a smile of intense sweetness and bliss, like nothing I'd ever seen before. I hoped it would give me the split-second I needed to make a leap for it, fling myself to the ground, scramble for a hedge or... anywhere. Unfortunately, I wasn't quick enough. Or she wasn't distracted enough.

"I do love you, you know," Jessica told him, and then she squeezed the trigger.

For me, nothing else continued out of that moment except blinding pain, like my whole chest had been taken away and replaced with angry fire ants dancing direct on my nervous system. Time did some odd doughnut-shaped thing whereby it both sped up—the whole thing just a blur—and slowed down until the seconds filled up eternity. The thought that shootings, portrayed on television, really weren't a thing like real life, filtered across my brain as I hit the ground.

Joss lunged at his wife, going for the gun, and Jessica yelled. He caught the stock in the stomach, bent double and gasping before he managed to wrest it from her. I thought someone, somewhere, might have been screaming, but I doubted it was me.

I closed my eyes, just to blink the grit from them, and saw no more.

Chapter Twenty-One

August 28ᵗʰ 1976

He didn't keep anything in any kind of order. Typical bloody Damon, Joss decided. Just piles of stuff banked up, pack-ratted around the leather sofa, the record player, and the outdated bits of equipment he used. Guitar on the wall, one on the floor; blue glass ashtray on a rickety coffee table, its shorter fourth leg chocked up with back issues of *Harper's* and *Vanity Fair*. That perfume advert Inez had done probably featured in some of them. Joss wondered if she knew where they'd ended up. 78s filled shelf after shelf, and the colours of different sleeves—some new, unopened, some dog-eared, passed down third or fourth hand like an old girlfriend—mixed before his eyes. Joss brushed through them, thumb rattling on slim spines, finding nothing but Damon's eclectic tastes and annoyed by it.

He had no right to be, he knew that. No right to be in here, either, and that knowledge beat tight in his chest. He ducked back over to the sofa, stooping to avoid hitting his head on the wonky wooden ceiling beam. Man, he was still firing on all four cylinders of browned off, that's what this was.

Downstairs, aggressive American rock pounded, muted a little through the floor, but not much. As if Damon felt out of place outside of sordid council flats with damp chipboard walls and noisy neighbours. That might be unfair, Joss supposed. Few council flats had views like this. The little window looked all the way down to the Severn, muddy and baked dry in a fringe of frazzled grass, monochrome with the last hours of the night. Even over the music—over the stifling, stale air—he heard those words repeat.

It's all changin', Cris! You can't hold me back no more, y'know what I'm sayin'? If I got a chance, I'm gonna take it, man!

Vince standing there red-faced and oily, cheeks puffed out, and turkey-gobbling, Cris inhaling like a sail boat at six knots, eyes bugging and knuckles white on his glass. Strings of vituperative bile. Joss had just stayed behind the cheese plant, not gone into the room. Listened in, but... he'd not wanted to get involved. He never did that, always stuck to what he knew, stuck to the task in hand, and that got things done. Because that's who he was. Mr. Dependable. They had their roles, he had —he had his job. Glue and sticking plasters. And Damon wanted to rip them off. He couldn't... no, he *could* believe it. Stumbled away, not listened to the details. They'd come out soon enough, like the work Day said he'd done. New songs. Whole new world. Shystering little—but who to tell? Joss didn't want to admit eavesdropping, didn't want to be the one to drag it into the open, not yet.... Jessie had the right of it, when she said to stay quiet.

His fingers closed on a sheaf of papers, folded into a notebook that lay on the arm of the sofa. These didn't look familiar. She had a point, that was the thing. And he'd just have a look, have....

Shit. This stuff was actually *good*.

Damon's handwriting, big and bold, spilled all over the pages. Same style Joss knew so well, the same broad beats, same snazzy riffs, but different. Newer, cleaner, better. He hadn't seen anything like this from Day's pen since *Only a Woman*. And words... words that actually *meant* something. No incessant mantra, no baby-girl-rock, but ruined clouds over faces of the past, hands stacked with apologies. Joss' thumb skated over the smooth gloss of the page.

> *I'd fix it if I could, if only you would*
> *Lay back and let me.*
> *Morning light splits the pillow in two*
> *Don't know why you*
> *Still mean what you do*
> *But you do.*

Joss frowned. Movement in the doorway, and he made to turn around, impaled on his own guilt.

"It's only me. Did you find anything?"

He returned his attention to the page. "Yeah."

Her presence flowed into the room, soothing him without the need to see her. The ink danced in front of him, deceitful and mocking. Fucking Damon. Joss jumped at the sound of a cassette player, the crackle of a microphone, the clearing of a familiar throat.

"One. Two. One-two." The sound of Day taking a last pull on a cigarette, amplified rustle of him leaning forward to drop it in the ash tray. "Uh... yeah. *Untitled*... for now. I'll get it. Take three. Two, three, four...."

Joss spun on one heel, almost falling. "Jessie! Shh! Turn that off, someone'll—"

She stood by the desk under the window, drifts of detritus, her head tilted to the side. Her hair—cut to the middle of her back now, half the length it used to be—hung down, her neck a curve of alabaster. She glanced back at him over one freckled shoulder, her long green dress patterned with pink flowers, and she smiled.

"It's all right."

"You're s'posed to be watching. What if—"

"No one'll come up."

She turned back to the desk, rifling through the tapes and papers like a jumble sale, no care for what order she put them back in. Joss moved towards her, 'cos they had to be careful how they did this, how....

"Jess?"

The tape played on: Damon's voice atop an overdubbed acoustic part, sketching the melody. A clean electric line, supple and soaring. Joss could hear what he was going for... what he so nearly had. The Gibson's mellow burr, the swoop and the glide, working in and out of the notes.

"What's that on your hand?"

She looked quizzically at him as he reached for her. Soft skin smeared red.

"Jessie?"

Blood on her frock too. Wet, the fabric crinkled across her stomach.

"Jess, what have you done?"

"You were right," she said, her voice low and her eyes unblinking. "It isn't fair. He hasn't got a *thing* you haven't. And pride always comes before a fall."

Joss searched her face for any kind of explanation, anything at all other than the suspicion that now slipped down his back, cold and slimy. He turned, darted from the room, bare feet out onto the landing, where the bathroom door stood ajar. There hadn't been anyone up here, surely. Everything had been quiet. All the doors shut.

He looked at the world through crowded eyes, hand reaching for the doorknob, and the breath choked off in his throat.

Holy shit.

Joss stared at the mess. Blood on the floor, slick and bright, bright red. Far brighter than he'd ever seen it. Pale skin pink-streaked where the thicker, redder smears didn't reach. Body oddly bent against the vinyl.

"What... oh, God. Oh, Christ, Jessie.... What did you *do*?"

She padded up behind him, arms around his waist, chin on his shoulder, sweet breath on his neck. "He was stoned. Really gone. Nobody ought to get into that state. See? He hit his head."

She hugged him tighter, the stain of Damon's blood on her frock wet against the back of his shirt. Joss' stomach flipped.

"He's d— Oh, fuck. Fucking hell! We should call an ambulance. We need to.... We can't just leave him like this. This is... fuck it, Jessie! Close his eyes, can't you? He's... oh, Christ, it's horrible."

Jessica murmured something he didn't quite hear, slipped free of him, and picked her way back into the bathroom. The pulse thumped in Joss' throat, all disbelief and panic. His whole body tingled with it, muscles bunched for flight or action. She held up the hem of her frock, balancing on pink-tipped toes, stepping lightly around the blood and the puke. She moved like a dancer, like a child gathering daisies. Her red-gold hair slipped against her shoulders, and he half-expected her to start humming as she reached one elegant hand down to those awful, staring eyes, but—

He wasn't *that* gone.

What came out of Damon wasn't even a groan. A stifled cry, stilted through slack lips, broken breath, and a feeble hand, clawing at her ankle.

Jessica screamed, leapt back. "Shit! Fuck almighty! Joss, do something!"

She whimpered, hopping around the blood, diving back to the door, clinging to the frame. It would almost have been comical but for the way Day was moving, flexing against the sticky floor, body mottled white and red against the pale vinyl... and the sounds. His mouth quaked, framed guttural, half-made noises, like a dog in pain or something caught in a trap, too weak to scream.

Joss crossed himself before he'd even known he'd done it. Face buried in his chest, Jessica shook and mewled. Joss tried to tear his gaze away from the bathroom floor, but there was something hypnotic about it. The face got him worst. The unseeing, blood-smeared face, loosely contorted, the... the wound. God. Was that bone? How hard had she...?

And *now* she cried?

In the studio, the tape was still playing... he flinched at the sound of Damon's voice working around some catchy tune, walking a melodic bass line through the chords. Downstairs, the party noise continued, muffled but unabated. Loud enough for now. He stroked Jessica's hair.

"Baby, what did you do? Oh, Christ, Jess. What are we gonna do?"

Joss swallowed, levered Jessica off him, wiped a hand across his mouth, and stepped gingerly into the bathroom.

"Make sure no one's coming."

Jessica lifted up the full skirt of her dress, dabbed at her eyes with the hem, let it fall again. The bloodstain resembled a butterfly, Joss noticed. She nodded. He looked down at Damon, fascinated briefly by the sense of detachment he felt. Because... she did have a point. But for him, it would all be so easy. And it was as good as already done, wasn't it? He wouldn't get up from this.

He fell.

Barely aware of his own heart pounding, the blood racing in his ears, Joss reached down, buried his fingers in that thick mane of dark gold hair, wet with blood and crusted with God knows what. Strange. Damon wasn't that small—too big, really, at five seven to play the pocket rocket Cris had always marketed him as—but he felt like a doll. Like paper. Funny, because Joss would have thought that... well, the phrase was 'dead weight', wasn't it? Skin like wet porcelain. It was too easy to do it. Too easy to bring him up, hard, against the edge of the sink. The blow reverberated all the way up Joss' arms, and the sound it made—the thick, sullen thump—echoed to the back of his teeth. Damon sunk limp in his hands, just a lump of nothing breathing one long, slurred, rattling sigh.

"Do it again."

Joss' head snapped round. She stood in the doorway, the red butterfly in the middle of her body, her hair shining in the light. A brightness to her eyes, her cheeks flushed. The roar in his ears filled him up, just like she did.

"Do it again," Jessica repeated. "Make sure."

Joss blinked and looked down at the blood on his shirt, his hands, his feet.... Who'd have known there was so much of it?

"No," he said, stepping back. "It's done."

He dropped Damon back to the floor. For a moment, Joss could have sworn his eyes flickered... but he wasn't there anymore. That wasn't him. It was over. He realised he was going to throw up and, just in time, lurched to the lavatory. Hand on the seat, Damon's blood wet between his skin and the wood, Joss pulled roughly away to spit and flush, and his palm print became just one smear among many. The lumbering stains of a drunk scrabbling for purchase. He wiped his mouth, felt Jessica move behind him. Turning, he saw her pull down the plastic shower curtain. It fluttered to the tiles, half-covering the body.

"He fell," Jessica said softly, and held out her hand. "We weren't here."

Joss felt her touch him, her fingers lacing through his, felt her pull him away, leading him like a child. It wasn't real. It couldn't be real. None of it seemed real. Sweat ran down his back and, through it all, he heard bloody Damon Brent, his gentle, self-mocking laughter and the warm gold tones of the Gibson. He followed Jessica back into the studio, scrubbing his itchy palm against his shirt and looking over his shoulder to make sure that they were leaving no traces behind them—no footprints in the sand—and he ripped the tapes from the deck, stuffing them in the pockets of his jeans. Jessica picked up the papers, the notebook, and looked at him darkly in the mellow morning light. Birds called, outside in the beeches. The dawn was almost here.

She crossed the room and kissed him softly on the cheek.

Because... what did Damon fucking Brent have that he didn't? Fucking nothing, that's what. And now, he was... he was dead.

"Baby? Come on. We need to go."

Joss blinked, glancing down at her. She tugged urgently at the waistband of his jeans.

"Yeah," he said distantly. "Yeah, we... oh, shit. Oh, shit, Jess...."

"Come on." She took his hand. "Quickly."

Jessica brushed off his worries about being seen. She was right, Joss supposed. Right about everything. There was no one about... people downstairs wouldn't hear them. Easy enough to slip through the connecting door, up here, that separated those private rooms from the guest bedrooms. She closed it after them, left them in the corridor faced with blank, eyeless doors. Moans and giggles issued from within some of them. Jessica dragged him along to the room Day had given them, right at the end. Joss stumbled over his own feet.

"We killed him," he murmured as Jessica shut the door behind them.

Because, it *had* happened, hadn't it? The corridor hadn't seemed so long before, an endless walk. Only, if it was real, then it *was* real... and people would find out. People were going to know, and people were gonna care. Really care. He was aware of her pulling his shirt off, which confused him because, though pumped and pounding with adrenaline, he was limp as a rag... she couldn't possibly want that, could she? 'Cos he might never have another erection ever again. *He's dead.* It had been the face—the eyes—that got him the worst. And the way Day had tried to talk. Hadn't he? Wasn't it real?

His hand already on the door, Joss fought the urge to go back, to look. 'Cos maybe it wasn't true. Maybe it wasn't real. Jessica wiped him with something wet and cold. A flannel, he realised, seeing red on damp white cotton. She'd taken off her dress, thick pink nipples tipping small breasts that brushed against him when she washed the blood from his face.

Had he had blood on his face?

Her eyes—deep green, hazel-flecked in muted gold—searched his face, but he didn't know what she wanted to find. He didn't understand how she could be so clean, either. She ran hot water in the sink in the corner of the room, squeezing the flannel over herself. He watched the water slip down her body in soft rivulets. Damon was dead.

Jessica sponged him down, washed his hands, and stroked his face. Hauled a black gym bag out from beside the bed. He didn't recognise it, but she took a clean frock out—didn't recognise that either—and packed away their bloody clothes, dress and shirt rolled up in each other. She slipped on the frock, not quite her size, took the tapes from his pockets, put those in the bag along with the papers and the notebook. Another dip in, another rummage, and she smiled at him, a tab of acid on her fingertip.

"What?" Joss frowned, confused.

Jessica opened her mouth and touched her finger to the end

of her tongue. She crossed to him and, cupping her hands around his face, pulled him in for a slow, deep kiss.

"Go," she whispered. "Go fly, baby. Make sure people see you. I'll be back."

She wiped his face and tidied his hair. Then she picked up the bag and slipped out of the door. Joss stared at the wood for a while. Nothing much happened to it, so he went downstairs, mingled his way through the happy people. Perhaps a half hour, a full hour later, he found Jessie again, dancing by the pool. The tab she'd given him was low grade stuff. He started to come up as she greeted him, the world shifting and slipping. Just enough to blur things… and it worked.

Jessie wound her body around him, around the solid shapes of the sunrise.

They watched it together, knots of people on the terrace and the lawn, appreciative murmurs at the beauty Joss was sure only he could *really* see. He put his arm around Jessica, kissed her hair. So beautiful. All that golden light. New and clean. Impossible, but there all the same.

"I left the bag up by the tennis court," she murmured. "I'll fetch it later, once things start moving. I can get lost then. You'll be here for a while, baby. But you know what to do, right?"

He didn't understand. Start moving? What would… oh.

She tucked a bag of weed into his pocket, told him it wouldn't look right if he didn't have anything on him. Kissed him again. Inside, the armchair he sat on massaged his bare back with a thousand tiny fingers, and the tea she fetched him was elastic, tawny liquid intensity. Jess sat in his lap, face pressed close against him, quiet susurrations of the morning, movement and stilted mumbles. She took him back up to the bedroom and told him how it had been. The story he'd stick to. How he was tripping now and how, then, they'd been upstairs, how he'd been drinking, smoking... how anything he thought he saw couldn't really be trusted.

Before long, he believed it. He understood it. Everything became indescribably clear, and he could see all the way through his own body, right down to the fibre of the earth. Her words kissed his brain, and he could recite exactly what he needed to, aching with a terrible clarity..

Chapter Twenty-Two

I should, by rights, probably not have survived the shooting. Bits of me should have been splattered all over Jessica's rose bushes, leaving nothing but stubborn stains on the patio and a sad, crumpled pile of uselessness. When I opened my eyes into total darkness, I assumed that's what had happened. However, I didn't feel dead. That, of course, begs the question of how that *should* feel... which probably isn't a question that ought to be answered.

There didn't seem to be much shape to me. No weight of body nor the intensity of pain I'd felt. Hard to tell whether that was good or bad.

The familiar touch of a well-known palm smoothed the forehead I might or might not have had, and other fingers squeezed my hands. Something wet nudged my leg. I wanted to move but couldn't, which seemed weird, because a definite sensation of movement appeared to be involved somehow. Just maybe not associated with me. Or not-me. Whatever I was.

"Stop thinkin' about it, baby. It's complicated enough, yeah?"

Day. I opened… *other* eyes. Mine, but not mine. Me but not me. Like being inside myself, the me of dreams and other waking oddities. He spun into focus somewhere to my left, looking concerned, the neckline of a purple smock riding low against one shoulder, fabric striped with gathered bands of beaded red lurex at the elbows. He twisted the hem of one flared sleeve in his fingers, mouth drawn into a tight bow.

Muffled forms, noises, and colours battled for acknowledgment around me. Beeping things, rattling things, voices… words like 'hemithorax' and 'shock'. I couldn't quite identify them. I tried to sit up, but unseen hands held me back. Shapes I knew I should recognise—*did* recognise—buoyed around me, in all their impossible, invisible familiarity. Sound, smell and touch… the same-shaped pieces of existence I'd never thought to see again, and yet couldn't see. Not truly. They floated just out of reach, flimsy whispers ever so slightly beyond proper hearing, beyond seeing.

Nice job, Tiger Cub.

That hand on my head again, the bubble of laughter that wasn't quite there. Mum, Granddad, Gran… the wet thing at my knee, a nose. Pepper, the spaniel we had when I was tiny. I wrestled again for movement but it wouldn't come. Damon touched my cheek, the backs of warm, firm fingers against my skin, the sweep of a thumb across my lips. The smell of cigarette smoke and soggy carnations, with overtones of white musk, sandalwood, and nutmeg. I couldn't work out if I was heading his way, or he mine. Kohl-banded eyes narrowed, and that muscle in his jaw jumped to a silent beat.

"I ain't 'avin' it," he said after a moment. "It ain't fair."

I'd have made some comment or other, pushed for at least a little bit of explanation as to what the hell was going on, but everything kept slipping away from under me.

He faded... *I* faded. What little focus I'd had—what little ability to see, to feel—petered away into emptiness and deposited me back into a dark sea, nothing to latch on to but myself.

Kata ton daimona eaytoy, I supposed.

* * *

About two days later, give or take, I woke up. From the smell of disinfectant, the rhythmic bleeping, and the pervasively shiny beigeness of everything, it became apparent that I was in a hospital. A Nigerian nurse of generous dimensions and capacious cheerfulness confirmed this suspicion and assured me I had been incredibly lucky. Still snared to the bed with a nest of tubes, I couldn't do much about that but croak a weak expletive. She laughed and said it was good I'd started to feel better.

Doctors, nurses, and police officers drifted in and out during that first afternoon, with careful explanations and cautious questions. I owed my life to Joss, they said. He'd wrested the gun from Jessica, administered first aid, radioed Ms. Brooks to get the ambulance. Taken control for what might have been the first time in thirty years. The general consensus appeared to be that, if the ten gauge had been loaded with buckshot instead of smaller birdshot pellets, if Joss hadn't grabbed the gun just before she fired, altered the angle of the shot, if I hadn't leapt for cover like I had... I wouldn't have made it. I was—my surgical consultant explained—the happy child of circumstance and should feel extremely grateful that my injuries were not more severe.

Privately convinced that his bedside manner could use some work, I just nodded as best I could and said 'oh, good'. I recycled his version of events for the police and hoped it wouldn't surprise Joss too much when he eventually heard it. I remembered the look on his face, just standing there stock still while Jessica squeezed the trigger.

I should have taken both barrels.

Bird or buckshot, I should have been in pieces. I should have died.

But maybe it didn't matter. Memory's a funny thing. Like reality. Belief, conviction... connection. Maybe the whole thing was just some cosmic game of chess, pawns sidling up to each other and whipping out dirks in the dark. Each square a battleground between what is and what isn't; perpetual negotiation full of jostled space.

They didn't let me have visitors for the first few days.

Instead, the nurses allowed me a phone and a long, tearful conversation with Auntie Jan... which led me to suspect visitors would have been easier. At least she hadn't found out from the police, or some nameless hospital staff member. Leon—who'd rolled up at the farm about an hour behind me, just as the police arrived—had taken that into his hands.

Auntie Jan wept and tried her very hardest to understand why I hadn't been at least a little bit more truthful, though without at any point actually expressing disappointment. Pretty excruciating. She asked to speak to the ward sister when I started to sound tired, said she'd come up to see me before I got moved back to Brighton. Given what she'd heard of my injuries, she guessed that would be a week or so, which matched up fairly well with what the doctors said. I told her she didn't have to come, winced at the ensuing telling off—of course she bloody well did—and obediently passed the phone back so Sister could have Jan's professional curiosity inflicted upon her.

Despite the fact I suspected I'd be in for a bollocking from virtually everyone who knew me, I looked forward to being able to have visitors. Any kind of distraction from the delicate little tube drain sticking out of the right side of my chest and the perpetual agonies of trying just to breathe deeply or move much would have been welcome. I shared the ward with three other women: one recovering from gastric surgery, who didn't say much, one elderly lady with a newly-fitted stent, and a Jehovah's Witness called Susan, whose entire extended family and local Bible study group came to sit with her every day for the entire duration of visiting hours. In shifts. Usually with board games to entertain the children. Impressive dedication, I had to admit. Also loud, and extremely talkative.

I waited out my solitude and tried to pretend I wasn't watching the corners of the room, wondering where.... Well, silly, really. I mean, the truth of Damon's murder had been uncovered. My little recorder was with the police. Arrests had been made, and the whole story had broken, messily, all over the news. At least, Auntie Jan said so, but no one would let me see a television or a newspaper. I told her to take cuttings, maybe buy a new scrapbook. She'd laughed damply, said she would.

It still felt strange, not seeing him around.

When I was finally allowed visitors, my Nigerian nurse, Katherine, got me tidy and respectable enough for them, still irritatingly cheerful about the whole thing.

"Everyone is coming to see *you*," she said, with a ridiculously big grin.

"Wh—" I began, but she needed to fiddle with my drain, so I closed my eyes and turned my face away. "Ouch!"

The gates opened for the hordes at ten. Susan's coterie flocked in, said hello to everyone, snabbled every chair in the place. I smoothed out a wrinkle on my bed's bobbly pink blanket.

"Ellis! You complete *tart*! What the bloody 'ell did you go and do, eh?"

I grinned. Ron, Jeremy in tow, bore down on me like an angry bantam, skinny chest puffed out and glasses almost steamed up with indignation.

Jerry smiled. "All right, Ell?"

"Not so bad," I said as they both fussed around me with cheek kissing, hand squeezing, and general talking over each other.

"We *knew* something wasn't right," Ron said haughtily, "when we couldn't get you on the phone. 'Away for a couple of days', you said. 'Could you feed the cat?', you said. Not a peep since. I said—Jer, get us some chairs, would you, love?—I said to Jeremy, it's not like her. And now bloody look at you. I don't know...."

Jerry went to commandeer chairs from the Witnesses.

"It, er, it really wasn't intentional," I said, but Ron had hit full flow.

"And we were so worried about you! Then, what with all that business at your place, and—"

"Shh!" Jeremy plonked the chair down on his foot. "Shut *up*."

"...obviously... what happened," Ron finished with a wince.

I tried to haul myself up against the pillow, but my body let me down, pain bursting through muscles too loose to hold me. I flopped back, useless and frustrated. At least the concussion had cleared up, though apparently I had something like six months of respiratory therapy in my future.

"Bugger! Wh-what business at my place? Is everything okay?"

"Yes. Oh, yes. Fine," Ron said, all false composure and transparent affectation.

Jeremy groaned and sat down in the other chair. "You're bloody useless, you are," he told Ron. "Now, look, Ell. You mustn't worry, all right? You just need to concentrate on getting better. Everything's fine. The cat's okay, and there wasn't very much damage."

"What?" My chest tightened, which bloody hurt. "Ouch...! Oh, G—what happened? What d'you mean, 'damage'?"

Katherine passed the end of my bed, oral syringe of laxative in her hand for the stent lady, who'd been telling us all about her constipation in far more detail than anyone ever needed to know.

"Someone tried to set your flat on fire," Ron interjected with a helpful nod.

"*What*? What the f—"

"It didn't take proper hold," Jeremy cut in. "It was your

neighbour from downstairs, they think. When the fire crew arrived, he wouldn't let them up to the flat. Kept running around the stairwell, yelling and trying to push them back."

I stared, throat dry. "Yel—what did he say?"

Jeremy frowned. "Uh… well, I don't— Ron, what did the lady in the garden flat tell you?"

Ron leaned forward conspiratorially. "She said he went really weird. Screaming about the balance of the world not being right and he had to mend it. Something about purging the demons."

"By setting fire to my sodding *flat*?" My voice rose, and Katherine gave me a chary look, so I made a more concerted effort to calm down. "All right. What ha—"

"Um. That's really all there is to tell." Jerry patted my hand. "They put it out. Like I said, not as much damage as there could have been. It'll be all right."

"But what about Mr. Do—*him*," I corrected, because Mr. Downstairs just sounded daft. In all the time I'd lived there, had I even asked his name? I didn't think so.

Busy blinking with the shame of that, I almost missed the shifty looks Ron and Jeremy exchanged.

"Well, um…." Jerry cleared his throat. "Of course, they tried to take him out, get him away…. He was obviously very, uh, disturbed."

Ron coughed meaningfully. "Jer, I don't think she needs to know—"

"Tell me!"

"Well, he…." Jerry shot Ron an apologetic glance. "He jumped out the window, love. Dropped three floors onto the road. Um, he didn't…. Bit of a mess, really. I mean, clearly he was a danger to people, and to himself, and…. Sorry, Ell."

I felt sick. Tears brushed the insides of my eyelids.

"God. That's… that's horrible." I sniffed, but more material concerns were already butting in for my attention. "Y-You said Mr. Tibbs is all right, though?"

Purging the demons.

Had he succeeded?

"Yeah, he's round at ours for now. Got him in the spare room. Bit shaken, slightly singed, but the vet says he's fine. Very lucky, really. They found him on the pavement outside, after… well, he must have run out when the doors opened." Jeremy squeezed my hand again, checking I was still with him. "The flat's still cordoned off. I think the hall and sitting room are a bit, er… toasty, and obviously the front door's knackered, but otherwise it's mainly smoke and water damage, from the hose."

"You can come and stay with us," Ron cut in, "when you're out of here. If—well, you're going to need somewhere to go. We're here for as long as you need."

"Thanks, lads." I put my other hand over Jerry's, and looked warmly between them. "Might well take you up on that."

Ron smiled. "Good. Well, we, um… we ought to shove over. Not the only ones who want to see you."

"Hmm?" I let go of Jerry's hand and had another go at pushing myself up, not really much more successful than the first. "What…?"

I caught sight of Leon lingering at the end of the ward like a spare part, silk blend suit topped off with a worried expression. Sister was talking at him, which I doubted he really deserved. He saw me look and—with a hand cupping her elbow and a polite apology on his lips—he excused himself and made his way over with an uncertain smile at Ron and Jeremy. Recognition bloomed on Ron's face, and Jerry got up, standing heavily on his partner's foot.

"Ooh, aren't you—*ouch*!"

"Are you all right?" Leon bent over my bed, apparently oblivious to Ron's yelp of pain. "Well, not... I mean, clearly you're not all—aw, crap. I was worried, y'know?"

He leaned in to kiss my cheek; I landed one on his lips instead.

"I've had better days, I'll admit," I said, enjoying his rather bewildered expression. "Um. Sorry. My friends, Ron Maddox and Jeremy Dalby. This is L—"

"Leon Fielding!" Ron grinned, enthusiastically pumping the hand that Leon offered him. "Hello! Well.... Dark horse, Ellis."

Jeremy cringed quietly in the background and smiled. "Hey."

Leon nodded. "Hi. Hey, don't feel you have to... 'cos of me. I...."

"Oh, we were gonna get a cup of tea anyway," Jeremy said pointedly, nudging Ron in the back of the ribs. "We'll maybe pop back in a bit, Ell, all right?"

I smiled my thanks. "Good to see you both."

Leon watched them go, then sat in one of the oddly-shaped plastic chairs and gave me a long, hard look. The ripples of interest among the nurses and Susan's varied visitors had begun to subside a little. A couple of the Witnesses' children— preternaturally well-behaved—were playing Junior Scrabble at a small table beneath the window. Outside, blue sky and fluffy white clouds. The duct from the hospital kitchens belched wavering steam across it.

"You should've waited for me."

I flexed one shoulder. Half a shrug. "Prob'ly."

He sighed. "I'm glad you're… no less okay, anyway."

"I'm all right."

"Ha-bloody-hah-ha."

His hand enfolded mine, not quite the way Jerry's had done. I squeezed back.

"Thank you. I mean, I couldn't have—"

"Recklessly endangered yourself without me? No, I appreciate that."

"Good."

We sat for a while, not saying very much. After a minute, Leon cracked a smile, and I marvelled at really how little he'd changed from all those centrefolds. I told him about my flat, which he didn't take that well, and he told me what the press had been saying, which made me swear quite a lot, too.

"You're gonna have to decide how you want to play that, when you're ready. There's a—well, phone's been ringin' off the hook. Gavin's delighted. Says it's great." He grimaced. "I've had proposals for two documentaries and a book deal so far, but I haven't committed to anything. I said they all ought to talk to you."

I groaned. "Oh, *hell*…."

"Aw, it's not so bad. Get you a good agent, it'll be okay." Leon glanced around the ward and lowered his voice a little. "By the way, are you all right here? Sure you wouldn't prefer a private—"

"No. Thanks. I'm… honestly, I'm fine. I'll be fine," I added, which seemed a more accurate statement, all things considered.

Maybe not yet, maybe not for a long while, but at some point. Probably.

Leon tilted his head to the side and looked dubious.

"Okay," he conceded. "If you're sure."

"Yes."

Dull fire licked at my lungs. I wanted... not to go to sleep, but perhaps to close my eyes. Just for a minute. Down by the nurse's station, Ron and Jeremy were back from their foray to the café, chatting away to Katherine and generally keeping an eye on me.

"Um." Leon rubbed his thumb over my knuckle. "By the way... there's somebody else waiting to see you."

I blinked. "Mm?"

If he'd wheeled Auntie Jan all the way up here, I wouldn't forgive him. But he mugged earnestly at me with the top half of his face, and I realised he didn't mean her, which confused me. He couldn't possibly....

"Jack!" Ron called out, at the other end of the ward, ceaselessly genial as ever. "All right? You look well. She's just up there, but sh—"

I stared at Leon. He smiled. A familiar voice wrapped itself around my ears, mixed up with footfalls on the shiny beige floor and the heavy waft of fag ash... so much stronger than before.

"Hello, lads! All right? Yeah, I know. 'Ere, they wouldn't let me bring flowers."

"I told you," Leon said, tearing his gaze from mine, leaving his words to echo dimly somewhere, "it's hygiene regulations."

"Oh, it's bloody *flowers*," retorted... not quite Damon Brent. "Ellis deserves somethin' to cheer her up. All right, darlin'?"

He beamed widely at me, sliding down the ward with an easy-going, natural stride, the mingled scents of tobacco and a classic aftershave preceding him. The hems of dark indigo, hip-hugging designer jeans brushed his red Converse trainers, while an Indy Star tee in fashionably retro red and grey peeped from beneath his dark green babycord jacket. A blue desert scarf looped his neck, but his *hair*....

He hauled up by the side of my bed and stopped just short of dipping to kiss my cheek, perhaps because of Leon sitting there with that vaguely, absurdly proprietary air. Ron and Jerry, moths to a flame and inquisitive noses twitching, dawdled in his wake. A bag emblazoned with the logo of an expensive boutique not far from my flat—my poor flat—dangled from his fingers, but that wasn't what held my attention.

"Your *hair*!" I breathed as Day sat down on the edge of the bed.

He grinned and ran a hand over it. Gel-tousled at the front, with the slight hint of a fringe, cut in close at the back and sides. It made him look, from the ears up, a very tiny bit like a young, blond Elvis, or at least the stylist's interpretation thereof.

"Different, innit?" he said.

"I haven't seen you look like that since 1968," Leon muttered.

Day winked at him. "Shh."

I reached out. "Can I—?"

"Yeah, sure."

He bent his head. My fingers met the stiffness of styling products—a hint of synthetic coconut rising to tickle my nose somewhere through the YSL—yielding to the softness of freshly razored hair around his ears. The feel of his skin and its impossible, indelible warmth. The pulse beating at the base of his neck. My palm rested against his chest. *One, two.* I couldn't wipe the stupid grin off my face, even when Day put his hand over mine and I felt the natural heat and the texture of his skin, the shape of each finger, the roughness of the calluses on their tips.

He bent my fingers, brought them to lips twisted in a mischievous smirk, and kissed them, dark eyes—for once devoid of kohl—fixed on mine. Somewhere, a thousand teenage girls probably fainted, a less than angelic choir.

"Thank you," he whispered.

I didn't mind blushing. Not all that much.

My mind kept returning to the flat, though, picking at all the destruction and devastation that awaited me. Wreckage that had already claimed at least one victim. Purging demons. Flames, and the total conviction that… *something*… must be destroyed. *You can't stay here.* What had changed? Maybe my chessboard analogy was right. Black and white always struggling for legroom, realities and negotiable worlds pressed cheek by jowl, just waiting for one pawn's chance to slip into another's place.

What had he said to me, that very first night?

Time and space, baby.

Day reached into the boutique bag he'd stood by the side of the bed.

"Here y'are. 'Fore I forget."

I frowned, perplexed, but any confusion soon slipped away into insignificance. A little bit charred at its very edges, but… my photo album. My pictures of Mum, of my grandparents, of all the childhood memories they'd worked so hard to give me.

Of Jan and Duncan, and family holidays at the beach.

He'd saved it for me. All those precious pages... and all the pages left to fill.

My chin wobbled, and I managed a damp and snotty: "'nk you."

"You're not supposed to make her cry," Leon admonished. "She hasn't got the lung capacity to cry."

I hit him with the photo album. "Oh, shut up."

Epilogue

I was still sore when the hospital released me, just over a fortnight later, the summer sun bright on tired eyes... and it had been turning into another long, hot summer. Concrete planters full of geraniums winked red by the automatic doors, obligatory cigarette stubs screwed into the compost. A black estate car occupied a space near the entrance, just one among many vehicles and a large gaggle of people, which—even though I'd expected to see them—still struck me with bowel-watering terror.

Leon's arm tightened around my shoulders.

"All right?"

I nodded, then reconsidered. "Wait, no. No, I'm not. Can we—"

"Yeah, you are. C'mon. One, two, three, go."

"Oh, *crap....*"

We stepped out. I wasn't quite sure what to make of it

when they rounded on me and the cameras started clicking. Overlapping voices called my name.

"Miss Ross! Got a comment?"

"What drew you to the story?"

"BBC News! When did you realise you were investigating a murder?"

"How did getting shot feel, Miss Ross?"

"Will you be releasing a formal statement about last month's events?"

"Is it true you're a Jehovah's Witness?"

I blinked, dislocated and disorientated by all of it, happy to let Leon propel me through the scrum.

"Thank you very much, ladies and gentlemen, Miss Ross is very grateful for your concern and appreciates that you've been waiting."

Did I? This was news to me.

"However, there will not be any comment at this time. As I'm sure you understand—*get in the car, Ellis*—she's still recovering and will be making a full public statement in due course. No, really. Nobody's got anything to say ri—excuse me? Uh, no. Nobody's answering any of *those* questions at all. Sorry. All right, that's it, thank you very much! *Now. In the damn car.*"

He bundled me into the passenger seat and shut the door. Flashes went off through the windows, and I made to shield my eyes with my left hand, forgetting for a moment about the twinges that kind of movement still sent through my ribs. Leon got into the driver's seat, smile fixed and eyes tight. He leaned over to help me with my seatbelt, fastened his own, then blew out a long breath.

"Shall we get the hell outta here? You feel up to some breakfast?"

"I could be tempted," I said, staring in vague horror at one photographer, pressed up close to the windscreen with the camera across his face like some gross protuberance, tongue poking out between fleshy, gurning lips.

"All right."

"Mm."

Leon kicked the engine into life, and we pulled away in chronically slow motion, journos still dogging us until we got out of the car park. Everything from my neck to my hips throbbed, and I leaned my head back against the seat, eyes drooping shut. The shadows of daylight bounced off the inside of my eyelids, and I relaxed into the thrum of the road.

"So," Leon said, after a while, "where d'you wanna go?"

It could be anywhere, I supposed. A new life of unimagined potentials and ridiculous possibilities had opened up for me, unasked for and unexpected. And yet, there were still so many questions. They lingered like ripe fruit just in front of my lips, perfumed and tempting.

I took a deep breath and, after a moment, cracked one eye open. A lazy arabesque of cigarette smoke curled past my cheek. And it stunk. Leon sighed and hit the window control, letting in a cross-current of fresh air.

"Do you *have* to do that in the car, man?"

A throaty chuckle rippled from the back seat. With some considerable effort, I turned as far around as I could.

Damon sat... no, that wasn't the right word. He *sprawled* —in an extremely stylish way—across the upholstery, cigarette in his fingers, skinny black fur boa at his neck, wearing ombre-dyed jeans and an extremely paisley shirt with the cuffs rolled back. A massive pair of tortoiseshell Jackie Os shaded his eyes. He pushed the sunglasses down to look at me, wicked grin on his face, and winked.

"I don't know about you, baby, but I'm *dyin'* for a cup of tea."